T0310057

Everything Is Now

Everything Is Now

NEW AND COLLECTED STORIES

Michelle Cliff

University of Minnesota Press
MINNEAPOLIS • LONDON

Stories in the second section of the book were previously published as *Bodies of Water* (New York: Dutton, 1990). Stories in the third section were previously published as *The Store of a Million Items* (New York: Mariner Books, 1998).

Published by the University of Minnesota Press
111 Third Avenue South, Suite 290
Minneapolis, MN 55401-2520
http://www.upress.umn.edu

LIBRARY OF CONGRESS CATALOGING-IN-PUBLICATION DATA
Cliff, Michelle.
Everything is now : new and collected stories / Michelle Cliff.
p. cm.
ISBN 978-0-8166-5593-9 (alk. paper)
ISBN 978-0-8166-5594-6 (pbk : alk. paper)
I. Title.
PR9265.9.C55E84 2009
813'.54—dc22

2008055597

Printed in the United States of America on acid-free paper

The University of Minnesota is an equal-opportunity educator and employer.

16 15 14 13 12 11 10 09 10 9 8 7 6 5 4 3 2 1

Contents

My Grandmother's Eyes

MY GRANDMOTHER'S EYES were green. The green of Ava Gardner. Smokey Robinson. The vale of St. Thomas, Jamaica. An iguana on a moss-covered rock. A wild parrot at one with the rainforest. The green of the shallows of the Caribbean Sea as seen from the air. There was so much green in Jamaica. I was told a songwriter—in Cuba as I remember it—wrote a *bolero* for her, after she proved elusive. *Ojos Verdes.*

After her death I was going through some of her papers and found these notes on her life—sealed in a manila envelope in her safe deposit box, addressed to me: "To Be Read upon My Death by My Granddaughter"—she had appended a footnote: "*I know this sounds melodramatic but remember, I was an actress."

Early Memories

I came to this country in 1923. By *this country* I mean the United States. Straight from our ruins. An aristocoon, I called myself to myself. But to no one else. It made me smile.

You asked for my first memory [I had asked her this in our last exchange]—it was January 14, the year 1907, the year after I was born. (I keep my birth date to myself at all times, except here. Oscar Wilde once said a woman who would reveal her age would reveal anything—that's a paraphrase.) I trust you will keep my secrets.

My first memory: I was naked in the middle of my mother's bed. My mother and father had separate beds, separate rooms. It was a very hot day, even for Jamaica, and I was covered in prickly heat. Mama was rubbing something into my skin. Some potion. Something concocted by some bushwoman, selling her wares from gate to gate as the dogs sounded their alarm. Suddenly, the bed began to shake, the iron bars at the head began to rattle. The sensation was far rougher than my nurse, Winsome, rocking me in my cradle. The second great earthquake had begun. (The first had been in 1692, when Port Royal was swallowed whole.) The ewer and basin slid off the stand next to the bed. They crashed to the tile and shattered. Mama's face came close to mine as I began to scream. Our house was right on the sea. Mama was afraid a tidal wave would follow. Papa was away at the time. He was involved in the building of the Panama Canal. Mama did not know where to turn. Her own family was on the North Coast near Discovery Bay. The only resource we had left was our stables near the racecourse in Knutsford Park. Mama gathered all four children—I was the youngest—and the servants and hired some men to carry us and some of our belongings and supplies to the stables. Of course we could not camp out in the stables. So she asked the groom to fetch some canvas, and there and then he and she manufactured a dwelling—a tent—in the infield of the racetrack. We lived like that for a few days, until Mama thought the danger past. Papa returned some months later to the house by the sea. There we were, as if nothing had happened. The house had suffered little damage. There had been no tidal wave.

Into the Past

When I was about five or six, I was sent to live with my mother's mother in their place near Discovery Bay. My brother and two sisters were away at boarding school. I was sent across the island by train with Winsome as my companion. Neither of us had been on a train before. I can still feel the wicker of the train seat. Hear the rattle of the metal on metal. I can see Winsome, who was probably in her twenties, her own children being raised away from her by relatives, her hands folded in her lap, a starched white cotton handkerchief smartly folded, peeping out of a pocket of her skirt—dark blue, I think it was. Yes, dark blue with a white sea-island-cotton blouse, embroidered with doctor birds. She was very sweet to me. Always.

I was never told why I had been sent away. There were whispers about "woman troubles," but I did not know what that meant. Suddenly, overnight it seemed, Mama took to her bed and I was sent away. It sounds very Victorian, I know. But that's what happened. Papa took Winsome and me in a horse-drawn carriage to the station. He gave her some money to buy us food along the way and instructed us not to speak to anyone except the train conductor. He took us to the platform and gave the conductor our tickets and probably tipped him to look out for us. We would be met at Discovery Bay by my grandmother's manservant. The trip seemed to take forever, especially with my small child's perception of time. At some of the stops Winsome bought food through the train window. We had our own compartment—cozy. In other cars people sat on long backless wooden benches. I glimpsed them when she took me to the toilet. What did she buy? Probably fried fish and bammy (cassava cakes) at Old Harbour. Tangerines and bananas. Paradise plums. Coconut water. Those are the tastes I recall.

Finally we reached our destination. The manservant, Victor, was waiting for us, and he fetched our baggage and drove us away. Our mode of transportation a trap drawn by a mule. I remember driving up a long avenue bounded by coconut palms leading to the house. Formerly the great house of a sugar plantation. Yellow stucco, I think, faded by sunlight, with a tin roof. There were chickens in the courtyard at the end of the drive. The place had seen better days. On the verandah, which was up a flight of stairs, stood my grandmother, in a long-sleeved ankle-length black dress, even in this heat. She draped herself in mourning clothes after my grandfather died.

The family said he died from TB. I'm not so sure. Like many a planter there was always a full carafe of rum beside his planter's chair in his study and a puncheons in a cabinet in the room to replenish the carafe. My grandmother did not allow drink at the table. Although surrounded by the stench of burning sugar, as the rum distilled, puncheons waiting in the yard, she never touched a drop, not even a dram when she had a toothache.

Behind the great house were what had been slave quarters. No buildings, but traces of their existence in the ground. Fragments of foundation. There were abandoned puncheons here and there—the place no longer served as a distillery—and a piece of looking glass as well. I saw my eyes in the mirror. My green-green eyes. "Lizard eyes," Mama had called them. I didn't know why. At least not then. I pocketed the looking glass.

The walls of the great house smelled of molasses, as if sugar held the walls together. The ground where the cane had been planted was overgrown. The orderly rows of sugar replaced by chaotic overgrowth, ruination.

My grandmother greeted us and Victor showed us to my room. Winsome would share the room with me. But it would always be known as "my room." The bedsteads—there were two—were iron. There were two kerosene lamps and a metal ewer and basin on a mahogany nightstand. Two enameled chamber pots sat under each bed. And a Persian runner between the beds.

My grandmother thought that educating girls was a waste of time, so I would not be sent to school. She expressed on more than one occasion her dismay that my sisters were wasting "good money" at the Convent of the Immaculate Conception. My education—I lived with her until I was about sixteen, maybe seventeen, I'm not certain as not much was made of birthdays—consisted of twice-weekly sessions with the local minister, who taught me how to read and write; that was all. The only books in the house had belonged to my grandfather, a failed poet. So at least there was something to read besides the Bible, which was the text of my literacy. My grandfather's study had been left as it was. My grandmother never ventured in. I was able to spend precious alone-time in there. I have always needed time to myself. Those books and Winsome were my company. So I never knew a children's book. No. The books I read were penny dreadfuls, and Dickens and Thackeray, an anthology of English poetry, the complete plays of Shakespeare. My encounter with the green-eyed monster, reading *Othello* when I was about eleven, had me staring at myself in the piece of looking glass at my "lizard eyes." Did jealousy have something to do with my banishment, with Papa's taking leave of me with not so much as a peck on the cheek?

There was a book of paintings by Constable, in which I saw landscapes bounded by the same stone fences that bounded my grandmother's land.

This was a childhood in which my contact with others was minimal. My grandmother barely acknowledged my existence. I had the distinct impression that her reserve toward me had something to do with the reason I had been "visited upon her."

She once told me I reminded her of Annee Palmer, Creole woman of legend, suspected of voodoo practices, murderer of husbands.

"They say the only possession left from her is her looking glass. I wonder if you would find yourself in it." My grandmother told me this when I was about thirteen.

Another Hint at My Point of Origin

"Beg you teach mi fi read and write," Winsome asked me when I was ten.

I may have been only ten but I knew the ways of this world. I agreed, but well aware of my grandmother's inevitable response, told Winsome we would have to meet in secret, and not anywhere in the house. And please don't tell the other servants, who might serve us up to curry favor with my grandmother. I suggested we meet outside, behind one of the stone fences. I would keep an exercise book and a pencil and the anthology of English poetry in a crevice in the fence. We would begin with Elizabeth Barrett Browning, whose family once owned property here.

I had read somewhere about the hedge masters in Ireland. The English occupiers—which included some of my mother's ancestors—forbade the teaching of literacy to the Irish peasants. So schoolmasters became hedge masters, teaching reading and writing behind the tall green hedges I could only imagine.

Winsome and I made a fair exchange. I would teach her to read and write. She would teach me about menstruation, and other "women's troubles."

I found a place for our lessons behind a stone fence, sheltered by a mango tree. There we sat in the guinea grass, the odd blue-green ground lizard scuttling around us. There I taught Winsome to "mek out words."

When I was fifteen or so I found a letter from my mother to my grandmother. I have gone back and forth in my life wondering if I was wise to have read it. It was left in plain sight on the dining table. Left for me to find? No envelope, just a sheet of folded paper. The date on the letter was the year I was sent away. Obviously it was left for me to find.

> My dear Mama,
>
> I hope this finds you well. Some years ago I committed a grievous error. Because of my mistake my marriage is in tatters. There is but one way to salvage it. I need you to take my youngest. For the sake of the other three children, whom I have reassured Frederick are his. He found me out. You can keep her and she will be your companion in old age. I will send along a servant to take care of her. Please do this for me. You are my last resort. . . .

That's all I can recall of the letter.

Just like that, Winsome and I had been relocated. Our fates decided for us, as of course they would be.

Soon after I found the letter, the bottom once again fell out of my world. Thrown out of the cauldron of family—cold, yet with a heat all its own—I was again to be relocated, displaced.

Another letter appeared—at the breakfast table, its script laboriously printed, it had a Victorian turn to its phrasing. My grandmother read it aloud, only pausing to sip her coffee and stare away from me.

> Dear Mistress,
>
> The time has come for me to take my leave of you. By the time you read this I will be long gone. I want to thank you for everything, especially for the use of the books. I want to thank my boon coon companion for the gift of literacy. I plan to use it wisely. For this is my possession forever.
>
> Your unwilling servant, Winsome Sophia Maxwell, Member, UNIA.

"You have a lot to answer for," her voice directed itself at me but her eyes remained elsewhere.

". . . I demand to know why you took it upon yourself to teach that girl. . . . You know if they get themselves educated, there will be hell to pay. They will come after what is rightfully ours. Look at Bogle and his mob. What a disaster that almost was. And what in God's name is the UNIA? Some sort of church group?"

(For those with short memories, or ignorant of history, or both, the UNIA stood for the Universal Negro Improvement Association, founded in Jamaica by Marcus Garvey. More about this later, when Winsome and I cross paths—perhaps—again.)

"I have sheltered you all these years. Some gratitude you have shown me. Blood will tell, as they say. You have betrayed the part of you that belongs to me."

Her previous coldness was now molten, a lava flow of words meant to smother me. Her voice raised as no lady of her station had been taught.

The only phrase she did not use, it seemed, was "Never darken my door again," which would have been fitting given my circumstances. Much had been made of the greenness of my eyes, my deep tan skin. My lizard eyes, as I mentioned before.

My grandmother rang for Victor, told him to make ready the trap, instructed me to pack my belongings.

"No books."

"Take her to the station, Victor. And come right back."

"Yes'm."

I was sent away with ten one-pound notes and a satchel to "seek my fortune," a girl of sixteen or so. I had read enough Dickens to fear what might come next. I knew this island was not steeped in the "kindness of strangers." (Remember, I was in a regional production of *Streetcar*—predictably I played Blanche. You know, one ruined great house is the same as another. Got good notices, too.)

It's very difficult to recall exactly what I felt. I think I was probably mourning the loss of Winsome. Ours was not one of those sentimental nanny-charge attachments of romantic novels or sanitized history, but she had been my only company in that place, and our little reading group gave me solace. It gave her something else.

Winsome had a righteous anger at spending so much time apart from her own children. Little did I know how much and where it would lead her. Among my grandmother's kind the assumption went unquestioned that "they" did not attach themselves to their children as much as "we" did. Even though "they" were expected to care for the children of "us." Such nonsense informed the social contract on that island. Even as a child—why? I've no idea—I found such beliefs and their practical applications unsettling.

I knew Winsome was biding her time, filling a knotted handkerchief with coins she saved from her meager salary. Still, I was surprised when she took her leave, and although we were not that close, I would have liked her to say good-bye to me.

I took my leave in jodhpurs and a white sea-island-cotton shirt; my black hair was tucked into a cap. I needed to look as boyish as I could make myself. In the pocket of the jodhpurs I secreted a gold and ruby ring I stole from my grandmother's chest of drawers. Ten pounds—even though a decent sum in those days—would not get me very far. All I knew is that I wanted to quit this island. The ring would be my ticket. I held the ring tight in my left hand. My ticket, my amulet. Three dark red stones set in a ring of white gold. The ring in the form of a coiled snake. The stones the snake's eyes and mouth.

I took a train headed for Montego Bay. As I looked out the window, as the land ran by, Brahmin bulls, white tickbirds on their humps, john crow vultures, coconut palms, cane fields, citrus groves, towering pimento and breadfruit trees, my chest became heavy with a great sense of abandonment, sadness. I was about to lose the only place I had ever known. But did I actually have any real knowledge of it? My life had been spent in confinement in that aged great house. Only in books did I find myself. That I remember, as I remember fighting back tears, trying to conjure every hero and heroine I knew from books. Each one who had risen above his or her apparent fate.

I opened the train window and the trade winds—one side of the train ran by land, the other ran by the sea—came through the railway carriage, hot and strong.

Then it hit me: I was going away to seek my fortune—another phrase I met in books.

The train stopped and I saw drays piled high with bananas. Like me, headed to the mainland.

I had no papers, no passport, no birth certificate—nothing to prove my existence. Except my looking glass.

I think my bravado had to do with youth, and a sense of having nothing to lose. Who can say?

Emigré or Refugee—

I came to America under the auspices of United Fruit—after the United States and Great Britain, the uncontested overlord of the region. I was transported with many bunches of bananas on one of the Great White Fleet of United Fruit. A banana boat. A stowaway, I lived on bananas for five days. To this day I cannot bear the smell of bananas. When I got to Montego Bay I found my way to the docks. There I asked about passage on the banana boat. You know, I have always wondered at my good fortune. No one bothered me—yet. Was it my demeanor? My green eyes? I asked a stevedore if I could come aboard and gave him a pound note when he said yes.

We entered the harbor sailing past the Lady with the Lamp, up the Hudson to a berth in the fifties. The city as we approached it was bathed in light. People used to come to New York City for its clarity of air. Imagine. Imagine me traveling from my nineteenth-century childhood, the mold of the great house, the mold of old books, slave tracks in the yard.

Suffice to say—you are my granddaughter after all, and not privy to everything—I disembarked the banana boat more or less intact. You don't need to know the gory details.

It was, as I said, 1923; the twenties had commenced their roar. All the clichés were in place: Stage door Johnnies. Speakeasys. Prohibition. Bathtub Gin. Neon. Texas Guinan.

Cotton Club: where I danced, one of the "Tall, Tan, and Terrific." Cab Calloway. Ethel Waters—I knew her. Josephine Baker—*La Sirène des Tropiques*—sporting bananas; bananas again! O'Neill's *The Moon of the Caribbees.* I had a bit part in that—by sheer luck I was spotted at the Cotton Club and asked if I would be willing to wear dark makeup for the part of a West Indian "Negress"—I swear they used that word. I said yes. I was tired of pretending to be a dancer. Why not pretend to be a "Negress"? I was staying at a hotel for women in the Village. I wore my dark makeup home one night during the interval and was asked if I had come for the maid's job! Too predictable, eh? I said no, left, returned to the theater, which was around the corner. (It was the Provincetown Playhouse on MacDougal Street, my hotel was on Bleecker.) After the performance I removed my makeup, returned to the hotel: "Good evening, miss," the same fool at the desk said.

I finally enter the Great White Way. 1927. I was in the original cast of Jerome Kern's *Showboat,* another bit part. I also understudied the great (and, alas, drunk) Helen Morgan in the role of Julie, the octoroon—typecasting, no? Even plastered she knew the show had to go on. Lucky for me. I would have been scared to death. She was Judy Garland before there was a Judy Garland. It was through Helen Morgan that I met Libby Holman—best known for introducing Cole Porter's "Love for Sale" and for shooting her husband (it was ruled a suicide), heir to the Reynolds tobacco fortune. Lady Day recorded "Love for Sale" later on. I heard her sing it at Café Society downtown—"The Wrong Place for the Right People"—also heard her sing "Strange Fruit" there—but that's getting ahead of the story.

Libby Holman introduced me to J. I don't want to use her whole name, not even between the two of us. She was a fairly well-known painter. We met in the lobby of the Algonquin for drinks one afternoon. J. ordered a Gibson. She specified Bombay Gin, the one with Queen Victoria on the label—the sun never sets, etc. The bluish tinge of the gin. Funny how some things are cemented into memory and others vanish. I was about twenty-two or -three. J. was a married woman in her thirties with two children and a stockbroker husband. They were riding high—this was a year or so before Black Tuesday, the Crash. (Her husband took a header onto Wall Street the very next week. Poor devil. Luckily J. had family money.) She asked to paint me and I agreed. She would pay me. (I did all manner of things to make ends meet. I worked in the theater. I worked as a dancer; over time I had improved. But I also sold blood. And I sold hair. And I was a numbers runner in the theater district—I'd met a gangster at the Cotton Club who took pity on me; he said my face was the dead stamp of the "Madonna." And a shop girl during the Christmas season. Still I held on to the ruby ring—it was my savings account. I think my early life among books somehow emboldened me. I had read widely and knew some of the pitfalls of life through words. But I also knew the vast possibilities of life through words. Do you understand?)

I went to her studio on 57th Street, nearby Carnegie Hall. The studio was one large high-ceilinged room with huge windows, letting in a golden light. At least that particular day the studio was bathed in sunlight. She was to paint me nude. She arranged me on a chaise. Her eyes were a dark blue, almost violet. She looked deep into mine as she arranged me. I could not disconnect from her gaze. I didn't want to. I think you will understand what I mean. I've never told anyone about this until now. It remained through my life, my marriages, my sweet secret. I remember or at least think I do—every moment of that afternoon. She painted for an hour or so. Then put down her brush and palette. And offered me some champagne. 1926 Veuve Clicquot. Brut, of course. It became clear that painting me was not the main reason I was invited. (She did finally complete my portrait—weeks later—but I refused payment. Things between us had changed.)

J. kept her life carefully divided. A townhouse on the Upper East Side with her husband and children. Then this studio where she entertained her lovers and led what she called her "secret life." We were high enough so no one could see in and so we could make love with the windows bare, that golden light flooding over us.

Afterwards she took me to one of those French restaurants—don't know if any are still there—on Ninth Avenue. I had mussels for the first time. We shared a bowl of *moules marinières*; we drank the broth from mussel shells. She asked me about myself, and I gave a carefully edited version of my life so far. She was suitably impressed by the great house and all it entailed; so many people were, it stood me in good stead to keep some at bay, draw others close.

She put me in a taxi and I headed back to my hotel room downtown, quite astonished by what had happened. No doubt the Freudians would make hay of my experience—unmothered woman, etc., seeks female companionship—but I honestly don't think that was the case. Certainly I yearned for a tenderness which I had never really known. And tenderness was at the very center of our lovemaking. "Underwater, the clownfish is drawn into the labial grasp of the anemone." Those are words I recall from that afternoon. We met off and on for quite some time, and no one was the wiser.

You know, you met her once. You were about four and living with me by then, and J.—her children grown—had sold the townhouse and was living in a penthouse in the east thirties. I had always treated you as a small adult. You ate what I ate and any guests we might have. J. served Hungarian goulash for lunch and was impressed that a four-year-old would decline when offered something more "childlike." After lunch we strolled around her garden. It was a gorgeous day. We could see across the East River. After we put you down for your nap, my one concession to your small self, she and I sat in the garden and made love.

Back to the twenties: J.'s life extended into a third division. These were the days of the Harlem Renaissance—a whole world away from the Cotton Club, although within blocks of each other. J. fancied herself more bohemia than society. This third division consisted of J.'s involvement in the Renaissance.

And not in the Carl Van Vechten, patronizing way. I met him once. No more need be said. Speak no ill of the dead.

J. knew Augusta Savage, the sculptor. Savage's father, a black preacher in Florida, forbade her to be a sculptor. He took the taboo against "graven images" literally. She fled north to Harlem. J. wanted me to meet her. She was a great champion of Savage's work. For a white American, J. had an interesting take on race. I don't know where she got it, but it was certainly refreshing given the quotidian racism of the day to this day. I don't know if her attitude extended to the help she employed to run her townhouse. I never once witnessed that realm of her existence. But as far as she was concerned, Augusta Savage was her equal in the arts. I expected that Savage would "recognize" me, but it did not concern me. I was, after all, a race of one, unto myself.

It was J. who took me to hear Billie Holiday at Café Society. Where we heard "Strange Fruit" and the audience trembled. I mention that here because of what we saw on our way uptown.

On our way to Savage's studio, we passed a parade on Lenox Avenue. A banner was hanging over the parade from a flagpole on a building: "A Man Was Lynched Yesterday." In perpetuity.

Now even more of a shocker, in another way. The parade was a Garveyite parade. Marcus Mosiah Garvey, born just so from the great house. I thought of Winsome's note of departure to my grandmother. My grandmother's assumption that the UNIA was a religious organization. The only sort of organization she could imagine for Winsome. I thought I saw Winsome—I cannot be sure—but I wanted this woman in the parade to be Winsome. She was carrying a banner reading "Poetry for the People." I wanted to know Winsome was here, and safe. "The New Negro Has No Fear" read another banner.

Savage's work was in keeping with the idea of the New Negro. She instilled nobility in the ordinary. For the Chicago World's Fair she created a sculpture based on what was then known as the "Negro National Anthem"—"Lift Ev'ry Voice and Sing." Human voices raised in song. It was bulldozed at the close of the fair. Across this clear window the drapes of racism were drawn—again. Darling girl, now that I know where your heart lieth, I will say such things to you.

Ruby Ring

Cuba in the thirties. I finally sold my grandmother's ruby ring for a pretty penny, and lit out with my friend Patrice—a Haitian *chanteuse* J. and I encountered in the Village at a club called Ambiguities—for Havana. We entered the harbor on a steamship—no United Fruit this time. Cuba would be the closest I would get to a return to Jamaica.

We were strolling along the Malecón, the seawall ringing the harbor. Patrice and I were sipping Cuba libres at an outdoor café. We were sipping Cuba libres and smoking cigars. Quite the sight we must have been. His café au lait skin and golden eyes set off by the white sharkskin suit he wore. A white silk turban on his head. My own bare shoulders browned by the Carib sun.

The ruby ring of Patrice's mouth. Blood-red lipstick. Another indelible image in my memory. We were asking each other questions about our respective islands. I've only ever lived on islands. Jamaica, Manhattan, the dreadful Long—my second husband's choice. That was ill fated.

Patrice told me that when he was a boy he had stolen money from his father to pay a voodoo woman. She promised to turn him into a little girl. She sacrificed a ground lizard, skinned it. She placed the lizard skin over his private parts and told him they would fall off. He was about eight years old. When he returned to tell her the spell had not worked, she put a curse on him. She said he would die an untimely death, dismembered by a pack of wild dogs. He was terrified and, as soon as he could, left Haiti for New York. Mecca.

In the midst of the story we were approached by a couple of army officers. They invited us to visit a cigar factory. Row upon row of workers at long tables rolling the cigars by hand. A man on a high chair on a platform, visible to all the workers, was reading the poetry of José Martí. Somehow the scene reminded me of Winsome. Our history: reading in the bush, away from the gaze of my grandmother. "Poetry for the People." I hoped that was Winsome in the parade. Again. I wondered what had become of her children.

It was in Havana that I met the lyricist of the bolero "Ojos Verdes." I think you know this bit of my story, legend really, already. Patrice's army officer introduced me to him. The song was his sublimation.

Cover Girl

After Cuba, Patrice and I returned to New York. He went back to singing at Ambiguities. I became a *Vogue* model, even making the cover twice. For the shoots I had to wear heavy panchromatic makeup. The hot spotlights would be almost touching my skin and the makeup would begin to melt. An assistant to the photographer would stand there, fanning me to stop the melting. As you can imagine it was terribly uncomfortable. I felt as if my skin were melting. All that for five dollars an hour! But a lot in those Depression years.

I was a cover girl in more ways than *Vogue*. I had managed to lose what accent I had. I claimed part-French ancestry. I felt this necessary for my survival.

The Cuba trip had been my adieu to the Caribbean. I was an American once and for all.

Memories of Pearl Harbor

I was on a stepladder. It was a wintry morning. I was dusting the wooden venetian blinds in a living room in Oyster Bay. The blinds were a pale green. I wore what was called a "snood" to protect my hair from the dust. By then I was married to my second husband. The one after your grandfather. That grandfather who refused to look at you when you were a teenager and met him for the first time because you had my eyes. Idiot. Anyway, I was on a stepladder dusting with the radio on and the news flash came over the air. "The attack came in two waves. 7:53 A.M. and 8:55 A.M. It was all over by 9:55."

My life at that time had settled. I had become a housewife/hostess. My husband was a banker/golfer. The attack on Pearl Harbor more than anything excited me—I know that probably sounds horrible, but I was bored out of my skin. Your father was a teenager and away at boarding school. I needed to do something for myself. I felt the air had been sucked out of my life. I had once been daring, adventurous. In one show I appeared in, I performed a monologue dressed as a pirate queen: I was Anne Bonney, wreaking havoc on the Spanish Main. I wanted that self back. The roaring girl.

I told my husband I was filing for divorce. I joined the Stage Door Canteen on 44th Street.

Third Husband, Not the Charm

At the Canteen I met an Army Air Corps pilot who would become husband number three. We courted for five years. I was on the road a lot of the time, in road companies of various plays. He seemed not bothered by my travels. He was charming, handsome, a facade that concealed so much. I don't know what possessed me to marry again. Except it—marriage—was expected. The War had been romanticized almost until the point of death. No excuses.

No one in those days spoke of the effect war has on the soul. Those poor unfortunates who showed signs were sent away—out of sight, out of mind. In more ways than one. Shell shock, they called it. Battle fatigue. The pilot drank when his memories, his terrors, got the better of him. A common enough thing, I suppose. And when he drank he hit me. And what's worse, I took the punishment. And even worse I saw it as punishment, not abuse. The marriage did not last long. At least I had the sense to get out. I had my three strikes.

I wonder if you remember our afternoons at the Ringling Brothers' Circus? I have a memory of one in particular. Of hundreds of children twirling flashlights (they were square in shape with some sort of image on them) on red plastic ropes. As you twirled next to me your flashlight highlighted the bruise under my left eye, which I'd tried to hide under pancake. Covering again. You were very sweet not to ask about it. Later we went to the sideshow and saw a girl with no arms or legs, writing poems with a pen in her mouth. Remember?

Number three had dropped by the night before. We'd been divorced for ages, but every now and then he tried to get back in. You were asleep upstairs. He pushed his way in and beat me. I conked out and when I came to I found he had left. He left a note, barely legible, asking that I forgive him.

You may be thinking why did I do this? Three husbands going from bad to worse. I don't know that I know. I had absolutely no model for marriage, or for motherhood. And I know I wasn't a very good mother. But I did know how it felt to be a granddaughter, a discard, so when you came into my life I could right my own childhood and give you your own.

I bequeath to you my looking glass.

I only hope that my moment of death resembles a thrilling orgasm, like those I shared with J. I do not wish to fall quietly, without a sound, into the Great Silence.

This is all I have time for right now, more later.

Everything Is Now

THE MIDWINTER DAY was glorious. Made more so by the fact that soon Cassandra would be wrapped in the legs of her lover. A fire alight in the hearth in the bedroom, softening the winter light. She turned her rented car—a red Chevy Tracker—onto a dirt road she was sure would lead to State Route 7 and to her lover's saltbox.

The snow had a bluish tint, reflecting the sky. Skeletal trees touched the only gray to the landscape. She opened the driver's side window. Cold air flooded the car.

"I have never been able to carry anything beyond that first glorious phase, when sex becomes more central than life, and demands to be called love. Does that make me a coward about life?" She spoke these words aloud; she asked no one in particular.

At the car rental counter at the airport she had debated snow tires versus chains. On the blacktop snow tires had worked fine. But now the dirt road had a thin crust of ice across it and she had skidded a couple of times. "Turn into the skid," she remembered. But she had never been sure how to do that.

Then: Suddenly:

On her left, down a hill, she could see a white-fenced horse farm. The snow had disappeared, had turned to green. Midwinter had become late summer. She found herself closing the window, turning on the air conditioning. The sun beat through the windshield. Soon she would have to stop, remove her jacket, her sweater.

In the distance a figure was walking up a slope of green.

A woman was approaching, waving in greeting.

Cassandra rolled down the window.

"You're not exactly dressed for today, are you?"

"I guess not."

By *today* did she mean weather, or time? The stranger—But could she be called a stranger? There was a familiarity between the two—was wearing loose khaki slacks, cut in the manner of the forties, and a white shirt. Around her neck was a black silk scarf held together by a clasp in the form of a scallop shell. Her cuffs were linked with pearls. The face of a magnifying glass peeked out of one breast pocket. Western Union peeked out of the other. Her hair was auburn, shoulder length, turned under in a pageboy. Remember the Breck girls? Lauren Bacall in *To Have and Have Not?*—like that. But a bit older.

"It's such a warm day, would you join me for some iced tea? I haven't entertained anyone in the longest time."

"Thank you." Cassandra shut off the ignition and got out of the car, noting that the red Chevy Tracker was now a hump-backed black Buick. She took off her jacket and sweater and tossed them into the backseat.

"You can leave your car here. Hardly anybody comes by on this back road. Especially with gas rationing. This damned war. Everyone is trying to conserve."

The two walked down a flagstone path toward a gray clapboard house, two-storied with white shutters flanking each window.

"We'll sit outside. I'll just get the tea. Be right back. I'm Grace, by the way."

"Cassandra."

Grace disappeared through a screen door and Cassandra settled herself at a round table with a glass top.

"Okay, just go with it. It's not like something like this hasn't happened before."

The air was wonderfully clear. Sunlight glanced off the surface of a small pond. In the distance a circle of horses grazed. A tabby moused in new mown grass. The desiccated head of a sunflower was nailed to the side of the house. Birds had pecked away at the seeds. The remains of a vegetable garden, run amok, were next to the house. Leaf miners had left behind filigreed chard and spinach leaves. A rosemary bush dominated one corner, spreading itself wide. Rosemary, remembrance.

On closer look the sunlight glanced off algae on the surface of the pond, highlighting them to a dark blue. On closer look the house could use a coat of paint and the glass top of the table was chipped. Cassandra ran a finger along the broken glass, drawing a drop of blood. This made it real.

Grace emerged with the iced tea.

"What's that noise?" Cassandra asked.

"You're hearing the river. The waters where the dead dissolve. Sometimes there are so many the water rises and floods the meadow. We can walk the path alongside if you like."

"Yes. Later."

"Do you want to see the telegram?"

"Pardon?"

"The telegram. The strip of words pasted on a sheet of paper. Telling me the worst thing had happened. The Western Union boy rode his bicycle all the way out here to hand it to me. I have it right here." She touched her breast.

But where was here? Cassandra wondered.

In her childhood when she had glimpses through the veil she told no one. At first she did not recognize what was happening. Later she grew to accept this way of being but knew her mother and father would not be so accepting. Somehow they would find it, and her, a blasphemy, transgressing the beliefs to which they clung. She later realized they only lacked imagination, so religion imagined for them.

The figure of a woman in a long dress, sometimes white, sometimes blue, perpetually standing by the bay window looking out, waiting for someone? The smell of gardenias and cigars in the backseat of her father's Mercury. An illustration in a book: black-and-white photograph of a Buenos Aires street in the thirties: a man seated at an outdoor café, a woman elegantly dressed, standing in front of him. A street at the bottom of the world framed by skyscrapers and chic shops, and her certainty: I have been on that street. I know these people. A man hanging in a corner of a dirt cellar. Just hanging there, surrounded by a cloud of sadness. She feels for all of them.

She has long given in to her gift. Why not? It was no more mysterious than anything else.

A friend dying three thousand miles away. Cassandra was sitting at her desk. Then: a blue marble dropped from the beak of a passing bird, on the deck outside her study. That friend's farewell.

"I had no idea where he was," Grace went on. "I tried to trace his whereabouts through newspapers, newsreels, the radio—*Life*. A neighbor came by one morning and said she thought she had glimpsed him in the opening frame of a newsreel at the Congregational church the night before. She said the newsreel showed a long line of soldiers trudging over a landscape that could be almost anywhere, and my neighbor thought she saw my lover—of course she said 'boyfriend'—walking with them. She wasn't certain but I held on to the image. That was a couple of months ago. Yes, we're in late August now, aren't we?"

Cassandra nodded and sipped her iced tea.

"Yes. Late August. When they sent the news they didn't give me any details. Nothing I could . . ."

"When was that?"

"Some weeks ago."

There was silence. Then Grace spoke again.

"This is his shirt. I've been living in it. I think I could smell him at first, now our scents are enfibered, intertwined. I carry this with me always," she said, indicating the magnifying glass. "I keep looking for his face in the crowd. In *Life,* in newspapers. I want one last glimpse. Just one. Upright. Not on a stretcher. They all look impossibly young, or impossibly ancient. Filthy faces, dangling cigarettes, dead eyes, frightened eyes."

"I think I understand."

"I know this is supposed to be a good war, if there can ever be such a thing. What do you think?"

Cassandra said nothing.

"Well, answer me, dammit." Grace raised her voice, then lowered it. "Please forgive me. My anger is only my inverted anguish. Are women even allowed to question war?"

"I really don't know what to say."

Cassandra first knew the War only from her parents' anecdotes—how the War had brought them together under the clock at the Biltmore Hotel—like so many others—or in the Astor Bar: in this way the War took on a romantic hue—underscored by black-and-white movies she watched as a kid in the darkened living room while her parents slept—she remembered one line from a movie with Margaret Sullavan—was it *Bataan*?: "They're Americans. They believe in happy endings"—*Since You Went Away,* Claudette Colbert on the home front—and of course Cassandra had been taught the War from schoolbooks—the War as a great adventure where as usual the USA saved the world. Later, as she grew older, as a student of history, and eventually a journalist, she cast a more critical eye. But that was now, this is then. Then is now.

Cassandra had sought the name of a classmate on the Wall in Washington—blown into a fog by a landmine. The day at the Wall had been an autumn day. It was raining. Cold. She traced the letters of his name as water streamed into the crevices of the black granite, distorting her own reflection. A group of tourists babbled behind her and she resented their presence tremendously.

Vietnam had been "her" war. She had marched against it, had seen friends sent to it, had the ROTC boy she was "pinned" to come home in a miasma of fear and sorrow, the nightmares and night sweats. Boys disappeared into that war the way girls in high school had disappeared into the Lily Pond Nursing Home.

"I simply can't let go. I don't know. I'm stuck here, you know?" Grace's eyes were the color of Cassandra's and were filling with tears. Cassandra saw her face reflected in Grace's tears. Grace put her head on the glass-topped table and began to weep. Cassandra leaned over and put her arm around Grace's shoulder.

"It's early days. You need to give yourself time. Isn't there anyone you can talk to?"

"Only you."

It must be a Saturday. Through the screen door came the sounds of the Met sponsored by Texaco. Was it *Tosca*? Who would be singing the title role in the forties? Tebaldi?

Grace suggested they take a walk by the river. The river ran behind the house, about a hundred yards away. The two crossed a meadow filled with late-summer wildflowers. They trod purple and yellow and green underfoot.

"Do you think there is any square inch in the world where there has not been bloodshed? I mean, this meadow, with its wildflowers, the stand of birches marking the line of the river, what has this landscape witnessed?"

Cassandra responded. "Yes. Battlefields are everywhere. Armies have no respect for landscape. I was at Antietam once, doing research. Working on a history of the year 1862. I was walking through the Maryland countryside, old farmhouse visible. A witness to the battle. It was a still autumn morning. Quiet but for the odd squawk of a raven. Then: a voice out of time, out of nowhere."

"What do you mean?"

"Just that: a voice out of time, asking, 'Is there someone baking bread?' That's all."

"Did you smell bread baking?"

"No."

"Who was speaking?"

"One of the twenty-three thousand fallen, I imagine. Twelve hours. A Wednesday in September. The bloodiest day in American history."

"At least on these shores," Grace said.

"Yes. The battlefield was covered in cornstalks. All dried out, sere. The only colors the blue sky, the black ravens."

Cassandra knew they were nearing the river. The stand of birches, the sound of rushing water told her so.

"A few days before the telegram I was lying upstairs, reading. Suddenly there was a noise as sharp as a gunshot. The noise echoed off the walls and windows of the bedroom, and I got up to see where it was coming from. There was a glass plate on my bureau. Heavy, purple—I bought it at a gallery in Boston. It had cracked in two. Just like that, I knew. The telegram only made it official."

Cassandra took Grace's hand.

Across the river—they could cross via a line of river rocks—was a small graveyard. The type that dots the New England landscape. It was almost too picturesque. The river. The flat rocks. A bullfrog in the mud of one riverbank. Small fish in the water, illumined by the dappled sunlight glancing through birches that lined the banks. And just beyond, the graveyard, which would tell the history of this particular common place. Puritan monuments giving way to Revolutionary soldiers giving way to Civil War soldiers alongside the domestic: *My amiable wife who lived belovèd and died lamented.* And of course the children. Each stone etched in the iconography of death. Wingèd death's head. Weeping willow undulating above an urn. A snake devouring its tail, reassuring endlessness.

"We made love here once. In this silence, in this light, among the reminders."

"Really?"

"Yes. Right over there." Grace pointed to one of the more elaborate headstones. "*Here sleeps the precious dust. She shines above, whose form was harmony, whose soul was love.* Right between the headstone and the footstone. Did you know they also had footstones? Some at least. It was a day not unlike today. Warm and sunny. The grass underneath sweet and thick. Nourished by *the precious dust* no doubt. The wonderfully plain wooden boxes disintegrating."

"You weren't afraid of stirring things up?"

"Our lives are contiguous. You must realize that. Sometimes I think I can see our contours in the grass. The ground in graveyards is very soft. It protects indentations. We touch them; they touch us. It's that simple. After a storm scraps of bone have been known to roam to the surface."

"Were you . . . ?"

"Going to be married? No. We were only lovers. Only," she repeated. "I guess I was fortunate to receive the telegram. He had put me down as his next of kin." Grace gave a shrug of her shoulders. "It is so hard to hold on to us, my memories keep sliding into the dark."

Memories woke Cassandra.

"I really should be going."

"If you must. I'll stay here a while. I want to trace our outline."

Cassandra turned and walked back to where, when she came in.

Back on the road it was snowing lightly and the red Chevy Tracker was waiting. She put the key in the ignition, started the engine and slowly negotiated the back road until it turned into Route 7. She took 7 south and saw the familiar stone fence, the spaces between the stones where in summer gray and blue violets thrived. Now there was a dusting of snow in and around the stones. She drove to the back of the house.

"Sorry I'm late, darling."

"I was a little concerned. Is everything okay?"

"I got sidetracked."

"How do you mean?"

"I encountered the shadow of a former self," Cassandra told her lover.

"What do you mean? An old lover?"

"Not that. That would be simple."

"What then?"

"You probably wouldn't believe me."

"Try me," she said, and took her lover's face in her hand.

"Maybe later," Cassandra said. "Let's just go upstairs. I need to make love."

Upstairs the bed invited them, the firelight glanced around the room. "*Vissi d'arte, vissi d'amore . . .*"

"Caballé?"

"Tebaldi. It's an old recording."

Ashes, Ashes . . .

THE FAMILY HAD A HABIT of falling, had fallen many times. Falls from grace. Falls from wealth, property. Fallen on hard times. Fallen angels. Falling stars.

The family had exited Eden more or less willingly. They were not expelled from paradise exactly; rather, they were impelled toward a land of promise, which theirs was no longer. The family left Eden without a backward glance. That was a shame. But the place had become contaminated.

Two died from their falls. One was two years old.

The child was the adopted son of a doctor and his wife who had emigrated to Boston in the 1920s. They lived in a comfortable, well-appointed house on Massachusetts Avenue. The doctor had trained at the University of Edinburgh Medical School. In Boston he had hospital privileges at the Peter Bent Brigham, as well as a private practice in his office at home. He treated the well-to-do.

The child had come to them through his practice. The daughter of a patient, a banker, found herself in what used to be called the "family way." The doctor was not asked to terminate the pregnancy; that was not her family's way. For that matter, the doctor shared the belief that termination was akin to murder. He was asked to recommend a place in the country where the girl might seek refuge and to find a decent home for the baby. The banker was not thrilled when the doctor told him he and his wife wanted the child. (This his wife had yet to know.)

"It's too close to home. Someone will find out." That was the banker's argument. But the doctor prevailed, telling the banker that doctor-patient confidentiality applied and that no one, repeat no one, not even his wife, would be the wiser. "The fewer who know, the better," he said. And maybe the day would come when the banker would like to meet his grandchild.

"I can't see that ever happening. All I want is to put this thing behind us." He had wanted to say "this mess" but censored himself.

"Very well, then. No one will ever know. Not your daughter, not my wife."

These were the kind of men who decided what was best for women. The doctor decided his wife needed a child. He feared she might become restless without one. The banker decided a suitable fate for his daughter, her child.

A retreat was found for the girl in western Massachusetts, near North Adams, on the Mohawk Trail. She was granted a medical leave of absence—"nervous exhaustion"—from Wellesley. The college was told she would recuperate in seven months or so. Doing catch-up work in the summer, she would only lose one semester.

She was delivered of a baby boy. The doctor was summoned to North Adams. The doctor took the child from the matron. He would never meet the debutante-mother. That was all to the good. The doctor named the child Michael. He took him back to Boston on the afternoon train and surprised his wife.

Two years later: the doctor's wife's sister, an actress, was visiting from New York. The run of *Show Boat* had just ended. She'd had a minor part and understudied Helen Morgan in the role of the octoroon Julie. She was waiting for another part to open up. She told stories of Helen Morgan, drunk, her hair falling into the scrambled eggs in some Harlem after-hours joint.

The doctor did not approve of his sister-in-law. She disrespected men for one thing. She used them up. And he knew she had had at least two abortions. He held her in contempt. Even her beauty, green eyes, raven hair—men fell for her all right—irritated him. Everything about her, according to his lights, was wrong. Everyone knew that actresses were one step removed from the street. He wished she had stayed behind in the corruption of paradise, kept her distance from her sweeter sister. He thought her a fallen woman. He kept this to himself.

But for his wife's sake he tolerated her sister and offered to take them both to dinner one Friday evening. Their little boy would be looked after by his nurse. The doctor's wife had adjusted to his gift of a child. At first when he brought Michael home she seemed almost hurt. She was still a young woman, barely thirty-five; why had he given up on her? But he was fifteen years her senior. "I think it's now or never for us. You'll get used to this, my dear. You'll learn to love him." As you learned to love me? The doctor had few illusions.

This Friday evening the three were having cocktails in the drawing room. The doctor had prepared a pitcher of Bombay gin martinis on a glass-topped cart. He poured each of them a drink, dropped in the obligatory pimento-stuffed martini olive, and toasted his sister-in-law.

"It's lovely to see you again, Bess." The only thing true about that sentence was her name.

"Thanks, Edward; delicious martini, by the way." Even though scotch was her drink.

No one in the room preferred rum, for obvious reasons.

The little boy came running, breathless into the drawing room at that moment, trailed by his Irish nurse.

"He wants to say night-night, sir."

Then: It happened so suddenly. Somehow the stool on which the doctor rested his legs got upturned, and the little boy fell into one of its feet. His excitement vanished and he started to whimper.

"There, there, it's all right," the nurse said, lifting him up, holding him close. "There, now."

"I'd better take a look," the doctor said. He took the little boy from the nurse and carried him out of the room, into the night nursery upstairs. The nurse followed behind.

The two women sipped their drinks. Neither had budged.

"Everything is fine," the doctor said as he came down the stairs. "Just a bit shaken up, is all."

The three emptied their glasses and the doctor called a cab to take them to Locke-Ober's.

"May I recommend the lobster Savannah?" their waiter inquired.

"Thank you. But we'll have the chowder for starters. And a bottle of the Pouilly Fuisse, if you please."

"Very good, sir."

The women were silent. The actress didn't want to rock the boat. Her sister's marriage had allowed her own emigration. The doctor and his wife were her sponsors into this new world. Whenever she visited she was on her best behavior.

. . .

Two days later: Michael died in the children's ward of his father's hospital. The doctor held his little hand. He wept beside the fallen child. The doctor had fallen in love with the little fellow. His son. Heir to all the doctor had become.

Michael's fall had caused a perforation in his small intestine. He developed peritonitis. And, these being the years before antibiotics, there was no hope for his recovery. A child's rhyme came into the doctor's mind:

> I do not like thee, Doctor Fell,
> The reason why I cannot tell;
> But this I know, and know full well;
> I do not like thee, Doctor Fell.

The doctor tried to blame the actress; she always brought instability with her. But in the end he blamed himself. He should have examined Michael more closely. Surgery at once would have saved him.

By and by, as they used to say in fairy tales, the doctor drank himself into oblivion. His wife returned to postlapsarian Eden. The actress returned to the stage.

That's the story as it came down to me, through narrow family channels. As narrow as our blood vessels, evidence of aristocracy beneath our skin. So it was told me.

The actress, hair still raven, eyes still green, but slightly bloodshot and always concealed behind dark glasses, is an old woman. Although she will have none of it. She has had three husbands. Two children. My father was her son.

She tells me she wants one more "fabulous orgasm" before she dies. She tells me she wishes she believed in God.

We are in a restaurant in Greenwich Village to celebrate her birthday. She orders a Dewar's on the rocks, water on the side. Some things never change.

"I need to tell you something. There's not a lot of time left. There was that week in Boston when I was visiting my sister and the doctor, her husband. I need to get this into the open. Everyone's dead except me and you. They had a little boy, adopted. But you know about him.

They couldn't have children of their own. The doctor bought him from an Irish girl a friend of his got into trouble, knocked up, you know. At least that's what my sister told me. He had another story, which turned the child's blood blue. That's the one you probably heard. Status meant the world to him. Poor devil. On the nursemaid's day off I was alone with the child. My sister had an errand and asked me to watch him. He and I were alone in the nursery. I had to take a long distance call from New York. So I left him in the nursery, told him to stay there. But he didn't. He took a fall, running downstairs, and fell into a doorstop. Into the mast of a cast-iron ship. He screamed bloody murder. Finally, he calmed down. He'd taken a tumble the evening before so that would explain any bruises.

"So I didn't say anything. The doctor resented me enough. I've never told anyone this. I let them think he died because the doctor didn't notice the damage done the night before. I was in this country under his sponsorship. I had a terror of being deported. There was nothing left for me back there. Can you understand?"

She gives me a half-smile. She wants to be forgiven. Not even forgiven; her action, or inaction, understood. I do not know what to say. I put my hand over hers. But I remain silent. I do not know what to say. I honestly don't know what to think about this truth-telling. The family channels can be so polluted.

Finally, I speak. "Did you tell Rebekah before she died?" I am asking about her sister.

"What possible reason would there have been?"

"To unburden yourself?"

She is silent for a moment or two, uncomfortable.

Then: she plays her trump card. I've seen it many times before.

"My sister was your real mother," she goes on. "Your parents weren't ready to have children. When you had diphtheria and nearly died, they would go out at night dancing at the yacht club and not even bother to look in on you when they got home. My sister sat by your bedside. She saved your life. You were one.

"She had never really cottoned to the little boy. He was the doctor's child for the most part. There's so much more you don't know."

"Tell me."

"I don't know if I should."

"Everyone's dead but us. You said so yourself. Why not?"

She asks me to order her another scotch. Then goes to find the ladies' room.

"It's downstairs."

"Be right back. I'll think about it but I'm not making any promises."

Her final words to me before she falls. Her final sound, a scream, echoing in the narrow stairway. Headlong she falls. Face-first down a flight of metal stairs, skull cracked open, an empty socket where one green eye had been, the other eye intact, surprised at the suddenness of it all.

I have her cremated. She would hate her damaged face.

Then As Now

THE FIRST TIME she had heard Martha Argerich live had been an evening at the Metropolitan Museum of Art. Twenty years had fled since then. At least.

In a row behind her—she could see the evening as if it were yesterday—she is blessed with a photographic memory—sat a man of about fifty and his much younger companion. The younger man was holding forth, expressing in emphatic tones arcane facts to do with the history of tea. She found she could still hear his voice and wondered why.

The spaces around her filled as people filed in, found their places, rustled, settled.

The young man spoke of tea bricks—"embossed with courtesans and dragons, all bound feet and firestorms"—used as currency during the years of the China Trade. He'd learned all this—"and much more; I fear I'm a dreadful cliché"—as a boy sailor in Her Majesty's navy.

"Shades of Madame Butterfly," the older man said.

"Hong Kong was ever so hectic."

The woman had to smile.

The pianist entered and the former boy sailor fell silent.

Other details came back as the evening took shape in her mind.

She recalled the stage as carpeted in red. Could that have been? No, she was remembering Bergman's production of *Hedda Gabler*, in London: before or after. She *was* certain that above the piano had been hung a painting from the museum's permanent collection. One of those paintings to which she returned again and again. Courbet's *Woman with a Parrot.* Auburn hair, elongated body not unlike her own. The model had been Whistler's mistress on loan to Courbet. Like the boy sailor she has her own store of knowledge on which she depends.

Argerich, black hair streaming, attacked the piano. Chopin, as the woman recalled.

That was then.

Now she was at another concert hall and the pianist, Argerich again, was playing something by Brahms. This time she was backed by a full orchestra.

The woman was again alone.

A man was seated next to her, on her right. On his right, as she glanced down the row, sat a woman in a sable coat even though it was a warm Indian summer evening. The man had a FedEx envelope in his lap and was presently sliding some papers from it. He shone a silver penlight across the papers. He tidied the papers into a stack and took a silver pen from his breast pocket. She glanced down and noticed there was a drawing on the top page. Unmistakable. The interior of a female. Laid bare. Orderly. Precise. One size fits all.

She'd never peered inside herself. She didn't want to.

The man took his pen and made a correction in the caption that ran under the drawing. Then drew an arrow from the caption to the likeness of the womb. His pen moved fluidly, making only the slightest scratching noise, across the galley proof. Acoustically above, or below, the Brahms.

She began in her irritation to invent a scenario. The sable woman, doctor's wife no doubt, greets her husband at the door of their apartment, overlooking—something—the Park, the River—and reminds him that they have tickets to a concert that evening and that it's almost a coup to get to hear Argerich live since she's notoriously difficult to book. The wife speaks with *New Yorker* authority. The doctor reminds his wife that his work means everything and his publisher needs the proofs sent back almost immediately. They strike one of those bargains. She will have her evening out; he uses the word *recital* to get her goat. He will bring his galleys. He often works with music in the background.

The woman tried to turn her attention to the music but too much intruded.

. . .

"Do you have a record player?"

She thought it an odd question, then what it implied came clear to her, and she was frightened. He was the friend of a friend; they were meeting for the first time. He was in his final year of medical school and would not be able to give her anything, he said, for fear of getting into trouble should anything go wrong. Of course, he said, what he'd agreed to would get him into plenty of trouble should anyone find out. No fear, she said; she wasn't talking. If she did, he said, he could kiss his future good-bye. She wouldn't. If anything went wrong, he could be arrested. She did understand, didn't she? If anything went wrong—there it was again. She didn't want to think about it. Just let it be over. But without anesthesia, he said, then anyone could be responsible, even her. It happened all the time. Okay? Okay. She really had no choice; he was doing her a favor.

In her one-room graduate student digs at the top of a triple-decker house she set up the portable stereo close by her bed. She could not for the life of her remember what music she'd chosen that evening. She made the bed with white muslin sheets, making the surface as smooth, as tight as possible. She did remember the volume of the record player turned up and her being afraid the landlady would complain. Then she remembered it was the landlady's bingo night and the house would be quiet as she was the only tenant.

She was lying naked under a top sheet, also pristine, her legs drawn up and spread. She thought of Courbet's nude and tried to remember the composition of the painting, but her store of knowledge failed her. The painting fell away. Its brilliant sensuality dissolved.

As he worked, her muscles began to cramp and tighten. Relax, he said. She felt a bruising and thought she could see inside herself. And saw herself purple, a hurricane sky. I'm almost there, he said. He scraped and hollowed her.

There was a rush, and she liquefied and poured out of her body, rushing onto the sheets.

Could her voice be heard above the music? She did not know.

Muleskin. Honeyskin.

In 1998 a woman is put to death via lethal injection in Texas. In Connecticut on Live at Five *a news anchor tells her viewers that the last female executed in the Nutmeg State was hanged in 1786. She adds that the female was twelve years old.*

FLOCK OF CROWS, feathered darkness, clack-clack against the leaded glass, clack-clack, each day at five without fail.

It is January. In the distance the western hills are starkly lit.

Crows are a constant in this place, fisher crows up from the river. A history of Connecticut says they are the embodied spirits of those hanged here, when this, the highest point in the city, held the gallows.

If this be true, and stranger things have been, then which is she?

Which "well-to-do Goody Ayres of Wethersfield"? She who received the "devil's instrument"—in the language of her time—and transmogrified into a fox. Convicted witch.

On this very spot, beneath the leaded glass windows of my short-term rental within the little ivy league, encircled by a rundown city of Caribbean immigrants, was hanged a twelve-year-old girl. Of course she haunts me. How can she not?

Who was she?

At the historical society near the home of the poet on Westerly Terrace, an offshoot of Asylum, a librarian in a polka-dot frock approaches me, her affect at once hushed and animated.

"How may I help you?"

I tell her. She nods and disappears behind a door with a milky glass window. *Reference* in black paint on the glass.

The librarian reappears with a box.

She slides a microfiche under the viewer on the darkened oak library table.

I scan the record.

The gray of stones. Stone fence with tumbled stones. Red. There's red as well as gray. Strawberries in a basket.

Smashed. Berries. Blonde of a girl's head. The path to the girl is gray. Dappled red.

And there's red skin.

The walls of the jail—spelled *gaol* in the recently postcolonial paper—are thick.

Also gray, veined gray-blue—mossed in the New England summer heat, wet.

It will stay light well into the night—extramural. Darkness and damp within.

I try to take myself there, inside.

Into the cell with its dung smells, scurryings, where a girl might find the bowl of a clay pipe. For the gaol had begun life as a tavern and bits of clay pipe and brown bottles emerged now and then from the hard earth floor. On one side of the bowl is the head of a king, porphyrial George perhaps, on the obverse his queen. She may run her fingers over these images again and again. She may find comfort in their concreteness, a remnant of company in the dark.

This is but wishful thinking.

Who is this girl?

Reportage: On the morning of July 28 a girl known for her malicious nature is sent to fetch water by the Widow Rogers.

Time and again the newspaper identifies the Widow Rogers as the girl's mistress. The girl has been—in the language of her time—bound out.

This girl, this malicious girl, is identified. Her name is spelled variously: Hannah Ocuish, Hannah Occuish, Hannah Oquish.

She is called mulatto, melatto.

Muleskin. Honeyskin.

"That's curious," the librarian says.

The paper goes further. The girl's mother, in thrall to drink, abandoned creature, Pequot, one of the remnant, long since vanished. Father unmentioned, anywhere.

So this half-breed, possibly half-black, perhaps half-slave, or slave in fact—we cannot be certain of anything—was sent to draw water; when, what?

A wall, stones tumbling.

The body of another girl is found in the road. Facedown nearby the tumbled stone fence. She is covered with stones. Head, arms, legs.

There are red marks on her throat.

Then: almost immediately: the culprit is caught red-handed.

The librarian slides another microfiche under the magnifier.

"Here"—

Arrest is swift. There is never any doubt. Of course it would come to this. Unbridled girl, renowned for temper. The worthless laying waste to the worthy.

After a few lies—she tried to blame some local boys—Hannah confesses.

She was, she says, punishing the other girl—Eunice Bolle, aged six—because Eunice accused Hannah of stealing strawberries from her a few weeks before—when strawberry time began.

Caught red-handed in the strawberry patch of the Widow Rogers, the woman to whom she was bound.

"I spied her on the public road."

"What did you do then?"

"I called out for her to wait."

"And?"

"And she would not answer me. She was a wicked girl."

"Why do you call her wicked?"

"She told lies on me."

"Yourself are a liar. And worse. Yourself are wicked."

"I put down my bucket and chased after her across the garden."

"She was a child but half your age."

"She was wicked."

"What possessed you to kill this child?"

"I caught up and beat at her until she stopped."

"Stopped?"

"Until her life stopped."

"And then?"

"Then I covered her body with stones and prayed for the devil to come and take her away to where she belonged."

"And where was that?"

"In Hell with the other liars."

"And the murderers?"

"She provoked me."

"Vengeance is mine, saith the Lord, I will repay."

Hannah is taken to gaol. Where—and this is curious as well—"My goodness," says the librarian—she is placed in a cell with other children, as if in a children's ward.

After two months she comes to trial.

The librarian whispers to me from the paper.

The trial takes no time at all. Hannah is convicted. She is then sentenced in the language, etc.

"That you be returned hence to gaol from whence you came, and thence be carried to the place of execution—and then be hanged with a rope by the neck, between the heavens and the earth, until you are dead, dead, dead."

It is reported that she made no response, but at the moment of her approach to the gallows she appeared small and frightened and surprised at what was to become of her.

December in New England. All is gray.

Trees, skies, chimney.

Inside the gaol, she is freezing.

Or maybe everything is whitened.

Snowfall, sign of God's grace, the night before.

Iced branches crack and fall in the night.

Her neck breaks.

Clack-clack against the leaded glass, clack-clack.

Belling the Lamb

On Friday afternoon the coroner and jury sat on the body of a lady, in the neighbourhood of Holborn, who died in consequence of a wound from her daughter the preceding day.

—*Times,* London, September 24, 1796

A WOMAN HELD TOGETHER by shoelaces hoards her imagination in a small room in a small house in north London.

She weaves and unweaves and reweaves the needlework in her lap, in her mind; her hands must never be idle.

She is alert to the clang of her mother's bell.

It *is* a clang rather than a tinkle. It vibrates through my brain. I put my fingertips to my temples to no avail. Her clang, followed by her bellow, is awful.

I am thirty-two, housebound, and a virgin.

November 26, 1796

That which I remember makes my hands tremble. The date is September 22, this very year. We are in the dining room. We, meaning the servant girl newly down from the country and myself. We are laying the table for the evening meal. Charles is in his usual place at the Salutation and Cat. The weight of the carving knife only adds to my tremors. The servant girl places the cake fork to the side of the place setting rather than above it. I have told her its proper place more than once but she may be a bit dim. Or merely frightened by her new surroundings and its denizens. We are not a pretty sight. The drooling old man who cannot remember from moment to moment. The bedridden tyrant—no other word for it—who is my mother, barking orders morning, noon, and night from her sanctum sanctorum. This must come to an end.

I am thirty-two years old now and am serving a life sentence, just as the serving girl who has misplaced the cake fork. This life unbearable.

The carving knife in my left hand, I pick up the cake fork in my right. Fling it against the wall. Another, then another. I do not speak. The servant girl is screaming bloody murder and dashes from the dining room to her drear, albeit safe, quarters at the roof of the house. I am flinging cutlery right and left, and each piece clatters to the floor, and eventually the old man staggers into the room.

I detest his pissed-upon self and the assumption that I will clean up after him.

I take a fruit knife—we are well-equipped for entertaining, though seldom have we visitors—and, taking aim this time, impale it in his neck. A thin trickle of his thin blood runs down his shirt, his eyes widen and he starts, but only briefly, and turns to leave the room, the knife stuck in place. By now he has forgotten it is there.

I pass his chair as I head upstairs, and he makes as if to read the evening paper. He who has forgotten language.

I take the stairs two at a time—if I pause I may lose my nerve.

The carving knife is firm in my left hand. I have ceased trembling. At the landing on the second floor I turn into my mother's room. I am stone cold. She is propped on pillows and has been woken from a nap. She asks me about the commotion downstairs and tells me her sleep was interrupted. I raise the carving knife shoulder-high. "Have you gone mad?" Her last words. I do not speak, instead draw back the knife and cut into her left breast, piercing her heart, which explodes across the sickroom. Her face is frozen in astonishment. Her mouth agape. This is not a crime of passion. I am stone cold.

Soon enough Charles will return home from the Salutation and Cat where over a tankard of ale and a pipe of oronoko tobacco he has been punning with his circle, his one blue eye and one brown eye sparkling in the firelight. (I have never been inside the Salutation and Cat, nor any other public house. I am not encouraged to venture out. Charles is generous with his recounting.)

Even with his stammer (acquired at boarding school when he was nine, under circumstances unknown to me, although we are exceptionally close; STC will write a poem, witness to this fraternal/sororal bond), his lambent wit comes through.

"Oh, sir, please come quick! It's a terrible, terrible thing that's happened!" the servant girl cries from her rooftop window. He glances up toward her noise, then spies me sitting on the steps outside, and his pace picks up. I must be a sight. My mother's blood spattered across my face, arms, bodice. Who knew the old woman would have so much blood! (*Macbeth* is in our future.) This would be the worst time to laugh—but I cannot stop myself. I roar as my brother approaches. I indicate with my right arm the way into the house as if he would not know.

This roaring virgin will go to trial for the "heinous crime of matricide."

My dear brother, his stammer drawing laughter from the crowd, will testify on my behalf. He cites our shared history of melancholia. Our "episodes of dread."

The coroner brings in an alienist to examine me. The "mad," as we are called, are thought to be estranged—strange—removed. *Aliené* is the French for insane. It crosses the Channel along with the latest fashions. I sew to help support the family. I am a mantua-maker. I cut and stitch loose cloaks for gentlemen and ladies. Free-flowing garments for the crowds who flow freely along London's streets. An alienist studies the alienated. The woman estranged from herself; what it is ordained she become. Who resists what she was meant to be.

"This court has no choice but to find the accused, Mary Lamb, having evinced no remorse for the murder of her mother, insane."

December 18, 1796

There are red rosebuds scattered across the walls of my room in Islington. These may transmute into bloodspots when I close my eyes, but this happens less and less. Charles is paying a mother and daughter sixty pounds per year for my upkeep. The mother and daughter run a private asylum. The irony of their pairing is not lost on me. But without this place I would be confined in the royal hospital—Bethlem, Bedlam—among the indigent lunatics. Some talk around and about that I belong there. Or worse. The food here is halfway decent. Mostly nursery fare, intended to calm us. The place settings simple. The dining table here is not my lookout. See, I can still make a joke. Charles brings me books and writing paper and pen and ink. I have a large and airy room all to myself. This is not punishment; matricide was a small price to pay for solitude. No more clangs! The window over my writing table overlooks the street in front. The only noises are the occasional bleat of one of the other inmates and the sound of carriage wheels on the cobblestones outside. STC visits me from time to time. He has promised a carriage ride if the mother and daughter concur. He sometimes brings laudanum, which brings on a benign dreaming. My brother fears the effects of these visits. He wishes me to be among cooler intellects and duller fancies—as he has written—but does he not realize I am freed of my demon (note: singular)? We both are. Am I mad to think such a thing?

Charles writes: "I am a widowed thing, now thou art gone."

September 11, 1797

They tell me Mary Wollstonecraft has died giving birth to a daughter. Not much else is there to say. On the day Godwin drew a black line across a page. What a business: to die in the putrefaction of childbirth. Charles will attend her burial at St. Pancras. What a business. The baby lived, poor thing.

September 22, 1797

A year to the day. Clang-clang-clang-bellow-bellow-bellow no more.

Soon I will depart this private madhouse. I cannot depart myself. Not that I wish for that.

October 15, 1799

The life of the old man is finally closed and we are released into our bliss of double-singleness. It is said among our friends that to see us strolling through Regent's Park arm in arm is the most natural sight in the world. And so it feels. It is I alone with whom he does not stammer, surrounding me in his eloquence. Such is his trust.

Which is the greater sin (or *is* it a greater madness?): not to love one's mother, to kill her and feel only relief that she is silenced? Or to love one's brother almost to death?

Truth be told, as I climbed those stairs I was afraid. She frightened me; she always had. I was a cat engaging a cobra. But a cat with a carving knife in my front paw.

August 30, 1800

I feel like a cat that has been belled. The act follows us wherever we go. Someone finds out. They hound us from place to place. They ask not why it was done; why I did it. They think only that I am mad, or evil, or both. As soon as they find out about us, we are put on the street and left to find other accommodation. It is trying. Not so much for myself but for Charles. Perhaps this is my punishment. Yet I have never felt a loss of his affection. I raised my hand to our last landlady and she screamed bloody murder. Running down the stairs backwards, away from me. Like someone in a farce. I was only defending myself against her hysterical rants, but who would believe that? Lock up your mothers! Mary is in town.

STC has invited us to Greta Hall, but Charles puts him off. He is afraid the gathered company will provoke my alienation. His constant vigilance of me can become tiresome. I argue that the mountain air will do us both a world of good after the soot, the dregs of London. We shall see. Charles worries too much. Far too much. I promise we can pack my straitjacket. I have embroidered my initials at the right shoulder in crimson thread; there will be no mistaking it is mine. M. A. L. *Malade.* Malady. *Mal de mere.* I will sew the outlines of a little lamb, with little black curls.

The alienist calls the straitjacket a camisole; like the garment women wear over their corsets. Soft cloth concealing whalebone skeleton, all lace and ribbon, eyelet cotton.

All this holding in . . . the straitjacket is well-named: it straitens, confines, narrows.

September 26, 1802

Finally. We arrive at Greta Hall. The wife glum, embodiment of gloom. Our host entirely opposite. I suspect the wife surmises our complicity in STC's misbehavior. Who can blame the poor man escaping into dream? Imagining his unhappiness be gone. Mistress Glumly is possessed of a foul temper. She once poured a pan of boiling milk over her husband's foot, making him lame for a time. He who loves more than anything to walk all over the landscape in search of waterfalls.

As I stand in the doorway I feel Charles's arm around my waist, sense his gentle restraint.

Is it so wrong that I do not regret what I did? It is as though that life did not exist. I am borne on the arms of my brother.

Crocodilopolis

BY THE TIME WE ARRIVED, at the beginning of September 1905, we had been traveling for one month, give or take a day. We landed at Alexandria, having embarked in Marseilles on the penultimate leg of our journey. From Alexandria we took the train to Cairo and there spent the night under the aegis of the British High Commissioner. We had sent letters of introduction ahead, the social instruments necessary for entry.

I do think that one of the only uses of Empire is ease of travel.

The place was of course terribly hot. My skin seemed to retain the heat so that at night in bed under the white netting it was as if I radiated. I thought I could see the heat waves in the darkness. Emanations. I longed to perspire, to be bathed in sweat, but I was bone dry, burning. More water, my girl. I got up and walked through the High Commissioner's residence and found myself inside a walled garden. The street sounds of Cairo were almost nonexistent at that late, or early, hour, a few voices raised here and there, a dog barking in the distance, its noise resonating off the walls of the garden, the air heavy with the scent of oranges. I sat on a bench and tried to ignore the heat in my body. After a bit, with no success, I got up and returned to my room.

After breakfast—tea and eggs and bacon and toast—in that heat!—we set sail down the Nile toward our destination.

On the boat there managed to be something of a breeze, and the heat was tempered by the blue of the waters lapping at us.

At least the blue purveyed a visual coolness.

I don't know what I was thinking. I had on a plaid taffeta dress which brushed the ground and a leghorn straw hat, tied under my chin with a ribbon of the same plaid.

I cannot tell you the relief when I gave myself leave to untie the ribbon.

I longed for white linen, loose.

I longed, I must say it—I have been avoiding it, even to myself—for you.

A month had gone by. A month had not cooled me.

Photographs of our peripatetic ilk are commonplace. Newsprint, family albums, postcards. "Millie is seated on the ship of the desert," begins the greeting, as Millie wobbles on the camel's hump. "Note Sphinx in distance." Millie will sally forth and burn. Oh, my goodness. Not very nice. I confess to an arrogance about the Millies of this world.

Perhaps I should have petitioned Worth. Not much hope there. The man had designed the bell sleeve after all. Confinement was the order of the day.

I had a desire to remove all my clothes, down to my underthings, venture even beyond that, and sink myself in the dark blue. Even as the man-eaters swarmed on the banks, in the bulrushes. I would open my legs and the Nile would flood me. The man-eaters, their hides as if islands. I'd straddle one and ride him downstream. As queer as Millie on her ship of the desert. For had I not partaken of the most forbidden thing?

The sun right now was heating the boards of the deck and traveling the railing where I stood. I felt the heat in my soles. Passing through my entire body.

In the distance a flock of ibis sat in the naked branches of a tree I did not recognize. Two birds seemed to duel, curved beak against curved beak. Or perhaps that was their mating ritual.

I turned from the river and returned to my cabin and my books.

We'd hired an Egyptian woman to do for us. The High Commissioner had recommended her. She was industrious and honest. And clean, Mrs. High Commissioner stressed. A rarity among these people, she commented, in that ordinary, predictable tone. Were it not for Empire, and its need for caretakers like herself and her hubby, she'd be setting a tea table in St. John's Wood or Mayfair with the help of her Irish maid, whom she would also commend as a rarity among her people.

Superiority must be claimed in all things, including one's choice of servants.

The Egyptian woman was presented to us. She was swathed in white cotton, almost blue in its coolness. Yes, she said, she was willing to accompany us; she had family near where we were going and was eager to see them.

Onboard she trod barefoot on the planks of the deck.

As soon as we reached the site I would free myself of this traveling regalia and dress likewise. I envied her way of moving, so unlike my own, except in dreams, and secrecy. As you know.

She spoke English well enough, which was to our advantage since none of us was particularly adept at Arabic. My second language was French, and I had studied Greek for ten months with a Miss Threadgill, a friend of the family. Shabby genteel spinster on the face of things. A woman who had come to grief, as the euphemism goes, but not in the usual way. She had spent a stretch of time in Bethlem Royal Hospital—Bedlam—having committed a crime beyond conventional punishment. I was not supposed to know anything about this circumstance.

Our party was four in number. Myself, the Egyptian woman, my brother Vincent, and his friend Hugh Waterman.

"I am Adventure!" my grandmother, whom I adored, would declaim at table after a few glasses—Veuve Clicquot Brut—but she was not a woman who depended on wine for her explosions of self.

No indeed.

As a girl I sat on her four-poster bed, and we traveled around the world she had never seen. She was rather like Prester John, imagining creatures in far-off places, at the edge of the world, tumbling off.

Beings with umbrellas growing from their foreheads.

Women with golden nipples, dripping Golden Syrup.

Volcanoes inhabited by fire-people who were in a constant state of burning but were unconsumed. Unlike one of Bosch's infernal landscapes. Here fire was a blessèd thing, lighting the chamber inside the volcano. And the unconsumed the opposite of damned. "Life should be made of fire," my grandmother said. "Not immolation but a blaze of light."

She died finally by sliding down a banister. I was in my room one night when I heard a sharp "Ooh!" and then a thud. I ran toward the sounds and found her in her nightdress, in a heap at the foot of the staircase, one thin line of blood at the corner of her mouth. I closed her eyes, now emptied of imagination, daring, and enfolded her in my arms. I sat there as she grew cold. The dawn began streaming through the stained glass window and lit upon us. One of the servants, on her way to light the morning fires in the bedrooms came upon our pietà and gave a cry and ran off to fetch my brother. That very day I moved into her four-poster where I wrapped myself in her counterpane and spent my grief.

The boys—now in their thirties—had met at Oxford. I had been educated at home—in the family library, my grandmother's four-poster, through the Greek lessons of an apparent madwoman. I followed where my own mind led me, unconfined by curriculum. That's one way to regard it.

It was I who had located Crocodilopolis in the first place. I found it quite by accident. In the library one evening after everyone had gone to bed I poured myself a cognac and found Strabo's *Geography* and decided to practice my Greek.

There it was: Crocodilopolis, Shedet, the separate one. "The oasis that was not an oasis," according to Strabo, "a place of dalliance."

The crocodile emerged in silence and in mystery from the waters of Nun, the primeval sea which drained into the Nile. Its back, an island, represented earth, its membraned eye, the sun, and it was given life by way of water, as are we all.

In the crocodile was all creation found.

In Crocodilopolis were his temples and his tombs.

Strabo described the sacred crocodile, vicar of Sobek, the crocodile god. A tamed creature decked out in ornaments of glass and gold, its forefeet braceleted and painted, he held court for pilgrims bearing offerings. The tamed creature lived in a lake on temple ground in a state of divine captivity. It drank milk sweetened with honey and was fed grains and meat. On its death the creature was embalmed by priests as if it were a pharaoh. Its mummy was carried through the streets of Crocodilopolis in a sacred procession until it reached the temple where the mummy was placed on an altar, its final resting place.

The internal organs, but for the heart, had been removed. A scarab was placed over the heart, the seat of brilliance.

Inside the mummy was a rumor of language, poetry. It was that we sought.

The table was set in the main cabin. An earthenware vessel of black olives sat at its center. As I was waiting on Hugh and Vincent to arrive, I poured myself a glass of red wine from a terracotta pitcher, decorated with a curve of blue, the Nile, running down its side. We were to join the captain for the evening meal. There were no other passengers. We had hired the boat to take us downriver to a place called El Wasta, where we would secure overland transportation to deliver us to Crocodilopolis.

The captain came in through the jalousied doors and greeted me. Behind him, through the opened doors, was the blue of the river. I listened for the yawns of crocodiles. All I heard were the sounds of the boys' approach.

Hugh's voice, high-pitched one moment, basso the next, as I imagined Oscar Wilde might have spoken, heralded: "I came upon Isis and Osiris: I had done a deed, they said, which the ibis and the crocodile trembled at. I was buried for a thousand years, in stone coffins, with mummies and sphinxes, in narrow chambers of the heart. I was kissed by crocodiles."

"I think you left a bit out," Vincent said.

"Only by way of improvement, old chap. I don't think De Quincey would mind, if in his stupor he managed to notice."

"Ah, the importance of being you."

The two entered the cabin.

"I believe the phrase was 'cancerous crocodiles,' dreadful image, the opium-eater's remorse, I expect." Vincent would not let go.

"Don't be tiresome," Hugh replied, as he cast his gaze across the brownness of the Egyptian woman, carrying a silver platter laden with tomatoes and cucumbers dressed with mint and olive oil, flat breads dotted with toasted sesame seeds, lamb kebab spiced with sumac, all of which she placed in front of us on the dining table. I tried to meet her eyes but was unable.

After dinner I went for a stroll around the deck. In the dark the half-moon reflected off the waters. And that which I had submerged—in my own waters—came up for air.

You turn onto a narrow lane which branches from a secondary road. The lilacs are on the verge, on the edge of a cow path, worn down over the years, widened by spring rains. It is May in the dream and we are in England. I follow you at a distance.

This is a chance encounter outside the bounds of our lives.

Is the house still there, are you, visible from the flagstone path? The trace of garden, the copper beech?

Rosebushes, "heavy feeders," as you once said. "As we are," I responded. Fragrant Cloud, deep-red with one dark petal as if bruised.

As we were.

Rosebushes are numerous in the Fayum—our destination. Most attar of the roses of Egypt is manufactured there. The air will be heavy with their scent. Even unbearable.

I dreamed about the date May 5, 1895. We were together in a small room with others, people I did not recognize. I told you about the dream. You said, "That was the day my mother died. And you don't think we are connected. You think this is some romantic adventure, some of the rule-shattering in which you like to engage."

Then: one last letter from one disastrous afternoon:

Yesterday when I chose those flowers I did feel, as I said, they somehow represented us. I think the depth of color, scent. The sweetness of roses, the sharpness of ginger. The strict cultivation of one, the ruinate wildness of the other. How one can have both, be both. As we

That's all I can remember.

On the narrow lane you stop suddenly. You turn and see me. Throw a kiss.

. . .

Your bed, still. The room clouded.

What a stunning secret.

Of which I cannot let go.

I woke in the dark of the cabin and ran my hands over my body. I slipped off my nightdress and felt the heat of my skin under the Egyptian cotton sheets.

A place of dalliance.

I knew I could not stay here in this bed. I knew I could not fall asleep. I got up and put on a robe and began to pour myself a glass of brandy to settle my thoughts. Then a light came on outside my door. And I swear I thought I would find you on the other side of the jalousie. I almost convinced myself. I opened the door and saw it was but moonlight. Idiot. I heard the boys' giggles a few doors down. Since there was nothing else I decided to take a stroll. I set out barefooted along the deck and felt the warmth of the boards flooding me again. Again I was drawn to my memories. Wanting now to banish them I stood at the rail and watched the outline of the crocodiles, their island hides riding the surface of the river.

Several days passed. We were nearing our destination.

I had hoped distance, the adventure, would aid forgetting.

That I could let go.

Our affair because of its nature had been parabolic. The passion between us, unlike anything I had known (had even imagined was possible, a young lady's imaginings should not venture there, into those dark, wet places), would not die down, did not take what I imagined would be its natural (that word!) course but existed in spurts, followed by bouts of rage, terror. What possible future could we have? Two intelligent, beautiful women (my grandmother taught me to detest false modesty) going at each other hammer and tongs, tongues, nipples, the glorious space between our legs. Madness. Complete. We had in our misbehavior no center of gravity.

"Do you realize they would have burned us at the stake?"

"At the very least, my love."

Forgetting is beyond me. Distance lends no comfort because I hold all of it inside of me and am lived in by thoughts of you. Us. The physical is one thing, one unimaginable thing, but there is another dimension to all this, which has captured me and—

And what?

Try to concentrate on what lies ahead, on what might be uncovered, discovered.

"I am Adventure!"

I am bewitched. I know that state. I lived there.

The body remembers what that mind thinks it has forgot. June. A rainy afternoon. Green outside the window. The commingled smell of earth, rain, green. A river behind the woods behind the cottage. Our nakedness in the rain, river. The body remembers, becomes wet.

Our party shall be landing tomorrow and taking a caravan the remaining distance to Crocodilopolis. It will be a journey of four or five days. We will lodge in tents.

Are we so different from other grave robbers? I wonder.

Nonsense. We seek poetry, not pots. The words the Aeolian lyre accompanied. The *disjecta membra* of a queer and brilliant people.

"The perfect love affair is akin to the perfect murder. Ideally, only two people should know about it."

One of the boys was pronouncing outside my tent. I could not ascertain which one; their speech patterns had become unnervingly similar.

The Egyptian woman very kindly has given me a pair of white trousers and a white shirt. I will use the excuse of ease of movement, coolness, for my masculine dress in case anyone inquires.

I am reading a book by Amelia B. Edwards, an Englishwoman who fled to Egypt in middle age when her parents' deaths freed her.

She writes: " . . . a magnificent fragment containing nearly the whole of the second book of the Iliad . . . . the three oldest Homeric texts previously known came from the Land of the Pharaohs. . . . Other papyri found within the century contain fragments of Sappho, Anacreon, Thespis, Pindar, Alcaeus, and Timotheus; and all, without exception, come from graves.

"The great Homer papyrus of 1889 was rolled up as a pillow for the head of its former owner. . . . its former owner was a young and apparently beautiful woman, with little ivory teeth and long, silky black hair. . . . She may have been Egyptian, but she was more probably a Greek. . . . She so loved her Homer. Her Homer is now in the

Bodleian. Her skull and her lovely hair are now in the South Kensington Museum."

The dream separated from the dreamer. Ensconced she is today in the Natural History Museum, among the taxidermy, on display. Her favorite poem, her chosen companion in the afterlife, is now the property of scholars, old men, young men, querulous, no doubt, of the intellect of this apparently beautiful woman, if they are even aware of her.

I am also reading John Addington Symonds on the Greek poets and take heart particularly in his outrage at the physical destruction of Sappho's poetry. But even in his outrage he cannot accommodate her passionate bent and so changes the pronouns in her hymn to Aphrodite from *she* to *he*. As with Swinburne's "Sapphics," which Symonds touts, the eternal scholarly struggle to combine respect and loathing.

The odor of roasting lamb is in the air. The Egyptian woman is preparing the meat on a spit over a bed of coals. The lamb was slaughtered this morning by two of the men who operate this caravan. They led it away a good distance so we, with our Western sensibilities, were spared its cries. Not so different from England, where our cruelties are left in the hands of others. But I would never become a vegetarian.

Later, after dinner, I strolled into the surrounding oasis and came upon the pelt of the slaughtered lamb. The pelt had worked its way to the surface from a shallow grave, or had been pulled there by another animal. I touched it with my bare foot. Soft, silky. Like my grandmother's coat of unborn Persian lamb.

The Egyptian woman is outside my tent, an envelope held in her left hand.

"For you."

"Thank you." I take the envelope from her, hoping against hope for news I crave. The letter is much traveled, as if you are pursuing me. How I wish that were true.

The Egyptian woman turns and leaves.

On the camp stool outside the tent I study her hand.

My heart,

I know not when, if this will reach you. I am sending it via the office of the High Commissioner in Alexandria. Please forgive me for interrupting your adventure. I must write you because I am afraid of what may happen to me, over which I have no control. I know, I think you will understand. I am afraid . . .

Whence is she writing me? From her bedroom where she conceals her correspondence in the webbing of a chair that she weaves and reweaves as if Arachne?

I can see her in my memory's eye. The straight-backed chair pulled up against her writing table. The gaslight casts a yellow glow across the wallpaper in her room. Primroses. The drapes on her two windows are heavy, velvet, dark green. If it is evening they will be drawn. Their greenness shutting out the light and noise of a street in Hampstead. On the mantel over the gas fire is a display of family memorabilia. Long-haired soft-featured women and sharp, mustached men. A print of Lady Butler's oil, *Calling the Roll after an Engagement, Crimea,* gift of an aunt and uncle, hangs over the mantelpiece. "Into the valley of death . . . valiant six hundred." The legend etched in brass on the frame. Over the bed a print of a crofter's cottage, two girls at play in a barnyard, puss sips milk from a blue-willow bowl with a chipped rim. On the bedside table are the books she dips into to pass the time, nothing out of the ordinary.

Our actions trespassed these virginal environs. Shattered them.

I turn the page.

I wish there were a safe place. There is no safe place. Not on your caravan. Not in an oasis in the middle of the desert. Not in some ancient ruins with lyric poetry for company. Safety is found only in the grave or in conformity. Safety—I crave safety. You were right to call me a coward. Passionate in your embrace, but at heart coward nonetheless. I am enslaved by things conventional.

We had not committed the perfect love affair. Her family had found out and was threatening a cure. For me there would be no going back. She hoped, she wrote, that they might forgive and forget. That a dowry might be settled on her, a suitable match arranged. But doctors had been brought in to evaluate her "case." She would be given milk and zwieback and put to sleep.

Ever after there would be silence.

The moon has set and the Pleiades; it is
midnight, and time goes by, and I lie alone.

—SAPPHO, fragment 169A

. . .

At long last: “Look,” the Egyptian woman says, indicating the horizon. “There.”

And there it is.

I am standing in the ruins of the Crocodile god’s temple. As promised the air is heavy with the flesh scent of roses. Their fragrance reigns. On either side of me are pink granite stumps, what remain of pink granite columns. Bits of mica and feldspar in the granite glitter as shafts of sunlight reach them. The temple floor had been paved with pink granite as well. According to accounts by Strabo and Herodotus the doors had been covered with sheets of hammered gold. These are no more.

I am almost overcome by the sweetness of the air, by what lies around me. Scattered over the temple floor, a sea of fragments, poetry, and the pink granite becomes the ocean floor.

I sink into the sea of fragments. Alive.

Lost Nation Road

"YOU TAKE A RIGHT out of the airport. At the second light take another right; you'll be on town road 9. Look for a homemade sign 'Lost Nation Road,' if you don't see a number. That's what people around here know it as."

Soon after she leaves the airport she's convinced she's lost. The road is pitch. It's about 11 P.M., a Sunday evening in mid-July. In this part of Vermont the road signs are few and far between. It's assumed the driver knows where he or she is going and how to get there.

She is driving a rental car in the middle of a midsummer night through foxfire and the night-wet scent of green. The darkness heavy and moist. Finally a sign. Hand-painted. Luminous orange against a dark background. She is on the right road after all. Relief.

The road winds and she takes care at the curves. The radio has found a French-Canadian station; she is close to the border here. The border that has been plugged. No more being waved across into our neighbor to the north.

She loves driving. She especially loves having the road to herself.

Then, suddenly, someone's brights in the rearview mirror. Closer and closer. She can make out a blue pickup filled with young men. They begin to tailgate, taunt. Toss empty beer cans at the trunk of her rental car. Honking now. Yelling. What, she can't quite make out. The road is narrow. She doesn't see anywhere she can stop to let them pass, but she knows she can't take much more of this. She is becoming afraid.

Finally she enters a village and manages to pull over at the common where a bandstand illumined by the nightlights of a Chevron station is covered with red, white, and blue bunting, left over from the fourth or maybe it's perpetual, given the times. The blue pickup pretends to sideswipe her, then veers off and speeds out of the village into the wet-dark of the countryside. As it goes by she notices the back bumper is covered with stickers. She thinks—ungraciously—one probably says TAKE BACK VERMONT. She lights a cigarette and sits there, feeling fortunate having rid herself of them, what they might have threatened, a truckload of young men, and herself, an outsider.

The village is fast asleep. The summer darkness hides what the daylight will reveal. Tarpaper shacks, rusted cars, trailers set on cinder blocks; the trappings of rural poverty—nothing the red, white, and blue bunting can conceal.

Flying over the country on her way to the Burlington airport, she looked down at human settlements, wondering how many people were making love at any given time. It's something she does to quell her fear of flying. Picturing the interiors of dwellings. Like counting baseball diamonds. Or imaging pterodactyls flying alongside a 737: past and present in combination.

"It is all now. Everything is now." Morrison. *Beloved.*

She takes her leave of the village. Heads out on luminous Lost Nation Road. The French-Canadian station is playing highlights from *Manon Lescaut.*

About ten miles up the road a dying deer is splayed across cat's eyes. Blood from her mouth trickles across the yellow reflectors. Her legs are in spasm. The blue pickup, former nemesis, has run off the road. Its front end badly dented. Someone will catch hell for this. The young men seem dazed, are wandering about. Staggering. More from shock than drink. Lost boys.

One of them, wearing camouflage, is carrying a rifle. Back from Iraq? Or did his daddy draw lightning in Desert Storm? Or is it both? Each a member of the poverty-stricken all-volunteer army, guiding a Humvee down another nation's roads. From father to son, and, yes, daughter. Shock and awe-inspiring.

She rolls down her window, shouts in his direction, "For God's sake, put her out of her misery." Suddenly embarrassed by the panicked tone, the B-movie words, of her own voice. Predictable, hysterical female—the sort of being she detests.

In her rearview she sees him walk over to the deer, straddle her, fix the barrel of the gun to her head, still. She thinks she sees his tears through hers but she is too far away. Then: the sound of one gunshot cracks the midsummer night in two.

She's heading to Lake Eden, where in 1929 García Lorca spent ten days.

While Underneath

ONCE AN ENCLAVE for the underachieving sons of New England money, the college had gone coed in 1970. The integration was half-hearted. *Wo* was added to *Men:* WoMen's rooms with tampon dispensers hanging alongside the urinals.

Underneath the campus was a network of tunnels dating back to the time when young men were accompanied to college by a manservant. The servant would run through the tunnels from the college kitchen preserving the heat of his master's meals. The servant slept in a room adjacent to his master. His room faced the street; the master's room faced the quad.

The tunnels were mentioned in passing in the college handbook as "Evidence of the college's active participation in the Underground Railroad. A sign of the college's commitment to equality for all." Ask the women in the kitchens behind the dining hall. Not all that much had changed. Like the city it lived in, the college was a banana republic.

I came to the college to teach in the nineties. A more complacent environment I had never known.

On a spring afternoon in 1992 I noticed a woman of about forty or so sitting in the student hangout—the Rooster's Nest, named for the school mascot. She was sitting alone at a table in a corner; arrayed in front of her were stuffed animals: cats, dogs, bears, one toy tiger. She was sipping something from a mug emblazoned with the college logo and whispering to her animals. There was an awkwardness to her, a rigidity about the motion of her hands. She had very short-cropped chestnut hair—severely cut—and wore a white sweatshirt with the name of the college in navy blue script across the front and faded Levis. On her feet was an ancient pair of penny loafers. She held her head tilted to her left side.

"Can I get you anything else besides coffee, hon?" one of the cafeteria workers approached to ask her. There was no table service here so I wondered why the attention. The woman mouthed, "No, thank you."

I was teaching a senior seminar that afternoon. My students welcomed any chance to talk about something other than the text of the week. I'd ask them if they knew who she was.

The seminar was experimental fiction. We had just begun *The Waves*. I really wasn't in the mood to lead them—it was a class of seven—through the streams of consciousness that laced the book—they were all seniors, but with the exception of one student, a female named Jean on loan from Mount Holyoke, all incurious; and often, even though the seminar did not meet until 2 P.M., hungover. The seminar became a dialogue between Jean and myself, with the other six in various stages of consciousness looking on. Next up would be McCullers's *Reflections in a Golden Eye*. What would they make of McCullers's sexual lunatics? (I mean that in the kindest sense of the term.) These kids were strictly missionary-position types. The year before, in a lecture on Emily Dickinson, I had discussed the poem that begins "On my volcano grows the Grass" as a poem about masturbation, female masturbation at that—the orgasm of a high-collared New England spinster; for this I was summoned by the dean of students, who raised the specter of "moral turpitude."

The experimental fiction seminar met in a small room in the Science building, which, one of the students informed me, had been used as an exterior on *All My Children*. This detail, for the student, seemed to make the college relevant. The soaps ran continuously on the big screen in a far corner of the Nest, displaying the comforting parallel world of television.

Jean was seated at the seminar table when I arrived.

We exchanged greetings. I opened my Woolf notes, glanced over them, and then addressed what was really on my mind.

"Jean, have you ever seen a woman in the Nest with stuffed animals on her table?"

"Really?"

I nodded.

"I noticed her today for the first time. There's a strangeness about her, and not just the stuffed animals."

"I've only been in the Nest two or three times. I usually head back to South Hadley as soon as we're done."

"I see."

The rest of the group dribbled in, and I asked them the same question.

One of the boys spoke up: "Are you talking about High-Stepper?"

"Why do you call her that?"

"Haven't you seen her walk?" He, like the majority of the student body, could have graced the pages of the J. Crew catalogs that littered the floor of the college P.O.

"No. And that nickname sounds rather cruel."

"Sorry, professor, but that's the only name she has here."

"Who is she? Where does she come from?"

A girl spoke next, in her manner more L. L. Bean than J. Crew: "I heard she was in the first coed class here, way back when."

One of the first *Wo-Men.*

"What's she doing here now?"

L. L. Bean spoke again, "She's here off and on. Who knows why?"

"Once I saw her being led out of the Nest by a couple of campus cops." J. Crew was talking.

"Did you ask them what they were doing?"

"No."

"Weren't you at least curious?"

"Not really."

"Didn't anyone help her?"

"A couple of the women who work there asked the cops to take it easy with her."

"Describe for me: how does she walk?"

"Like she's stepping over something on the ground. Like she's afraid of touching it."

We turned to *The Waves,* and it soon became clear that only Jean had cracked the book. So she and I engaged in our customary dialogue. The catalogs our audience.

After the seminar I walked across the campus to my car. On a field below the main quad the women's field hockey team was practicing. In a field beyond that the men's baseball team was playing the visiting team from Williams. It was a Wednesday afternoon, a warm day in late April; the lilacs were in bud, the jonquils in bloom. Though the year was 1992, the place had a sense of time suspended forty years earlier. A college in aspic.

But for the presence of *Wo-Men.*

I was driving back to my sublet in my red Escort, behind a pickup with the bumper stickers HONK IF YOU THINK I'M JESUS and I STILL MISS MY EX BUT MY AIM IS GETTING BETTER—the driver was a woman, her long braid interrupted by the gun rack behind her head. Odd sight in urban Connecticut.

Between figuring out what takeout to get for dinner—I hate cooking for myself—I was haunted by the mystery of the woman in the Nest.

I'd ask the department secretary, Dorothy, about her; she knew where the bodies were buried, so to speak. And, she was not fazed by academic pretension. I decided to stop at Circe's Feast and pick up a bottle of Pinot Grigio, some of their house pâté and a sweet baguette, and a tomato salad.

The next morning I stopped by the department office and asked Dorothy about the woman in the Nest.

"Yes, I know who you're talking about. That's some story. The kid in your seminar is right. She was a student in the first coed class here. That was the year after I was hired. I think she was an art history major . . . or music. I'm not sure. She went to a fraternity party, around homecoming, where she was gang-raped by at least five of the so-called brothers. A word—don't ask me to say it—was inscribed on each of her thighs, with arrows pointing the way."

"Jesus Christ."

"Campus police found her in the tunnel underneath the frat house the next morning. Someone phoned in a tip. A fountain pen with Greek letters was beside her."

Dorothy delivered this information in a flat voice that let the images stand alone.

"Oh, my God. What happened to them?"

"You know this place. . . . Nothing. Nada. They either said she made the whole thing up, or that she asked for it. The usual crap; you know."

"Nothing?" I said, stupidly.

"The fraternity did bring in a lawyer, to hedge their bets. He told the college it was a clear case of self-mutilation, a cry for attention, and he had a shrink in his pocket who would prove it. He added that she showed signs of kleptomania—she'd swiped the fountain pen. Nice touch. Without even interviewing the girl. It was their word against hers. She was all alone."

"Christ."

"There was something else that happened: the next weekend one of the brothers hanged himself, in the same tunnel where the campus cops found her. There was a rumor that he had taken part in the rape. There was a rumor that he was gay and couldn't live with that. There may have been no connection between the two events—that was the term used in the college paper; that and 'unfortunate incidents.' But this place is lousy with rumors, as you well know. Maybe he just couldn't live with what he knew and done nothing."

"And her?"

"She was brought before the dean of students, with the fraternity lawyer present. You can imagine how that went. She was told that she was trying to bring disgrace on the college. She was told to recant or she would be asked to leave. She was told to keep her mouth shut. The dean's secretary left the intercom on and reported back to the rest of us. And soon after, the girl cracked up, or her parents said she cracked up. How could she not? They hid her away in one of those places Wasps hide their embarrassments. A place just outside Simsbury. And she's been there ever since. She talks to the gals in the cafeteria. About what I don't know, and they wouldn't say if I asked them. You know the tiers in this place: faculty, staff, workers. Imagine: twenty years at a few hundred dollars a day. Talk about a stolen life."

"So why were the campus cops bothering her?"

"She goes missing from the nut farm, excuse the expression, every now and then and ends up here. The parents have instructed the college to return her. That's her story as far as I know it."

"Why do you think she comes back?"

"Damned if I know."

"Do you know her name?"

"Ellen . . ." and then Dorothy named a prominent New England family, one of the most prominent. I started to say something, but she went on, anticipating my response. "It didn't matter who her family was, you know that. In fact, I think the trustees counted on her family's desire to avoid any publicity. What happened to her was the sort of thing that happened to other people.

"Do you want to hear something else? After it happened the president—the guy looked like the papier-mâché groom on a wedding cake, complete with painted-on smile—suggested to the trustees that they plant rosebushes around the frat house, because, he said, 'Bad things don't happen in beautiful places.' Are you ready for that?"

Just another signifier of where we were.

"If you want to know more, maybe you should ask Tom Maxwell. I think they were in the same class."

Tom was a colleague in the department, specializing in the English Renaissance; his specific focus was censorship of texts.

Since my arrival at the college three years ago I had counseled my share of party- and date-rape victims. But I had heard of nothing like this.

I had also known two students who had committed suicide. One boy on returning from a Christmas ski vacation in Aspen with his mother and father and sister blew his brains out in the family garage. Another, a girl, dropped dead on the treadmill in the college gym, her bones protruding through her flesh, her grades a perfect 4.0. This in a place where the most sought-after grade was the gentleman's C.

That night after I got home the temperature dropped suddenly, without warning, and without warning there was a freak snowstorm. The lilac buds would be frostbitten, the jonquils as well.

My neighbor at the apartment I was renting was a blind woman. During the snowstorm, which raged all night long, I woke to her screaming underneath the bedroom window—my apartment was on the second floor. The fluorescent hands of my watch read 3 A.M. I got up and looked outside. She was circling in the snow whirling under the streetlight. She had lost her bearings. I threw on jeans and a sweater and ran downstairs to help her out.

"Carmen? It's okay. I'm here. Your neighbor. Take my hand." I stretched out my hand toward her. She was covered in the white wetness, trembling. Clouds of snow encircled us. She and I were the only two people on the street at that hour. I took her hand and tried to guide us out of the snow. In my snowblindness I had entered into her nightmare. I tried to focus on the thin yellow of the streetlight. Finally we reached the front door.

"Where's your dog?"

"Somebody stole him. No. I'm joking. That's not it. He got sick. I think the super poisoned his food. He had to go to the vet's overnight."

I did not ask her what she was doing outside at that hour. She had eccentric habits, like playing the television twenty-four hours. Or maybe that's not eccentric at all. She was alone, but for the dog—and lonely. I got the impression that if I made any overture to friendship at all I would become trapped. I was not proud of this emotion but it was there nonetheless.

Tom Maxwell was in his office. An 1818 first edition of Bowdler's *Family Shakespeare* was open on his desk. He had it on interlibrary loan from a college in New Hampshire. Tom explained that Bowdler—a member of the English Society for the Suppression of Vice—had taken it upon himself to eviscerate the Bard, to remove all "words and expressions . . . which cannot with propriety be read aloud in a family." Tom said he was writing an essay about the censorship of Elizabethan texts by "the self-appointed guardians of family values."

Poor man, he couldn't help holding forth.

"As if the family exists as a discrete entity, safe from the world."

(I recalled having to get my father's permission to use *Hamlet* in the original version in my high school English AP class, in Manhattan in 1968, rather than the Bowdlerized version assigned me by the school.)

"I can't get over this guy," Tom said, laughing. "What possessed him?"

"What possesses any of them? Then or now."

"You might well ask. Their obsession with sex coexistent with extreme aversion. Intent on bleaching all the color out of life."

"Tom, you were a student here in the seventies, right?"

"Slight change of subject, but yes."

"Do you recall anything about a case of gang rape and a subsequent suicide?" And I named the year and the frat house and said that it was around homecoming.

"Only vaguely." And he returned to his family Shakespeare.

I lied. I knew about both things.

The boy from the frat house who hanged himself left behind a letter addressed to no one, in which he described what he called an "ache" when he watched his roommate—myself—undress. He described lying awake listening to his roommate—me—breathe. It became too much for him to bear. The brothers found the letter and disposed of it to protect the reputation of the house. I was not held accountable. I was a star center on the lacrosse team: we were the reigning little ivy league champs.

The hanging was gruesome. He'd cut the piece of bedsheet too long, and when he kicked the chair out from under him his feet hit the ground. He'd had to strangle himself.

They did not know, he did not know I shared his longing. I could not say it out loud. Not to him, not to anyone. Not then; not now. It was natural that I become a scholar of censorship.

As for the rape: I was away that weekend, avoiding homecoming and the peacockery that particular weekend entailed—no pun(s) intended. So was he. Probably for the same reason. Of course we were told about the rape, although that word was never used. It was a situation that began as a prank but "got out of hand." That capacity for boys-will-be-boys brutality terrifying me. A recklessness that was apparently a birthright. "No harm done."

Maybe my roommate feared for himself should he be found out.

And no, I didn't resign from the fraternity. I went on with my Bowdlerized life.

My animals protect me. I carry them in a duffel bag on the bus from Simsbury. (I who as a child detested the false comfort lent by Steiff; I thought stuffed animals were stupid things. Not so. Not at all.) The bus driver is a woman; she recognizes me and lets me ride for free. Once when the bus was almost empty she let me off right at the gates of the college so I wouldn't have to walk up the hill past the gauntlet of fraternity houses. Maybe somehow she guessed their resonance for me?

The students laugh at the way I walk. Right in my face. At the very least they stare at me. The only people I can talk to are the real people I encounter, the people outside. The bus driver, the cafeteria workers. I don't talk to the doctors or the nurses or the occupational therapists, the people inside. They cannot help me. I don't talk to my fellow inmates. I can only be helped by being in the outside world among the real people. They are usually kind to me. I think it's because these are people who cannot afford to put away their problems. They may have someone like me at home, or at a relative's house. It wasn't *their* sons who led to this. My mother and father are afraid of me, I think. Ever since that night twenty years ago. Or maybe they see me as a disgrace, a shame brought on their hallowed name. Ruined. They're not about to tell me anything real. The circumstances that imprisoned me have never been articulated. Imagine. I doubt my name is mentioned in company. "You'll be as good as new." "It's for the best." Their mantra of twenty years.

Why do I return?

To remind the powers-that-be? To punish myself? To try to push back time? To return to the scene of the crime? But they told me there had been no crime. Of this they were certain.

I will only tell you what exactly happened when I know your motive. Do you really give a damn? Or are you just another voyeur? Like the shrinks whose curiosity is a barely disguised prurience. That's how it feels.

Allow me to set the scene for you who seem so interested.

A redbrick house on the hill leading to the campus.

A warm October evening, a Saturday, 1972. I was wearing cutoffs and a canary yellow T-shirt and penny loafers with no socks.

I was sitting on the steps at the front of the house.

A boy sat down beside me.

Then came a banal exchange:

An icebreaker:

"Hi, I'm—" even now I don't like to say his name. I didn't get the names of the others; only his.

"I'm Ellen."

"What's your major, or are you 'undecided'?"

"Art history." I was not an enthusiastic student; I liked looking at paintings, deciphering them. "What's yours?"

"American Studies."

The dialogue continued along this predictable line, and then he asked me if I wanted another beer, and then if I wanted to visit the tunnel under the house. And being interested in hidden places, hiding places—I said yes. That was all.

My family said a cave on our place in the Berkshires had been a stop on the Underground Railroad. There had been abolitionists in our past,

I was taught; one was hung over the mantelpiece in the drawing room. Abolitionists in New England families exist in about the same ratio as Frenchmen in the Resistance.

When I was about twelve I explored the cave. A narrow, low passage opened into a round chamber. There was nothing I could find to suggest human habitation. Not on that visit. The next time I took a flashlight, and when I sprayed the walls of the chamber with light I saw that lines had been drawn on the walls. A map perhaps.

I said yes. That was all. Because hidden places, hiding places interested me.

And there, underneath, the unbelievable happened.

The residue from the freak snowstorm melted rapidly the very next day as the temperature spiked at sixty. I drove to the campus in the late morning through streams of gray wastewater rushing down the city's streets.

I stopped in the Nest for coffee and there she was. Same as the day before. Stuffed animals arrayed in a semicircle in front of her. Apparently oblivious to anyone but the cafeteria workers who stopped by her table to greet her and refill her mug. I wondered where she had spent the night. A group of girls were giggling and staring. I probably judged them too harshly. In their ignorance how could they know?

After a while I walked over to Clemens House. The weekly department meeting had been called. We were to meet in the front room where the school's collection of yearbooks was kept. On the mahogany sideboard one yearbook was open to a centerfold page with snapshots of homecoming, 1972. Someone had broken the back of the yearbook so that it lay flat. A collage of the frat houses showed occupants and guests in various stages of hilarity. Cutoffs and Topsiders and Lacoste polo shirts. Everyone golden. Everyone exuding the gaity of entitled youth. *While underneath* had been scratched in the mahogany veneer, the characters faint, spidery.

Ecce Homo

Dream . . . on black wings . . . you come whenever sleep . . .
sweet god, truly . . . sorrow powerfully . . . to keep separate
. . . I have hope that I shall not share . . . nothing of the
blessed . . . for I would not be so.

—SAPPHO, fragment 63

THE STORY, as I was told it, begins in Rome.

There is a man who is a linguist. He is accomplished in several languages. Western and non-Western. He gets a job as a translator in the U.S. Embassy. He translates for Italians who clamor for visas. Jews among others.

His is a low-level position for a man of his qualifications.

He is black, which is of concern to his country.

He is homosexual, but they seem unaware.

He counts his blessings beside the Trevi Fountain.

All in all he has been comfortable in Rome.

His is an adopted country.

He was brought to America when he was fourteen. His are a nomadic people. Strivers, always in search of a better place. His mother and father—he was blessed with both—settled in Philadelphia. He did well in school, near the top of his graduating class.

He availed himself of Lincoln, the Black Princeton.

. . .

One evening in the Piazza Navona he is sitting at an outdoor restaurant. He has ordered a glass of Pinot Grigio—Campanile '36—and is lighting a Muratti cigarette. The restaurant—the storyteller cannot recall the name—is located at the south end of the piazza, and from his table the linguist can see Bernini's *Il Moro* and takes heart.

That very evening he meets a man, an Italian.

A simple meeting: the Italian stops by the linguist's table, asks for a cigarette, a match.

They stroll the Roman streets, light at the Italian's apartment.

They become lovers.

On the weekends they spend time in a hill town beyond the hills of the city the Italian knows from childhood.

They speak freely.

The storyteller says that was when they fell in love.

But too soon Americans have to leave. The linguist—like it or not—is a naturalized American. As such he must go.

But the linguist does not want to abandon his beloved. The linguist—the Negro who speaks in tongues—of rivers—unlike the tongues of the women back home (home the place that is un-America) in the Pocomania shacks—twirling their spirituous tongues—was once tongue-tied—

"What's the matter, boy?" "Wha' do you, bwai?"

"Is Cat got you tongue?"

"Don' mek me give you one tongue-lashing."

Now his tongue is the most skilled part of him.

He works with his tongue. He makes love with his tongue.

He knows when to hold his tongue.

The linguist tries to arrange a visa, but the beloved is a known quantity and the application is denied.

He will not leave.

And that—the storyteller says—is the beginning of the end.

. . .

One night the fascists descend on the rooms the two men share in the Piazza della Repubblica. They are removed suddenly, without incident, but for the incident of their removal.

When he was a boy, before the family left for America, he read in a newspaper about two men apprehended because they were found together. A laborer, a casual laborer, the paper had reported, and a bank clerk. They were discovered in "an obscene condition"—a child, he did not know what this meant. When the two men were arraigned on a charge of public indecency (they'd been discovered under a pier near the Myrtle Bank Hotel), hundreds packed the courtroom—including mothers and their children. Later the two men were given twelve strokes of the Cat and five years hard labor.

The police take the two men to the nearby train station where they are loaded on a car bound for a camp.

Do you remember the end of *The Garden of the Finzi-Continis*? The film, this does not happen in the book. The schoolroom where the deportees are taken to be sorted and shipped. The train station in this story has a similar feel right now. There are still the stalls selling bottles of Acqua Mia and San Benedetto, bunches of grapes in white paper, newspapers, magazines, paperbound libretti—the air smells of cigarette smoke and oranges and damp—the ordinariness of it all—strikes them—commerce, train travel—the schoolroom smelling of chalk dust—and people who have been tagged.

The two men arrive at the camp together. Thank God they have not been separated. But they will do well to ignore one another. To ignore one another while looking out for the other—that is their task.

They mask their longing.

They are assigned forced labor. Breaking rocks. Drawing the rocks, wagonload by wagonload, up the side of the quarry, stacking them in pyramids. The guards, wielding sledgehammers, smash the pyramids;

the prisoners return to the pit of the quarry and break more stones, draw them to the lip of the quarry, stack them.

The two men are mocked, called names only the linguist understands.

Outside the windows of the storyteller's flat the sun is going down over the Pacific, beyond the Golden Gate.

The storyteller does not know how the two managed to escape. We will have to bring our imaginations to bear.

It must be night. Under cover of night they drift to the edge of the camp. In the darkness they burrow out under the barbed wire. Something like that. An opportunity has presented itself and they take it.

They find their way into some woods.

They live in the heart of the woods in the heat of a war as lovers. They live on mushrooms and lamb's quarters and wild birds the Italian traps. And the storyteller knows this is romantic, but let's let them have it. They make a place to sleep in a tree trunk heavy with moss and shelved with lichen.

A decayed, decadent nest.

The gunfire that seems to encircle them is coming closer to them. They whisper about which course to take. They sleep with their legs wrapped together. One man's penis nestles against the other's flank. When it rains, the rain draws a curtain around them.

They decide they will try to find Switzerland. They laugh. At least they have a plan. The linguist will pretend to be the Ethiopian servant of the Italian: "A spoil of war," the linguist whispers.

Now they're getting somewhere.

Suddenly luck finds them. They stumble upon a company of American troops—Negro soldiers encamped nearby. The linguist explains—omitting the triangle—now but a ghost on his chest.

Time passes. Switzerland is forgotten.

The Negro soldiers get orders to move north and drop the men at a way station where displaced people wait.

The two are processed.

The linguist is returned to his adopted country.

The Italian is made a prisoner of war.

The linguist says, "When this is all over I will send for you."

This is a slender thread.

In the end it is no use.

The beloved hangs himself shortly after he is taken prisoner.

The linguist, this being postwar New York City, gets a job in the kitchens of the Waldorf-Astoria. He translates for the Hungarian chef.

When he hears of the Italian's death he breaks down.

He is committed to the Metropolitan State Hospital where he will die.

A man is seated under a silk cotton tree in the Blue uniform of the mad.

There are no silk cotton trees anywhere near this place.

Epiphytes—plants that live on air—disport themselves above his head. Bromeliads whose sharp pink blooms last months.

The rainforest just beyond the man in mad dress reminds him of the forest where they hid, two men trying to be safe. But, his mind's eye moving closer, he notes the difference.

In a contest—in a fancy dress parade of Green—the rainforest would win: a dead heat between the iguana and the breadfruit.

Home.

He places the beloved on the bench beside him. They face the Green impenetrable, listen to its suddenness of sound: shrieks, howls, echoes from within brick walls.

The constrictors would tie with the man in mad dress for silence.

He holds his tongue.

Water Signs

I

OCTOBER is one of the most lucid months on the central coast of California.

On October 7 she was driving down the coast, home from Point Reyes where she had been spending some time at the National Seashore.

A vee of tundra swans sung over her head on the wetlands near Limantour Beach, their wow-wow sound encircling them. Early migration, she thought; they usually arrived later in the year, winter, all the way from the Bering Strait.

A brown wren interrupted, his head thrown back, mouth wide, and a song huge for the tiny body came forth, and saltwater stung her eyes.

All manner of birdlife could be found in that place, between wetlands and dunes, lagoon and coastline. It never failed she thought of Hitchcock. Tippi Hedren imposed on Bodega Bay.

She drove over thousands of oyster shells on a mother-of-pearl road alongside oyster beds. Oysters dangling in the marshes, fast by the dark, salty estuary.

Two ancient toothless dogs stood guard among three rusted pickups in the dooryard of the oyster farm at the end of the pearled road.

On the path to Abbott's Lagoon, where snowy plovers nest, she found a shard of blue and white china risen through the sediment from the days of the Yankee Clippers. Maybe even before; after all, Drake made landfall here.

She dreamed that night that Duke Ellington and Satchmo had composed a suite for Emmett Till, who is always in her dreams, and were playing it in her head. She wished she had a musical memory so she could recall the sounds.

She saw a golden eagle's nest on the road to McClure's Beach.

In the morning at North Beach, with her chrome thermos of coffee, the ocean roiled and seagulls congregated among whips of seaweed.

Now she was driving home.

She had stopped at San Gregorio, and was at this moment looking out over the Pacific, watching the pelicans make vertical plunges, knifing the water.

Her father once told her that pelicans had an affinity with Christ. It had to do with their willingness to pierce their own breasts so their young could drink their blood.

"You people are bleeding me dry," he said over Sunday dinner.

Then: her face smarting from her father's five-finger tattoo—for her twelve-year-old smart talk.

The pelicans turned from the water and she turned with them, and tried to turn from that particular talking picture.

The parking lot, almost empty, was now in her line of vision. The pelicans flew south toward Pescadero. They gathered on a rock offshore, their own alcatraz.

Before she could turn back to the ocean something captured her attention.

A woman drove into the almost empty lot in a nondescript white car. She parked and got out and left the door to the driver's side ajar. Not just unlocked, open slightly.

The woman was tall, lanky, with long auburn hair. Dressed for the City, elegant in black trousers and white blouse. She was carrying a large black bag.

She bolted from the parking lot, ran fast up the slope to the north of the beach.

The other woman, rapt, lost sight of her as she disappeared into the foliage at the top of the bluff above the ocean.

Signs warned of unsteady ground up there. Eroding cliffs, unpredictable surf.

She was only out of sight for ten or fifteen seconds, then reemerged. She ran full speed down the hill and back to the car.

The black bag was nowhere to be seen.

She got into the car, tore out of the parking lot, turned left up the highway, north toward the City whence she'd come.

Questions flooded the other woman as she watched.

What had just taken place?

Why leave the door open? Was she unfamiliar with the car? Had she rented it? Had she come from somewhere far, taken a flight to SFO, rented a car—all to fling something into the Pacific?

And get away—with what?

What had been in the black bag?

Whatever it was, was likely irretrievable. The currents, the rocks at the foot of the bluffs would discourage any search.

Not that the watcher would presume to make one. Was she afraid of what she might find?

Anything thrown over was gone for good. Anything thrown over might be washed up on another coastal shelf. That was the unpredictable thing about the ocean.

Predictable—feminine?—images come back in response.

Infanticide. Stillbirth. Wrapped in a towel, then swathed in plastic. But she soon realized such disposals were to her mind in the hands of the very young, inelegant, terrified, whose idea of a final resting place was the dumpster behind McDonald's. Heartless, perhaps, but her sentiments nonetheless.

Her stranger, she would never forget her, was possessed of a certain coolness.

The noir kicked in. The bag contained a weapon. Somewhere a lover lay dead. Shot—heart? head? Point-blank range. Don't be idiotic. That's the stuff of *Lifetime*. Better yet, Lizabeth Scott with a smoky voice, smoking gun. Stanwyck—cool beyond cool: plotting murder among the baby food jars and boxes of soap powder. "Straight down the line, Walter." Bang.

Where would any of us be without the movies?

Little did she care.

She recalled a woman she once knew, who carried her mother's ashes around in a coffee tin—Medaglia D'Oro, no less. "Why not Chock Full o'Nuts, the Heavenly Coffee?" she'd asked, and knew she'd said the wrong thing. The woman slept with the tin on her bedside table.

Had there been a hasty burial at sea?

What was in the black bag? The question nagged.

What would she relinquish to the sea?

Even as she drove off in the opposite direction, artichokes and brussels sprouts running into the Pacific, leaves were melting into water, words drawn out by salt.

Little did she know.

II

Having acquitted herself, seen she insisted by no one, not that it should matter—she'd done nothing wrong—she sped up the coast, north toward the City, then home.

The sea lapped at her words, her once-unwritten past, recaptured briefly, inscribed, released, detritus now—destroy, she said.

At first, she'd retreated to the *OED*: nightmare: ME *nihtmare*: *niht* + *mare,* demon; AS *mara*; akin to *mahr,* incubus, spirit, or demon thought in medieval times to inspire nightmare; anything oppressive, a burden.

From *mare* to *mar* to *mere.* Demon to sea to mother. And back again.

In nightmare did the past declare itself, tentatively, then relentlessly, and she woke, wet with sweat and tasting her own salt. Trying to break the codes.

Fog shrouded the coast at Half Moon Bay.

In one dream, four roads cross an island. She has crossed three. The fourth one is the roughest. The most difficult to realize. Dirt, way up in the mountains, snow on peaks. Or are they seashells? This is supposed to be a tropical island. It—the crossing—will be arduous but well worth it, the guide tells her.

"There's just this one left, miss."

She screwed up her courage.

She took the fourth road and saw what she had feared, no doubt about it: her face held down in a basin of water. White enamel with yellow stenciled flowers. A room in a farmhouse at the side of a mountain. Her eyes open underwater. The chipped places in the enamel become enlarged. Turn into maps. Struggle. She is struggling. A small child resisting. The hands release her. Gasps. "Serves you right." No code here. Clear as a bell. Her face contorted, small hands open a side door, stumble down steps; she runs into the cane fields. Her legs crisscrossed, striped, and burning from the canebrake. Her face red from her mother's anger.

At boarding school she had been terrified of putting her face in the water. She swam the Australian crawl with her head held high, and the teacher said she looked like those grainy photos of the Loch Ness monster.

There is never any warning. Someone has the upper hand. A girl is running toward a racetrack—of all places. She sees low-lying flowers. She throws herself into them. She disappears.

And then: in the center of the notebook now drowning in the ocean:

She finds herself in a temple—she has been singled out for a rite (purification and/or repentance, no one says) and is decked in veils, jewels, thin red cloths. She faces a giantess, attired as she is, but wearing a headdress of some sort. Her vulva is revealed by a vent in the dress—huge and terrifyingly hairless (prepped for birth?). The giantess takes the girl into an alcove, and touches, barely, her clitoris with her tongue. The girl turns to the congregation and asks to be forgiven.

Time passes. She fights her fear of water, mirrors. Teaches herself to think the unthinkable.

Then: finally: reward:

She is with other children in the vault of space—black yet light. The stars are huge, close. The children say, "Look, it's a new galaxy; there's nothing to be afraid of." She looks and is not frightened, is amazed. She is passing to another level: so black and so bright. She has been washed onto a deserted island in the midst of space. Safe.

Castaway. Cast away.

She floored the accelerator as her memories were consumed by the seawater. *Suffering a sea change.* She was entirely unaware she had been watched, the subject of another's wondering.

III

South, at Pescadero, the watcher has caught up with the pelicans, gliding in line at the edge of the land, landing on their offshore rock. Deciding not to stop, deciding she could never know what she had seen—had the black bag been a dream?—she drove straight home.

It's All Yours

A WOMAN, about sixty or so, is living in a small house in the Sierra Nevada, not far from Truckee.

In this part of California there are approximately two people each square mile.

The woman has a two-car garage even though her house is quite small. In the garage right now is a two-tone (beige and brown) Plymouth Valiant; "Detroit's finest hour," her ex-husband used to say. Her son would disagree.

Under a black plastic tarp next to the Plymouth is a 1959 hunter green Stingray convertible. Vintage, magnificent. This car belonged to her son—his pride and joy—hard-won—and for a time she thought nothing would come between them—but then her son was killed just south of the DMZ in 1968.

Today a young man, local, self-employed, comes to fix her water heater—it is now May 1980—which is also in the garage. The water heater stands next to the breezeway attaching the garage to the house. The young man sets down his tools on the concrete floor. He walks over to the cars and lifts the edges of the tarp. He is all alone and cannot resist looking, but he is already certain from the contours of the tarp what magic resides underneath, what beauty.

He is crazy about Corvettes and knows he will never make enough money to buy one. Not without going into debt, which he was trained not to do. His was a strict upbringing; he carries it in his body. "Neither a borrower nor a lender be." That sentiment rattled against the thin walls of his parents' rented house.

The car captures his gaze. It has obviously been loved. Not a mark on it.

He walks back to his tools, turns his attention to the task he was hired to do.

When the young man knocks on the side door of the house, the door to the kitchen, to tell the woman her water heater is fixed and will be good for a few more years, she invites him into the kitchen and offers him a glass of water.

"It comes from a spring nearby," she says. The spring is fed by the melting snowpack; each week she walks a path behind her house, down a slope toward the sound of water running along a granite hillside. A spring, she thinks, such a constant thing—Paiutes and Pioneers, and who knows who else, thirst quenched by its water way back when.

The young man sips from the glass. "This is great," he says.

He looks around the room. It's a tidy place. White enamel stove and porcelain sink. Pale yellow refrigerator. A table at which the woman is now seated while he leans against a wall next to a curtained window. On the table are some spring wildflowers, arranged in a jar on a blue oilcloth. Once royal blue, now faded to pale by a morning sun raking the table.

She has gathered the wildflowers as she gathered the water. They grow along the path she walks to the spring. They splash color in the pale room.

"That's some car," the young man says. And the woman knows he's not talking about her Plymouth, her faithful if homely Valiant.

"Yes; it is," she says, and takes a sip of what may be iced tea.

"Is it yours?" he asks.

"Why not?" She allows herself a smile.

"Oh, you know . . ." his words trail off.

"Actually it belongs to my son."

"Oh."

The young man places the now-empty glass in the porcelain sink.

"Thanks for the water."

"I'm sick to death of it, of taking care of it."

Where is her son now? he wonders. Prison?

She gets up from her place at the table, sets her own glass in the sink. Turns to face him.

"Would you like to have it? The car?"

"But . . ."

"Technically it belongs to me."

Birdsong can be heard through the window, from the meadow outside.

"I'll let you have it for five hundred dollars."

She must know that it's worth more than that, much more.

"Take it or leave it."

He says nothing but, "Okay."

He throws in the day's labor for free. It's the least he can do, he figures.

He does not want to know anything about her son. He does not want to know anything. He's afraid the car, the deal will disappear if he knows too much. What he doesn't know can't hurt him, his own mother would say.

"I'll come by tomorrow with the money, if that's okay with you."

"Fine."

He goes to his bank in Truckee on the way home and withdraws five hundred dollars from his savings account. He wants to feel good, to celebrate. So he goes somewhere he's never been: to one of those old hotels on the main street, once sanctuary for forty-niners and copper miners, and orders a JD on the rocks at the restored brass-railed bar where a naked woman hangs above the silver-tipped bottles advertising a beer that's no longer brewed.

He wants to slowly drink his drink and convince himself that this is only good fortune, well deserved. He knows he's a good man. He's never cheated anyone in his life.

"Care for a refill?" The barmaid has a heart-shaped tattoo on her shoulder where he has a smallpox vaccination scar. There's a name carved in the heart, which in the dim light of the bar he cannot make out.

"Had it done in Reno." She's noticed him looking.

"No, thanks," he answers. "I'd better be going."

The next morning he gets a friend to drive him back to the woman's house so he may claim his purchase, his gift. He has the friend drop him at the end of the driveway and tells him he'll be in touch.

The woman is standing just inside the open mouth of the garage. She has removed the tarp shrouding the Stingray. The young man strolls up the driveway and looks into the dark of the garage, interrupted by sunlight filtering through the tamaracks overhead. His eyes adjust; he greets his benefactor.

"Go ahead; it's all yours. I haven't changed my mind on you."

He manages a smile and hands her an envelope with the five hundred dollars inside.

"Keys?"

That's all he wants.

"In the glove compartment."

He flips open the glove compartment and finds the keys.

He walks around to the driver's side and opens the door.

"Thanks," he says as she turns and walks away from him, through the breezeway, back into the house.

"Don't mention it," she says, without turning, slipping the envelope in her shirt pocket, not bothering to count the bills. "It's all yours, free and clear."

The young man slides into the driver's seat. He turns the key in the ignition and the car comes to life. Very gently he presses on the gas pedal. The car glides forward.

As he drives away he hopes he will never see this woman again.

Despite possible appearances, hers was not a snap decision.

She'd grown apprehensive.

The Corvette had become her living room, the place of her haunting.

At first—right after she received the regrets of her government—she couldn't bear the sight of the thing. But neither could she bear to be parted from it. Her son had been inseparable from it; he had loved it so much.

In the time since, she had approached the car with caution. Only glancing at it now and then. Lightly touching the tarp that had become its skin. Removing the skin from time to time and paying the boy from down the block to wash the car, polish the chrome, Windex the rearview and side mirrors and windshield.

Her son's body had not been retrieved.

There was something else about the car.

One evening about a year ago for no apparent reason, after pouring herself a drink, she walked into the garage, unsnapped the tarp, peeled it away from the car. She folded herself inside the passenger's seat, lit her cigarette, sipped her drink. She took the key from the glove compartment and turned it in the ignition just far enough to activate the battery so she could play the radio. She didn't really think about what she was doing. It just felt right. Music came up. The dial set at the rock station where he had left it. She left it there and sat back.

And then—

And there he was. In the side-view mirror on the passenger's side her boy appeared from nowhere, no man's land. His eyes sunglassed, his mouth open but no sounds came.

At first she was frightened. She turned down the volume on the car radio and called his name.

"Jim?" she whispered, afraid of speaking it too loud.

In response the mouth closed, its corners turned in the faintest smile.

Silently she left the car and went back into the house.

In her bedroom she took a wooden box from a shelf in the closet and sat on the bed, going through his letters.

The place suffered torrential rains, he'd written her, nothing like he had ever known. The heat rising through the rain, visible. Trees steaming. Skeletal, stripped trees. Eighty degrees, he'd written, felt like a cold snap.

The next night he appeared again. Again his eyes were dark-glassed, his mouth open but no words came. When he saw her, the mouth closed and the smile such as it was reappeared.

"This can't be. No."

The thought of painting the side-view mirror black passed through her mind, but she dismissed it. Certainly her son, not-her-son, this phantasm, was in her mind.

Of course he was. He must be. Am I going crazy? Who could blame me?

What if the glass, the chrome-backed mirror, was the place of his afterlife? Quicksilver holding him in silence.

Was she crazy for imagining such a thing?

After death she reckoned there were as many possibilities as there were people.

She decided she'd dreamed the whole thing.

He'd been vaporized just south of the DMZ. A cloud of flesh and blood and bone. Imagine that. Leave it at that. If you can. Try to think clearly.

She promised herself she'd visit the Wall, see her own face reflected in the black granite where his name was carved. "When I get the time."

She stopped visiting the car. She replaced the tarp.

All she had was time.

Now her son had company, climbing across the Sierra, descending into Nevada.

She only wishes the best for this young man.

She only hopes he will never return.

Her mind goes back and forth. Figment. Fragment.

He drives into Reno in his dream come true. The ghost in the machine.

Carnegie's Bones

Dinosaur remains from Utah eventually found their way, much like Carnegie libraries or American steel, throughout the nation and the world. A beautifully articulated skeleton of *Diplodocus* was found and named *Diplodocus carnegiei.*

—PHILIP L. FRADKIN, *Sagebrush Country*

NOT ONLY THAT. Another dinosaur was christened *Apatosaurus louisae*—after Carnegie's wife. Apatosaurus is also known as brontosaurus—thunder lizard—some honor, eh? And they named the great Saguaro *Carnegiea gigantea*—this is a stickup. Fleshed and skeletal.

[I wanted to live where I could smell the sea. I have spent my life among inland waterways. In Pittsburgh near the confluence of the three rivers—above the black-smoked delta. Here, alongside the Green River, nesting in a sandstone gorge. Excavating bones.]

I run a motel in Vernal, Utah. We're located between Dinosaur Gardens—featuring full-size replicas—and the turnoff for Dinosaur National Monument, State Route 149.

During slow periods at the motel I work for an old lady here in town. Her house overlooks the fiberglass dinosaur on Main Street.

There's no getting away from it. We're surrounded by Carnegie's bones.

[The first big find was in August 1909. On a hogback near Split Mountain. Eight vertebrae embedded in the sandstone. Intact. I was still in Pittsburgh waiting to leave. Both our families deplored the idea that I would take their grandchild and enter into the unknown—as they put it—as though we were going back in time—even though my husband was waiting—albeit from the cliff faces of the Morrison Formation, remains of an enormous floodplain. I agreed I wouldn't budge until the baby turned a year, but after the find, the tremendous excitement as the entire skeleton emerged, I could wait no longer. I took off. Just like that. They couldn't stop me.]

I helped the old lady with things around her place. Odd jobs. Everything from hauling trash to installing a new water heater. I'm a quick study at do-it-yourself, which serves well in my line of work. She was clearing out the attic and asked me to give her a hand. She said she didn't want her accumulation left to strangers. Didn't want anything left behind.

"The way it was with my neighbor," she said. "All those unopened sets of china, flatware, linen still in the cellophane. What on earth was she waiting for? Armageddon?"

I didn't ask why you'd need place settings at the end of the world.

"Maybe she was waiting for life to start. Some people are like that."

"More likely she was afraid. Heaven will do that to you. And hell."

The way into the attic was one of those ladders that come out of the ceiling. Sturdy enough for me but awkward for the old lady. So we agreed I'd manage it myself and she'd just have to trust me with it, clearing out the attic, I mean.

I'd call out all what I saw, and she'd tell me what she wanted given away and what thrown out.

"And he shall come to judge the quick and the dead," she said, then laughed—and there was no capital *H* in her voice either.

There'd been a billboard outside of town painted with that warning. Underneath the words was someone's idea of a world consumed by a fireball. But the sun out here is wicked, and over a short time everything faded. Some people are crazy.

Once I was up in the attic I switched on the light, a single hanging bulb, couldn't have been more than sixty watts, if that. I shone the light across the space—low eaves, dark wood—things upon things—it looked as if nobody had been up there since God knows when.

Don't even think about the dust, I said.

I turned and caught my face in a caul. Cobwebs, nasty things.

There was the usual stuff you'd find in an attic that's been filling up since preatomic times.

A lineup of glassy-eyed dolls. One naked with the outline of her crybox showing through the cloth of her body. I bent her forward and a rusted sound came out. Nowhere near the mama cry, fake as that was.

A pair of black ice skates were hanging by their laces next to a shelf of books. I ran my fingers over the blade of one skate. Dull.

The spines of the books had faded and I couldn't make out the lettering. Could've been anything, for all I could tell. Still, books.

I had plans.

I keep a lending library next to the ice machine at the motel. Too many people, you know, glued to America's domestic god. That's one way of controlling people. And, no, I'm not paranoid. I post a hand-lettered sign in each room. Black magic marker, block capitals: DO NOT TURN ON TV. YOU WILL RISK LOSING RECEPTION. BOOKS ARE AVAILABLE FOR YOUR ENJOYMENT.

I've had a few complaints, sure, but not as many as you might think.

"What about these books?" I yelled down.

The old lady yelled back up, "Just make sure my name is removed from the flyleaf."

Strange old bird.

"Okay if I take them?"

"Be my guest. Just remove my name, please. No traces."

"As you say." Who was I to argue?

[The closest town to the quarry site was Vernal, twenty-two miles to the west. We went there for all our supplies, and from there we shipped the bones back to Mr. Carnegie, Railway Express. Tons and tons. With instructions as to their assembly, of course. He'd asked for something "as big as a barn" to give to the King of England. We went one better.

In the winter we stayed put. There wasn't much of a choice. When the skies came clear, we hiked the ridges, walking over bones we would only recognize from a distance. Underfoot they were but rough terrain. The air was blue-cold. We were far from the black-smoked delta. In winter the ice on the Green River was more than two feet thick. We skated it, zigzagging shore to shore. At times the temperature dropped to thirty degrees below, and the wind howled—honest—through the gorge.

Our first home, before we built our cabin, was made of canvas-covered 2 × 4s—we lived in one tent, the other was for storage. I used to wrap the baby tight and prop him by the stove just so he wouldn't freeze. But for the work we might have judged the place the end of the world. It was no such thing. It was magic. Every time we found a skull, I made a complete Thanksgiving dinner.

Once we found a head turned, as if glancing back, as if in flight.]

There were three old trunks in one corner of the attic, one stacked on top of another. A hatbox was balanced on top of them. Cardboard with big reddish flowers—peonies maybe.

I have to watch my imagination. The hatbox made me think of that movie with Robert Montgomery. The one where he carries a head in a hatbox. A woman's head, naturally.

Naturally—how easy that comes.

Night Must Fall.

Then I remembered Winnie Ruth Judd. What if the peonies were something else? I stopped myself.

Don't be crazy.

I turned and yelled down the ladder, "What about these trunks? And there's a hatbox on top of them."

The old lady did not answer.

Couldn't hurt to look.

I reached up and caught the edge of the hatbox with my right hand. It tumbled to my chest. I shook the contents; they rattled—loud.

"What's going on?" The old lady had returned from wherever.

"What about this hatbox?"

"Bones, my dear. Stolen property."

What on earth did she mean? I shook the hatbox once more. Could be.

"How about these trunks?"

"Same. An embarrassment of bones."

I thought better about asking what sorts of bones. Whose were they?

"Don't fret. They don't belong to anyone you know."

[I found myself sitting on the ridgeback of a stegosaurus. The sun was high; it was midday. I'd taken a picnic and absented myself from the site—just for a few hours. I tried to imagine the place as it must have been. Dark-green, blue-green, foliage swollen with water. Where now there was the gray-green of sage. Wet where now all was dry. But for the river. An inland sea lapping against land. So much weight of water that the crust of the earth dented. What noises then?

Now there was for the most part silence. Once I heard the rattle of a snake. Heat. The smell of something burning far off.]

Dream Street

> It is perhaps fitting that the literal Dream Street, which formerly ran for several blocks in the vicinity of Pittsburgh's West Liberty Avenue, is no longer on the map. The area where the street used to be is overgrown with vegetation, and the opening through which the street ran is barely discernible today.
>
> —W. Eugene Smith exhibit, "Dream Street," Carnegie Museum of Art, 2001

THE BOY LIVED in his family an inconvenient stranger. He remembered one particular afternoon. A cold rain, not unexpected; they lived where it rained a lot. "Often rebuked . . ." He held in his hands an anthology of English poetry borrowed from the local Carnegie library. The air inside the small farmhouse was heavy with the smell of roasting beets. The damp of the outside seeping inside. Dark, earthly. And the beets, sweet. The only sweetness to be found inside these walls. Too soon the sweetness would be disappeared, be devoured. All that would be left to him: cold, damp. Once he left, never would he be "back returning." And everyone would say he'd turned his back on his people. Or worse. So what? One too many words hurting him. He'd take care they'd never find him.

He was their Heathcliff, yet of their flesh and blood. Dark like the foundling on the ash heaps of Liverpool, late eighteenth century. We are at the tail end of the twentieth century, just outside Pittsburgh. A few miles south of Frank Lloyd Wright's Falling Water. A world and a half away.

He begins his life at seventeen, on his own. What impelled him was nothing more or less than words. What fed his deed: every word of which he heard before. Many times before, but he had been too young until now to take his leave. To silence them, finally.

"You can't be one of us. I refuse to believe it." This from his father.

"Where could you have come from? Why have you been visited on us?" This from his mother.

"What a sin." Their duet. His life was their cross to bear, all because of a night in the backseat of his father's father's hump-backed Dodge. They came from people who, once caught, "had to get married." Never mind the law of the land. "You stupid, stupid kids." Her father's words.

They were told they had to get married or the girl would be shipped off and put away. Stashed with some nuns who would remind her perpetually of the failures of the flesh. Her father forced the marriage. That would be a fitting punishment. Two, then three lives lived in the purgatory of a loveless union. They heaped their lovelessness upon him.

The ceremony was performed in a church on Troy Hill known for its collection of relics—the most extensive collection outside of Rome. Fetishes. The finger joint of a saint. St. Anthony's tooth. Rags and tatter worn or touched by martyrs.

They met at the altar of the reliquary and took their vows.

What saved them, what united husband and wife, drew them toward each other, was their mutual feeling this boy had blacked out their futures. And he made it come true, finally.

The boy had enough, finally. He suffered no bruises brought on by punches, slaps. Only words. Words and occasional confinement. No other sibling as buffer. He and he alone. He had never learned to duck. To feint. To talk back.

Their words drove him away; others' words sustained him.

He only ever wanted to live in peace and quiet. And light. He had only known the dark interiors of lovelessness, of poverty as well. Newsprint holding out cold, also light.

He taught himself to love beauty, beautiful things. He found these things among the stacks in the local Carnegie library. Who can say how many lives have been saved by books? His was certainly one. When they locked him in the closet in his room, he secreted a flashlight in his waistband. There was a stack of library books waiting for him in a dark corner. Others' words waiting for him. He propped himself against the door of the closet, and read. Company.

On his way away he met a man in a diner near some train tracks. He had followed these tracks from the village to the city. Over black coffee—he was seventeen; *this* was living—in thick white mugs, he asked the man if he knew any place that was hiring.

"That depends; what do you know how to do?"

The man laughed when the runaway said, "I know how to read and write. I'm pretty good at it."

"That's it?"

"I guess so."

The man smiled, "Then, good luck to you; you'll need it."

The runaway left the diner and walked farther into the city. He walked across every one of the three rivers—Pittsburgh has more bridges than Paris, he read that somewhere—and up and down the hills.

After some weeks of searching he found himself at the Carnegie Museum of Natural History, taking a break one afternoon. He struck up a conversation with the man at the front desk, an old guy—he said he was close to retirement—with a nice smile and a smart uniform.

"You seem kind of young to be on your own."

"I'm an orphan. I've been on my own for some time now. One way or another."

It wasn't exactly a lie.

"Let me see what I can do." And the man made a call from the white phone on the front desk.

Another man, also in uniform, soon appeared and spoke briefly with the boy.

"Can I see some ID?"

"There was a fire."

"I don't know about that. I need to see something."

"I really need to work, mister. Honest." He lowered his eyes.

"What do you think, Ed?" He turned to the man at the desk.

"Give him a break, Frank. He seems like a nice kid."

"Okay, kid. Just don't make me regret this."

"I won't."

Right there, on the spot he got work as a night watchman in the museum. He got fitted out with a uniform, and a flashlight and a nametag. He gave his name as Tom Finn, after two of his favorite characters: Tom Joad and Huckleberry Finn. He was sent to a shop down Forbes Avenue to buy a pair of heavy, steel-toed black shoes.

He was on his way.

In the museum: he thought of Rembrandt's painting *The Night Watch.* His was a cluttered mind, filled with myriad images, littered with information. "Useless information," the parents had remarked. Stop! No more of those voices. Banish them from your thoughts once and for all. They have no place here, in your new life. This life you have given yourself. Besides, have you not silenced them once and for all?

He rented a room on Dream Street.

He talked to himself, a quirk developed in childhood. He needed the company of his own voice. He needed its reassurance, telling himself the two were wrong. In his night perambulations around the museum he passed vitrine upon vitrine of dead birds—who had once been wild, nesting, engaged in migration, he said out loud, his language typical of an isolated soul, engaged in a solitary dialogue. After the hall of birds he found himself beside a freestanding glass-eyed buffalo. Nearby was the enormous white jawbone of a sperm whale—his belovèd *Moby Dick*—one step removed from the actual thing. Next to the immense, bleached jawbone, a small black-and-white etching of the whaler *Greyhound*—her men whipping over the waves—the caption read, "Nantucket sleigh ride."

In another room scarabs, the dung beetles so dear to the Egyptians, who remade themselves time and again, were pinned to a board behind glass, iridescent blue-green. Hundreds of butterflies, also pinned.

Polar bear—mouth open in midroar—or scream—as strange men approached him for capture.

On a lower level was an elevator with one clear glass wall that took its occupant down and down into the geologic layers of the city. He travels down and down and down until he becomes frightened; he fears he is being buried alive. A self-service elevator has become his casket. What if it stalls?

He sends it upwards, leaning on the emergency bell all the while. He thinks there probably will be no one to hear it—there are other guards but the museum is vast; he takes care to avoid them—the clang comforts him. No one will hear it; maybe someone will come. Such is his logic.

Each night ends when he finds himself among the magnificence of dinosaurs. Brontosaurus, thunder lizard. One night he climbs the ribs of *Tyrannosaurus rex* as if they were the rungs of a ladder. Sits astride the spine, almost at the huge head, his feet nestled in the tiny forelegs like stirrups. "Whatever became of you?" he whispers. He asks this each and every night.

Dismounts.

The two will become skeletons soon enough. He'd left the door to the farmhouse open, inviting scavengers. One too many words attacking him. That's all.

He leaves the museum as the city is becoming light. Stops at the all-night diner, where the waitress fails to meet his eyes but brings his usual—scrambled eggs and corned beef hash, orange juice and rye toast. He eats slowly—this is his main meal of the day—pays his check, leaves a tip. He walks all the way to Dream Street. Up the steps of the semidetached house with battleship gray siding. Inside the heavy oak door with beveled window—details of birds, incongruous beauty against the plainness of the siding. Past the half-open door to the landlady's parlor. With luck she won't stir, won't disturb his progress. Up the main staircase to his room, where he wraps himself in a coarse wool blanket and falls asleep. To dream. He crowds his dream-mind with images, keeping memory at bay. He dreams of thunder lizards and raptors and sperm whales and iridescent insects. Glassy-eyed buffaloes roaming the once-wild landscape where the city now was. He dreams until it's time to leave for his nocturnal turn through the silent museum. And encounters with the creatures of his dreams.

"What the hell?!" He hears from his tyrannosaurus perch. "Are you tryin' out for the next Jurassic Park?"

Because he had not been loved, he'd not developed a sense of humor. So he didn't crack a smile at the voice's remarks.

The voice breaks into his dream-state.

"Hey, you. Up there. You better come down before you do some damage."

He stays still. He says nothing. Just go away. Please go away, he pleads silently.

"Here. I have a thermos of coffee. Want a cup?"

He wishes, as he wished times before, he was invisible.

"Look, if you won't come down from there, I'll have to call the boss. He won't like this one bit."

He does not budge.

"Okay, you asked for it." The voice turns on his walkie-talkie.

He atop the skeleton wishes he could channel the raptor's voice. What a roar he must have had.

Instead he begins to bellow, his own hollow, frightened sound. He is back in that small house with those two people who despise him. Where he barely speaks. Where one afternoon he brings a hammer to the kitchen table. He shivers. His sound bounds around the hall.

He only wishes his own flesh would fall away and he would be a skeleton atop this skeleton of a monster, his protector.

The head watchman is summoned.

"What are you, anyway? Nuts?"

The bellow ceases. The boy comes to, is told to calm down, is warned.

"This better not happen again. I've got my eye on you. Remember, the guys in charge gave you a break."

He will not do it again; he promises, securing his word with a nod.

Here is a boy hanging by a thread. He must not draw attention his way.

"I am on trial here," he says to himself.

At the same time there are headlines in the *Pittsburgh Post-Gazette,* day after day: SKELETAL REMAINS . . . REMOTE FARMHOUSE . . . COUPLE FOUND . . . BLOODSTAINED HAMMER IN KITCHEN . . . SON SOUGHT. The papers spread across the front desk at the museum in the hands of the man at the desk. "Rotten kid," he says to no one in particular. A woman proffering her membership card nods. Headlines blare from the vitrines at the corners of Forbes Avenue, Fifth Avenue. Reports drone from the son's landlady's drawing room, tuned relentlessly to Court TV. "Police seek couple's son for questioning," the commentator says. They name his given name on the TV. There are no photographs of him. None was ever taken. As is true in many cases, no one interviewed seems to recall anything about the family. "They lived their lives away from the rest of us," is one comment.

By and by this matter became a cold-case file, just one among the many.

He goes on among the vitrines of dead birds. The displays of bones and feathers and mummies and replicas of Indians. The jawbone of the sperm whale. The polar bear in midscream or roar. The dung beetles and the butterflies. His belovèd *T. rex.* These keep him company.

After a solid season of record-breaking rainfall: a warm rain this time. The green obscures the way into Dream Street and conceals him. In his dreams the wild reclaims the street. He feels safer, walking to the museum under an arcade of green.

Columba

WHEN I WAS TWELVE, my parents left me in the hands of a hypochondriacal aunt and her Cuban lover, a ham radio operator. Her lover, that is, until she claimed their bed as her own. She was properly a family friend, who met my grandmother when they danced the Black Bottom at the Glass Bucket. Jamaica in the twenties was wild.

This woman, whose name was Charlotte, was large and pink and given to wearing pink satin nighties—flimsy relics, pale from age. Almost all was pink in that room, so it seemed; so it seems now, at this distance. The lace trim around the necks of the nighties was not pink; it was yellowed and frazzled, practically absent. This wisp of thread that had once formed flowers, birds, a spider's web. Years of washing in hard water with brown soap had made the nighties loose, droop, so that Charlotte's huge breasts slid outside, suddenly, sideways, pink falling on pink like ladylike camouflage, but for her livid nipples. No one could love those breasts, I think.

Her hair stuck flat against her head, bobbed and straightened, girlish bangs as if painted on her forehead. Once she had resembled Louise Brooks. No longer. New moons arced each black eye.

Charlotte was also given to drinking vast amounts of water from the crystal carafes standing on her low bedside table, next to her *Information Please Almanac*—she had a fetish for detail but no taste for reading—linen hankies scented with bay rum, and a bowl of soursweet tamarind balls. As she drank, so did she piss, ringing changes on the walls of chamber pots lined under the bed, all through the day and night. Her room, her pink expanse, smelled of urine and bay rum and the wet sugar that bound the tamarind balls. Ancestral scents.

I was to call her Aunt Charlotte and to mind her, for she was officially in loco parentis.

The Cuban, Juan Antonio Corona y Mestee, slept on a safari cot next to his ham radio, rum bottle, stacks of *Punch, Country Life,* and something called *Gent.* His room was a screened-in porch at the side of the verandah. Sitting there with him in the evening, listening to the calls of the radio, I could almost imagine myself away from that place, in the bush awaiting capture, or rescue, until the sharp PING! of Charlotte's water cut across even my imaginings and the scratch of faraway voices.

One night a young man vaulted the rail of a cruise ship off Tobago, and we picked up the distress call. A sustained SPLASH! followed Charlotte's PING! and the young man slipped under the waves.

I have never been able to forget him, and capture him in a snap of that room, as though he floated through it, me. I wonder still, why that particular instant? That warm evening, the Southern Cross in clear view? The choice of a sea change?

His mother told the captain they had been playing bridge with another couple when her son excused himself. We heard all this on the radio, as the captain reported in full. Henry Fonda sprang to my movie-saturated mind, in *The Lady Eve,* with Barbara Stanwyck. But that was blackjack, not bridge, and a screwball comedy besides.

Perhaps the young man had tired of the coupling. Perhaps he needed a secret sharer.

The Cuban was a tall handsome man with blue-black hair and a costume of unvarying khaki. He seemed content to stay with Charlotte, use the whores in Raetown from time to time, listen to his radio, sip his rum, leaf through his magazines. Sitting on the side of the safari cot in his khaki, engaged in his pastimes, he seemed a displaced white hunter (except he wasn't white, a fact no amount of relaxers or wide-brimmed hats could mask) or a mercenary recuperating from battle fatigue, awaiting further orders.

Perhaps he did not stir for practical reasons. This was 1960; he could not return to Cuba in all his hyphenated splendor, and had no marketable skills for the British Crown Colony in which he found himself. I got along with him, knowing we were both there on sufferance, unrelated dependents. Me, because Charlotte owed my grandmother something, he, for whatever reason he or she might have.

One of Juan Antonio's duties was to drop me at school. Each morning he pressed a half-crown into my hand, always telling me to treat my friends. I appreciated his largesse, knowing the money came from his allowance. It was a generous act and he asked no repayment but one small thing: I was to tell anyone who asked that he was my father. As I remember, no one ever did. Later, he suggested that I say "Good-bye, Papá"—with the accent on the last syllable—when I left the car each morning. I hesitated, curious. He said, "Never mind," and the subject was not brought up again.

I broke the chain of generosity and kept his money for myself, not willing to share it with girls who took every chance to ridicule my American accent and call me "salt."

I used the money to escape them, escape school. Sitting in the movies, watching them over and over until it was time to catch the bus back.

Charlotte was a woman of property. Her small house was a cliché of colonialism, graced with calendars advertising the coronation of ER II, the marriage of Princess Margaret Rose, the visit of Alice, Princess Royal. Bamboo and wicker furniture was sparsely scattered across dark mahogany floors—settee there, end table here—giving the place the air of a hotel lobby, the sort of hotel carved from the shell of a great house, before Hilton and Sheraton made landfall. Tortoiseshell lampshades. Ashtrays made from coconut husks. Starched linen runners sporting the embroideries of craftswomen.

The house sat on top of a hill in Kingston, surrounded by an unkempt estate—so unkempt as to be arrogant, for this was the wealthiest part of the city, and the largest single tract of land. So large that a dead quiet enveloped the place in the evening, and we were cut off, sound and light absorbed by the space and the dark and the trees, abandoned and wild, entangled by vines and choked by underbrush, escaped, each reaching to survive.

At the foot of the hill was a cement gully that bordered the property—an empty moat but for the detritus of trespassers. Stray dogs roamed amid Red Stripe beer bottles, crushed cigarette packets, bully-beef tins.

Trespassers, real and imagined, were Charlotte's passion. In the evening, after dinner, bed-jacket draped across her shoulders against the soft trade winds, which she said were laden with typhoid, she roused herself to the verandah and took aim. She fired and fired and fired. Then she excused herself. "That will hold them for another night." She was at once terrified of invasion and confident she could stay it. Her gunplay was ritual against it.

There was, of course, someone responsible for cleaning the house, feeding the animals, filling the carafes and emptying the chamber pots, cooking the meals, and doing the laundry. These tasks fell to Columba, a fourteen-year-old from St. Ann, where Charlotte had bartered him from his mother; a case of condensed milk, two dozen tins of sardines, five pounds of flour, several bottles of cooking oil, permission to squat on Charlotte's cane-piece—fair exchange. His mother set up housekeeping with his brothers and sisters, and Columba was transported in the back of Charlotte's black Austin to Kingston. A more magnanimous, at least practical, landowner would have had a staff of two, even three, but Charlotte swore against being taken advantage of, as she termed it, so all was done by Columba, learning to expand his skills under her teaching, instructions shouted from the bed.

He had been named not for our discoverer but for the saint buried on Iona, discoverer of the monster in the loch. A Father Pierre, come to St. Ann from French Guiana, had taught Columba's mother, Winsome, to write her name, read a ballot, and know God. He said he had been assistant to the confessor on Devil's Island, and when the place was finally shut down in 1951, he was cast adrift, floating around the islands seeking a berth.

His word was good enough for the people gathered in his seaside chapel of open sides and thatched roof, used during the week to shelter a woman smashing limestone for the road, sorting trilobite from rock. On Sunday morning people sang, faces misted by spray, air heavy with the scent of sea grapes, the fat purple bunches bowing, swinging, brushing the glass sand, bruised. Bruises releasing more scent, entering the throats of a congregation fighting the smash of the sea. On Sunday morning Father Pierre talked to them of God, dredging his memory for every tale he had been told.

This was good enough for these people. They probably couldn't tell a confessor from a convict—which is what Father Pierre was—working off his crime against nature by boiling the life out of yam and taro and salted beef for the wardens, his keepers.

Even after the *Gleaner* had broadcast the real story, the congregation stood fast: he was white; he knew God—they reasoned. Poor devils.

Father Pierre held Columba's hand at the boy's baptism. He was ten years old then and had been called "Junior" all his life. Why honor an unnamed sire? Father Pierre spoke to Winsome. "Children," the priest intoned, "the children become their names." He spoke in an English as broken as hers.

What Father Pierre failed to reckon with was the unfamiliar nature of the boy's new name; Columba was "Collie" to some, "Like one damn dawg," his mother said. "Chuh, man. Hignorant smaddy cyaan accept not'ing new." Collie soon turned Lassie, and he was shamed.

To Charlotte he became "Colin," because she insisted on Anglicization. It was for his own good, she added for emphasis, and so he would recognize her kindness. His name-as-is was foolish and feminine and had been given him by a pedophile, for heaven's sake.

Charlotte's shouts reached Columba in the kitchen. He was attempting to put together a gooseberry fool for the mistress's elevenses. The word *pedophile* smacked the stucco of the corridor between them, each syllable distinct, perversion bouncing furiously off the walls. I had heard—who hadn't?—but the word was beyond me. I was taking Latin, not Greek.

I softly asked Juan Antonio, and he, in equally hushed tones, said, "Mariposa . . . butterfly."

Charlotte wasn't through. "Fancy naming a boy after a bird. A black boy after a white bird. And still people attend that man. . . . Well, they will get what they deserve," she promised. "You are lucky I saved you from that." She spoke with such conviction.

I was forbidden to speak with Columba except on matters of household business, encouraged by Charlotte to complain when the pleat of my school tunic was not sharp enough. I felt only awkward that a boy two years older than myself was responsible for my laundry, for feeding me, for making my bed. I was, after all, an American now, only here temporarily. I did not keep the commandment.

I sought him out in secret. When Juan Antonio went downtown and while Charlotte dozed, the coast was clear. We sat behind the house under an ancient guava, concealed by a screen of bougainvillea. There we talked. Compared lives. Exchanged histories. We kept each other company, and our need for company made our conversations almost natural. The alternative was a dreadful loneliness; silence, but for the noises of the two adults. Strangers.

His questions about America were endless. What was New York like? Had I been to Hollywood? He wanted to know every detail about Duke Ellington, Marilyn Monroe, Stagger Lee, Jackie Wilson, Ava Gardner, Billy the Kid, Dinah Washington, Tony Curtis, Spartacus, John Wayne. Everyone, every name he knew from the cinema, where he slipped on his evening off; every voice, ballad, beat, he heard over Rediffusion, tuned low in the kitchen.

Did I know any of these people? Could you see them on the street? Then startling me: what was life like for a black man in America? An ordinary black man, not a star?

I had no idea—not really. I had been raised in a community in New Jersey until this interruption, surrounded by people who had made their own world and "did not business" with that sort of thing. Bourgeois separatists. I told Columba I did not know, and we went back to the stars and legends.

A Tuesday during rainy season: Charlotte, swathed in a plaid lap robe lifted from the *Queen Mary,* is being driven by Juan Antonio to an ice factory she owns in Old Harbour. There is a problem with the overseer; Charlotte is summoned. You would think she was being transported a thousand miles up the Amazon into headhunter territory, so elaborate are the preparations.

She and Juan Antonio drop me at school. There is no half-crown this morning. I get sixpence and wave them off. I wait for the Austin to turn the corner at St. Cecelia's Way, then I cut to Lady Musgrave Road to catch the bus back.

When I return, I change and meet Columba out back. He has promised to show me something. The rain drips from the deep green of the escaped bush that surrounds us. We set out on a path invisible but to him, our bare feet sliding on slick fallen leaves. A stand of mahoe is in front of us. We pass through the trees and come into a clearing.

In the clearing is a surprise: a wreck of a car, thirties Rover. Gutsprung, tired and forlorn, it slumps in the high grass. Lizards scramble through the vines that wrap around rusted chrome and across black hood and boot. We walk closer. I look into the wreck.

The leather seats are split, and a white fluff erupts here and there. A blue gyroscope set into the dash slowly rotates. A pennant of the Kingston Yacht Club dangles miserably from the rearview.

This is not all. The car is alive. Throughout, roaming the seats, perched on the running board, spackling the crystal face of the clock, are doves. White. Speckled. Rock. Mourning. Wreck turned dovecote is filled with their sweet coos.

"Where did you find them?"

Columba is pleased, proud, too, I think. "Nuh find dem nestin' all over de place? I mek dem a home, give dem name. Dat one dere nuh Stagger Lee?" He points to a mottled pigeon hanging from a visor. "Him is rascal fe true."

Ava Gardner's feet click across the roof where Spartacus is hot in her pursuit.

Columba and I sit among the birds for hours.

I thank him for showing them to me, promising on my honor not to tell.

That evening I am seated across from Charlotte and next to Juan Antonio in the dining room. The ceiling fan stirs the air, which is heavy with the day's moisture.

Columba has prepared terrapin and is serving us one by one. His head is bowed so our eyes cannot meet, as they never do in such domestic moments. We—he and I—split our lives in this house as best we can. No one watching this scene would imagine our meeting that afternoon, the wild birds, talk of flight.

The turtle is sweet. A turtling man traded it for ice that morning in Old Harbour. The curved shell sits on a counter in the kitchen. Golden. Delicate. Representing our island. Representing the world.

I did not tell them about the doves.

They found out easily, stupidly.

Charlotte's car had developed a knock in the engine. She noticed it on the journey to the ice factory and questioned me about it each evening after that. Had I heard it on the way to school that morning? How could she visit her other properties without proper transport? Something must be done.

Juan Antonio suggested he take the Austin to the Texaco station at Matilda's Corner. Charlotte would have none of it. She asked little from

Juan Antonio; the least he could do was maintain her automobile. What did she suggest? he asked. How could he get parts to repair the Austin? Should he fashion them from bamboo?

She announced her solution: Juan Antonio was to take a machete and chop his way through to the Rover. The car had served her well, she said; surely it could be of use now. He resisted, reminding her that the Rover was thirty years old, probably rusted beyond recognition, and not of any conceivable use. It did not matter.

The next morning Juan Antonio set off to chop his way through the bush, dripping along the path, monkey wrench in his left hand, machete in his right. Columba was in the kitchen, head down, wrapped in the heat of burning coals as he fired irons to draw across khaki and satin.

The car, of course, was useless as a donor, but Juan Antonio's mission was not a total loss. He was relieved to tell Charlotte about the doves. Why, there must be a hundred. All kinds.

Charlotte was beside herself. Her property was the soul of bounty. Her trees bore heavily. Her chickens laid through hurricanes. Edible creatures abounded!

Neither recognized that these birds were not for killing. They did not recognize the pennant of the Kingston Yacht Club as the colors of this precious colony within a colony.

Columba was given his orders. Wring the necks of the birds. Pluck them and dress them and wrap them tightly for freezing. Leave out three for that evening's supper.

He did as he was told.

Recklessly I walked into the bush. No notice was taken.

I found him sitting in the front seat of the dovecote. A wooden box was beside him, half-filled with dead birds. The live ones did not scatter, did not flee. They sat and paced and cooed, as Columba performed his dreadful task.

"Sorry, man, you hear?" he said softly as he wrung the neck of the next one. He was weeping heavily. Heaving his shoulders with the effort of execution and grief.

I sat beside him in silence, my arm around his waist. This was not done.

The Ferry

THE CARS ON THE FERRY below decks were kept from the waters of the harbor by a slender gate. Once in a while a car might slip its emergency brake and slide forward. Were it a car at the front of the line, the gate would break its momentum, giving slightly, returning the force it received like a slingshot.

The boy's mother was dating a man who drove a '59 Chevy with dual controls; freaky thing. The man, whose name was Jimmy, borrowed the boy's new sports coat at his mother's request so that she and Jimmy could go to church on Sunday and make a good impression.

The boy, Vincent, did not accompany them. He had given up on church shortly after his father died. Not that he had been particularly close to his father and was left angry at God. Not that he suffered any dramatic loss of faith. His father's death was as good an excuse as any to remove himself from the tedium of the hour of worship, the drone of a minister, the heads spinning to see who was coming down the aisle with whom, what they were wearing, where they would sit—dying for something to talk about.

He knew the sight of his mother and Jimmy would set them calculating the span of widowhood, approving or disapproving, as if their opinions mattered.

The only thing that had kept him going as long as he had was not his mother's wishes (as she thought), but the voice of the paid soprano, the one brilliant space in the tedium. Something he found more beautiful than the stained-glass windows, the marble memorial plaques, the psalms. As she launched into Mozart's "Alleluia" on Palm Sunday, "O Holy Night" on Christmas Eve, "Be Still, My Soul" on some less sacred day, Vincent would turn his head and regard her in the choir loft, high above him, against his mother's admonishings. You were supposed to pretend the voice came directly from God, the paid soprano a vessel of God's noise. You were not supposed to note her effort, imagine the sweat on her top lip, the phlegm in her cotton handkerchief.

He watched her in the choir loft, hands clasped tightly, eyes focused on some vanishing point on high, singing out over all of them. She was, in her isolation, magnificent.

The others, including his mother, called her dumpy, dowdy, and said she earned her living in the basement of Gimbel's. The twenty dollars they gave her each Sunday, when she traveled on the ferry across the water, was more than enough—someone else would not charge. But, they agreed, they needed her.

Vincent noticed the contradiction in them.

Not even the sound of her voice could hold him.

Jimmy was a small man—*dapper* was the word some used; Vincent, at seventeen, tall and broad as a swimmer, quiet for a boy. The man swam in the sports coat, but the mother did not ask Vincent if the sleeves might be shortened: that seemed to be going too far.

The boy did not hesitate to hand over the coat: he usually did as his mother asked, whether he wanted to or not. Neither mother nor son cared for confrontation. She had taught him that only "low-class" people raised their voices, disagreed openly, caused "scenes." Born among such people, she wanted nothing more than to leave them behind—thought she had when she married Vincent's father.

And here she was, dating a man who didn't own a jacket, whose prized possession was a crazy mixed-up car. Her son kept mum.

"You can't judge a book by its cover," she might say, not extending that charity to the paid soprano.

Vincent did own a blue serge suit, but his wrists extended way beyond the ends of the sleeves, and in it he looked like a Dead End kid dressed up. The sleeves had been let out as far as possible by the tailor in the shop downstairs, but no help. And besides, he had worn it to his father's funeral the year before, and it saddened his mother to see him in it. But she did not toss it away or give it to the Salvation Army. Now it hung in the back of the hall closet behind his father's World War II dress uniform, under the shelf that held a white wedding album with gold lettering, and a furrier's box containing ancient glassy-eyed stone martens. Signs of a person's history. Mementos.

They would never have said it to each other—not "in so many words"—but each was relieved at the father's death. "He's at peace now. He's out of pain," was what she said.

He wasn't a falling-down drunk, or public embarrassment—not at first—just a man who dosed himself a few ounces each hour of each day. But soon his disability checks couldn't maintain his needs, and he began to hock things (she must have redeemed the stone martens a dozen times if she'd redeemed them once) and, later, more desperate, to plead break-ins by large, dangerous Negroes, or hopped-up Puerto Ricans.

Soon, he was verging on public embarrassment. People pitied him when they saw him on the streets, weighed down like a peddler, as glassy-eyed as the stone martens draped around his neck. The cops at the local precinct thrilled to the idea of nabbing a few marauders—they'd been pouring onto the island ever since the bridge was opened—and were disappointed when the pawnbroker identified the plaintiff as the perpetrator. "We'll let you off with a warning this time. Understand?"

Why did he drink? Misery. Oblivion—the need for. Something to do.

The usual.

His wife passed him off as a casualty of war. Wounded. Shell-shocked. Too genteel for his own good.

A man who had helped liberate Paris.

Actually his wound had been caused by a jeep accident. "Just like Patton," he joked with her when they first met.

In fact he'd never left Fort Dix. But he went along with her story; it was the least he could do. And when the minister and a few of the elders dropped by, he splashed some cold water on his face, sucked on a peppermint, and told them about weeping Frenchmen and girls craving nylons and children screaming for Hershey bars—just like in the movies. And he knew not a damned soul was fooled. Not for a minute.

They hardly spoke of him after he passed on.

Jimmy was grateful to have the loan of the sports coat and in return—for he was not a man to take something for nothing—offered Vincent driving lessons.

Jimmy's car in 1969 was too young to be classic and too old to be cool, but it had an individuality to be built upon, and he set about making it one of a kind. He had it painted and the seats recovered, the words AL'S DRIVING SCHOOL removed from one door, and CAUTION IS OUR MIDDLE NAME from the other. It became yellow, with red and black and green upholstery. Jimmy stood back: it looked "jazzy."

To his eye. "One of a kind," he repeated, while Vincent's mother hoped she could convince him to trade it in, or at least have it painted black, if they were to have any future together at all.

That was future. Fun, the here-and-now, was something else. And what she called her "serious side" was quiet when she took her place in the death seat and worked her set of controls. Riding shotgun. Some Sundays after church she and Jimmy would compete against each other on the black gravel roads around Wolfe's Pond, roaring up and down, one accelerating while the other slammed the brake, black clouds rising, chasing them.

Careening past the edge of other people's picnics, skirting the Arthur Kill, around and around, out of breath, as if they were powering the car themselves.

"Wonder what your son would say if he could see you."

"I'm still a young woman, you know. Not just someone's widowed mother."

"I know."

"This is where they shot part of *Splendor in the Grass,*" she told him, claiming fame. "Ever see it?"

"I'm not much for the movies," he answered, telling her something she already knew. He told her he was not a watcher; he was a man of action.

"Natalie Wood is a doll." She closed the subject, and pressed hard on her gas pedal.

"Say," he yelled over the roar of the Chevy.

"What?"

"Let's go over to Jersey."

"What for?"

He spun them out of the park and onto Hylan Boulevard, passing the house where schoolchildren were taught year in, year out, Washington signed some papers, and then slept. To the Outerbridge Crossing, then down the Jersey shore.

The car in its original incarnation had been spotted by Jimmy on the Staten Island Ferry early one morning—on the *Mary Murray,* to be precise, as Jimmy was whenever he told his story; one of the oldest vessels in the fleet, with a huge greased-over portrait of its namesake in the main salon opposite the steaming Sabrett's hot dogs in their glass case. The words under the painting told people that Mary Murray, who also gave her name to Murray Hill, held off a band of Red Coats during the Revolution—single-handed.

"I was standing there, having a cup of coffee," Jimmy explained, "when something told me to go below. You know those feelings you get?"

The car was at the foot of the stairs. He walked around it, just knew he wanted it, made an offer to the driver—who said he was Al's brother-in-law—and got it cheap.

It had potential, he said.

"You weren't afraid it was 'hot'?" she asked him.

He didn't really care. "You get a nose for these things," he answered her. Why worry? He'd made the car his own. Not even its own mother would recognize it.

The two men clinched the deal below decks where cigarette smoke from commuters blocked any possibility of a sea breeze, but at least cut across the aroma of the garbage scows, plowing back and forth between Manhattan, Brooklyn, Jersey. The stench of Camels, Luckies, Winstons was surely better than the smell of decay: the mountains of bones, letters, tin cans, Kotex, leftover spaghetti, condoms, sour milk, razor blades, fetuses, party favors—all mingling on the flat-bottomed barges, passing in Dantesque procession to their dumping grounds.

The thick blue smoke of the cigarettes, even at eight in the morning, cast a romantic shadow. You could summon up the fog of a film set, and you could see Fred Astaire in *Shall We Dance,* singing to Ginger Rogers, "They can't take that away from me."

Vincent also knew the ferry. He went to school in the City—as island people called Manhattan—and took the boat every morning. Riding the waves, dodging the garbage barges, ice floes, tugs nudging a liner in or out, Vincent moved among the commuters, among the old Italian men barking "Shine? Shine?" among the hair-netted counterwomen, weary, fresh, serving up coffee, Danish, among the oddballs lolling around the urinals. He walked the length and breadth of the boat, around the deck, watching the sooted skyscrapers coming closer, the openness of the harbor narrowing.

He usually ended up in the smokers' cabin, below decks, puffing a forbidden Lucky, listening to the talk around him while desperately trying to memorize a poem for the first period, English Lit. He sat among people he knew only by sight—the 7:45 was unvarying in its cargo—people he had been taught he was not a part of. He could put the book, the poem between them, protecting himself from them.

You could be sitting in a smoky, overheated, crowded cabin on a boat on the water and the life of your mind could keep you in total isolation.

"Quinquereme of Nineveh / From distant Ophir," he spoke in his head, certain that at that moment not another soul in the cabin, on the boat, was echoing him.

"Look up any unfamiliar words in the poem and be prepared to use them in a sentence," had been the teacher's command.

He might make a joke of it. "A quinquereme is a galley ship not unlike the Staten Island Ferry," he might say. And the teacher would call him a smart aleck and never suspect the poem had gotten to him.

And he'd grin in the back of the room, tilting his chair dangerously, while the rest of the IGC's sat straight, dull.

Maybe, maybe not.

His dreams were still fresh at this hour of the morning, sometimes stealing his attention from his homework, the people around him. He loved dreaming, loved the colors, the strangeness, the freedom of them. One he rehearsed over and over, sometimes excited by it; so excited that he had to snuff his Lucky and get out and move; sometimes he was ashamed. What would they think if he told them about the paid soprano and how he had fucked her in the back of Jimmy's Chevy? Would they be shocked at the fucking, or the fact that she was old enough to be his mother? *Toda la vida es sueño, y los sueños, sueños son.* Spanish class; fifth period. "Tell me what does Calderón mean by this"—another teacher's command.

When the fog enveloped all of them and the horns sounded their warning across the water, it could have been a scene from *Outward Bound,* and he might shudder if he thought these people would be his company for all eternity. Or would he?

People laughed in the smoke one morning at a boy, about seventeen also, who asked, pleading with the commuting women (for on the early morning trips the boats held mostly women) to let him rub the high heels of their office shoes against his face. When the women refused, laughing, the boy retreated.

Vincent felt his face redden.

Voices, against the quarreling of seagulls thick after one of the scows, against the thumping pistons of the engine, raised in counterpoint.

"And he has such *nice* skin."

"What does that have to do with it?"

"People like that usually have pimples."

"How many people like that do you know?"

"I've lived."

"Like the guy that killed those nurses?"

"Someone said that if they weren't nurses, they wouldn't have died."

"That's nuts."

"There's always someone."

"What do you mean?"

"Authorities, so-called."

"I had enough of that shit when I was in school."

"They said that they were trained to take care of people."

"They were women, weren't they?"

"I'd pull the switch."

Heads nodded. There was no verbal response to that—except: "You said it."

"But him," someone said, meaning Vincent, "he's an all-American boy."

He tried not to hear, even as they commented on his build, his attention to his book, how he never bothered anyone.

Silence.

Then, soon enough, their talk turned elsewhere. Stories of the night before, predictions of the day to come. Who was getting married, when, and did they have the hall lined up. Puerto Rico as a honeymoon spot.

"It's really empty. Most of them are here."

Bosses.

As they spoke, they smoked, sipped their coffee from cardboard containers with fanciful little boats drawn on them grabbed at the counter upstairs, or snatched on the run from the Commuter's Spa in the terminal; between the Food Farm where some of them would grab the makings of dinner on the way home, and the Normandy Bar & Grill, named by a man who had landed at Omaha Beach.

Between coffee and dinner was the day-at-the-office, where they were employed in companies clustered around Wall Street. High finance. Cargoes. Speculation. Import. Export. Banks. Stockbrokers. Shipping Lines. They were the women who answered the phones. Typed and typed and typed. Fluently decorated steno pads with the grace of Pitman. The romance of capital, far-flung places, exotic teas and coffees, was lost on them. They sat in swivel chairs, wired to headsets. Ran errands. Welcomed clients. Ate their bag lunches in Trinity Churchyard in the shadow of Alexander Hamilton, or in Battery Park in the shadow of cannon, or splurged for a sandwich and coffee in Chock Full o'Nuts.

Most of their husbands, were there husbands, did not travel by sea to their jobs. They were truck drivers, plumbers, pipe fitters, mechanics, worked the docks. The fortunate ones were their own men. Others were stationed in Da Nang, and elsewhere. One man shared the sea with his wife—he was on a cruiser in the Gulf of Tonkin.

"Jesus, I wish I had a dollar for every time I passed that," a woman said, as the Statue of Liberty or Ellis Island passed by: the hollow female, her cracked arm held aloft. The collection of red buildings, suggesting cavernous insides, echoes, pushing, shoving, people with tags tied to them, quarantine.

Many of these women lived in houses in which an old woman or an old man could recollect their first sight of either thing.

Almost every woman on the boat had someone in Vietnam, knew someone there, at least had a neighbor whose son, husband, nephew was way the hell across the world. One woman wore a watch in the shape of a beetle around her neck, sent from Saigon. She didn't regard the pickets around the recruiting office she had to walk by to get to work with kindness. She called them "spoiled brats," and worse.

These were Vincent's shipmates.

At first Jimmy's presence didn't bother Vincent—he didn't let it bother him. His mother had been alone for a long time, even when his father was alive. But more and more they would take to her room, saying they were going to watch TV, locking the door—he could hear the skeleton key turn each time. He listened for it.

After each turning he felt his face go hot and a fury rose in him that was frightening. He had never been so angry before in his life. He didn't really understand it.

The fury invaded his dreams, interrupted them, so he no longer remembered them; just slivers of color remained. His encounter with the paid soprano vanished. His sleep was broken, and he woke exhausted.

In the morning her door would be ajar, and each morning he would push it in farther, gently, not to wake her, not to say good-bye before running down the hill to the ferry, but to check. And seeing her alone, curled on one side, peaceful, eased his fury, and he wondered if he might have imagined the skeleton key turning the night before.

This slight doubt calmed him, but the calm did not last. He would find Jimmy's razor on the porcelain ledge above the sink, or a used coffee cup on the kitchen table. Who does he think he is? He got hot all over again, slamming the front door, running down the stairs, down the side streets to the boat, feeling the cobblestones bruise his feet through his sneakers.

Son of a bitch! he yelped in the morning air.

She slept through his departure most mornings. If he woke her she put it down to his haste to get to school—they had told her he was an Intellectually Gifted Child, hadn't they?—and not miss the early boat, a boy's natural exuberance. Especially a boy like him.

She rose slowly, showered, took coffee in her robe, switched on the *Today* show, tidied up the place, took something out of the freezer, then went to her job at the diner down the street where she worked the late-morning, early-afternoon shift.

With Jimmy around she was relieved of some of the financial terror she had known. He was generous; he paid his way, gave her money for groceries, toward the rent and utilities. That, and the money she got paid on her husband's death, made her almost a lady of leisure. At least she could relax. At least she no longer had to work two jobs, running from the diner to the public school, where she cleaned and polished banisters, steps, bathrooms.

Now that the diner was adding on, she was going to be kicked upstairs, called "hostess"; things were looking up.

As soon as she had some extra cash she was going to buy Vincent a graduation suit—from Barney's, in the City.

When he was not locked behind her door, Jimmy taught Vincent how to drive, trying to enter his life as a friend.

"I guess you miss your old man."

Of course he didn't—he didn't miss the pretense, the covering up.

The not knowing what would be missing, what the poor slob had bartered away. “I guess so.”

“Your mother says he was a hero in the war.”

“Yeah.”

“I would’ve loved to have been in that one.”

“How come you weren’t?”

“Too young. You want to stop here for a beer?”

“My mother doesn’t like me to drink.”

“C’mon. I won’t tell if you won’t. What she don’t know won’t hurt her.”

“You don’t understand.”

“Understand?”

“My father had a problem. She’s afraid. That’s all.”

“I had an old man who drank and I’m just fine. But if you don’t want to, you don’t want to. Just decide for yourself. Be— ” he hesitated—oh, what the hell—“a man.”

“Okay.” Vincent felt the fury beginning and quickly turned down the window, almost yanking the handle out of the door, begging the cold wind to take the heat away.

But it couldn’t.

“I bet you weren’t too young.” He had control of Jimmy’s prized possession. “I bet you were a faggot.”

“Watch it!” Gray water cascaded across the windshield.

Vincent tried to concentrate on the rutted street, doing his best to hit every puddle left from the rain of the night before.

“Hey! Watch it! I’ve got whitewalls, you know.”

“Okay,” he said. “Okay, faggot,” he spoke to himself.

Vincent drove with deliberate caution after that, studiously avoiding every pothole and body of stale water.

“Okay,” Jimmy conceded. “I get the message. I didn’t mean to give advice. I know I ain’t your old man. But don’t you ever say that to me again, or I’ll knock your fucking teeth down your throat. I don’t care if you’re her son or not.”

“Sure.”

“I mean it.”

“I get the message.”

Vincent slowed the car almost to a stop. Jimmy gently lowered the accelerator on his side, floored it, while the boy struggled with the brake. Sailor’s Snug Harbor flew by. Vincent was losing control.

"I'll show you who's boss."

There was a sudden turn and the car skidded in the wet street. Feet lifted from the pedals in synchronicity and the car rolled to a stop outside the gypsum plant.

Vincent got out of the car.

They switched places silently; Jimmy took the wheel.

"Do you mind if I turn on the radio?"

"No," Jimmy responded. "Be my guest."

Leaning forward the boy turned the knob of the radio and tuned to WINS. "Give us twenty minutes and we'll give you the world."

His mother seemed not to notice his elaborate sullenness whenever Jimmy was present. At least she never asked him, "What's the matter?"

He had no one to talk to, and the fury was bearing down on him. The thing drove him. He had to move.

Each night, after the skeleton key turned, he would sneak out of his room in the dark apartment, sneak into the living room and find the porcelain dish on the coffee table where each night Jimmy deposited his keys and wallet. He slid the keys in one pocket and a few bills from the wallet into another.

"You want her, it'll cost you," he whispered into the dark; the only other sound was the hum of the television from her room.

He'd crack open the front door, slide out, go down the stairs, and find the car.

He drove and drove and drove. Sometimes straddling the hump in front and working both sets of controls, one foot playing chicken with the other. "Gas father, brake mother; brake father, gas mother." Back and forth, back and forth. Was this hate?

He'd drive up to the parking lot at Silver Lake and regard the steamed-up windows of the cars, laughing when the cops rolled in and flashlights were pointed, played over crotches, faces, warnings given.

Maybe if he had a girl?

Maybe he should see the minister and—what? Confess to what?

Once, he drove the full length of Victory Boulevard on the passenger side, steering with one hand out of view, honking the horn so people would think he was the captive of a ghost-driver.

No cops came.

He ended each night at a car wash, scrubbing the precious whitewalls so he wouldn't be found out. Wishing he could run through the jets and brushes himself.

Of course he was caught.

Jimmy could let the missing cash, the rising odometer go only so far.

One morning before church he confronted Vincent.

"I know you've been using my car without asking."

"And you've been using my mother without asking."

Jimmy was no match for him. The little man drew his right hand back, and Vincent only laughed at him, skirting the chair that separated them and ran out the door.

"Where's Vincent?" His mother was making the final arrangement of her Sunday veil.

"How should I know? He's your kid."

"Did something happen?"

"No."

They walked to church that morning.

What happened that Sunday morning was the talk of the boat on Monday.

"Jeez, just like Chappaquiddick."

Not exactly.

He revved the engine of the yellow car and ran it full force against the gate. At the last second, like James Dean in *Rebel without a Cause,* he rolled out of the driver's side, rolling until he came to a stop in a pile of ropes used to secure the boat to its berth. The car's ass stuck up in the air, then slid rapidly down into the green-gray, like the *Titanic.*

The few people below decks that Sunday were sitting in their cars, snoozing off a hangover from the City or reading the papers. No one noticed him in his pile of ropes. Eyes rose from papers, woke from dozes at the sound of the gate breaking, not giving, and watched Jimmy's "Yellow Peril" sink to its watery grave.

Vincent found himself at the Seaman's Mission, was given Sunday dinner, pulled on a bottle of wine offered by one of the guests, slept in a green-blanketed cot. Slept through the night and into the next morning, when he strolled to the recruiting office near the Battery.

A Hanged Man

This story is based on two historical details. The first is the suicide of a man who hanged himself from his whipping post in a building used for the punishment of slaves. Such whipping houses—removed from the plantations—were not uncommon in the years immediately preceding the Civil War, when abolitionists, in groups, came south to investigate reports of the mistreatment of slaves.

The second detail is the life of a man named Peg-Leg Joe, a one-legged sailor (we do not know if Joe was black or white or Indian—or a combination thereof), who led slaves to freedom from as far away as Mobile, Alabama. The following verse from an American folk song is one of the only reports we have of Peg-Leg Joe: "De riva's bank am a very good road / De dead trees show de way / Lef' foot, peg foot goin' on / Foller de drinkin' gourd."

THERE IS A CLEARING in the woods. A heavy rain has fallen the night before. Water stands around the foundation of a building in the clearing, seeping into brick. The slate roof is washed clean, shingles glint in the early summer sun.

A brick walkway in the form of a cross leads to the front door of the building. It is lined on every side with roses, begun with caution and formality, now loosed, each challenging the fitness of the other; thorns from one cane cut into the cane of another, drawing blood. Musk, Damask, Isfahan, Old Blush, captured on trails blazed by Crusaders, wild scents flashing in the clearing, fetid, fleshy, sweet. An archway of Persian lilac cascades around the entrance to the building.

To the side by itself is the sport of the Apothecary, Rosa Mundi, her striped red over pink ground; red from her parent, the rose of Lancaster, about which every schoolchild in those days knew.

The building began life as a station, set in the middle of nowhere, beyond the trees and fields pertinent to the town. *Began life* is not quite right, since the place never actually came to life. Set at the end of a failed spur line where day-trippers had been meant to disembark, admire the roses, the design of the place. Visions of country excursions with parasoled ladies in tasseled carriages held together by chains fell flat. Baskets of sweetmeats and biscuits and chicken legs went unpacked. Jugs of syllabub unpoured. The place seemed too far, not far enough, from home. These people not suited to day trips. The spur line in the end was impractical, not suited to any real cargo.

Now a slender minaret—exotic doodad embellishing the delicate structure—poked up, brushing against the budding branch of an oak. On one balcony a pair of mockingbirds fought and sang, with more repertoire than a muezzin ever had.

The whole establishment became a sort of shame. A waste. Good money poured out. Almost a complete disgrace until someone suggested another use and saved the town's face—in more ways than one.

The building was well-suited to its new found purpose—its setting in a clearing in the woods beyond the town was exactly what was needed, and the architect, dead and gone, was praised as a man of foresight.

Albeit one with a taste for what one town father called "Byzantine," referring not only to the minaret, the roses known to Saladin, but to the plaster replica of Powers's *Greek Slave,* set on a pedestal in the waiting room, all the rage at the Crystal Palace, the architect had patiently explained.

Noise could not travel to town from this place. Visitors suspect nothing. Sensibilities spared.

No one would hear a thing. Not even the Powhatan with his ear to the iron rail.

Anyway, the rail had been torn up, interrupted. The Powhatan long gone.

The only one to hear would be the ones waiting their turn. That was not a bad thing.

. . .

He was facing west. Rivers. Smokies. Expanse. Prairie. Monuments.

Behind him was the ocean. Traders. Clippers. One point of a triangle. Cotton. Tobacco.

These were at his back.

He was hanging motionless. Drab. Drab in his work-clothes. Gray. Brown spots where blood had dried. Hands hung at his sides. Eyes stared. He was rigid. Stiff. Dead weight. Tongue swollen and thick in his mouth.

Beneath him sawdust covered the floor. Stained and wet, it had not been changed in some time. At his side, within arm's reach, were that not absurd, was a rack that held his tools. Cat-o'-nine. Rope. Bull. Each suspended by a hand-carved handle, smoothed by sweat and use.

He might hang there for days. Not be found until someone had need of him, his craft. He had no people of his own.

Sunlight passing through the minaret illumined him. Mockingbirds fought above him, then burst into song. Would they swoop down and peck out his eyes?

Early summer. Buds heavy.

The time of the year when Yankees thawed and headed south to investigate. Poking and probing into the "wrongs," the inquisitive little bands were well received. (To be impolite would be impolitic.)

Returning home to their mills and factories and righteous societies, their girl-workers twisting filaments on looms, living, if you could call it that, jammed in bleak whitewashed rooms, fighting damp and cold—and dust. Clinging to eyebrows, lids, lips, skin whitened, chest heavy—the cotton dust was everywhere, was in the air when Whittier came to speak. Eyes watered.

But they can at least read, a visitor might say. Our nigras, the host might reason, have at least the sun.

Now just where did those Yankees reckon the cotton on those looms came from?

India? Egypt?

Blest be the tie that binds, the thread of connection.

Right now, at this very moment, as this hanging man waited on discovery, soul God knows where, if, evensong was being sung in the stone church, for the benefit of women in black and men in black, unused to such elaborate service, severe and shunning any excess.

"To our distinguished visitors," the pastor spoke, "brothers and sisters, welcome."

He paused. "Let us pray."

Then:

My soul be on thy guard,
Ten thousand foes arise;
The hosts of sin are pressing hard
To draw thee from the skies.
O watch and fight and pray;
The battle ne'er give o'er;
Renew it boldly every day,
And help divine implore.

Each recognized the song as theirs. Weighed down by righteousness, they sang their hearts out.

But one woman, black taffeta under a stained-glass window, who wished for something gentler.

After the service there was a somber and sedate dinner, with Bible readings, pan-roasted oysters, watermelon pickle, meat cut high off the hog. A pale old man standing in the shadow of the breakfront, silver salver at the ready. Darkness masking the line running from his eyelid to his jawbone. A lady tinkled Mozart on a spinet.

Over port and cigars the visiting men—the ladies had taken their leave, even now were being helped into their night-things, awkwardly, by women who did not speak, did not respond to them—the men were left the delicate questions, the thing they had come all this way to probe.

Upstairs a woman cries out, seized with gripes, wondering if the stories about poisoning are true. Ashamed for wondering. We are their friends, she says to herself, not knowing these dark silent women at all. Don't they realize that? The trichina worms its way into her muscle. She muffles her cry. She lies back in the featherbed, praying for the pain to pass, not wanting to wander around this house, huge and dark, in search of help.

Downstairs the conversation, inquisition, continues.

We have heard . . .

Sir, I beg you . . .

Of brutality . . . branding.

Consider your sources . . .

Iron necklaces . . .
Sir, would you willfully . . .
An excess of punishment . . .
Damage . . .
There are reports . . .
Something on which your livelihood depends?
No.
Well, sir.
We have heard of the lightening of the Africans . . .
Much exaggerated . . .
Their skin . . .
You and your companions . . .
The pale old man, right eye droopy as he tires, as the line to his jawbone tugs at him, pours port.
Are most welcome to look into any nook and cranny on this farm.
Or mine. Or mine. Or mine.
The chorus chimes in.

The company adjourns. The old man replaces the decanter in the breakfront. Thinks again and pours himself a glass. Drinks. Then marks the level on the crystal for the mistress to note where the gentlemen left it. He regards the ruby liquid, himself in it, the line that pains him, then snuffs the candlelight.

Near dawn the figure stiffer than before. A rat sniffs at the leg of the upended stool, moving on to nibble at the dangling thongs. The wind through the minaret imitates human sounds.

The sideboard creaks from the weight of meat. All is laid out in silver. Silver is set on white linen that covers the fine veneer of mahogany. The same pale old man stands against the wall.

The stench of dead humanity is high. The rat has made her way across the floor to where the salt is kept. She licks at the crystals.

All hell breaks loose at breakfast. Well, at least temporarily. Temporarily, good manners are suspended. Tempers, held tight last night, loosed. All because a visitor raises the question of Mrs. Stowe and her Uncle Tom.

The host explodes. Melodrama! Sheer melodrama! Written by a homely woman to buy a black silk dress.

There is silence at the table.

Upstairs a woman vomits into a silk pillowslip.

A young woman is standing outside the door of the station, a slip of paper in her hand. She is too frightened to care about the roses. She has not been here before but knows too well the stories. She wears an apron on which she has appliquéd figures, as if they will protect her. Jonah in the belly of the beast. Keep her company. The women at the foot of the cross. Remind her that this life is not all. Shàngó aloft, riding a chariot. Swing low.

She knocks. Loud. Then louder.

Please, marster, don't prolong my agony.

She does not dare turn the knob.

She cannot look through the windows. They are painted black.

She slides the slip of paper underneath the door.

Cap'n: fifty lashes and charge to account.

She sits on a stump to wait.

She sat there for a long time and the door did not open; no one else appeared. In her entire life she had never had this much time when she had been completely alone, not called on. But anticipating punishment robbed her of the use of solitude; she was only frightened.

The fright built in her over the hours, the tension in her pitching so high that her ears began to ring, and she felt she would explode unless she could move. So she got up and began to walk around, more to relieve her terror than for any other reason.

At first she explored the grounds, trying to ease her mind with the smell and color of roses. Trying to trace the red stripes of the flesh of one she was only reminded of the stripes awaiting her, which would make ditches across her back.

The only interruption in the stillness was birdsong, and she tried to follow the changes of the two mockingbirds atop the building's tower. Listening, she walked back and forth on the path, toes tracing the moss between the brick. Soon this was as bad as sitting on a stump—she turned to walk away.

Running did not enter her mind; she began to walk away.

When she had walked as long as she had spent by that blasted, haunted building, she had the nerve to look behind her, and ahead of her, to her left and to her right. Behind and ahead were woods; to her right, woods. To her left she sensed running water and turned to walk toward it.

It was too sweet. Soaking her feet in this rushing, cold water. Concealed by woods, not a soul to hear her. No break in the stillness here but the breaking of water on rock. She grabbed a bunch of cress from the riverbank and let her mouth enjoy its heat. A cold, wide river was at her side, running—daring her: escape! Bless me, Oshun, she prayed to the *orisha* of sweet water. With that prayer she cast her lot.

She got up, wiped her mouth with the corner of her apron, and walked on. She looked down at the muddy bank and recognized the trace of a track: human foot beside the circle of a peg leg. The mark of the journeyman. Spying this she walked forward. There was another track, then another, and after a hundred such tracks she was able to breathe deep, and take heart in this other human presence.

A Woman Who Plays Trumpet Is Deported

This story is dedicated to the memory of Valaida Snow, trumpet player, who was liberated—or escaped—from a concentration camp. She weighed sixty-five pounds. She died in 1956 of a cerebral hemorrhage. This was inspired by her story, but it is an imagining.

SHE CAME TO ME in a dream and said, "Girl, you have no idea how tough it was. I remember once Billie Holiday was lying in a field of clover. Just resting. And a breeze came and pollen from the clover blew all over her and the police came out of nowhere and arrested her for possession.

"And the stuff was *red* . . . it wasn't even white."

A woman. A black woman. A black woman musician. A black woman musician who plays trumpet. A bitch who blows. A lady trumpet player. A woman with chops.

It is the thirties. She has been fairly successful. For a woman, black, with an instrument not made of her. Not made of flesh but of metal.

Her father told her he could not afford two instruments for his two children and so she would have to learn her brother's horn.

This woman tucks her horn under her arm and packs a satchel and sets her course. Paris first.

This woman flees to Europe. No, *flee* is not the word. Escape? Not quite right.

She wants to be let alone. She wants them to stop asking for vocals in the middle of a riff. She wants them to stop calling her *novelty, wonder,* chasing after her orchid-colored Mercedes looking for a lift. When her husband gets up to go, she tosses him the keys, tells him to have it washed every now and then, the brass eyeballs polished every now and then—reminds him it's unpaid for and wasn't her idea anyway.

She wants a place to practice her horn, to blow. To blow rings around herself. So she blows the USA and heads out. On a ship.

And this is not one of those I'm-travelin'-light-because-my-man-has-gone situations—no, that mess ended a long time before. He belongs in an orchid-colored Mercedes—although he'll probably paint the damn thing gray. It doesn't do for a man to flaunt, he would say, all the while choosing her dresses and fox furs and cocktail rings.

He belongs back there; she doesn't.

The ship is French. Families abound. The breeze from the ocean rosying childish cheeks, as uniformed women stand by, holding shuttlecocks, storybooks, bottles. Women wrapped in tricolor robes sip bouillon. Men slap cues on the shuffleboard court, disks skimming the polished deck. Where—and this is a claim to fame—Josephine Baker once walked her ocelot or leopard or cheetah.

A state of well-being describes these people, everyone is groomed, clean, fed. She is not interested in them, but glad of the calm they convey. She is not interested in looking into their staterooms, or their lives, to hear the sharp word, the slap of a hand across a girl's mouth, the moans of intimacy.

The ship is French. The steward assigned to her, Senegalese.

They seek each other out by night, after the families have retired. They meet in the covered lifeboats. They communicate through her horn and by his silver drum.

He noticed the horn when he came the very first night at sea to turn down her bed. Pointed at it, her. The next morning introduced her to his drum.

The horn is brass. The drum, silver. Metal beaten into memory, history. She traces her hand along the ridges of silver—horse, spear, warrior. Her finger catches the edge of a breast, lingers. The skin drumhead as tight as anything.

In the covered lifeboats by night they converse, dispersing the silence of the deck, charging the air, upsetting the complacency, the well-being that hovers, to return the next day.

Think of this as a reverse middle passage.

Who is to say he is not her people?

Landfall.

She plays in a club in the Quartier Latin. This is not as simple as it sounds. She got to the club through a man who used to wash dishes beside Langston Hughes at Le Grand Duc who knew a woman back then who did well who is close to Bricktop who knows the owner of the club. The trumpet player met the man who used to wash dishes who now waits tables at another club. They talked and he said, "I know this woman who may be able to help you." Maybe it was simple, lucky. Anyway, the trumpet player negotiated the chain of acquaintance with grace, got the gig.

The air of the club is blue with smoke. Noise. Voices. Glasses do clink. Matches and lighters flare. The pure green of absinthe grows cloudy as water is added from a yellow ceramic pitcher.

So be it.

She lives in a hotel around the corner from the club, on the rue de l'Université. There's not much to the room: table, chair, bed, wardrobe, sink. She doesn't spend much time there. She has movement. She walks the length and breadth of the city. Her pumps crunch against the gravel paths in the parks. Her heels click along the edge of the river. All the time her mind is on her music. She is let alone.

She takes her meals at a restaurant called Polidor. Her food is set on a white paper–covered table. The lights are bright. She sits at the side of a glass-fronted room, makes friends with a waitress, and practices her French. *Friends* is too strong; they talk. Her horn is swaddled in purple velvet and rests on a chair next to her, next to the wall. Safe.

Of course, people stare occasionally, those to whom she is unfamiliar. Once in a while someone puts a hand to a mouth to whisper to a companion. Okay. No one said these people were perfect. She is tired—too tired—of seeing the gape-mouthed darky advertising *Le Joyeux Nègre.* Okay? Looming over a square by the Panthéon in all his happy-go-luckiness.

While nearby a Martiniquan hawked *L'Étudiant Noir.*

Joyeux Nègritude.

A child points to the top of his crème brûlée and then at her, smiles. Okay.

But no one calls her nigger. Or asks her to leave. Or asks her to sit away from the window at a darker table in the back by the kitchen, hustling her so each course tumbles into another. Crudités into timbale into caramel.

This place suits her fine.

The piano player longs for a baby part-*Africaine.* She says no. Okay.

They pay her to play. She stays in their hotel. Eats their food in a clean, well-lighted place. Pisses in their toilet.

No strange fruit hanging in the Tuileries.

She lives like this for a while, getting news from home from folks who pass through. Asking, "When are you coming back?"

"Man, no need for that."

Noting that America is still TOBA (tough on black asses), lady trumpet players still encouraged to vocalize, she remains. She rents a small apartment on Montparnasse, gets a cat, gives her a name, pays an Algerian woman to keep house.

All is well. For a while.

1940. The club in the Quartier Latin is shut tight. Doors boarded. The poster with her face and horn torn across. No word. No word at all. Just murmurs.

The owner has left the city on a freight. He is not riding the rails. Is not being chased by bad debts. He is standing next to his wife, her mother, their children, next to other women, their husbands, men, their wives, children, mothers-in law, fathers, fathers-in-law, mothers, friends.

The club is shut. This is what she knows. But rumors and murmurs abound.

The piano player drops by the hotel, leaves a note. She leaves Paris. She heads north.

She gets a gig in Copenhagen, standing in for a sister moving out—simple, lucky—again. Safe. Everyone wore the yellow star there—for a time.

1942. She is walking down a street in Copenhagen. The army of occupation picks her up. Not the whole army—just a couple of kids with machine guns.

So this is how it's done.

She found herself in a line of women. And girls. And little children.

The women spoke in languages she did not understand. Spoke them quietly. From the tone she knew they were encouraging their children. She knows—she who has studied the nuance of sound.

Her horn tucked tight under her armpit. Her only baggage.

The women and girls and little children in front of her and behind her wore layers of clothing. It was a warm day. In places seams clanked. They carried what they could on their persons.

Not all spoke. Some were absolutely silent. Eyes moved into this strange place.

Do you know the work of Beethoven?

She has reached the head of the line and is being addressed by a young man in English. She cannot concentrate. She sweats through the velvet wrapped around her horn. All around her women and girls and little children—from which she is apart, yet of—are being taken in three different directions. And this extraordinary question.

A portrait on a schoolteacher's wall. Of a wiry-haired, beetle-browed man. And he was a colored genius, the teacher told them, and the children shifted in their seats.

Telemann? He wrote some fine pieces for the horn.

The boy has detected the shape of the thing under her arm.

She stares and does not respond. How can she?

The voices of women and girls and little children pierce the summer air as if the sound were being wrenched from their bodies. The sun is bright. Beads of sweat gather at the neck of the young man's tunic.

It should not be hot. It should be drear. Drizzle. Chill. But she knows better. The sun stays bright.

In the distance is a mountain of glass. The light grazes the surface and prisms split into color.

Midden. A word comes to her. The heaps of shells, bones, and teeth. Refuse of the Indians. The mound builders. That place by the river just outside of town—filled with mystery and childhood imaginings.

A midden builds on the boy's table, as women and girls and little children deposit their valuables.

In the distance another midden builds.

Fool of a girl, she told herself. To have thought she had seen it all. Left it—the worst piece of it—behind her. The body burning—ignited by the tar. The laughter and the fire. And her inheriting the horn.

American Time, American Light

As the leaves thinned the days shortened and the winter light cast everything cold. As the cold advanced quiet became the village—all sound was muffled. But for the fingers of ice cracking like gunshots in the night when the tree branches could no longer bear the weight of frozen water.

A lake formed in a valley, soft hills ringing around it. In these hills the forest waited. Beyond the homes of summer people, boarded and shrouded in winter; beyond the hill towns named Florida and Peru (with a long *e*) and Baptist Corner; beyond the churches, some abandoned, doors flung wide, molded ceilings scrolled and curlicued, chipped and darkened here and there; beyond the shops laying bare the artifacts of spinners and weavers and printers and merchants, decaled and prettified; beyond those spindles and spools and moveable type and adding machines; beyond the spruced, converted factories sporting cool cellars and underdone meat; beyond the deserted academies where dissenters sent their sons, strains of the Faith burgeoning, the sons soon giving, heading West to new terrain and wild naive flocks, excitement fit to burst; beyond the remains of spas, once gay, water flowing like there was no tomorrow, ladies sunk in porcelain tubs, breasts covered by a square of Irish linen by an Irish maid, good for what ails you; beyond the long, plain tobacco barns, green leaves browning, hung by Micmacs down from Nova Scotia; beyond the long green porch of the Independent Order of Scalpers, Narragansett on tap; beyond the ancient lilacs, French and English, some woman's pride and joy way back then; beyond the mounds stark, shards, bones, beads, unearthed, encrusted, feathers molted, gracing a vitrine in a county seat museum, legend typed on a manual with a chipped *t*; beyond a diorama in the same museum, class project of an eighth grade, settlers, miniature iron pot swinging over a blazing cardboard hearth, hasty pudding, silhouette cut from red construction paper, peeking through a cellophane window; beyond the libraries, Webster and Britannica, *Poor Boys Who Became Famous* and *Girls Who Made Good,* Olive Higgins Prouty and the *Christian Science Monitor,* benefactor smiling from the wall; beyond LIVE DEER, PETRIFIED CREATURES, NIGHT-CRAWLERS; beyond the hiding places of slaves (still secret), the homestead of W. E. B. Du Bois, the dining room where Mumbet served the table, tin ceiling curling from artificial heat; beyond the meeting places of Abolitionists, the collisions of Douglass and Brown and Phillips and Truth—beyond all this human interruption, this stopping and starting—memory, relic—the forest waited patiently to return, as it had done before and before.

In spaces between birch and pine and maple, soft indentations marked a cellar hole. A forsythia strained near where a porch had been. Stone steps, mossed and cracked went nowhere. In the dark of the cellar hole, a wreck of a stove lay, its place of origin—FLORENCE—embossed on its oven door.

Potatoes—all eyes—seeded themselves in the soft black of the forest floor, and Vietnam veterans, alive in this dark, abandoned space, had found them. Underground springs lay frozen in wait, to explode into freshets. The movement of worms in the earth was suspended. Fish slept. Cress would grow thick and green once the water flowed.

You might live off the land, and water.

Middle-aged men, stubbled and yellowed, camped out, making do with potatoes, beer bought from the nearest Mini-Mart—where a cat name Mama-San prowled—and grass dried over the past summer.

A man named Frank nested in an overgrown dooryard.

Black Minorcas (once the rage—"prolific layers of an extremely large egg") long absent. Packed squawking into a wagon headed West, amid bedclothes, irons, seed corn. The farm had failed; the family abandoned it—in 1895. With their children, those surviving, the mother and father crossed to Nebraska. Two pieces of granite marked the remains of two boys lost to measles.

Almost a century gone and no one had come to claim the land.

Frank felt in this deserted place, hidden and dark, as the last survivor—of he knew not what. The man who wakes up after the bombs have gone off? The one standing after a duel in a missile silo? The man the earth swallows, then vomits up? War? History? Family? His own life?

Survival, he knew, was not what it was cracked up to be—you bet your life.

He had no company, no spirit guides, not much of anything. He was alone. And glad of it. And scared of it.

Elsewhere men gathered together, and not to ask the Lord's blessing. "Misery loves company," his mother might have said—in her way capturing the human condition—and he wondered where that sudden recollection of her words had come from; his mind was practically wiped clean of memory.

"Not quite a tabula rasa," the smartass VA doctor had said, "but almost."

At least Frank could remember to say, "Fuck you."

Frank kept to himself, even at the hospital.

On his way to his nest he had stumbled on a group, sitting around a fire, drinking beer in the freezing cold. He quickly pulled back, to the edge of their circle. They took little notice. They were drinking and talking and smoking. Blue and gray wisps wreathed each of them, converging into a nimbus, traces of fire, cigarettes, joints, their own warm breath hitting the frigid air.

One of them wore a doughboy's hat and offered Frank a Bud. "Here, man, take it." He did, and began to retreat.

"Hey, later!" someone yelled after him.

All quiet on the western Mass. front. Little flashes. The lost boys. Little flashes. Robin Hood's Merry Men. Little flashes, lights in his miserable old head.

Looking over his shoulder he saw their firelight at the pinpoint center of their circle; the red of the fire against their camouflage and olive drab, and the white of the landscape, and the gray sentinels of bare trees. Nimbus drawing them together, blessing them.

Now, in the dooryard, he looked around. Everywhere the forest masked humanity. A hundred yards beyond the dooryard did not exist. He had no idea how to find the circle again.

He wanted only to stay in this place now he had found it, settle, wrap the wreck around him. He had done nothing wrong.

He was a forty-one-year-old man. He had walked away from somewhere he did not belong. Where the air was black with smoke, and blue from other men's misery, and flickering from the infernal light of the television.

What made him leave?

It just got to be too much.

In the dead of night he opened the footlocker under his bed and slid into his fatigues under the thin blanket. They hung on him and he felt like a kid trying on his father's clothes. His body was wasted, from too much smoke and not enough food. His chest caved and he could trace the bones in his pelvis. He had to move deliberately because his thoughts swirled and did not follow. He had to will himself—to dress, get up, sneak past, out, away. Down in the lobby, walls decorated with murals of the Lafayette Escadrille, a dim light barely illumined the desk of a night watchman, away from his post. Across from the desk, under a painting of an aircraft spiraling to earth, was an exhibit set up by the local historical society: CONTAGIOUS DISEASES IN NEW ENGLAND. A child's contagious bed, iron rectangle with barred sides, receptacle of nightmare, was the centerpiece of the exhibit, and in the dim light from the desk it cast a huge shadow against the mural, bisecting the plane. "They get you coming and going," Frank whispered to himself, and began a soundless laugh.

A mannequin of a nurse, crisp and white and capped, stood to one side of the empty bed, pointing a plastic finger, fake mouth smiling into the emptiness. He started at the ghost, fought a desire to look up her skirt; he laughed again, knowing she would be as unreal, as ill defined as the inflatable woman who made the rounds upstairs.

He fell to his belly, moved past the angel of mercy, and out of the lobby. He reached his right hand up to the knob of the front door, slid out, away.

He made his way up I-91 on foot, in stealth. One foot in front of the other, one foot in front of the other. At a rest stop he poked through the top layer of a dumpster. Hungry now, cold, he finished off a stranger's Big Mac, which had been barely touched. "You deserve a break today," a TV chorus echoed. And he sang it into the cold night. He wished he had a flashlight and could search the dumpster—who knows what he might find? The wind hit at his ears, and he seized a newspaper from the top of the trash and made himself a hat. He walked on, looking like an overgrown boy playing soldier; all he needed was a wooden sword. Hayfoot, strawfoot, hayfoot, strawfoot, he repeated to himself, to the frozen landscape, as he made his way away.

Sitting there, in his nest, he suddenly remembered, he who was not supposed to remember, in a little flash, suddenly and clearly, with a clarity of glass, a book he had loved as a boy, when books were his solitary, constant comfort.

He could not conjure the title, did not expect to, but saw a picture—the cover—as if he held it in his hands. A boy in blue jeans and a white T-shirt. A bridge is in the background, massive against the boy's slender body; the boy has walked across the bridge from one part of the city to another. The glint of a steel key is at the boy's feet. The picture begins to move. The boy picks up the key and wanders over to the pier of the bridge, as thick and as gray as an elephant's foot. Set into the pier is a heavy fire door. The key fits and opens to a clean room. Small. Cot made with white sheets and a green wool blanket. One pillow. A table in the room, with a chair that slides under it. A stall shower and toilet off to one side. This might seem to be a cell but for the key. All a body needs. A room prepared for a caretaker or watchman, but it is not in use. Someone has forgotten about it.

The boy in the book, in flight from home, has found a home. He moves in, gets a job in a supermarket, buys a hotplate, gets a library card.

He is on his own.

He must have been sixteen when he read that book, maybe younger. Who is he to say? Finding it on one of his weekly treks to the branch library. He was working his way through the books and away from his parents' wars.

Lying on his bed, or on the grass under the fire escape, his forefinger holding the place, looking, again studying the book itself. Then turning back to the page, the words and the sentences—the life of it. Trying to shut out the world while the world is exercising its influence—birdsong, a parent's voice, traffic noise, the smell of cooking, shouts at a pickup game.

He was the boy who read. And it came to him now, in his nest, that the reading muscle had been severed and replaced by a plastic shunt.

He savored the picture of the boy, the room. Nothing else came. Surely it had been only a book? Only? Read a book and you will never be lonely. Who said that?

He sat back on the hard earth and the cold began to seep into him. He worked his way into the failed farmhouse. Beams blocked him, and he was afraid to budge them and have the place cave in on him. Afraid to make a noise—why? There was no one to hear. He worked his way under the beams, on his belly, across someone else's kitchen floor, his face flat against flagstone—ice, ice cold.

He will find what the family has left behind.

A blue-backed speller is visible across the floor. Snow, ice dapple the surface. Snow and ice are over everything. Snow and ice cover the brown remains of a newspaper under a crashed beam. The black of the type emerges through the white and against the brown. He traces the type with the forefinger of his right hand. Nothing makes sense.

United Opinion Erisypelas Bright's Disease Heart Failure THE ONLY SUBSTITUTE FOR MOTHER'S MILK Croup Eczema Diphtheria LIFE SENTENCE FOR STEALING BACON Ovarian Neuralgia Gout Scrofula LUCY CHILDS HAD A SHOCK LAST WEEK SO THAT SHE IS UNABLE TO SPEAK. IT IS WITH GREAT REGRET THAT WE CHRONICLE THE SAD NEWS Chautauqua Circle THE TRAINS ARE AGAIN DRAPED IN MOURNING ON ACCOUNT OF THE ACCIDENT ON THE SOUTH-BOUND MAIL WHEN AN ENGINEER AND A FIREMAN WERE KILLED Dr. LeSure's Magic Compound Drs. Starkey and Palen's Compound Oxygen Dr. Keneally's Favorite Remedy Electric Bitters Hood's Sarsaparilla Blood Purifier Pain Balm OSCAR WILDE ON TRIAL Ripan Tabules THE LISTERS ARE BUSY TRYING TO SURPRISE PEOPLE BY APPEARING UNEXPECTEDLY Green Mountain Sarsaparilla Recommended by the Clergy "I am a well man today and weigh 200 pounds" Lydia E. Pinkham "Young girls must know that self-preservation is the first law of nature" ROADS IMPASSABLE.

His eyes brush against the type. Nothing. He picks up the sheet and it flakes in his hands. Carefully he puts the bits in his breast pocket.

If he goes to sleep, he will not wake.

He sits back. Pulls the newspaper hat down so that the paper brushes the bridge of his nose. Words are folded into each other.

He closes his eyes.

Some children were gathered at a creek. Boys and girls. On the shore lay a magnificent fish, scales rainbow in the light. A small boy is watching as it writhes in the stones and the dirt. He bends over, squeezes its middle, and a mustard-yellow ooze comes out. The children laugh. A girl moves forward and plays her finger through the ooze. The waters are rushing. A boy bites into the fish on a dare. The fish moves its mouth open and shut, open and shut, gasping, a place in its side, from the boy's teeth, leaks. Shoes are caked with mud, gathered around the daring boy, the fish.

The thaw, the spring, is on.

The black ink of the type from the newspaper hat runs down his cheeks, streaking him like war paint.

The children find him.

Burning Bush

LAST SUMMER the forest shuddered as a Winnebago passed through, obscured by foolish fire.

The paper blazed a headline in Second Coming type—ELDER SISTER MISSING: POLICE FEAR FOUL PLAY—starker, darker than the one the day before.

The missing sister was a seventy-five-year-old odd quantity, so people thought. Not someone anyone really knew, certainly harmless enough. Who would want to hurt such a little old lady? A rounded little woman with a covered head and soft brown coat who walked up and down the main street of the village, eager to speak with almost anyone, whom a few remembered as a strapping girl.

As she walked, casting a shadow, in line with the season, in line with the time of day, she remembered the events of her life and what she had come to.

One stood out: being taken to a sideshow at the tri-county fair when her father was alive. Where for a dime—when a dime meant something—you could peer at the freaks.

Why did people dress up their little children and march them hand-held tight into the dark world of those deformities and dishonesties, for some of them were not to be believed, the sun hidden by the canvas of the circus tent, sawdust wet and sticking to black shoes like at a butcher's shop. Surely there was a space for those people—the genuine ones, the fakes were another matter—out West (Wyoming? Utah? Badlands? Black Hills?), where Sister told them a place had been found by a Dominican with sympathies for the misshapen.

Ahead of them in the darkness a tall man with a stovepipe hat named Doc welcomed the visitors—step right up, step right up. Was he the physician in charge? Behind him, lined side by side on a raised platform, were the gaudy freaks. Tattooed Lady. Smallest Mother in the World. Black Lobster Man. White Penguin Boy. Alligator Woman. Just there. See me. Two-Faced Man. Woman with a leg growing from her armpit, her wedding ring brightly displayed, two-legged children at her side. Look at me. Armless, legless poet, a trunk of a girl penning verse with a contraption fixed to her tongue. Regard me.

And the main attraction, the reason so many dimes shone in the collection plate held by Doc's spangled assistant, sat above this chorus on a throne of bamboo and feathers and soft red cloth. The Girl from Martinique, born in slavery, so the legend read, for these people did not speak, did not announce themselves. And no one seemed to mind, or even notice, that slavery had ended in Martinique almost a hundred years before. But few if any in this landscape of skunk cabbage and fiddleheads and birches shaped like corkscrews and rock-bearing fields had even heard of such a place. Did they eat one another?

Never mind. The Girl from Martinique was a sight all right and well worth the price of admission. A piece of cloth wrapped her breasts and wound itself behind her, crossing her body beneath her navel. She was uncovered for the most part, for she was *parti-colored,* so read the legend, as if you had to be told, had to have it pointed out to you, and this was her uniqueness. Patches of black bumped against ivory. *This checkerboard of a woman owes her skin to certain practices of her native land brought with her ancestors from the Dark Continent. She comes to you direct from Paris . . . appearances before the crowned heads . . . main attraction at the Hippodrome . . . the subject of study by the greatest scientific minds of the century . . . etc.*

The legend was barefaced, bold. And no one had trouble believing she was genuine. Her eyes were flat, cloudy.

Well, here I am again. The poor man's Josephine Baker. Without the bananas and with an added panache. Or the poor man's Hottentot Venus—without the butt. I concentrate on keeping my eyes out of focus. If I do, the people below me become indistinct. Just little patches of color, bright, dull. Sunday-best dims. As their shapes fade and soften, their noises seem to dim also: "Oh!" "Paris!" "My God!" "Wait your turn!" "Indecent!" "What a shame!" Better not mind what people say, or think.

You know, it's not easy being a freak; not even a pretend one—don't tell me you believed it for a minute. The Girl from Martinique was my idea. Yes indeed. In this business exotic is good, means a livelihood. I'm really the girl from Darktown. Left. One day just left. Took off to seek my fortune. Better to get fifty cents a day, room and board, for sitting here, white-washed and mysterious, than for lying on my back, or kneeling for that matter.

I live in a trailer with the Lobster Man. Nothing personal. We're the two coloreds in the show. Even freaks have their standards. But he's a nice man. No fake there. Born that way. Midwife had to twist and turn to get him out. Thought he would never walk, but his mama prayed and rubbed and rubbed and prayed and slowly, slowly he began to move sideways. Can a nigger manage? I mean.

I mean he's down on all fours but he gets around. Well, you probably couldn't call it walking but he's under his own steam, and that's good for something. He sleeps in a wooden box, he can fold himself up so small. Handy when you're sharing a trailer. I'm a big girl myself. Need all the room I can get. Never was enough room at home.

Last time I saw my mama was when I had to leave the show. Usual female reason—well, the Lobster Man said it didn't matter whose it was, we could raise it as ours. Thanks but no thanks—you know what I mean? So it was born back home and I left it—her—with my mama, and that was the last time I was there. The place was still too small. My mama was glad of the new company, even though the baby sported evidence of *certain practices of her native land.* Dig? Mama's always been a race woman. I told her not to worry. Children darken as they grow. Lifting as they climb—Now girl, she interrupted me, don't you go on being disrespectful. Oh, Mama, just take the little wood's colt and leave me in peace. You always wanted to start over with me. Here's your chance.

Yes, the Girl from Martinique was my idea but I didn't make her up. I read in a book that there was this little child back in slavery time—came out as a patchwork. So I got a couple of bottles of white shoe polish and—as La Bakaire would say—voilà! The child's name was Magdelaine. They put her on show as a baby. Called her *La Fille du Martinique.* I translated for the hometown crowd. Poor little thing. What a life!

. . .

There but for the grace of God, Agnes's father said, with no apparent logic.

She thought as she walked the village main street so many years from then, my God, I am more misshapen than they, stranger than she. Why think about that now? Other fairs had passed, other freaks. Why remember the Girl from Martinique?

Because she gave me nightmares?

Stove polish had probably achieved her effect, her father had reassured her, wondering why anyone white would ever want to be black, even partly so, even to make a living.

Isn't she real, Papa?

Only as real as any entertainment, Agnes.

Her father's hands.

Something stirred as she saw them, folded in front of him, as he calmly regarded the freaks. Gloved, at rest.

Agnes switched.

No. No, she must have started black. Must have. But wasn't it against the law for a colored person to be white, even partly so? Even a patchwork?

Feeling sick at beholding her, Agnes was eager to stare. In the dark, under the tent, one hand moved, slid itself under her armpit and rested on her breast.

She had been given an unfortunate name. Her mother chose it, hoping her little lamb of God would feel the call, would be given the call by virtue of her name. But she had not. Had not felt the heat of vocation. Had not, but ought, she thought, to have been drawn to Him. She could have been saved, safe, with the Sisters of Mercy in Providence, rather than in the dangerous place her life had become.

But she did not feel the call, was at fault, and could not pretend—besides, she was damaged goods.

And then her father died, and her mother went legally blind from grief—the priest declared—and as the eldest daughter all choice was removed from her.

She should probably have pretended—to have spoken with the Blessed Virgin cloud-borne over the lake, ringed with stars, draped in her blue gown, roses blooming through the ice—bloodred and fragrant. Beseeching, commanding, begging Agnes to follow her. Forgiving. Or at least she could have conjured St. Teresa, or Kateri Tekakwitha, the Lily of the Mohawks, whose sacred lake this had once been. But Agnes was afraid of Our Father's wrath should she pretend, and she had not the heart for devotion.

And no one would believe her—false or true.

The sisterhood had called her first cousin Cecelia, now Sister Augustine, splashing around in holy water, teaching math to city children. Fixing her coif looking into a spoon.

Agnes did as she was told. She stayed within the family's bosom; in fact became the bosom, upon which they rested their heads, wept, which her brother John clasped to him.

At the inquest—in her absence—the villagers said she had seemed happy. Always cheerful, content, no sign of anything. Not an enemy in the world. She could be neither victim nor—what was the word used on TV?—*perpetrator.* Neither one. They thought further, paused. Just a little too eager for conversation. Yes. Wanted to know too much about other people's families, lives; asking, pressing them for details, past, business, children. She was hungry, it seemed. As if she had no family of her own. Wasn't there a son? someone asked. Didn't he die at birth? another wondered. No. No, that must have been someone else.

By and large she seemed happy—they concluded.

A woman held inside her a question Agnes had asked on the corner by the common just a few months before—did your father ever teach you how to love a man?

None of the village had seen the Dalys—save Agnes—since the death of the father, and until the night of BOOM BOOM BOOM BOOM, as a bonfire raged by the church celebrating Independence, thinking at first the noise was fireworks, part of the festivities—some thought the rest of the Dalys had passed on and that Agnes had had them quietly buried on the farm.

Until the next morning, quite by chance, when they were laid bare for all to see, and pity, the Dalys kept to themselves—but for Agnes. The house in which she lived with her brother, son, sister, mother was caught at the time of the father's death. A time of great need, loss, Depression. In the dark front room, entered by an unhinged door, screen torn and dusty, one wall was covered, decorated with pictures. Covers of *Life*—their window to the world. Black-and-white images—Hoover Dam, Shirley Temple, WPA workers, Brenda Frazier—against a bright red logo. As the black-and-white images had become darker and fainter from the smoke of the wood fire, the red logo seemed to gain in brightness, so that if anyone entered the house, he or she was struck by LIFE LIFE LIFE LIFE emblazoned on the wall in front of them. But no one but the family was ever admitted, and that was part of the problem. Intercourse with outsiders took place through the scrim of the door, as if in a convent of Poor Clares.

Rita Hayworth's smoked-over face, kneeling in her lace negligee, head turned, gave credence to the church's explanation of the Black Madonna, held dear by the French-Canadians over the river.

The things women endured. God Almighty! Agnes had in her mind the story of a grandmother, told by an aunt some years before—at some family reunion, wedding or funeral or baptism, events her branch attended before their father's death, before they cut themselves off. The aunt threw back a tumbler of whiskey and proceeded to recite, as God is my witness that is what happened.

Her father, Agnes's grandfather, had stuffed a potato into his wife, her mother, Agnes's grandmother. This became family lore and a family joke because of the famine and all that entailed. Hardship.

Working on the railroad Agnes's grandfather was away a good deal of the time and needed to be clear in his mind. The job was dangerous, the foreman a bigot, the grandfather did not need the added concern. He'd seen men lose limbs.

So he took a spud—a small new potato, mind you—and stuffed it inside his wife. A potato from her own plot. The tale was told over whiskey and laughter, and that was that.

Agnes did not know—or know to ask—what this did to her grandmother. Did she wrench the potato out, after seeing him safely off? Did she sleep with him ever after only under protest? Was she quietly relieved behind her widow's weeds when he fell from a trestle in the West and was returned to her in a square Railway Express box?

At school the other girls took out after Agnes and chastised her. It was as if she gave off a scent. They could not explain why she was chosen.

The nun in charge would occasionally swoop down on the mob, scattering those in her path with threats and slaps, habit trapping some of the girls, but for the most part Sister let the girls blow off steam, their violence contained by the dirt floor and iron fence of a schoolyard.

Agnes had to stick up for herself, Sister reckoned. It was necessary, to get by in this life—unless, of course, the girl was to embrace martyrdom.

"Poor Agnes Violet Daly," Sister told the Mother of her order, "she is violated, is in agony daily." Black habit trembling at this cleverness.

"Puberty often lends itself to frenzy," the Mother put aside her *Boston Globe* to declare. "There's always one."

"Yes."

"Have you spoken to Agnes yourself?"

"Mother?"

"I thought not."

"Well, I did speak to her last week; rather, she spoke to me."

"About?"

"She asked me if nuns were allowed into sideshows—"

"As exhibits?"

Sister smiled. "I told her yes, and she wanted to know if I had seen the sideshow at the tri-county fair this past summer."

"And?"

"I said no, and she walked away."

"Curious child."

The distance from the family farm to the parochial school was a long walk. A long walk but the only time Agnes had to herself, except those hours when she was asleep, and those were disturbed more and more, claimed by another.

On these walks, Agnes tried to come up with some strategy to counter the other girls, some clever words to defeat them, at least draw their attention away from her. But she found herself at a loss for words even when alone, and inevitably her search for words ended instead with images, full-color fantasies of a magnificent and startling fury. Walking the dirt road, kicking pebbles, Agnes's visions kept her company.

Some she gleaned from the *Tales of the Wild West* her grandfather left the family, others came from the *Lives of the Saints,* her grandmother's bequest. Agnes combed details from each anthology. These were the only real books in the house, and they sparked Agnes's imagination; they held *true* stories.

Agnes buried girls to their necks in anthills, smearing their faces with honey, sitting out of harm's way as the huge red ants took apart the mouth and eyes of a classmate. Girls screamed and wept their agony, turning to Agnes. She did not heed their pleas; in life, they did not hers.

Agnes led girls into an ambush of Redskins, flaming arrows arcing a blue sky, piercing the white sea-island-cotton breasts of the girls. Agnes stood back, to the side of the vision, as if invisible to the Redmen, watching and watching and doing nothing to save the sweet girlish bodies—unlike hers—against this pagan desecration. Accepting a flaming arrow from a fierce Apache, Agnes draws back the bow, lets loose, and watches as the fiery tip ignites the black of Sister's habit and she goes down in flames.

Girls spin on flaming wheels. Girls are impaled on iron spikes. Girls have their nipples torn off with red-hot pincers. Girls line the Via Appia, nailed to crosses. And blessing this panorama, judging the punishment meet, was the Girl from Martinique, on her jungle throne, queen of Heaven, intruder into Agnes's hagiography. Somehow she seemed right, and Agnes let her be.

And in this company Agnes walks to school, and home again.

Her father told her King Solomon was the wisest and holiest of men and by right could have any virgin in his domain. Any one.

Agnes closed her eyes but the hagiography would not be summoned. Her father crashed against her imagination, and she became part of his.

Her brother inherited her.

Her mother and sister said nothing.

Her brother was the father of her son.

Her mother told her to quit her job at the watch factory.

Her brother told her to keep the boy at home or else someone would find out.

She did.

She handed in her apron, brush, and small container of radium.

BOOM BOOM BOOM BOOM. Jesus, Mary, and Joseph, I should have done this years ago.

This seventy-five-year-old odd quantity is flying through the dirt of the country in a Winnebago, on the run, heading for parts unknown. It is hot. She is alone.

The lake smokes behind her. The will-o'-the-wisp rising.

It was quite premeditated.

The week before, in the village, Agnes bought her ammunition. Barreling on in her jittery way to the man at the Mini-Mart about crows and scarecrows.

"I need to thin out the blackbirds. They're flying wild through the corn. Getting ready to devour it and it's nowhere near ready. The scarecrow's been stripped again. During the Depression, hoboes would do that—for the clothes. Guess it's kids now . . . or maybe them vets. Hear about the one that was defrosted in the woods?" Agnes's voice slid into a cackle of a laugh, covered almost immediately by, "Poor thing, poor thing. Must've been crazy.

"Happened last year, too—stealing from the scarecrow. Had put one of my grandfather's old railroad vests on him . . . and my papa's doughboy hat. Don't know why the vets would want those old things . . . must be kids. Poor old scarecrow will be kindling soon enough . . . sad to see him standing there all naked in the field.

"Guess I'll just have to shoot the crows. So if anyone hears a noise you remember that. . . . Then I'll string them on a clothesline and let the dead be a warning."

She wondered if the man had even listened, and if he had, had she made sense? She'd never be able to do it in the light. And who went after crows in the pitch dark of a summer's night? Black on black. No full moon. Never mind. The man's head was down under the front counter where he kept the ammunition.

"One box do it?"

"Oh, mmm. I guess so. I can always come back for more."

Funny. The hardest thing had been sliding the keys to the RV from her brother's pocket. Afraid he would sit upright and grab them from her—"Now, Agnes, this doesn't concern you."

But he was long gone.

His keys to the road, he had said. After a lifetime of working like a dog, and now that Mama is nearly dead, and summer people clamoring for the farm. Don't worry, we'll split it fair and square.

Well, not quite.

Inside the thing was nicely fitted out. Pots and pans and a TV set and linens and a CB radio and even a bathroom.

She was sad to leave the scrawny old scarecrow behind. All naked and miserable. Soon enough his limbs would freeze unless some kind soul cut him into kindling. Anything was better than being cold. Even burning.

After the blasts of the shotgun warmed her, Agnes prepared to leave the farm.

Before she started the Winnebago, before she slid into the seat and set off on her own, before she roared into the night, she lit the burning bush at the side of the porch. She wanted to light their way.

There was a soft whoosh as the gas ignited.

Screen Memory

THE SOUND OF A JUMP ROPE came around in her head, softly, steadily marking time. Steadily slapping ground packed hard by the feet of girls.

Franklin's in the White House. Jump / Slap. *Talking to the ladies.* Jump / Slap. *Eleanor's in the outhouse.* Jump / Slap. *Eating chocolate babies.* Jump / Slap.

Noises of a long drawn-out summer's evening years ago. But painted in such rich tones she could touch it.

A line of girls wait their turn. Gathered skirts, sleeveless blouses, shorts, bright, flowered—peach, pink, aquamarine. She spies a tomboy in a striped polo shirt and cuffed blue jeans.

A girl slides from the middle of the line. The woman recognizes her previous self. The girl is dressed in a pale blue starched pinafore, stiff and white in places, bleached and starched almost to death. She edges away from the other girls; the rope, their song, which jars her and makes her sad. And this is inside her head.

She senses there is more to come. She rests her spine against a wine-glass elm. No one seems to notice her absence.

The rope keeps up its slapping, the voices speed their chanting. As the chant speeds up, so does the rope. The tomboy rushes in, challenging the other to trip her, burn her legs where she has rolled her jeans. Excitement is at a pitch. Franklin! Ladies! Eleanor! Babies! The tomboy's feet pound the ground. They are out for her. A voice sings out, above the others, and a word, strange and harsh to the observer's ears, sounds over the pound of feet, over the slap of rope. *Bulldagger! Bulldagger! Bulldagger! Bulldagger!* The rope sings past the tomboy's ears. She feels its heat against her skin. She knows the word. Salt burns the corners of her eyes. The rope-turners dare, singing it closer and closer. Sting!

The girl in the pinafore hangs back. The girl in the pinafore who is bright-skinned, ladylike, whose veins are visible, as the ladies of the church have commented so many times, hangs back. The tomboy, who is darker, who could not pass the paper bag test, trips and stumbles out. Rubbing her leg where the rope has singed her. The word stops.

Where does she begin and the tomboy end?

Fireflies prepare to loft themselves. Mason jars with pricked lids are lined on the ground waiting to trap them. Boys swing their legs, scratched and bruised, from adventure or fury, from the first rung of a live oak tree. Oblivious to the girls, their singing—nemesis. The boys are swinging, talking, over the heads of the girls. Mostly of the War, their fathers, brothers, uncles, whoever represents them on air or land or sea.

The woman in the bed can barely make out their voices, though they speak inside her head.

Sudden lightning. A crack of thunder behind the hill. Wooden handles hit the dirt as the rope is dropped. Drops as big as an elephant's tears fall. The wind picks up the pace. Girls scatter to beat the band. Someone carefully coils the rope. Boys dare each other to stay in the tree.

The girl in the blue pinafore flies across the landscape. She flies into a window. To the feet of her grandmother.

Slow fade to black.

The woman in the bed wakes briefly, notes her pain, the dark outside.

Her head is splitting.

She and her grandmother have settled in a small town at the end of the line. At the edge of town where there are no sidewalks and houses are made from plain board, appearing ancient, beaten into smoothness, the two grow dahlias and peonies and azaleas. A rambling rose, pruned mercilessly by the grandmother, refuses to be restrained, climbing across the railings of the porch, masking the iron of the drainpipe, threatening to rampage across the roof and escape in a cloud of pink—she is wild. As wild as the girl's mother, whom the girl cannot remember, and the grandmother cannot forget.

The grandmother declares that the roses are "too showy" and

therefore she dislikes them. (As if dahlias and peonies and azaleas in their cultivated brightness are not.) But the stubborn vine is not for her to kill—nothing, no living thing is, and that is the first lesson—only to train.

While the rose may evoke her daughter, there is something else. She does not tell her granddaughter about the thing embedded in her thigh, souvenir of being chased into a bank of roses. Surely the thing must have worked its way out by now—or she would have gotten gangrene, lost her leg clear up to the hip, but she swears she can feel it. A small sharp thorn living inside her muscle. All because of a band of fools to whom she was nothing but a thing to chase.

The grandmother's prized possession sits against the wall in the front room, souvenir of a happier time, when her husband was alive and her daughter held promise. An upright piano, decorated in gilt, chosen by the king of Bohemia and the Knights of the Rosy Cross, so says it. The grandmother rubs the mahogany and ebony with lemon oil, cleans the ivory with rubbing alcohol, scrubbing hard, then takes a chamois to the entire instrument, slower now, soothing it after each fierce cleaning.

The ebony and the ivory and the mahogany come from Africa—the birthplace of civilization. That is another of the grandmother's lessons. From the forests of the Congo and the elephants of the Great Rift Valley, where fossils are there for the taking and you have but to pull a bone from the great stack to find the first woman or the first man.

The girl, under the eye of the grandmother, practices the piano each afternoon. The sharp ear of the grandmother catches missed notes, passages played too fast, inarticulation, passion lost sliding across the keys. The grandmother speaks to her of passion, of the right kind. "Hastiness, carelessness will never lead you to any real feeling, or," she pauses, "any lasting accomplishment. You have to go deep inside yourself—to the best part." The black part, she thinks, for if anything can cloud your senses, it's that white blood. "The best part," she repeats to her granddaughter seated beside her on the piano bench, as she is atilt, favoring one hip.

The granddaughter, practicing the piano, remembers them leaving the last place, on the run, begging an old man and his son to transport the precious African thing—for to the grandmother the piano is African, civilized, the sum of its parts—on the back of a pickup truck.

A flock of white ladies had descended on the grandmother, declaring she had no right to raise a white child and they would take the girl and place her with a "decent" family. She explained that the girl was her granddaughter—sometimes it's like that. They did not hear. They took the girl by the hand, down the street, across the town, into the home of a man and a woman bereft of their only child by diphtheria. They led the girl into a pink room with roses rampant on the wall, a starched canopy hanging above the bed. They left her in the room and told her to remove her clothes, put on the robe they gave her, and take the bath they would draw for her. She did this.

Then, under cover of night, she let herself out the back door off the kitchen and made her way back, leaving the bed of a dead girl behind her. The sky pounded and the rain soaked her.

When the grandmother explained to the old man the circumstances of their leaving, he agreed to help. To her granddaughter she said little except she hoped the piano would not be damaged in their flight.

There is a woman lying in a bed. She has flown through a storm to the feet of her grandmother, who is seated atilt at the upright, on a bench that holds browned sheets of music. The girl's hair is glistening from the wet but not a strand is out of place. It is braided with care, tied with grosgrain. Her mind's eye brings the ribbon into closer focus; its elegant dullness, no cheap satin shine.

Fifty cents a yard at the general store on Main Street.

"And don't you go flinging it at me like that. I've lived too long for your rudeness. I don't think the good Lord put me on this earth to teach each generation of you politeness." The grandmother is ramrod straight, black straw hat shiny, white gloves bright, hair restrained by a black net. The thing in her thigh throbs, as it always does in such situations, as it did in front of the white ladies, as it did on the back of the old man's truck.

The granddaughter chafes under the silence, scrutiny of the boy who is being addressed, a smirk creasing his face. She looks to the ceiling where a fan stirs up dust. She looks to the bolts of cotton behind his head. To her reflection in the glass-fronted cabinet. To the sunlight blaring through the huge windows in front, fading everything in sight; except the grandmother, who seems to become blacker with every word. And this is good. And the girl is frightened.

She looks anywhere but at the boy. She has heard their "white nigger" hisses often enough, as if her skin, her hair signify only shame, a crime against nature.

The grandmother picks up the length of ribbon where it has fallen, holds the cloth against her spectacles, examining it, folding the ribbon inside her handkerchief.

The boy behind the counter is motionless, waiting for his father's money, waiting to wait on the other people watching him, as this old woman takes all the time in the world. Finally: "Thank you, kindly," she tells him, and counts fifty cents onto the marble surface, slowly, laying the copper in lines of ten; and the girl, in her imagination, desperate to be anywhere but here, sees lines of Cherokee in canoes skimming an icebound river, or walking to Oklahoma, stories her grandmother told her. "They'd stopped listening to their Beloved Woman. Don't get me started, child."

The transaction complete, they leave—leaving the boy, two dots of pink sparking each plump cheek, incongruous against his smirk.

The woman in the bed opens her eyes. It is still, dark. She looks to the window. A tall, pale girl flies in the window to the feet of her grandmother. Seated at the piano, she turns her head and the grandmother's spectacles catch the lightning.

"I want to stay here with you forever, Grandma."

"I won't be here forever. You will have to make your own way."

"Yes, ma'am."

"We are born alone and we die alone, and in the meanwhile we have to learn to live alone."

"Yes, Grandma."

"Good."

They speak their set piece like two shadow puppets against a white wall in a darkened room. They are shades, drawn behind the eye of a woman, full-grown, alive, in withdrawal.

"Did something happen tonight?"

"Nothing, Grandma; just the storm."

"That's what made you take flight?"

"Yes, ma'am."

"Are you sure?"

"Yes, ma'am."

She could not tell her about the song, or the word they had thrown at the other girl, to which the song was nothing.

She could not tell her about the pink room, the women examining her in the bath, her heart pounding as she escaped in a dead girl's clothes. They had burned hers.

Two childish flights. In each the grace that was rain, the fury that was storm chased her, saved her.

In the morning the sky was clear.

. . .

"Grandma?"

"Yes?"

"If I pay for it, can we get a radio?"

"Isn't a piano, aren't books enough for you?"

Silence.

"Where would you get that kind of money?"

"Mrs. Baker has asked me to help her after school. She has a new baby."

"Do I know this Mrs. Baker?"

"She was a teacher at the school before we came here. She left to get married and have a baby."

"Oh." The grandmother paused. "Then she is a colored woman?" As if she would even consider having her granddaughter toil for the other ilk.

"Yes. And she has a college education." Surely this detail would get the seal of approval, and with it the chance of the radio.

"What a fool."

"Grandma?"

"I say what a foolish woman. To go through all that—all that she must have done, and her people too—to get a college education and become a teacher and then to throw it all away to become another breeder. What a shame!"

With the last she was not expressing sympathy for a life changed by fate, or circumstance beyond an individual's control; she meant *disgrace,* of the Eve-covering-her-nakedness sort.

"Yes, Grandma." The girl could but assent.

The woman in the bed is watching as these shadows traverse the wall.

"Too many breeders, not enough readers. Yes—indeed."

"She seems like a very nice woman."

"And what, may I ask, does that count for? When there are children who depended on her? Why didn't she consider her responsibilities to her students, eh? Running off like that."

Watching the shadows engage and disengage.

"She didn't run off, Grandma."

No, Grandmother. Your daughter, my mother, ran off, or away. My mother who quit Spelman after one year because she didn't like the smell of her own hair burning—so you said. Am I to believe you? Went north and came back with me, and then ran off, away—again.

"You know what I mean. Selfish woman. Selfish and foolish. Lord have mercy, what a combination. The kind that do as they please and please no one but themselves."

The grandmother turned away to regard the dirt street and the stubborn rose.

The granddaughter didn't dare offer that a selfish and foolish woman would not make much of a teacher. Nor that Miss Elliston—whose pointer seemed an extension of her right index finger, and whose blue rayon skirt bore an equator of chalk dust—was a more than permanent replacement. The bitterness went far too deep for mitigation, or comfort.

"Grandma, if I work for her, may I get a radio?"

"Tell me, why do you want this infernal thing?"

"Teacher says it's educational." Escape. I want to know about the outside.

"Nonsense. Don't speak nonsense to me."

"No, ma'am."

"And just how much do you think this woman is willing to pay you?"

"I'm not sure."

"What does her husband do, anyway?"

"He's in the navy; overseas."

"Of course." Her tone was resigned.

"Grandma?"

"Serving them coffee, cooking their meals, washing their drawers. Just another servant in uniform, a house slave, for that is all the use the United States Navy has for the Negro man."

She followed the War religiously, *Crisis* upon *Crisis*.

"Why didn't he sign up at Tuskeegee, eh? Instead of being a Pullman porter on the high seas, or worse."

"I don't know," her granddaughter admitted quietly, she who was half-them.

"Yellow in more ways than one, that's why. Playing it safe, following a family tradition. Cooking and cleaning and yassuh, yassuh, yassuh. They are yellow, am I right?"

"Yes, ma'am."

"Well, those two deserve each other."

It was no use. No use at all to mention Dorie Miller—about whom the grandmother had taught the granddaughter—seizing the guns on the *Arizona* and blasting the enemy from the sky. No use at all. She who was part-them felt on trembling ground.

Suddenly—

"As long as you realize who, what these people are, then you may work for the woman. But only until you have enough money for that blasted radio. Maybe Madame Foolish-Selfish can lend you some books. Unless," her voice held an extraordinary coldness, "she's sold them to buy diapers."

"Yes, ma'am."

"You will listen to the radio only at certain times, and you must promise me to abide by my choice of those times, and to exercise discretion."

"I promise," the girl said.

Poor Mrs. Baker was in for one last volley. "Maybe as you watch the woman deteriorate, you will decide her life will not be yours. Your brain is too good, child. And can be damaged by the likes of her, the trash of the radio."

Not even when Mr. Baker's ship was sunk in the Pacific and he was lost, did she relent. "Far better to go down in flames than be sent to a watery grave. He died no hero's death, not he."

> Full fathom five, thy father lies;
> Of his bones are coral made;
> Those are pearls that were his eyes.

The baby with the black pearl eyes was folded into her chest as she spoke to him.

> Nothing of him that doth fade,
> But doth suffer a sea-change
> Into something rich and strange.

She imagined a deep and enduring blackness. Salt stripping him to bone, coral grafting, encrusted with other sea creatures. She thought suddenly it was the wrong ocean that had claimed him—his company was at the bottom of the other.

> Sea nymphs hourly ring his knell:
> Ding-dong.
> Hark! now I hear them—Ding-dong bell.

She heard nothing. The silence would be as deep and enduring as the blackness.

The girl didn't dare tell the grandmother that she held Mrs. Baker's hand when she got the news about her husband, brought her a glass of water, wiped her face. Lay beside her until she fell asleep. Gave the baby a sugar tit so his mother would not be waked.

The girl was learning about secrecy.

The girl tunes the radio in. Her head and the box are under a heavy crazy quilt, one of the last remnants of her mother; pieced like her mother's skin in the tent show where, as her grandmother said, "she exhibits herself." As a savage. A woman with wild hair. A freak.

That was a while ago; nothing has been heard from her since.

It is late. The grandmother is asleep on the back porch on a roll-away cot. Such is the heat, she sleeps in the open air covered only by a muslin sheet.

The misery, heaviness of the quilt, smelling of her mother's handiwork are more than compensated for by *The Shadow.* Who knows what evil lurks in the hearts of men?

The radio paid for, her visits to Mrs. Baker are meant to stop—that was the agreement. But she will not quit. Her visits to Mrs. Baker—like her hiding under her mother's covers with the radio late at night, terrified the hot tubes will catch the bed afire—are surreptitious, and fill her with a warmth she is sure is wrong. She loves this woman, who is soft, who drops the lace front of her camisole to feed her baby, who tunes in to the opera from New York on Saturday afternoons and explains each heated plot as she moves around the small neat house.

The girl sees the woman in her dreams.

On a hot afternoon in August Mrs. Baker took her to a swimming hole a mile or two out in the country, beyond the town. They wrapped the baby and set him by the side of the water, "Like the baby Moses," Mrs. Baker said. Birdsong was over them and the silver shadows of fish glanced off their legs.

"Come on, there's no one else around," Mrs. Baker told her, assuring her when she hesitated, "There's nothing to be ashamed of." And the girl slipped out of her clothes, folding them carefully on the grassy bank. Shamed nonetheless by her paleness.

Memory struck her like a water moccasin sliding through the muddy water. The women who would save her had her stand, turn around, open her legs—just to make sure.

. . .

She pulls herself up and comes to in her hospital bed. The piano in the corner of the room, the old lady, the girl, the jump rope, the white ladies recede and fade from her sight. Now there is a stark white chest that holds bedclothes. In another corner a woman in a lace camisole, baby-blue ribbon threaded through the lace, smiles and waves and rises to the ceiling, where she slides into a crack in the plaster.

The woman in the bed reaches for the knob on the box beside her head and tunes it in; Ferrante and Teicher play the theme from *Exodus* on their twin pianos.

Her brain vibrates in a *contre coup*. She is in a brilliantly lit white room in Boston, Massachusetts. Outside is frozen solid. It is the dead of winter in the dead of night. She could use a drink.

What happened, happened quickly. The radio announced a contest. She told Mrs. Baker about it. Mrs. Baker convinced her to send her picture in to the contest: "Do you really want to spend the rest of your days here? Especially now that your grandmother's passed on?" Her heart stopped. Just like that.

The picture was taken by Miss Velma Jackson, Mrs. Baker's friend, who advertised herself as V. JACKSON, PORTRAIT PHOTOGRAPHY, U.S. ARMY RET. Miss Jackson came to town a few years after the war was over, set up shop, and rented a room in Mrs. Baker's small house. In her crisp khakis, with her deep brown skin, she contrasted well with the light-brown, pasteled Mrs. Baker. She also loved the opera and together they sang the duet from *Norma*.

When she moved in talk began. "There must be something about that woman and uniforms," the grandmother said in one of her final judgments.

Miss Jackson, who preferred "Jack" to "Velma," performed a vital service to the community, like the hairdresser and the undertaker. Poor people took care to keep a record of themselves, their kin. They needed Jack, and so the talk died down. Died down until another photographer came along—a traveling man who decided to settle down.

Jack's portrait of the girl, now a young woman, came out well. She stared back in her green-eyed, part-them glory against a plain white backdrop, no fussy ferns or winged armchairs. The picture was sent in to the contest, a wire returned, and she was summoned.

She took the plain name they offered her—eleven letters, to fit best on a marquee—and took off. A few papers were passed.

"Will you come with me?"

"No."

"Why not?"

"I can't."

"Why not?"

"Jack and I have made plans. She has some friends in Philadelphia. It will be easier for us there."

"And Elijah?"

"Oh, we'll take him along, of course. Good schools there. And one of her friends has a boy his age."

"I'm going to miss you."

"You'll be fine. We'll keep in touch. This town isn't the world, you know."

"No."

Now there was nothing on the papers they sent—that is, no space for: *Race?*

Jack said, "And what do you propose to do? Say, hey, Mr. Producer, by the way, although I have half-moons on my fingernails, a-hem, a-hem?"

She was helped to her berth by a Pullman porter more green-eyed than she. In his silver-buttoned epauletted blue coat he reminded her of a medieval knight, on an iron horse, his chivalric code—RULES FOR PULLMAN PORTERS—stuck in his breast pocket. He serenaded her:

> De white gal ride in de parlor car.
> De yaller gal try to do de same.
> De black gal ride in de Jim Crow car.
> But she get dar jes' de same.

He looked at her as he stowed her bag. "Remember that old song, Miss?"

"No."

Daughter of the Mother Lode. The reader might recall that one. It's on late-night TV and also on video by now. She was the half-breed daughter of a forty-niner. At first, dirty and monosyllabic, then taken up by a kindly rancher's wife, only to be kidnapped by some crazy Apaches.

Polysyllabic and clean and calicoed when the Apaches seize her, dirty and monosyllabic and buck-skinned when she breaks away—and violated, dear Lord, violated out of her head, for which the rancher wreaks considerable havoc on the Apaches. You may remember that she is baptized and goes on to teach school in town and becomes a sort of mother-confessor to the dancehall girls.

As she gains speed, she ascends to become one of the more-stars-than-there-are-in-the-heavens, and her parts become lighter, brighter than before. Parts where "gay" and "grand" are staples of her dialogue. As in, "Isn't she gay!" "Isn't he grand!" She wears black velvet that droops at the neckline, a veiled pillbox, long white gloves.

She turns out the light next to the bed, shuts off the radio, looks out the window. Ice. Snow. Moon. The moon thin, with fat Venus beside it.

The door to the room suddenly whooshed open and a dark woman dressed in white approaches the bed.

"Mother?"

"Don't mind me, honey. I'm just here to clean up."

"Oh."

"I hope you feel better soon, honey. It takes time, you know."

"Yes."

The woman has dragged her mop and pail into the room and is now bent under the bed, so her voice is muffled beyond the whispers she speaks in—considerate of the drying-out process.

"Can I ask you something?" This soft-spoken question comes to the actress from underneath.

"Sure."

"Would you sign a piece of paper for my daughter?"

"I'd be glad to."

If I can remember my name.

The woman has emerged from under the bed and is standing next to her, looking down at her—bedpan in her right hand, disinfectant in her left.

The actress finds a piece of paper on the bedside table, asks the girl's name, signs "with every good wish for your future."

"Thank you kindly."

She lies back. Behind her eyelids is a pond. Tables laden with food are in the background. In the scum of the pond are tadpoles, swimming spiders. Darning needles dart over the water's surface threatening to sew up the eyes of children.

A child is gulping pond water.

Fried chicken, potato salad, coleslaw, pans of ice with pop bottles sweating from the cold against the heat.

The child has lost her footing.

A woman is turning the handles of an ice-cream bucket, a bushel basket of ripe peaches sits on the grass beside her. Three-legged races, sack races, races with an uncooked egg in a spoon, all the races known to man, form the landscape beyond the pond, the woman with the ice-cream bucket, the tables laden with food.

Finally—the child cries out.

People stop.

She is dragged from the water, filthy. She is pumped back to life. She throws up in the soft grass.

The woman wakes, the white of the pillow case is stained.

She pulls herself up in the bed.

The other children said she would turn green—from the scum, the pond water, the baby frogs they told her she had swallowed. No one will love you when you are green and ugly.

She gets up, goes to the bathroom, gets a towel to put over the pillow case.

"Hello. Information?"

"This is Philadelphia Information."

"I would like the number of Velma Jackson, please."

"One moment please."

"I'll wait."

"The number is . . ."

She hangs up. It's too late.

"She did run away from them, Mama. She came back to you. I don't think you ever gave her credit for that."

"And look where she is now, Rebekah."

"She ran away from them, left a room with pink roses. Sorry, Mama, I know how you hate roses."

"Who is speaking, please?" The woman sits up again, looks around. Nothing.

. . .

What will become of her?

Let's see. This is February 1963.

She might find herself in Washington, D.C., in August. A shrouded marcher in the heat, dark-glassed, high-heeled.

That is unlikely.

Go back? To what? This ain't *Pinky*.

Europe? A small place somewhere. Costa Brava or Paris—who cares? Do cameos for Fellini; worse come to worst, get a part in a spaghetti western.

She does her time. Fills a suitcase with her dietary needs: Milky Ways, cartons of Winston's, golden tequila, boards a plane at Idlewild.

Below the plane is a storm, a burst behind a cloud, streak lightning splits the sky, she rests her head against the window; she finds the cold comforting.

Election Day 1984

A WOMAN STANDS on a snake of a line in the back of a born-again church in a coastal town in California. In places the line is slender, in others it bunches like a python after swallowing a calf, in a shot from *Wild Kingdom.* This is the polling place.

On the wall to the woman's right is a map, straight pins with colored heads indicating the positions of missionaries. She glances at the map, to see if any pins are fixed to her native land. Indeed. Her island so small that the huge blue head practically obliterates its outline.

On her left, through a glass, brightly, a Bible study class sits around a conference table on red plastic chairs, lips moving without a sound behind a window; all are women. She begins to hate them, fights it; whatever have they done to her? God.

She recites in her head: *Though I speak with the tongues of men and of angels and have not charity I am as a sounding brass or a tinkling cymbal.* If there is a hell (which she doesn't really believe, but childhood is hard to shake) and if I am chosen to burn, it will be because of this—which a teacher noted in the third grade, Palmer script flowing across the report card: *She holds herself aloof from the others.* There it was. Way back then.

"Where you from?" The woman in front of her, in a tan raincoat, a yellow fisherman's hat on her head, brown leather handbag strapped across her chest, turns suddenly to make conversation.

"New York." She answers with the place she last was, not the place she is made of. Anyhow, she belongs there no longer. Her voice would not be recognized by her people. They are background.

"How long you been out here?"

"Two months."

She is not being very friendly. The land is about to slide for Ronnie, and surely this old lady is part of it, partly to blame, just as the parroting Bible class is. *Live and let live.* Her mother echoed in her head. *Slow to anger and abounding in steadfast love.* I hate their hate. *Two wrongs don't make a right. Judge not lest ye be judged.* Your father and I want for you and your brother a better life. There's no chance back there, that's all.

"How'd you get out here?"

"I drove."

"Married?"

"No."

"Alone?"

"Yes."

"You weren't scared?"

"Not really." *Liar.*

The line inches forward. People drip with unaccustomed rain. Every now and then someone says, "But we need it." And someone else nods.

"Isn't this country something?"

"Yes, it is." She does not say beautiful, desolate.

"And where did you stop?"

The younger woman begins to recite her route. Her mind glosses her spoken words. Images flash like lantern slides. As if someone dropped the tray. Out of order.

"Detroit first. I visited friends."

A rat sprints across the highway and a woman in a big Buick brakes—hard. Laughing with her friends in their backyard: we brake for rats. The Heaven Hill is out of hand. She brakes hard, just like a woman. The totem pole—eagle on high—shadows them. Inside a turtle shell is sweet grass. Indians inside cities raising corn. Totems. They turn to her, serious. Has she made the right decision? She strokes the sweet grass, traces the quadrants of the turtle shell. Yes. I think so. The center fell out.

You're not running, are you? No. I don't think so. Sure?

Desert. In the distance a cluster of trailers. Wires crossing like spiders' webs. Smoke rises from thin pipes. Pickups. Children. Laundry supported on a slender thread. Everything slender, small, minute, at this distance. Nothing in the Rand-McNally. A cluster of people against red monuments, landscape laced with barbed wire. Dust cloud raised in the foreground as a roadrunner speeds by.

Labor Day Parade. Union floats. Reagan in an outhouse at the back of a UAW flatbed. A woman asks for a cigarette. "Got a light, too, sugar?" A dime? A dollar? A house? A home, honey?

"You got a place to put your head?"

"Yes."

"You got kids?"

"No."

"God bless, sister."

River Rouge. Black Madonna. GOSPEL CHICKEN—OUR BIRD IS THE WORD! boarded up.

FREEDOM ROAD USED CARS: WE TOTE THE NOTE—rusts.

Mississippi. A plain green sign announces the King of the Waters. The Mici Sibi of the Chippewa. The final resting place of de Soto. The river nobody wanted to be sold down. As wide as the Styx.

This is a country of waters and no water.

Glorious, ordinary the river runs.

Platte. Republican. Ohio. Little Blue. Des Moines.

In a backwater town of grain elevators and railway lines, roundhouses and old hotels, three women run a lunchroom. The wall behind the register is hung with their families. Beyond the lunchroom, the town, fields are a deep gold, pumps bow and rise, rhythm breaking the still of the landscape, in the distance a windbreak shelters a house.

She remembers from a history book in the eighth grade the photograph of a family, posed outside their sod house, amongst their valuables, chattel—Singer, piano, settee—brought into the light. *Moses Speese Family, Custer County, 1888.* That plain identification, with this opinion: *not all Negroes were downtrodden.*

FDR smiles from a wall in a lunchroom.

In the converted bank in Red Cloud hangs a letter from Langston Hughes to Willa Cather. Upstairs a diorama illustrates the Professor's room. Ántonia's cup and saucer are found behind glass. A few streets away is the perfect small white house. A small white house with an attic room where a girl plotted and planned to get away.

1961. Small apartment over a drugstore. World map over her bed. Jam jar with babysitting geld. Lying there in the heat of a summer night, regarding France, her goal back then, the woman above them playing over and over, "I always knew I'd find someone like you, so welcome to my little corner of the world." Husband shouting to shut the goddamned phonograph off. The woman chanting, "Hit me, hit me, go ahead and hit me." Quiet then.

Farmland turns high plains.

A stone is fixed to the ground. ON THIS SPOT CRAZY HORSE OGALLALA CHIEF WAS KILLED SEPT 5, 1877.

This one will stand for the others.

She sends a postcard of the marker to her brother.

> Dear Bill,
>
> I'm okay. Thought you'd like (stupid word) to have this. Visited Cather's house and museum in Red Cloud. Lots of stuff. But no red carnation. Was it a *red* carnation?
>
> Love, Jess

Salt Lake. A city set in yellow. In the tabernacle, imposing, a family, intact, divine, walks on air.

At a gas station a man throws her change at her and calls her a wetback. What tipped him off? Her speech is plain. Her skin has a tinge but could deceive the untutored eye. Her hair curls at the edges. But permanents are "in." Perhaps not in Salt Lake. She almost laughs but realizes the danger. She revs the Mustang and lets the silver rattle on the floor.

She fought the desire to call out "Adiós!" Spanish is her third language.

A tired waitress in an all-night diner serves her eggs and coffee, her skin sallow from the atmosphere. "You're not from around here are you?"

"No."

The great white lake lies on either side of her. Black highway a thin ribbon between water and salt. Light refracting color here and there.

She turns on the tape deck and Bob Marley sings about loss and future and past and, no, woman, no cry. And she does. Her tears run salt into her mouth.

She crosses into Nevada. Stops at a restaurant on a bright Sunday morning and feeds a machine until she feels refreshed. An old man with a cup of quarters wedged in his belt feeds the one beside her. As she turns to leave, a woman in a cowboy hat, wild bird feather garnishing its rim, storms in, pushing the old man from his spinning cherries, bells, oranges. "Jesus Christ! A person can't even go get something to eat!"

"Don't mind her," the old man says, "she's just protecting her investment."

In her silver Motown prairie schooner, packed with books and all else she owns, she is driving west. She crosses into California at the Donner Pass, observes the monument to the pioneer spirit, and heads down the Sierra to the Pacific.

"My last stop before here was Reno."

"When you passed through Nebraska, did you drive through Omaha?"

"Yes. Is that where you're from?"

"No. I'm native Californian. From Bakersfield. But I was in Omaha once. In and out."

"Oh."

"Did you visit Boys Town when you passed through?"

The old woman asks this matter-of-factly, as if an orphanage was one of the top-ten tourist attractions. Right beside Disneyland, Mount Rushmore, Wounded Knee.

"No."

"That's too bad. It's a wonderful place. At least it was when I was there. Nineteen thirty-five. Of course, everything changes. That Father Flanagan was a saint. But you're probably too young to remember him."

The younger woman nods politely. She sees only Spencer Tracy, in black and white, on a nineteen-inch screen, getting tough with Mickey Rooney.

"I took a boy there once."

The old woman declares this quietly, dropping her voice, moving closer, beckoning the stranger closer, at once transforming the dialogue.

The younger woman is startled. Brother? Cousin? Nephew? Son? Who? She doesn't dare ask. She thinks she has met an ancient mariner, one who walks the coast, telling.

"Really?"

"Yes. Really. Like I said, it was nineteen thirty-five. The depth of the Depression. Just took him and drove from Bakersfield to Omaha. Almost nonstop. Didn't take that long, you know. Most of the traffic was going in the other direction." She smiles.

The child slept in the back for most of the journey. Covered with a plaid blanket. He twitched in his sleep, whimpered now and then. The desert. Her black car eating up the rays. The child remained wrapped in the blanket, suffering from a coldness, seeming not to notice the heat, light, LAST CHANCE FOR GAS BEFORE wherever. She was washed in sweat.

She sang to pass the time, to keep them—herself—company. The desert past, they cross the Sierra. Oh, mine eyes have seen the glory of the coming of the Lord / He is trampling out the vintage where the grapes of wrath are stored. It is written in her will that they will sing it at her graveside.

She tried to get the boy to join her, but he hadn't the heart to sing. Else he didn't know the words, but she did try to teach him. The boy was too shy, frightened, to ask for food, for a drink of water, to use the bathroom. So she stopped when she thought it might be necessary, and that seemed to work. It was a spinster's best solution—what did she know about children?

She stopped the car for a rest. Poured a canvas bag of water into the desperate radiator. Sitting on the running board while the car drank, sitting there they watched the people from the Dust Bowl pass them by. Each traveling band had a song. California, here I come.

People sang back then. Sang themselves through all kinds of things.

"Just you and the boy?"

"Yes." Yes, me and the boy, and I didn't even know his name. Finally got it out of him in Colorado. He didn't know the year of his birth, so I made one up.

"Yes. Just the two of us. We were in a big hurry, you see, so they picked me. I had the most reliable car, for one thing. And there wasn't any reason for anyone else to come along."

"Who was 'they'?"

"A group of women from my church. Baptist. Anyway, my car was pretty good, four new tires, and I was unattached and could get away at a moment's notice, and there wasn't anyone to miss me. Being a single woman and all. I just put a sign on the door. Closed due to illness. I ran a small grocery store. Inherited it from my father. The kind of place you hardly ever see nowadays."

"What happened?"

"Well, we got to Omaha and I turned the boy over to Father Flanagan."

"I mean what happened before? Why? Why did you have to take him there? Didn't anyone want him?"

She, the child-immigrant, knows intimately the removal of children. She takes the boy's part, her suspicion drenched in assumption. "Didn't you want him?"

"Wasn't mine to want, dear. Listen, it's a long story, but I've come this far. And this line is moving awfully slow—and not much at the end of it." She smiled again, and the younger woman couldn't help but join her.

"He was ten years old about. He lived with his mother and father on a small ranch at the edge of town—they were tenants, not owners—poor people. Once, when one of the church women visited the ranch with a basket for the family—which is what we need to be doing now, especially with Thanksgiving just around the corner; you can't just do it holiday time, though. Well, anyway, this was in the summer, and the church woman called on the family. She noticed, couldn't help *but* notice, that the woman who answered the door, the boy's mother, was bruised, all purple and yellow, on her face, hands, neck—everywhere not covered by her clothes. So the visitor gave the woman the basket and asked her who had beaten her—not right out, mind you, but as clear as she could make the question. And of course the woman said no one. What else could she say? The visitor told the woman that if things got so bad she couldn't stand it, she should call the minister's wife and talk to her, and the minister would come and talk to the woman's husband.

"Well, the woman explained to the visitor that they had no telephone, but the visitor persisted, so the woman said, okay, if things got too bad she'd call from the pay phone at the filling station down the road. I don't think she ever intended to call on her own account. I mean, getting a minister, a stranger . . . it wasn't the brightest suggestion . . . probably would have only made things worse for her . . . anyway, the visitor left and the woman nodded and thanked her for the basket, and that was that.

"Then one night the minister's wife took a call, and the voice at the other end was expressing itself in these fierce whispers. The voice was upset, but the woman was taking care not to be overheard. Finally, the minister's wife put two and two together; she called me and I called a couple of other women—we were the ladies' auxiliary of the church, you see. Well, we got in my car and went out to the ranch."

She paused for breath and looked around, but no one else was listening.

Her voice slowed, each syllable carefully pronounced. "It was the damnedest sight I ever saw, or ever hope to see. Not even as a Red Cross girl, in the war, in New Guinea.

"The ranch house had a Dutch door—remember those?—the kind where the top is separate from the bottom?"

The younger woman nodded. Fifties TV. A woman dressed in a frilly apron calls the boys in for brownies.

"Well, the top half was swinging wide open. On the porch, outside the door, was this man, lying on his back, his face just gone. Blowed off. Nothing.

"Inside, you could see this little boy sitting on some steps, holding a shotgun, crying and wiping his nose on his sleeve. His mother was sitting next to him, face as blank as they come. Ugly red line under her chin.

"We decided then and there to get him out of town. I mean, he had his whole life ahead of him. Why should he be punished? It was an easy choice, believe me.

"It was much harder convincing these Baptists that Father Flanagan's place would be the place to take the boy. But *we* were the Baptists, Lord knows what the boy and his people were. Better there than a reform school. I told them about an article I had read in the *Saturday Evening Post* and all about Father Flanagan and him saying, 'There is no such thing as a bad boy,' and so on, and it was decided. And we didn't even think to call the men in on this, that was for later.

"We packed up and left that very night. We told the mother it was for the boy's own good and she seemed to agree, though she didn't say much. Shock."

"Did *he* say anything?"

"Hardly a word between there and Omaha. Not even when we reached the Freedom Road—you know, where the Mormons are supposed to have planted sunflowers along the way? I wanted to tell him what I knew, tried, too, to tell him it wasn't the Mormons, it was the Indians—his people, you see."

"You didn't say they were Indians."

"Well, I think they were. They never said for sure. But I think it was a safe guess. They looked like it. Even if he wasn't, it was a nice story I told him: how they weren't just flowers, but holding the flower to the ground was something like a potato. Food the Indians planted during the wars on the plains. But I don't know how much got through to him, all wrapped up in the back."

"Couldn't you have found out from his mother where their people were?"

The old woman sighed. "I was trying to do what I thought was best. There wasn't time and, well, the woman wasn't talking. Indians can be difficult, but coming from New York you wouldn't know that."

The younger woman says nothing.

"I tried to tell him that if someone bullies and beats up on people, they have to expect what they get—shouldn't expect no better. And he was only trying to come between his mother and another beating—or worse. Are you listening?"

"Pardon?"

"I didn't think so . . . Look, better Boys Town than some God-forsaken reservation . . . where he would drown in whiskey or die from TB."

"I understand what you are saying. But . . ."

"His mother wouldn't talk. He wouldn't talk—even if he knew who his people were. Even if all the Indians had mailing addresses and I had all the time in the world . . . I don't know. Maybe his mother didn't talk because she thought I was doing what was best for him."

The younger woman withdraws further into silence, waiting now only for the end of the story, the end of the line.

"I don't know how much he understood of what I told him. Most of the time he seemed to be sleeping. Or I could hear him crying. Most of the time I talked—or sang. What a pair, eh?"

She will not relinquish her reminiscence, the flavor of it, the goodness of it. And what did you get out of it? Adventure? Righteousness?

The younger woman thinks she sees the boy clearly. The tracks of children running from the Christian boarding schools, feet frozen in the snow. She's not a historian for nothing.

She asks the inevitable question: "Whatever happened to him?"

"I don't know. I never saw him after I left him at Boys Town. But the police never found out where he was, either. That was good. I mean, that was the point of the whole journey. A safe place."

"What about . . . ?" The younger woman is caught up again.

"The mother? She wasn't so lucky. She went to prison for life. Manslaughter."

"Didn't she try to get away? I mean why didn't she run?"

"And where would she go? A woman like that—traveling alone?"

"Maybe she was heartbroken."

They reached the voting booths, having traveled the last few yards in silence.

Bodies of Water

I

AN OLD WOMAN is sitting in the middle of an icebound lake. She has a basket and a Thermos and is herself wrapped in layers of wool and down. She is seated on a campstool. Her lips move.

She is singing to bring in the fish, she would say, should you ask her, gather them into the round opening at her feet, cut with the saw now wrapped in a flannel rag set beside her on the ice. She has spent a lifetime cutting. Ice. Wood. Stone. Her maul handled anew many times by now, her wedge gray steel, no trace of the manufacturer's gay blue paint.

As she sings, mist escapes her mouth. She is cold. What fish? Trout; maybe perch. At this time of year? *I want something small.* She needs to feed no one beside herself, and has no heart for freezing.

The cold drove them to the deepest, cleanest part of the lake. Would her sound reach them as they slept? Would anyone underwater hear the singer? Or is her voice lost? "Sweet Molly Malone" caught in the winter light.

The gray of the afternoon rests on the old woman's shoulders, and she sips her whiskey-laced tea between snatches of song.

Truth be told, she sings to keep herself awake. No fish come. She is fighting sleep.

In a stone cottage at the water's edge a younger woman watches the old woman.

The house is new to her: hers, not-hers. Frozen into the silence of the season, where no birds sing. White flakes glance against the window frosted from the cold and heat cast by the woodstove. She draws her hand across the pane and watches. The old woman.

The lake. Enclosed, deep, cold. A cold that could stop time—she likes to think. The best lakes were hidden, safe, glacial. She is drawn to lakes, yet afraid of water.

She could see with her mind's eye her girlhood—one day, one afternoon. Her rising womanly from the waters. At twelve, or thirteen. The water laps at her and the black snakes of a mountain lake whisper past her. A tangle of hair reaches past her shoulders. The smell of freshwater is around her. Hard, black water bugs play around her legs. That is the picture in her mind. Standing in the shallows, moving forward, the Lady of Legend emerges from her element. And that image is joined in memory to another—lying belly-down on her single bed, the soft reds and muted blues of N. C. Wyeth in a storybook. She couldn't read yet; her brother could. It was his book, won in a citywide reading competition. The Lady's upraised hand, the sword.

"Your brother reads too much."

That summer at that mountain lake he had not been with them. Sent to some tough place, while she had the parents to herself. Two weeks in a rented cabin. The smell of knotty pine overwhelming. Counting the knots, trying to bring on sleep.

Six cabins circled a towering pole, Stars and Stripes flapping over families, brought down each evening by the owner's Boy Scout son. He set the flag at half-mast the summer Marilyn Monroe died; his mother thought that was disrespectful and yanked the banner to full height, warning her boy not to be so smart.

The younger woman sees herself rising from the waters of that mountain lake. In the frozen glass beyond which an old woman sits on the ice.

Her father's laughter as he saluted his little mermaid.

Her mother: "Mind! Snakes!" And the girl ran out of the water, convinced a snake had wrapped around her legs; a water bug made its way into the tangle of her sweet new hair—of which her parents were ignorant—and in that instant, giving way to her mother's warning, the delicacy of her relationship with snakes, bugs, water, weeds had been violated, changed. That simple.

The younger woman is warm in the cottage. She feels hidden, safe.

In thick wool socks and plaid Pendleton, soft brown corduroys wrapped around her legs.

In the foreground a cardinal is poking through drifts. His flash of color the only color of the afternoon. He captures her attention, draws her from herself, the old woman. Tomorrow she will venture forth, walk to the village to buy birdseed. There is a wooden feeder, handmade, hanging from a bare catalpa. In that tough place they taught her brother carpentry.

The old woman had thought it too cold for snow, but flakes are swirling around her. The wind is coming down hard from the hills and sweeping across the lake, no break in sight. No break but a few tall pines—*scorned as timber, belovèd of the sky.* She remembers another old woman's words; one who lived alone in the wild and painted totems.

She sniffs at the snow and sticks out her tongue to catch a few flakes, rocking her head from side to side. Too much whiskey, old girl, she tells herself.

"Or are you entering your second childhood?"

She recalls the familiar taunt of a niece, her dead brother's elder daughter, who takes it upon herself to keep family members in line. Not a dreadful woman, merely unimaginative, and terrified of any imaginative act. Little things set her off. Once the old woman sent the niece's daughter a book about the witch trials at Salem. The niece responded as if the old woman was a purveyor of magic.

Poor soul. But dangerous, too.

She would sometimes follow the taunt with a definite threat, one determined to get the old woman's attention.

"For if you are, we shall have to make arrangements."

Yes, *arrangements.* For what? A nursery? Padded cell? A bit of both. A room (shared with a stranger, strangers) where she would be spoon-fed—everything mashed beyond texture or recognition. Probably tied to her bed by night, her chair by day. Where the stench of urine would be as unrelenting as a bank of lilac in bloom. Where she—who had chosen childlessness, another of the niece's peeves—would be perpetually asked: Where are your children? Grandchildren?

She had seen these places for herself. She had seen enough friends locked away in places where a sign on the door warned visitors: DON'T LEAVE KEYS IN CAR. As if a horde of old women (for the inmates of these homes were mostly women) would seize the day, the chance to escape, and take the curves of the Mohawk Trail at unsafe speeds, endangering innocent bystanders.

At first the sign made her smile, but nothing about this was funny.

The physical restraints, the lack of movement, were not the worst of it. She had seen women shrivel before her eyes, with nothing to occupy their minds but the pettiness of people in a confined space, where one group had total control over the other. Where the library consisted of *Reader's Digest* condensed books, the Bible, out-of-date magazines. And, as unrelenting as the stench, the noise of the television.

The niece had erupted most recently when another old woman died, and her aunt was named—for all the world to read—in the weeklies and dailies of the valley as "sole survivor."

"Jesus, I've always suspected as much, but why did she have to advertise it?"

"You worry too much," her husband tried to calm her. "Any reasonable person will see it for what it is."

"Which is?"

"Two old maids. That's all."

The niece forwarded the old woman yet another brochure, enclosing a note. "This seems a pleasant place—now that your 'friend' is gone."

Not if she could help it. No. She had her own money stashed where they couldn't find it. If need be, she would take off, head west, change her name. She had her escape hatch. They wouldn't take her alive.

She thought about crazy old Agnes, disappearing without a trace while the village gathered to salute the Bicentennial, erasing her family in cold blood.

Now, *that* was wrong.

The escape?

The murders.

She is murmuring to herself.

Really? Even after what they found out?

No. That sort of thing is always wrong. There are certain absolutes.

They had gone to school together. She could see Agnes, off somewhere, cowed by the other girls, and her other life—the one lived away from the nuns. A strong girl, red hair, green eyes, Irish to a T. Never able to give as good as she got. She was outnumbered.

And she, old woman now, girl then, had done not a thing to lessen the odds.

That was wrong.

Did I know it then?

Get up, old girl, before they send the wagon for you.

Now—to home. Stir the fire. Choose a volume for the evening. See if the old black-and-white stray is around, as hoary and as sweet as the older Whitman. As she imagines the older Whitman. She will invite him in—never does he accept. She speaks softly to him on the porch, in the dark, his eyes like hard glass reflectors. He will take the pork chop bone, the remains of the baked potato, the dish of warmed milk—but not the shelter. Each time she makes the invitation, then leaves him to eat in peace.

She longs for warmth suddenly and wishes she could float to the clapboard house far older than she is.

Her head sinks forward and she knows she will either sleep there and freeze, or make her way home. She rises, carefully, her breasts have sunk into her belly; she lifts them.

She pours the remains of her Thermos onto the ice, as libation for the spirits, the manifestations. Next time they may guide the fish to her, if they are not too busy with better things. Tea dances. Bridge. Gossip. However they occupy themselves in their watery parlors.

She pictures them not draped in gossamer, but bugle-beaded, ghosts who dangle chain-mail evening bags from their thin wrists. These ladies of the lake.

Do they make their own music?

And how do they get on with the others? All draped in bombazine, the heavy black of mourning clothes.

Widows and glamour girls—together forever.

And the others?

How many souls collide underwater?

Enough.

She folds the campstool and gathers her creel and rod and reel, snapping the rod into a walking stick. Her gear is slung over one shoulder, and she moves forward on the ice.

The younger woman watches still. Watches as the old woman makes a false step and slips. Starts, and wonders if she should run across the lake. Immediately the old woman has risen again, and is off again—strongly. The younger one relaxes, sipping her coffee, turning back to the desk.

Raising her head as a snow-cloud crosses the lake, the younger woman fancies a shape, not able to make it out, the wind swirls so.

II

The old woman retreated in winter to one room at the back of the eight-chambered house. Built on and on, on one level, from parlor to bedroom, to kitchen, to birthing room, to mud kitchen to breezeway to woodshed. The peaked roof gave the house the illusion of two stories but held only a crawl space, the habitat of bats.

One room was hers, which she wrapped around her, and cushioned with all manner of souvenir, which she sometimes regards as comfort, sometimes as detritus. Recently she has needed her stuff more than before. That's natural, she thinks, sometimes.

A horsehair sofa stands in one corner opposite the fire—unto itself. Severe—as it had been when it stood in the waiting room of her father's office.

A child sitting in this waiting room, on this high-backed sofa, legs crossed at the ankles, as her father taught her, waiting, reading; always reading. Hour upon hour waiting, while her father searched deeds, negotiated rights of way, delayed liens. Property, the ownership and distribution thereof, had been his specialty. A man of substance, but not without compassion. The less fortunate, as she had been taught to call them, came to him. Flocked. The men and women and children who perched on the edge of this selfsame sofa, lacking the surety to sit back, leaving no mark on the hard black hide. Unlike some others—there was a scar on the armrest where the monsignor, visiting from Holy Cross, had set his cigar.

She sat reading, always reading, unless one of her father's clients, or two, or three, spoke to her. Politeness was valued: a child did not withdraw when addressed by an adult, no matter who, no matter how fascinating her book, how urgent her inner life. People she knew only by sight asked after her school, her brothers, her aunts and uncles, and, finally, her father, carefully avoiding the subject of mother, since the girl's birth had been the occasion of the woman's passing. Poor child, she needs a woman's touch, they said to each other in one breath, in another, slightly resenting this girl who had made her father a lonely man.

They would talk and she would respond, lower her eyes, smile, nod, whatever the litany called for. But she was uncomfortable with them, and forced herself not to withdraw when they addressed her, and did as they demanded. In between their words, their eyes were fixed on the wavy glass window, bathroom glass, distorting the shapes inside the inner office—what her father called his sanctum sanctorum—the gilt lettering stating, EDWARD DILLON ATTORNEY-AT-LAW. The brass knob turning from time to time and a tall dark man, Black-Irish, as handsome as the devil, calling "Next."

She sleeps on this sofa in winter, her heavy contours denting its surface, her scent entering it. The black leather cracked in a few places, but the piece, the structure, intact. They don't make things the way they used to. That's a fact.

At night she spreads a white muslin sheet, places pillows at one end, and covers herself with a quilt pieced by another woman, for which she herself cut the template.

Wrapped in these bits and pieces, a stack of books on the floor beside her, she allows her mind to wander. Now, even with *The Years* propped on her chest, her mind strays—she lets it—eyes lighting on a patch, determining its beginning, as sundress, robe, silk blouse with jabot, boastful intricate stitches fixing each piece to the other—she is gone somewhere beyond the book. Back.

Bessie taught her about quilts. They spoke of cartography, biography, history, resistance. Drunkard's Path. Road to California. Underground Railroad. Mohawk Trail. Bessie taught her about patterns, taught her how to cut, let her watch as she threaded the needle, leading steel and thread through cloth, stopping to consider direction, contrast, harmony, shade, color.

Theirs was a friendship begun in girlhood. Picking strawberries in thin cotton. Hands stained where the red tenderness gives way, thin cotton sticking to their upper legs. The redness of them, from berries, the August sun. They were in an old peach orchard near the lake. Someone else's land—abandoned. Gorged on berries they attack the peaches, the heavy fuzz of the fruit against their mouths. Their skin itches from the fuzz and they fly to the edge of the water and plunge in fully dressed.

"Ever been really kissed?" Who had been so daring as to ask that? In their wet dresses, sun sparkling the water on their red cheeks, two pink tongues met, and the two held fast.

On this cold night the snow flies around a mailbox at the side of the road. ANNE DILLON. ISABELLA STRANIERE.

She had not had the heart to remove the other name.

She could barely tell the bees.

III

January something,
the year of the piano

Dear Jess,

Hope you are able to find everything. The cupboard next to the fridge is well stocked and should hold you until you begin to find your way around. Nothing fancy. For essentials you can try the Mini-Mart at the edge of the village. Otherwise you'll need to "go to town."

Booze is underneath the breakfront by the dining table. Coffee beans in the freezer. Seasoned wood in the box just inside the back door—extra in the shed out back.

Défense de fumer. At least, I hope you've abandoned that particular death-defying habit. Listen to me. Hah! One good thing about all this, I won't have to quit after all. I can turn my fingertips burnt sienna if I please.

I've told the postmaster that I am going away and that you are using the place while I'm gone. No need to be specific. As long as they have some sense of what's happening with people's places, they're content. Curious but not nosy. Great happiness—but not now. Remember?

(She did. Her Greek landlady in London when she was in full flight, who read her coffee grounds and intoned the same prophecy each time. With henna hair and black eyes, in perpetual mourning for her White Russian husband and the baby she aborted in a bathtub.)

Don't know what they'd think if they knew, but probably no different than urban types.

Don't worry. Even if your ears ring when they hold town meeting. Smile.

God love you. Smile.

Seriously, I hope you stay well and that the place gives you what you need. At least something of what you need. It's been too long not seeing each other, but you'll glimpse me here. More than glimpse. And, let's face it, we're very different people, and probably would be at each other's throats before long.

(She lit a cigarette, inhaling deeply. Watching the ember flare, then fall. Turning to watch the roads of fire in the stove. The smoke only made the eye-water worse.)

It will be frozen and cold for weeks to come, but the spring will be worth it all. Watch for false hellebore—it has greenish-white flowers and grows on the floor of the pine forest beyond the lake. After the skunk cabbage they are about the next sign to appear. Then you will see trillium, pink and white, rampant green. You will know it's truly spring when you see a lady slipper. They're warm pink and lavender, like a wild orchid. O'Keeffe could never do them justice, the sensuality of them.

Probably no one could.

I don't think I will ever just see the lady slipper, the pine, the sun dropping without, you know, thinking O'Keeffe, Carr, Friedrich, or another trio. I have never been able to behold nature alone. But then you know that. Behold—funny word. I think it has to do with the need for human description, definition. Unless we describe it, oh, I don't know.

Don't you find O'Keeffe's work unbearably cold? I do. Cold old bitch of the desert. Our Lady of the Obvious. Sorry. Sorry. Sorry. *Mea Culpa. Mea Maxima Culpa,* aka Maxine Culpa, the famous nun-cum-scat-singer.

Rude boy!

Sorry, my love, I am meandering. Pray that this thing doesn't get me in the head, will you? I think I could take anything but that. This old head has already been through a lot. But do you know when it's that, or are you so far gone . . . no . . . God . . . I didn't mean to lay that out here. Of course it must be a matter of degree. A slice of bread going slowly stale, finally the soft spot at the center hardens—that's it.

To this day jelly sandwiches make me puke. And they said I wouldn't remember.

Last spring I found a beaver lodge at the far end of the lake. You could hear the babies.

I hear that in the city there's a run on all the channeling books, medium (media?), whatever. Well, I think I'll get me a Ouija board and call up Winslow Homer. Silly old queen. What makes people think the dead have time for the living? Or that someone you wouldn't be caught dead with in life deserves a hearing? Pathetic, isn't it? God, listen to me.

Why don't people channel Carole Lombard—I ask you that. Instead of all these drunks, bores, extraterrestrials?

Because Shirley MacLaine isn't a faggot, that's why. You heard it here first.

Poor old Carole Lombard, the last thing she needs is fans nagging her in the Great Beyond.

I should be burned at the stake, like Joan of Arc. Burned at the stake, scattered on the quenelles of Rouen, fed to the mayor, and my heart put in a box above the altar. My relic. Now where did all *that* come from?

(She got up and walked over to the stove, playing a poker through the coals. Choosing a thin log of birch, she watched the bark catch and curl.

She wrote him a letter on birch bark, pretending she was an Indian. Crazy Horse was his hero when they were kids.)

Characters. Not to change the subject, but . . . yes, there are plenty of characters. You will no doubt see Miss Dillon fishing on the lake. As I write this I can see her, all wrapped up and sitting on her campstool. She doesn't seem to catch anything—mostly I think it's a form of meditation. I know her by sight and from things overheard at the P.O. I think I've been here too long. Over-concern with country matters.

Anyhow, if you see an old woman on the lake—and you will—that's who she is. I gather her lifelong friend passed on (Jesus! Why can't I just say died?) a while ago. The friend (and why, for God's sake, can't I say lover?—the old girl *was* listed in the obits as "sole survivor") was a schoolteacher, Miss Straniere. The "sole survivor" thing caused a little bit of talk. The postmistress stopped one group cold with, "Well, I reckon that's what she is."

You know and I know why I can't say "died." So much easier to think of passing, floating, dancing on a fucking moonbeam. It's like waiting for a fucking car crash . . . head on . . . but very, very messy (say that like Bette Davis, please) and in slow, slow motion. As for "lover," my prejudice, I guess.

Miss Dillon kept the house and garden, sold maple syrup and watercolors to the summer people. (Mostly scenes of the lake, some quite surreal. Lots of mist and foxfire. Skeletal trees at the borders. Perhaps you'll get to see them; the Mini-Mart exhibits them during the season.) I know that sounds like Patience and Sarah on Golden Pond or something. She must be very lonely. No, that's presumptuous.

I am the one that's lonely.

This is the fifth draft of this letter. I *am* trying not to be morbid. Bear with me.

Try to enjoy yourself.

When you go to town—as opposed to village—to shop, you might want to check out the Atheneum. Wonderful woodwork inside and an actual Bierstadt. El Capitan. How he lit those huge landscapes.

Here I am again. You go to El Capitan (although I'm glad California did not claim you), probably sleep outside or something. I look at the Bierstadt three thousand miles away and have seen it.

After the thaw, you never know what might show up. Last spring a bunch of kids found a guy who had run away from the VA hospital. Poor bastard. Propped against a wall in a wrecked old farmhouse in the woods. Fell asleep in the cold. Yesterday's news on his head.

After the thaw and once the frost is behind you, the garden will make itself known in earnest. There are perennials, herbs—rosemary, thyme, sage, tarragon.

A thought: do you realize that if Joe Orton had lived, he'd probably be dead by now? His diaries are in the bookcase by the bed. I found them particularly moving. That desire to create oneself as far from family—mother and father, that is—as possible. And the assholes would say he paid a price for that, but that's not it at all. No.

Don't let the North Africa stuff horrify you. Boys will be boys—especially the English variety.

I guess I think of Orton as as much of an immigrant as you and I are/were. I mean, at least we were brought here at ages young enough so that . . . That's not clear. What I mean to say is that he didn't know the customs of his new world. Christ, I don't know why I'm going off like this. I should stick to describing paintings and let you do the political analyses. I think I'm afraid you're going to disapprove of him and therefore of me. Simple as that. After all this time. Crazy.

Also—not to change the subject—onions, garlic, asparagus. I dug the ditch for the asparagus myself three years ago. They will be in full power now. Two weeks in June—maybe three.

I remember a drive across the country years ago—the same route you took, I think—recognizing along the side of Highway 80 the flowers of Jerusalem artichoke. Everywhere. In such abundance I doubted my perception, and Jack thought I had become dangerously obsessive. I was like a kid counting Fords to pass the time. Into Iowa, Nebraska, and on and on. Not an artichoke at all, of course. Girasole, turning to the sun. Sister (or brother) to the sunflower. The small yellow heads will bloom in summer—I planted the garden boundary with them.

Being a big brother dies hard. Remember *Night of the Hunter*? Big brother and little sister running, finding Lillian Gish and her rifle—"I've got something trapped in the barn." Whatever. My need to look out for you, teach, worry. Even after all the years of separation, and the early rupture we both endured.

The food of the Indians. In the deep freeze of the ground across those thousands of miles; spreading and spreading in spring and summer, then blooming, stretching. Crazy Horse may have roasted their ancestors over a fire on the run. I still love him.

I remember you writing to me a few years ago about the old woman you encountered; you know, the one with the story about the boy she took to Father Flanagan? How she told him about the same thing? You were so angry when you wrote. So she wasn't Lillian Gish with rifle, house filled with castaway children, evil lurking in the barn, wounded, at bay. Who is? At least it wasn't a nuthouse. Boys Town, I mean.

Anyway, I planted them after I got your letter, the following spring, thinking about the boy. He may have been okay, you know.

(She smiled. Poured a small glass of vodka. Returned to her place at his desk.)

Okay. Back to practical things: if you feel like it, you can have Sam Haines at the service station till the garden for you. He'll refuse money but likes a bottle of Scotch. A nice big man. Very quiet. Almost startlingly ugly; something ate away a good deal of his lower jaw. The Mini-Mart woman says cancer (in a stage whisper), her husband, shrapnel (in a booming voice). Country matters again. But you soon get past his scars. He's the one that told me the lake's haunted. Yes, indeed. Quite a crew supposed to dance among the weeds.

Let's see: movie stars from the time the place was a summer colony; *exclusive,* Sam says. People arrived by private railway car at Northampton and were driven here in a chauffeured Packard, owned (of course) by the local undertaker. Sam's uncle was the driver for a time—for both sets of occasions. It was, still is, a small village, even with the arrival of summer people, and the undertaker had a hard time making ends meet—even during epidemics. Sam explained all this as if excusing the undertaker, his uncle, himself. People here have to make money off outsiders, but they don't like it. Well, the undertaker's long gone now, or else I might be tempted to stick around and do one last good deed. "Die for the nice man, Billy." Smile.

Back to . . . Sam's a discreet man, shy really, but did say that the cases of booze usually equaled the cases of clothes. And that there was "talk." I ask you, where would we be without "talk"? The usual stuff: loose women, drinking, skinny dips, and one old boy saw—for this Sam dropped his voice—"an unformed baby peeping out the drain at one end of the lake." Sam's uncle was called, the undertaker notified, and the little thing was taken care of. After that, no more were found, but the place was finally abandoned when one of the "stars" died of blood poisoning. Her death, Sam said, was blamed on Christian Science.

The ghosts, by the way, are ladies only.

Who else? Civil War widows. Sam says those are the furious ones. When the waves roll across the lake in summer before a storm, there may be whitecaps. If so—although this seems highly unlikely—but who am I to say?—if so, you will know the widows are especially pissed off. There will be a whiff of salt in the air, because the widows, Sam says, are weeping. And the lake turns for an instant—salt. I suppose the kind of tears you shed when your fury has no place else to go—concentrated, thick.

It seems the place had an inordinate number of men die at Antietam (what would be ordinate?), and the ladies never quite regained their cool.

Finally, there are those known only as the tongueless women. These really are the most interesting, probably for me because they are the ones closest to us: watchmakers. If you look across the lake from the cottage, you will see a slender chimney. That's all that remains of the factory where they worked, except for some bricks scattered around. They were not under some spell or hexed. (Except they were.) No call for ducking stool or scold's bridle. Their tongues fell out, rotted in their heads, Sam says, because of the radium they used to dot above the numbers on the watch faces. They licked the brushes with their tongues.

Sam says they want to warn people that there's radium in the waters of the lake, but they can't speak. Of course they can't, they have no tongues—and if that weren't enough, the poor dears are dead. You'll know they're there by the shimmer of light on the water—early in the morning—a foolish fire.

Atmosphere, my dear.

It's too much sometimes.

Seed catalogs and seeds from last year (still good) are in the basket on top of the fridge. And you can get sets of tomatoes and peppers and lettuce, etc., from the farm up the road. "Up" means away from the village. It's run by a woman who takes in teenagers every summer. Sends them back to the city on Labor Day and waits for them to return. And they do, most of them.

Now, look, don't worry about me. You were sweet to offer but it's really better this way. These people know what to do, and my mind (or what's left of it) will be at rest. And I still have friends in the city. Yes.

Would that I were going to a villa in Tuscany and we were ten friends telling stories; wonderful, strange, bawdy stories to lift our spirits and pass the time, while the cloud forsakes us.

Speaking of the ladies under the lake, remember that incredible image of the mother in *Night of the Hunter*? Shelley Winters sitting upright in a Model T with her hair mingling with the weeds? Perhaps it's something like that? No.

I'm glad you're in the house. I hope you'll want to stay. It's yours in any case. I want a smooth transition.

More practical matters: I have had the place gone over by a cleaning woman—very thorough. Not to worry.

You have the number where I'll be. I'm sure I gave it to you.

(He hadn't.)

Anyway I'll call when I have the chance and see how you're getting along.

(Will he?)

I hope you love this place as much as I have.

Take care of yourself. And remember what they taught us, or what we learned by trial and error: God bless the child that's got his/her own.

Love, Bill

P.S. Some old clothes you might want to toss are in the oak bureau. Obviously the Goodwill won't want them. Forgive bitterness.

P.P.S. The family pall is stored in the crawl space. On to Berlin!

IV

She put the letter aside, rubbed her hands along the worn ridges of corduroy, trying to raise his scent.

Out of nowhere came their great-grandmother, speaking of the cholera in her girlhood and how the dead were wrapped and swaddled and rolled outside the door, to be carted away, carried off by a man who actually sang, "Bring out your dead." An office, the great-grandmother told them, given him for some trespass or other. "For no one would choose to handle the plague-dead, you see."

She did not say if he brought artistry to his street-cry. Was he as thrilling as the "freshee-fishee" man she remembered when their mother opened a box of frozen fishsticks? As looked-forward-to as the "icee-icee" man she imitated whenever Good Humor rang the bell outside the apartment house? The great-grandmother did not say.

She only said that to this day, on their island of origin, which neither child could remember, there was a cemetery with dirt so alive it was a crime to enter in.

The great-grandmother was impossible—so they all agreed. Telling Bill to stop blowing his nose in the sheets in the middle of the night, telling Jess that boys would sniff at her "like dogs" once her periods started. Jess was eleven, Bill thirteen, when the old woman died in a state hospital, sitting in a corner running an imaginary iron over an imaginary suit of clothes.

Jess had resented her sorely. Resented particularly being the girl, that she had the responsibility for the old woman while their parents worked and Bill played after-school games. Resented the old woman as a portent—this is what little girls turn into.

She stirs herself to the larder and finds a package of Carr's water biscuits—carefully crumbling a few in her hand she turns her attention to the cardinal puffed out in the snow.

The cardinal receives the crumbs and pokes at them with his beak. What is he doing here all alone?

Back inside she tries to shake off the chill. Laying more wood on the fire, she puts a kettle on, changes her mind, pours another vodka.

She sets the glass on the desk beside her brother's folded letter.

She reads it again.

She tries to compose a response, but he has given her no forwarding address, and for the moment she allows this to stop her.

Tomorrow, she determines, on her way to buy birdseed she will stop at the P.O. and get his new address. Surely he must have told them?

V

A child is shut on a glass porch. The panes are painted shut. It is early autumn. Through the glass he can hear the hum and crack of someone's radio broadcasting the World Series. It is a hot Indian summer day.

1959. The Dodgers in L.A. are about to clinch it. He strains to listen to noises from three thousand miles away. But it's so hard to keep his mind on the game.

1959. Jess is twelve; Bill is fourteen. Jess is at this moment sitting in the back of the family's '51 Nash, head out the window, staring at the running board. Tread almost worn away. Her eyes trace the remaining lines. Her mind is on her brother who is shut on the porch. Should she raise her head and focus her eyes two stories up, she might see him. She can't.

Mother and father are in the front seat, in their customary places, as she is in hers. They are in the front seat of the car, looking ahead. To the familiar street, comforting, two-family shingle houses, four-family, six-family apartment houses, streetlamps reaching across the pavement in graceful arcs. Children are pedaling two-wheelers with brakes in the rear wheels. Striped polo shirts zip down the hill. The whole scene could be a postcard, advertisement for a heartbreaking state of well-being—but for one thing.

The father presses the gas pedal and the car moves forward—carefully. Away from the house. Away from her brother.

A boy in a glass booth.

It is just past midday. The sun is magnified in the glass and seems to pinpoint the child on the closed-in porch, his skin reddening. There is no shade. Nowhere to hide from the brightness. Sweat gathers at his temples. On his top lip. He drips. The sweat curls his dark-brown hair. There is no relief in this heat, this light. He draws a breath and feels his throat closing. He gags in the heat and the light. Vomiting orange juice and milk and shredded wheat onto the floor of the porch.

In the front seat of the car is a bound notebook. Black-and-white marbled cardboard cover, it could have held spelling, geography, the dates of historical events. In the blank space for *subject* is written DIARY—PRIVATE PROPERTY. This notebook is wedged tight between the parents, cotton spine against gray wool upholstery.

The parents say nothing to her, nothing at all. There is silence in the car but for her mother's whimpers.

The parents do not explain why they have brought her along. Why should she expect an explanation?

All that has been directed at her all morning is "Get in the car! Get in the car!" as if a getaway were at hand and she was jeopardizing their lives by dawdling.

The parents say nothing to her, or to one another, and the father swings the heavy Nash around an intersection, down a hill, and into the parking lot of the Medical Arts building, brick with Tudor detail.

The sky is a cold blue. Amaranthus trees, prehistoric—as prehistoric as the roaches that congregate under the sink—what she and her brother call "A-Tree-Grows-in-Brooklyn-trees"—surround the cars, yellow.

She is told to wait.

Her mind is on her brother. The wildness of the morning.

His notebook spread wide open at their father's place. Between the toast and coffee and the eggs over-easy. Is he about to catch hell for doodling Crazy Horse across a geometry lesson?

Nothing that ordinary.

A thin film of yellow—almost hard—is over one sentence where she glances. *I think I am.* Her father catches her looking, she knows to look away.

Her father ignores his son, looks directly at her mother, then back at the page.

"Jesus Christ! Jesus Christ!"

He chants it into silence.

"What?" Jess can't help herself. She is commanded to leave the table. "You, stay." Bill must remain.

As she leaves, she glances back at the three. Bill's head is hung. "And don't I have any rights?" She barely hears him; he speaks the words into the placemat.

Later, when she asked him—much later, when they were all grown-up—when she asked him if she should have stuck up for him that morning, he reminded her she was younger, and a girl, and probably had no idea what it was about, and to forget about it.

But she didn't.

"What in Christ's name do you know about rights?"

The father silenced the son.

In her bed, where she lay staring at the ceiling, Jess heard the noises of tears, whispers. A sudden shout from their mother: "Goddamit! Stop it! Goddamit! Stop it! Don't you know it's a sickness?"

Then silence.

And then the rustle of parents summoning an expert: calling the minister, informing him the son of a cousin was in trouble, getting a name to call. Apologizing that it is an emergency, a Saturday morning, a beautiful day.

They arrange the visit.

The smell of vomit on the glass-enclosed porch only made things worse for him. He began to sob.

She is not at all certain what has gone on. Only that there is something wrong with her brother, and she wishes that she had never wished him dead because he was a boy, and the logical favorite.

She must have waited in the car for more than an hour. Needing to use the bathroom. Afraid to leave and ask the people in the diner across the street. Afraid her parents will return and find the Nash abandoned. Their daughter gone.

"Are you trying to worry us to death?"

He thought briefly about smashing the glass with the heavy brass lamp and driving the shards into his wrists, his neck. He did not think about smashing the glass with the heavy brass lamp and sliding through an opening, dropping to the lawn below like a cat, getting away. Nor about taking the lamp by the base and swinging it faster and faster, spinning with it, laying waste to his mother's Hummels, carefully displayed on bric-a-brac shelves.

Jess watched the parents leave the front of the building. They looked as if in mourning, and she realized they had put on their best clothes, the ones they had worn to the great-grandmother's funeral the year before.

They were strangers in a strange land.

They opened the door of the Nash and slid into their places, the mother clasping the notebook to her. With a sigh the father started the car.

"Did you see the doctor?" Jess asked.

"Yes, dear," her mother responded.

"Is Bill going to be okay?"

"In time."

The landmarks of the neighborhood went by again: candy store, luncheonette, branch library, the Store of a Million Items, statue to the war dead, bar with pictures of Miss Rheingold contestants in the window, church, and then, almost home, the houses.

VI

Bill took his treatment one afternoon a week, heading at the last bell in one direction while his classmates went their own ways.

Sitting in the office of Dr. Blanke, in the Medical Arts, Bill focused his attention as best he could on the figurine on the table beside him. His mind, in this waiting room, could not hold on to words printed on a page. His schoolbooks remained in his schoolbag, resting against the leg of the green leatherette chair in which he sat. The magazines arranged on the low table in front of him went untouched.

Each time he sat there, the fluorescent light flickering overhead, he began by staring at the three-dimensional portrait beside him; an old man with a spindly beard and straw hat, someone's idea of a Chinese fisherman. His bare porcelain feet were drawn up under him on a porcelain rock. He dangled his thin line from his rod, a sliver of bamboo.

Bill thought the old man was one of a kind, like himself, and would probably have been startled to be faced with a line of identical old men on a shelf in the Store of a Million Items. A crate of old men unloaded onto the docks at the foot of the hill from the Medical Arts, all the way from Taiwan, excelsior clinging to their feet.

Bill had not even spoken to the other boy about it, just noted in the diary, *I think I may be. I think I am.* Following those speculations with the only word he had ever heard to describe it.

At the end of the old man's line hung a fish, from a small hook, a fish made of a deep green glass, with tiny bubbles inside. Bill stared at the figurine, then put his head back, curved his spine into a question mark, and shut his eyes. He imagined the old man in a safe place, ten thousand miles away, at the edge of the river, clean and cold, in which there were smooth, flat rocks. A thick fog settled around his shoulders, embracing him.

Behind him, on the bank, was a fire that warmed him, over which he would cook his fish.

You could detach the fish from the line. Each time, as the nurse was about to summon him, Bill pocketed the fish, feeling its smooth glassiness, hard and cool, his fist tightening around his amulet, the thing between himself and *cure,* as they fixed the electrodes to his head.

The green fish. Burning. Jelly sandwiches on white bread. A bruise over his left eye where he convulsed against a radiator.

The treatments were expensive. The family left their apartment in the six-family house and moved into a smaller place over a drugstore, underneath a man and a woman who battled almost every night.

The treatments were expensive, and they did not take. He was sent to a tough place up the Hudson, where they taught him carpentry. And when he returned, he knew enough to build some shelves for his mother's spices, and to ask a girl to the Junior Prom.

VII

Jess has read the letter yet again. She is not ready to compose an answer. She folds the letter and puts it between the pages of her ill-kept journal. Ill-kept by moonlight, proud Titania—silly joke.

She begins to arrange her things on top of her brother's desk but cannot make a dent in his presence—nor does she want to.

She sits at the desk for some time.

Bill's green glass fish, which he's had since God knows when, is sitting on a bookshelf. The fish reflects the red of the firelight. Hiroshima fish, she thinks, all of a sudden. And just as suddenly can hear her brother's voice: "Jesus Christ! Do you have to find images of oppression everywhere?"

Later, in the bath, she slides down against the porcelain. As she lowers her body, the water comes up to her breasts, and two dark knobs break above the surface of the water like buoys. The water rises to her neck as she lowers herself farther.

She has tried her entire life, or so it seems to her, not to see that Indian summer morning as the beginning of the end. The moment when she measured her parents for terror, and saw them as two frightened strangers. She has tried not to blame her brother for this terrible revelation that made her feel unsafe, alone. And the aftermath of that morning only confirmed this, so that when the family finally exploded, she was left only numb.

They had gone on pretending for years. Taking two-week vacations in the tiny summer cottage by the lake, even though finances were stretched to the limit. Without Bill at first, then with him, and she could see them measuring him all the while, and her as well.

There is a window next to the tub, and she can see the moonlight skating across the ice. No ghosts yet. Except family.

Their great-grandmother believed in ghosts. Had seen them, she said, "as clear as day." Her cinnamon eyes would light at the memory of a handsome sea captain she had encountered in the upstairs gallery of a country house where she had gone for a dance. "And when I told my host and hostess," she paused, "they told me he had been dead for many years."

Like most children, Jess and Bill had loved the idea of ghosts and begged for more. And the great-grandmother was at her best in the telling.

The water is getting cool. She rises, dripping.

Dry now, clean and robed and warmed, she sits in front of the desk again.

She tacks postcards to the white wall above the desk: Billie Holiday; Chief's robe from the Third Phase; the Second Bible Quilt of Harriet Powers; ANC women.

See, Bill—also the resisters—and the artists. People like you. How long it has taken for her to say that.

Above her postcards Bill had hung the *Magic Glasses* of Edwin Romanzo Elmer. Crystal sugar bowl on a marble counter. Into the crystal is placed the magic—the magnifier, prism, divider of light. The magnifying glass has split the landscape, which comes into the scene through a window. On either side is reflected a farmyard, woodpile. The concern for sustenance—marble surface for kneading bread, sugar bowl, woodpile—warmth, future. In the center of the magnifying glass—where the light has been split—is a sliver of dark.

VIII

She had seen no ghosts, took the foolish fire over the lake for what it was.

But the spring was as Bill had promised. On a walk one morning in the woods around the lake she found the first (at least, the first to her) lady slippers. Dewdrops clung to them. They seemed to have sprung out of the dry needles of the forest floor.

She found herself at the end of the lake, near to the slender chimney Bill had written about. Bricks scattered on the ground, the consistency of stale cake, crumbly. She picked up a brick and could trace the cracks in it, the pieces of sand, clay, whatever came together to make it into something that would support a building, become a building. Poking her foot through the needles revealed something shiny. The delicate wand of a sweep second hand.

IX

May 31, 1988

Dear Bill,
Today they had a celebration on the common for Memorial Day—you probably remember.

Nothing like beginning a letter with a memento mori—sorry.

I drove by as it was going on and saw men in uniform, fatigues, women in hats and summer dresses and white gloves, a few children and a few old men. The minister presiding over all. Then a roll call by a woman wearing a Gold Star. Everyone gathered around the statue to the Union dead, the drummer boy. The scratch of the "Battle Hymn of the Republic" in the air, broadcast over a loudspeaker set on the porch of the church. And then some lanky boy in blue jeans and white T-shirt—straight out of *Seventeenth Summer*—blew Taps. And after that people drifted away.

The whole thing moved me, appealed to the historian in me. Later, Sam Haines came by the house (he asked to be remembered to you) and offered to rototill the garden. He told me it was a little late but figured I was too shy to ask, or maybe didn't know to ask. He said it was the usual arrangement that he could keep any pieces of glass or china or metal he might find during the tilling. Said he used the stuff "for decoration." I said sure. You only mentioned a bottle of Scotch to me and I'll get that in the morning. Maybe he never told you about the other? Well, it's no big deal. Interesting though.

His face is at first startling, as you say, but there's something so calming about his presence.

I am sitting at your desk, writing this, watching the lake, but no whitecaps yet. I would have thought Memorial Day, the remnant of Taps carrying across the water, would have stirred your widows?

Overheard at the Mini-Mart:

First woman: I hope the Democrats get in in November and do something about this homeless problem. I'm tired of tripping over people when I go up to Boston. All the Republicans know to spend money on is guns.

Second woman: Do you want to be invaded by the Russians?

First woman: At least we'd have free housing.

Second woman: Yes, but what kind of housing? Twenty people in one room.

Oh dear.

I'll also go up the road tomorrow and get some sets. Tomatoes, mostly, lettuce, broccoli. Sam asked me what I intended to plant and then advised me about bugs. Cutting a collar for the broccoli out of aluminum foil to deceive the cutworms—one piece of advice. Here again I'm telling you something you already know.

The place just gets more beautiful. The asparagus is coming along. Would it be worth it to you to have me send some down by bus or something? Let me know. Or do you just want it here—that's what I figured, but thought I'd ask anyway. It's a spectacular green right now and the spears are beginning to poke through the earth. The Jerusalem artichoke is on its/their way too.

You know, it's funny. What's funny is that you still see me as this hothead—as hotheaded as the little girl in the schoolyard (one of the "not-born-heres," as the principal called us) who smashed a girl's glasses when she made another girl cry. "I am in the world to change the world," the grown-up version of that little girl told you once, and you called the words (and me too?) "impossibly dangerous." Why didn't I, that morning, do something? If I could fight for a stranger why couldn't I fight for you? Because they were our parents? Because the whole scene was so crazy, the threat of calamity so pervasive? Ma always said I cared more for strangers than for family, remember? A place was cleared in me that morning twenty-five years ago. I was emptied. I never saw any one of us the same way again.

For years I blamed you of course. Thinking that I had to be the good girl par excellence to make up for you, the bad boy who left the task to me. Thinking, "Why couldn't he just take his medicine?" You went off without a word and at night, night after bloody night, I would hear Ma crying as Pa slipped deeper and deeper into his silences. Two terrified people.

. . .

She looks up from the letter; across the water are two figures, strolling arm in arm, out of a tintype. No. Probably just a couple of aging hippies, never having outgrown their granny dresses, still seeing the world through their granny glasses.

I thought for a moment I saw your ghosts.

Oh, shit. She tears the page across and begins the letter again.

Keeper of All Souls

NOVEMBER 2 was the day Sam made.

Just after the hullabaloo of Halloween, as hand-carved pumpkins shriveled on folks' porches and stoops, the parade of weekend leaf-peepers diminished, and fall began to bump against winter, Sam's day came and went.

The air was crisp, the church glistened white on the common, fallen leaves crunched underfoot, the sky reflected in the cold waters of the lake.

A postcard, yes, but it did look like that.

A rack of postcards spun inside the door of SAM'S SERVICE STATION, as the sign in front read. Spun slowly, urged on by the hot-air vent in the floor below. Fall and winter scenes mostly, since Mrs. Sam rearranged the rack every few months. Mostly scenes shot during the forties and fifties, or so, but a stranger would never know, since there were neither cars nor people in the pictures to give the time away. Timeless—but only to the eye ignorant of the history of the village, someone passing through in haste, eager to get somewhere else. In one shot, elms stood bare against a blue sky, when elms encircled the common before the Dutch Elm struck. In another, the watch factory was intact, had smoke streaming from its chimney, and a legend reading: FINEST TIMEPIECES IN NEW ENGLAND MANUFACTURED HERE.

Sam's was an old-fashioned gas station; no fancy pumps, one grease pit, outdoor thermometer advertising Royal Crown Cola, a ladies' room with chintz curtains and a calendar from the local undertaker—put there by Mrs. Sam, "to make women think."

Sam had switched petroleum companies several times over the years. On the disk atop the pole in front of the station you could detect the shadow of a star underneath the faint outline of a flying horse that rested on a delicate scallop shell. These pentimenti reminded Sam of times past, and he would not neaten the sign, not even when the new dealer offered to replace the entire thing, pole and all, with the logo of the latest corporate giant—huge and ugly letters, no image at all.

Mrs. Sam had charge of the ladies' room, and Sam took charge of the men's. On the wall above the single urinal and over the rusted sink, bright painted letters spoke:

IDLENESS IS THE SEPULCHRE OF THE LIVING MAN
KEEP NO MORE CATS THAN WILL KILL MICE
THERE IS AN ALL-SEEING EYE WATCHING YOU

Once one man emerged, hands dripping, eyes lit, asking Sam, "Did you write those words?"

"Which ones?"

"The ones about the all-seeing eye."

Sam nodded.

"I'm a Christian too," the man spoke too enthusiastically, "read this." He thrust something printed into Sam's hands.

Sam acknowledged the man's offering with another nod, then let the booklet slide to the floor.

"A man's beliefs are his most intimate thing," he spoke aloud, softly, then went out back for his brush and paint, adding that thought to the wall.

Out back, behind the station, was another, much smaller building where Sam kept his paints and other things. This had a sign over the door also: SAM'S WORKSHOP. KEEP OUT. And people did. Even his wife.

This was Sam's place of retreat and meditation, where he got his ideas and planned things. Here, he said, he became "plain."

Against one wall he had fashioned an altar from aluminum foil over wood. The altar rose from floor to ceiling, and stretched from side to side of the small room. On its front shelf were things Sam arranged and rearranged, as his vision moved him. Things collected. Things the earth had yielded after a summer downpour, the spring thaw. Things the blades of his tiller turned up. Shards working their way back to the surface. Sam walked through the village, pushing his tiller with one hand, a canvas sack in the other, eyes downcast. You never know what you might find.

Pieces of colored glass, fragments of medicine bottles, Sunday china, everyday ware. A piece of brick. Rusted watch face. Glass-headed, cloth-bodied dolly. Spent shells. Rubber nipples. Ribbon. Wooden letters from a printer's tray. Ring of skeleton keys.

Every place on the altar is cluttered with relics. Everything man-made.

A small clothbound book with *Record* scrolled across the cover is at one end of the shelf. This is "Sam's Book of the Dead," as is written on the first page, in which he enters the names of the dead on the day of All Souls.

That done, he sits back and sings the dead to sleep. He thought it was the least he could do.

Transactions

I

A BLONDE, BLUE-EYED CHILD, about three years old—no one will know her exact age, ever—is sitting in the clay of a country road, as if she and the clay are one, as if she is the first human, but she is not.

She is dressed in a boy's shirt, sewn from osnaburg check, which serves her as a dress. Her face is scabbed. The West Indian sun, even at her young age, has made rivulets underneath her eyes where waters run.

She is always hungry.

She works the clay into a vessel that will hold nothing.

Lizards fly between the tree ferns that stand at the roadside.

A man is driving an American Ford, which is black and eating up the sun. He wears a Panama hat with a red band around it. He carries a different brightly colored band for each day of the week. He is pale and the band interrupts his paleness. His head is balding and he takes care to conceal his naked crown. In his business, appearance is important.

He is practicing his Chinese as he negotiates the mountain road, almost washed away by the rains of the night before. His abacus rattles on the seat beside him. With each swerve and bump, and there are many, the beads of the abacus quiver and slide.

He is alone.

"You should see some of these shopkeepers, my dear," he tells his wife. "They make this thing sing."

His car is American and he has an American occupation. He is a traveling salesman. He travels into the interior of the island, his car packed with American goods.

Many of the shopkeepers are Chinese, but like him, like everyone it seems, are in love with American things. He brings American things into the interior, into the clearing cut from ruinate. Novelties and necessities. Witch hazel. Superman. Band-Aids. Zane Grey. Chili con carne. Cap guns. Coke syrup. Fruit cocktail. Camels.

Marmalade and Marmite, Bovril and Senior Service, the weekly *Mirror* make room on the shopkeepers' shelves.

The salesman has always wanted a child. His wife says she never has. "Too many pickney in the world already," she says, then kisses her teeth. His wife is brown-skinned. He is not. He is pale, with pale eyes.

The little girl sitting in the road could be his, but the environment of his wife's vagina is acid. And then there is her brownness. Well.

And then he sees her. Sitting filthy and scabbed in the dirt road as he comes around a corner counting to a hundred in Chinese. She is crying.

Has he startled her?

He stops the car.

He and his wife have been married for twenty years. They no longer sleep next to each other. They sleep American-style, as his wife calls it. She has noticed that married couples in the movies sleep apart. In "Hollywood" beds. She prevails on Mr. Dickens (a handyman she is considering bringing into the house in broad daylight) to construct "Hollywood" beds from mahogany.

The salesman gets out of his car and walks over to the little girl.

He asks after her people.

She points into the bush.

He lifts her up. He uses his linen hanky to wipe off her face. He blots her eye-corners, under her nose. He touches her under her chin.

"Lord, what a solemn lickle ting."

He hears her tummy grumble.

At the edge of the road there is a narrow path down a steep hillside.

The fronds of a coconut tree cast shadows across the scabs on her face. He notices they are rusty. They will need attention.

He thinks he has a plan.

At the end of a narrow path is a clearing with some mauger dogs, packed red-dirt yard, and a wattle house set on cement blocks.

The doorway, there is no door, yawns into the darkness.

He walks around the back, still holding the child, the dogs sniffing at him, licking at the little girl's bare feet.

A woman, blonde and blue-eyed, is squatting under a tree. He is afraid to approach any closer, afraid she is engaged in some intimate activity, but soon enough she gets up, wipes her hand on her dress, and walks toward him.

Yes, this is her little girl, the woman says in a strangely accented voice. And the salesman realizes he's stumbled on the descendants of a shipload of Germans, sent here as convicts or cheap labor, he can't recall which. There are to this day pockets of them in the deep bush.

He balances the little girl in one arm—she weighs next to nothing—removes his hat, inclines his balding head toward the blonder woman. She lowers her blue eyes. One has a cloud, the start of a cataract from too much sun.

He knows what he wants.

The woman has other children, sure, too many, she says. He offers twenty American dollars, just like that, counting out the single notes, and promises the little girl will have the best of everything, always, and that he loves children and has always wanted one of his own, but he and his wife have never been so blessed.

The woman says something he does not understand. She points to a small structure at the side of the house. Under a peaked roof is a statue of the Virgin Mary, a dish of water at her feet. On her head is a coronet of lignum vitae. She is rude but painted brightly, like the Virgins at the roadside in Bavaria, carved along routes of trade and plague. Her shawl is colored indigo.

"Liebfrau," the woman repeats.

He nods.

The Virgin's shawl is flecked with yellow, against indigo, like the Milky Way against the black of space.

The salesman is not Catholic, but never mind. He promises the little girl will attend the Convent of the Immaculate Conception at Constant Spring, the very best girls' school on the island. He goes on about their uniforms. Very handsome indeed. Royal blue neckties and white dresses. Panama hats with royal blue hatbands. He points to the band around his own hat by way of explanation.

The royal blue will make his daughter's eyes bright.

This woman could not be more of a wonder to him. She is a stranger in this landscape, this century, she of an indentured status, a petty theft.

He wonders at her loneliness. No company but the Virgin Mother.

The woman extends her hand for the money, puts it in the side pocket of her dress. She strokes the head of her daughter, still in the salesman's arms.

"She can talk?"

"Jah, no mus'?"

A squall comes from inside the darkness of the house, and the woman turns, her dress becoming damp.

"Well, good-bye then," the salesman says.

She turns back. She opens her dress and presses a nipple, dripping, into the mouth of her little girl. "Bye, bye," she says. And she is gone.

He does not know what to think.

The little girl makes no fuss, not even a whimper, as he carries her away, and he is suddenly afraid he has purchased damaged goods. What if she's foolish? It will be difficult enough to convince his brown-skinned wife to bring a white-skinned child into the house. If she is fool-fool God help him.

Back at the car he tucks her into the front seat, takes his penknife, and opens a small tin of fruit cocktail.

He points to the picture on the label, the glamorous maraschino cherry. "Wait till you taste this, darlin'. It come all the way from America." Does she have the least sense of what America is?

He wipes away the milk at the corners of her mouth.

He takes a spoon from the glove compartment.

"You can feed yourself?"

She says nothing, so he begins to spoon the fruit cocktail into her. Immediately she brightens and opens her mouth wide, tilting her head back like a little bird.

In no time she's finished the tin.

"Mustn't eat too fast, sweetheart. Don't want to get carsick."

"Nein, nein," she says with a voice that's almost a growl.

She closes her eyes against the sun flooding the car.

"Never mind," he says, "we'll be off soon." He wraps the spoon and empty fruit cocktail tin into a sheet of the *Daily Gleaner,* putting the package on the floor of the backseat.

Next time he will pour some condensed milk into the tinned fruit, making it even sweeter.

There's a big American woman who runs a restaurant outside Milk River. She caters to the tourists who come to take the famously radioactive waters. And to look at the crocodiles. She also lets rooms. She will let him a room for the night. In return he will give her the American news she craves. She says she once worked in the movies. He doesn't know if he believes her.

He puts the car in gear and drives away from the clearing.

His heart is full. Is this how women feel? he wonders, as he glances at the little girl, now fast asleep.

What has he done? She is his treasure, his newfound thing, and he never even asked her name. What will you call this child? the priest will ask. Now she is yours. He must have her baptized. Catholic or Anglican, he will decide.

He will have to bathe her. He will ask the American woman to help him. He will take a bathroom at the mineral spring and dip her into the famous waters, into the "healing stream," like the old song says.

He will baptize her himself. The activity of the spring, of world renown, will mend her skin. The scabs on her face are crusted over, and there are more on her arms and legs. She might well have scurvy, even in the midst of a citrus grove.

But the waters are famous.

As he drives, he alternates between making plans and imagining his homecoming and his wife's greeting. You must have taken leave of your senses, busha. She calls him busha when she's angry and wants him to stand back. No, busha. Is who tell you we have room fi pickney? He will say he had no choice. Was he to leave this little girl in the middle of a country road covered with dirt and sores and hungry? Tell me, busha, tell me jus' one ting: Is how many pickney you see this way on your travels, eh? Is why you don't bring one home sooner? Tell me that.

Everybody wants a child that favors them, that's all.

She will kiss her teeth.

If she will let him have his adoption, he will say, she can have the other side of the house for her and Mr. Dickens. It will be simple. Once he plays that card, there will be no going back. They will split the house down the middle. That will be that.

Like is drawn to like. Fine to fine. Coarse to coarse.

There are great advantages to being a traveling salesman in this place. He learns the island by heart. Highland and floodplain, sinkhole and plateau. Anywhere a shopkeeper might toss up, fix some shelves inside a zinc-roofed shed, open shop.

He respects the relentlessness of shopkeepers. They will nest anywhere. You can be in the deepest bush and come upon a tin sign advertising Nescafé, and find a group of people gathered as if the shed were a town hall, which it well might be.

Everything is commerce, he cannot live without it.

On the road sometimes he is taken by what is around him. He is distracted by gorges, ravines possessed of an uncanny green. Anything could dwell there. If he looks closer, he will enter the island's memory, the petroglyphs of a disappeared people. The birdmen left by the Arawak.

Once he took a picnic lunch of cassava cake and fried fish and ginger beer into the burial cave at White Marl and left a piece of cassava at the feet of one of the skeletons.

He gazes at the remains of things. Stone fences, fallen, moss-covered, which might mark a boundary in Somerset. Ruined windmills. A circular ditch where a coffle marked time on a treadmill. As steady as an orbit.

A salesman is free, he tells himself. He makes his own hours, comes and goes as he pleases. People look forward to his arrival, and not just for the goods he carries. He is part troubadour. If he's been to the movies in town, he will recount the plot for a crowd, describe the beauty of the stars, the screen washed in color.

These people temper his loneliness.

But now, now.

Now he thinks he'll never be lonely again.

II

The Bath is located on the west bank of Milk River, just south of where the Rio Brontë, much tamer than its name, branches off.

The waters of the Bath rise through the karst, the heart of stone. The ultimate source of the Bath is an underground saline spring, which might suggest a relationship with the sea. The relationship with the sea is suggested everywhere; the limestone that composes more of the land than any other substance is nothing but the skeletons of marine creatures.

"From the sea we come, to the sea we shall return." His nursemaid used to chant this as he lay in his pram on King's Parade.

The water of the Bath is a steady temperature of ninety-one degrees Fahrenheit (thirty-three degrees Centigrade). The energy of the water is radiant, fifty-five times more active than Baden-Baden, fifty times more active than Vichy.

Such is the activity that bathers are advised not to remain immersed for more than fifteen minutes a day.

In the main building the bather may read testimonials to the healing faculties of the waters. These date to 1794, when the first bathrooms were opened.

> Lord Salisbury was cured of lowness of spirit
> Hamlet, his slave, escaped depraved apprehensions
> MAY 1797, ANNO DOMINI
>
> Mrs. Horne was cured of the hysteria and loss of spleen
> DECEMBER 1802, ANNO DOMINI
>
> The Governor's Lady regained her appetites
> OCTOBER 1817, ANNO DOMINI
>
> Septimus Hart, Esq., banished his dread
> JULY 1835, ANNO DOMINI
>
> The Hon. Catherine Dillon was cured of a mystery
> FEBRUARY 1900, ANNO DOMINI

The waters bore magical properties. Indeed, some thought the power of the Lord was in them.

. . .

The salesman's car glides into the gravel parking lot of the Little Hut, the American woman's restaurant. She named it after a movie she made with Ava Gardner and Stewart Granger. A movie she made sounds grandiose; she picked up after Miss Gardner, stood in for her during long shots.

She hears the car way back in the kitchen of the restaurant, where she's supervising Hamlet VII in the preparation of dinner. Tonight, pepper pot soup to start, followed by curried turtle, rice and peas, a Bombay mango cut in half and filled with vanilla ice cream.

The American woman, her head crowned with a thick black braid, comes out of the doorway onto the verandah that runs around the Little Hut and walks toward the salesman's car.

"Well, well, what have we got here?" She points to the passenger seat in front. "What are you? A kidnapper or something?"

She's wearing a khaki shirt with red and black epaulets, the tails knotted at her midsection, and khaki shorts. The kitchen steam has made her clothes limp, and sweat stains bloom on her back and under her arms. Her feet are bare. She wears a silver bangle around one ankle.

"Gone native" is one of her favorite ways of describing herself, whether it means bare feet, a remnant of chain, or swimming in Milk River alongside the crocodiles.

Still, she depends on the salesman to bring her news of home.

"I've got your magazines, your *Jets,*" the salesman says, ignoring her somewhat bumptious remark.

It was late afternoon by now. A quick negotiation about a room for the night and then he will take his little sleepyhead, who has not stirred, to be bathed. He has great faith in the waters from all he has heard.

He asks the American woman about a room.

"There's only one available right now," she tells him. "I've been overrun."

The room is located behind the restaurant, next to the room where Hamlet VII sleeps.

The salesman, she remembers his name is Harold (he was called "Prince Hal" at school he told her), hers is Rosalind, is not crazy about sleeping in what he considers servants' quarters and tells her so.

"My daughter," he begins.

Rosalind interrupts him. "You may as well take it."

He's silent.

"It's clean and spacious," she tells him, "lots of room for you, and for her." She nods in the direction of the little girl. She can't help but be curious, aware from his earlier visits that he said he had no children, that his wife had turned her back on him, or so he said, that he equated being a traveler for an import firm with being a pirate on the Spanish Main, right down to the ribbon on his hat and his galleon of a car.

"Footloose and fancy-free" was how he described himself to her, but Rosalind didn't buy it.

He seemed like a remnant to her. So many of them did. There was something behind the thickness of green, in the crevices of bone; she wore a sign of it on her ankle.

"Very well, then. I'll take it."

"You won't be sorry."

"I need to take her to the Bath presently. Will you come?"

"Me? Why?"

"I need a woman to help me with her."

"I thought you said she was your daughter."

"I did."

"What's wrong with her?"

"Her skin is broken."

"Well, they have attendants at the Bath to help you."

"Okay, then."

Rosalind had in mind a stack of *Jets,* a pitcher of iced tea, and a break into the real world, Chicago, New York, Los Angeles, before the deluge of bathers, thirsty for something besides radioactive waters, descended on her.

"It will be fine. Just don't let her stay in too long."

"I won't."

"How much do I owe you for the magazines?"

"Not to worry."

"Well, then, the room is gratis."

That was fair. He felt a bit better.

At the Bath a white-costumed woman showed him and the little girl into a bathroom of their own. She unveiled the child and made no comment at the sores running over her tummy and back. As she dipped the child into the waters, an unholy noise bounded across the room, beating against the tile, skating the surface of the waters, testing the room's closeness. "Nein! Nein!" the little girl screamed over and over again. The salesman had to cover his ears.

The waters did not bubble or churn; there was nothing to be afraid of. The salesman finally found his tongue. "What is the matter, sweetheart? You never feel water touch your skin before this?"

But the child said nothing in response, only took some gasps of breath, and suddenly he felt like a thief, not the savior he preferred.

"Nein! Nein!" she started up again, and the woman in white put her hand over his treasure's mouth, clamping it tight and holding her down in the temperate waters rising up from the karst.

She held her down the requisite fifteen minutes and then lifted her out, shaking her slightly, drying her, and only two bright tears were left, one on each cheek, and he knew if he got close enough, he would be reflected in them.

The woman swaddled the child in a white towel, saying, "No need to return this." She glanced back, in wonder he was sure, then turned the knob and was gone.

If the waters were as magic as promised, maybe he would not have to return. He lifted the little girl up in his arms and felt a sharp sensation as she sank her baby teeth into his cheek, drawing blood.

The salesman had tied the stack of *Jets* tightly, and Rosalind had to work the knife under the string, taking care not to damage the cover of the magazine on top. The string gave way and the stack slid apart. The faces of Jackie Wilson, Sugar Ray Robinson, and Dorothy Dandridge glanced up at her. A banner across one cover read EMMETT TILL, THE STORY INSIDE. She arranged herself on a wicker chaise on the verandah and began her return to the world she'd left behind.

She took the photographs—there were photographs—released by his mother—he was an only child—his mother was a widow—he stuttered—badly—these were some details—she took the photographs into her—into herself—and she would never let them go.

She would burn the magazine out back with the kitchen trash—drop it in a steel drum and watch the images curl and melt against turtle shell—she'd give the other magazines to Hamlet as she always did—he had a scrapbook of movie stars and prize fighters and jazz musicians.

The mother had insisted on the pictures, so said *Jet*. This is my son. Swollen by the beating—by the waters of the River Pearl—misshapen—unrecognizable—monstrous.

Hamlet heard her soft cries out in the kitchen, over the steam of turtle meat.

"Missis is all right?"

She made no answer to his question, only waved him off with one hand, the other covering the black-and-white likeness of the corpse. She did not want Hamlet to see where she came from.

America's waterways.

She left the verandah and went out back.

Blood trickled from the salesman's cheek.

"Is vampire you vampire, sweetheart?"

"What are you telling me?"

They were sitting on the verandah after dinner, the tourists having strolled to Milk River, guided by Hamlet, to watch the crocodiles in the moonlight.

"Are they man-eaters? Are they dangerous?" one tourist woman inquired.

"They are more afraid of you than you could possibly be of them," Hamlet told her.

The little sharp-toothed treasure was swaddled in the towel from the Bath and curled up on a chaise next to Rosalind. Tomorrow the salesman would have to buy her decent clothes.

If he decided to keep her.

But he must keep her.

"I gave the woman twenty American dollars for her."

"What is she?"

What indeed, this blonde and blue-eyed thing, filled with vanilla ice cream, bathing in the moonlight that swept the verandah.

Not a hot moon tonight. Not at all.

He rubbed his cheek where the blood had dried.

"Her people came from overseas, long time ago."

They sat in the quiet, except for the back noise of the tropics. As if unaware of any strangeness around them.

Silence.

His wife would never stand for it.

He might keep his treasure here. He would pay her room and board, collect her on his travels. A lot of men had outside children. He would keep in touch with his.

Why was he such a damn coward?

Rosalind would never agree to such a scheme, that he knew.

But no harm in asking.

It would have to wait. He'd sleep on it.

But when he woke, all he woke to was a sharp pain in his cheek. He touched the place where the pain seemed keenest and felt a round hardness that did not soften to his touch but sent sharp sensations clear into his eyes.

When he raised his eyelids, the room was a blur. He waited for his vision to clear but nothing came. The red hatband was out of sight.

He felt the place in the bed where his treasure had slept. There was a damp circle on the sheet. She was gone.

Monster

MY GRANDMOTHER'S HOUSE. Small. In the middle of nowhere. The heart of the country, as she is the heart of the country. Mountainous, dark, fertile.

One starting point.

My grandmother's house is electrified in the sixties. Nothing fancy. No appliances. A couple of bare light bulbs sway on black queues in the parlor, dining room, cast a glare across the verandah, cutting moonlight. Now scripture can be read at all hours, no fear of damaging eyes.

There are two pictures on the walls of the parlor. Two photographs, hung so high the images are out of reach, distorted as they rest against the molding, slanting downward. Her two living sons. Each combed and slicked to resemble a forties movie star. The one with the blue-black hair and widow's peak thinks he favors Robert Taylor. This alone will draw the girls to him, he thinks, somewhere back in time.

Today he is bald and rubs guano into his scalp over morning coffee to ignite the follicles. His wife belches loudly and slaps her feet across the tile floor, her soles as wide as a gravedigger's shovel.

Pictures taken in a studio in downtown Kingston, where touched-up brides (lightened to reflect the island obsession) grace the window.

My grandmother's faith is severe and forbids graven images (she makes an exception for her sons), dancing, smoking, drinking (except for the blood of the Lamb, bottled and shipped from another end of the Empire).

Does she look the other way when her boys take a dark girl into the bush? Does she object? I have no way of knowing and wouldn't dare to ask.

Graven images include motion pictures, of course. Although she has never seen a movie, she has seen advertisements for them in the *Daily Gleaner,* right next to the race results. Nasty things.

Like most evil, brought from elsewhere.

My father loves the movies to death, as do I. Some of our best times are spent in the dark, thrilled by the certainty that in the dark anything can happen. It's out of our control. The screen says: sit back and enjoy the show!

We lived some of my childhood in New York City, visiting Jamaica once or twice a year, down the way where the nights are gay and the sun shines daily on the mountaintop. These were the fifties, sixties. In the City we go (at least) twice a week to the local movie house, the St. George, where we escape, comforted by the smell of popcorn mingling with disinfectant.

We are comforted also by the name. We live in America, as we will always call it, but are children of the Empire. St. George is our patron, his cross our standard. We are triangular people, our feet on three islands.

The interior of the movie house is overwhelmingly red, imaging Seville, Granada. The St. George sports no dragon, no maiden chained to a rock, no knight in shining armor, but is decorated as if a picture book of Spain sometime after 1492. A trompe l'oeil bullfighter makes a pass outside the men's room. Señoritas with mantillas and filigreed fans hang above our seats, gossiping across wrought iron balconies, duenna watchful.

Built in the heyday of the movie palaces, the delicacy of the Alhambra arches across the screen; whose dream was this?

"Someday, Rachel, someday, when we're long gone and people, archaeologists, dig this up, like Schliemann at Troy, they'll think it was one of our cathedrals. You mark my words."

Against his projection of the future our time spans come together; the barest ellipse separates us. We're practically contemporaries. "When we're long gone." Imagine saying that to a child.

"Our lives are written in disappearing ink."

I lie awake, terrified.

I am about nine or ten, but I know all about Schliemann and the four levels of Troy; in the time before the theater darkens my father instructs me in things that fascinate him. Victoriana. The ripping. "From crotch to crown, my dear, from crotch to crown."

When the chandelier in the ceiling begins to blink off and on, signifying the start of the show, we fall into silence.

We prefer mysteries, war movies, westerns. Love stories and musicals are for girls. Like my mother, who never joins us in the dark.

Science fiction is our absolute favorite, with horror close behind. The disembodied hands. The Man with the X-Ray Eyes.

THEM!

The redness of the Forbidden Planet.

"You must make allowances for my daughter, gentlemen. She's never known another human being except her father."

At night all hell breaks loose.

"What do you think they eat, Rachel?"

"Vienna sausage and asparagus straight from the can," I respond with my favorites.

We dare each other to eat raw meat, "like cannibals," he says. Slice the muscle that protects the littleneck and devour him whole, "in one gulp."

In my mind my father and the movies will be forever joined. Dana Andrews in the Flying Fortress graveyard. The decorated boy.

My father found himself in the Army Air Corps of the U.S.A. They filled his teeth with Carborundum, something to do with nonpressurized planes. Up there, in the wild blue yonder, flying high into the sun, he heard music in his head and thought he'd been shot down and gone to heaven, until, and this is a true story, until he heard, "Oh, Rochester."

"Coming, Mr. Benny."

And he realized that it hadn't been an angel singing but Dennis Day, the Irish tenor on *The Jack Benny Show,* and my father's teeth were behaving like a Philco, as he told the story.

My father would like to be an exception, like my grandmother's sons, and hang in the parlor on high.

My father tries to tell her that Cecil B. DeMille's *Ten Commandments* is a work of devotion and respect and could be used in Sunday school to illustrate the wonders of God.

She only smiles.

As if to say, when you need a graven image to perceive the glory of God, you're as bad as Aaron and them who worshipped the golden calf. As if to say, when your people were running fire through the cane fields, I was cutting cane.

She doesn't even have a cross in her house. Jesus is in her heart. Is he Black in there?

When she dreams of him, who does he favor?

I don't know why she agreed to it, probably for the sake of her daughter, but on a Boxing Day—called by some "*their* Christmas" in answer to the childish question, "How come Lillian isn't with her children today?" "Don't fret; Boxing Day is their Christmas"—anyway, on a Boxing Day in the seventies, the last time I was on the island, she allowed my father to show a movie, casting the images on a white sheet spread across the verandah, straining the Delco almost to the point of collapse.

She sits on the verandah behind the sheet, to the side of the mouth of the parlor. Night begins to come on, she rocks.

The people in the surrounding area look to her for judgment, guidance, the food she generously gives them, and if she has let her big, strong, American-sounding son-in-law bring a movie to them, how can it be wrong?

At dusk they begin arriving. Trudging up the red clay hill (vainly assayed for alumina by my uncles), dressed in almost all white are the women, looking as if they are headed for a full immersion baptism.

They come out of curiosity, respect, but not all are convinced of the rightness of the occasion. Some of the women nestle asafoetida bags between their breasts, just in case; acridity rises in the heat, damp from Christmas fat (as December rain is known) of the evening. A woman in the line has sewn pockets into her sea-island-cotton underpants, in which she places chestnuts, one in each pocket, so when he sleeps with her tonight, her husband will not impregnate her.

My father has planned the evening carefully. He is ringmaster, magician, the author of adventure. He is eager, nervous. He is to reveal the world beyond their world—of red dirt that sticks in every human crevice; teeth darkened by cane, loosened in the dark; eye-whites reddened by smoke, rum. He wants to become crucial to them.

He's lost interest in me, given me up. He began to lose interest in me when I grew breasts, kept secrets in a diary, bled. Not an unfamiliar story, I imagine. He tried to harness me, driven to extremes that I now regard as pathetic, but then—then I recalled the reins they held me by when I was two, three. He eventually realized it was no use, but not without World War III.

Still, I was there that evening. The last time I spent on the island.

Before the picture show there is a short display of fireworks. A taste of magic, unfamiliar, before the greater magic. Fireworks bought from a Chinese shopkeeper, a man from Shanghai, for whom there wasn't enough room in Hong Kong. Bought behind colored strands masking the storeroom in the Paradise Lost & Found. The island is ripe for explosion, people crave gunpowder. But for American currency, caution is suspended.

The sky lowers over us, black. The promise of magic is everywhere, natural, unnatural. Magicians, natural, unnatural. The woman with chestnuts in her drawers. My father, a pint of Myers's in his back pocket.

An Otaheite tree hosts the sputtering end of a St. Catherine's wheel.

The sputtering wheel is the only light but for the bulb of the projector. My father threads the film, fitting into the sprockets the Hollywood version of *Frankenstein.* One of the greatest movies ever made, he tells them, a classic like the book, he says, written by the wife of Percy Bysshe Shelley, the great Romantic poet.

"Me preffer Byron," a voice breaks in.

My father makes no sign that he has heard.

It could be worse, will be with any luck.

"Me preffer McKay."

"Me preffer Salkey."

"Me preffer Mikey Smith."

"Me seh me cyaan believe it."

My father doesn't mention that the author of *Frankenstein,* since we're identifying her through family ties, was the daughter of Mary Wollstonecraft.

The night is alive with the scent of women. Asafoetida. Sweat. The ash of St. Catherine. Talcum powder.

My father wouldn't know Mary Wollstonecraft from Virginia Woolf, or know they had more in common than some stones in their pockets, or know the significance of stones, or care.

Shelley is far more to the point. They have memorized "Ozymandias" in school. Most of them. Or had their knuckles split across. Their own people came from an antique land.

Most of the ships landed no more than fifty miles from here, in either direction.

The sound of the projector. A soft rattle across toads, insects. Nightflyers. A family of croakers, somewhere ghost-white in the middle of the night. Lizards that mate for life and walk upside-down on ceilings, sucking the whitewashed plaster to their feet. Moon rises, grazing the screen. The doctor throws the switch. Caliban stirs. Peenie wallies are attracted, their luminescent ends flashing past the black-and-white.

My grandmother's shade.

I use the light cast from the projector, the images on the sheet, the lurching monster, to glance across the audience.

On a girl apart from the group, unto herself, is an ancient dress of mine. What was once called polished cotton, blue with a pink rose in the center of the bodice, pink streamers sewn at the neck cascade down the wearer's back. Colors faded to paleness by now, from sun, river-water, the battery of women against rock. I remember trying it on in a dressing room in Lord & Taylor. I must have been about eleven, worried about what I'd heard in the girls' bathroom, that department store dressing rooms were equipped with two-way mirrors. Right now a stranger was scanning me, my undeveloped chest, panties, baby fat. I got to wear it for Easter Sunday. Now it reappears on the body of the daughter of the butcher's wife, apart from the group. Reddish skin. Almond-shaped green eyes.

Her eyes could make her my sister. Stranger things have happened. It is not uncommon here to be strolling down a dirt road and come up against someone who is your "dead stamp."

While I stare at this girl, while the gathered company watches the progress of the monster, a Roman candle has settled into an eave on the roof of the house, nestling between the mahogany shingles. Slowly the fire takes root. Slowly at first, then gathering frequency and height, sparks shoot into the night sky and fall dying on our shoulders like shooting stars.

Bats fly from under the peak of the roof, screaming as one, furious.

The monster is talking to a little girl at the side of a lake.

FIRE! someone finally yells.

The little girl is gone.

My father is wild.

"Rachel, take over!" he shouts, as if he still trusts me, then runs toward the house.

"Whatever happens, don't stop the movie!" He shouts back to me as he runs.

The mob is chasing the monster by firelight, torches raised above their heads, as sparks cascade across the sheet, across my grandmother's silhouette, and the bats make another pass, demanding attention.

No one moves. This is not their house. No one stops watching.

Poor lickle white child.

Is what happen?

Him nuh kill she?

My father has vaulted onto the roof, is stamping out God's wrath with his tenderized American feet.

Contagious Melancholia

"DID YOU NOTICE they didn't even have a piece of evergreen tacked to the walls?"

"Poor devils."

My parents, sitting in the front seat of the Vauxhall, are reminiscing about a visit just completed, to the house where an old family friend, Miss Small, and her invalid sister, live. We visit them only on Christmas, the most exciting day of the year for the likes of us. We recognize how fortunate we are.

"How the mighty are fallen." In this sliver of the island such language applies.

Almost the same exact exchange takes place year after year, followed by a recitation of the vast holdings once enjoyed by the Smalls, where there are now developments, hotels, alumina operations. And the Smalls realized little profit, the fault of an outsider who mismanaged the properties. There are a thousand such stories on this island; my father seems to know them all.

Miss Small is called by her family (none left but the sister) and friends (which you can count on one hand, so few remain) Girlie. She lives up to her name.

She is tiny in stature, each year growing smaller. At eleven I overwhelm her in height. She is dressed this particular Christmas Day in what looks to be an old school uniform, down to the striped tie and tied-up brown oxfords. She wears tortoiseshell spectacles. The huge, seagoing ancient beasts are an island treasure. We do not worship them, as did the Arawak; but we know they are worth a lot. Their shells are sold for eyeglass frames, their flesh for tinned soup. I drank them once in the Place de l'Odéon in Paris.

Miss Small's chestnut hair is bobbed and turns under at her neckline. The spectacles make her eyes big, two surprised circles, dark brown, against a pallid, lineless skin.

Her girlishness seems intact. She claps her hands in excitement when my father presents her with a tin of Huntley & Palmer's Christmas assortment.

As we enter the house the wireless is tuned to the Queen's message, coming to us live from what my father calls the Untidy Kingdom. He believes this puts them in their place, as when he refers to our neighbor to the north as the Untidy Snakes of America.

We sometimes live in New York City but always return home.

One return took place a week after Emmett Till's body was found. I heard my mother behind their bedroom door, "I've had enough of this damn-blasted place!"

That's another story.

I have never seen Miss Small's sister, Miriam. I have only heard her voice, calling from the room where she is bedridden. When I ask what is wrong with her, why doesn't she get up, my mother demurs, muttering something about "disappointment."

"What kind of disappointment?" I ask, hoping for a true-romance response. At best a fiancé killed in a war; at least an outside child.

"In life," my mother sighs.

In a few days, believe it or not, only ninety miles away, on another island, where turtles were also worshipped, the rebel forces are to take Havana.

"Rachel, go into the kitchen with Miss Girlie and see if you can be of help."

I follow my tiny host down the hall to the back of the house, to the kitchen, where my eyes are met with an excitement of roaches, another huge and ancient beast known to us. They scramble across a mound of wet sugar someone has spilled on a counter.

"Bitches," Girlie mutters under her breath. I do not know if she refers to the cockroaches, who know no shame, continuing to scramble over the mound, their feet gloriously crystalline with sugar, even after she has flattened one with a teacup, or does she mean the two women who are visible to me through the slats in the jalousie window?

"Pardon, Miss Girlie?" I say, not quite believing a word she would never utter in the parlor has escaped her mouth in the kitchen.

"Nothing."

The two women are no longer in my line of vision.

The remains of the cockroach cling to the bottom of the teacup in her hand.

The sugar mound appears to be the only food in sight. The safe, as it's called, a screen-fronted cabinet designed to stay flies and roaches, stands before me, apparently empty, not even a tin of sardines.

She catches me looking.

"Damn bitches nuh tek all me foodstuff?" She speaks for them to understand.

Cigarette smoke rises outside the jalousie. Someone is listening.

"Listen to de bitch, nuh. Listen to she. Nasty man-woman."

Miss Girlie gives a little shrug and places the teacup on a tray.

"Shouldn't we rinse it off?"

She nods and hands the cup to me. I turn on the tap. Nothing.

"You will have to use the standpipe in the yard. This tap does not function at the moment."

I find an enamel pan to catch water and head out back. I know my entry into the yard will cause comment. We live in an oral society in which everything, every move, motion, eye-flash, is commented upon, catalogued, categorized, approved, or disapproved. The members of this society are my writing teachers, but I don't know this yet.

The two women wear the dark blue dresses and white aprons usual to Kingston maids. I don't know their names. We visit only once a year, and the personnel is never the same.

"You raise where?" I am immediately spoken to.

"Pardon?"

"Me say is where dem raise you?"

"Why?"

"Far me wish fi know why you nuh wish we a Happy Christmas?"

"Happy Christmas, missis."

"You hear de chile? Is too late fe dat. Better watch de man-woman nuh get she."

I am reddening, which will cause more comment. About the resemblance my skin bears to a pig, for one thing.

I am too young to understand it.

I bend over the standpipe and pray that the trickle soon fills the enamel pan. I have set the teacup to one side.

"Me name Patsy." The second woman is speaking to me.

"Happy Christmas, Patsy."

"Change a come."

I slowly rinse the cockroach shell and guts from the flowered cup.

"Me say change a come. It due."

"Lord Jesus," the woman who is not Patsy is speaking.

"Missis?"

"Is what dat on de teacup?"

"Cockroach."

"Lord Jesus, what a nasty smaddy."

Back in the kitchen Girlie is standing in a corner, her eyes focused on the floor.

"I must make some tea for Miriam, my sister," she says.

"Where is the tea?" I ask her.

"In the safe."

I open the door into the emptiness, and with great care, and certain knowledge my hand is about to encounter something truly dreadful, feel around for Earl Grey or Lapsang souchong. Something wet is on my finger; I quickly draw it back. Without looking I wipe my hand on my best clothes. Another foray into the darkness of the safe and I manage to find an envelope with the words "Tower Isle Hotel" stamped on it. Inside there is a handful of miserable leaves.

"Miss Girlie, where is the teapot?"

"In the breakfront in the drawing room. I will fetch it."

I know I must venture again into the yard to fetch water for the tea.

The woman who is not Patsy has left. Patsy has her back against the wall of the house, one leg bent for balance, the foot flat against grayish wood.

She is staring into space.

"I'm just here to get some more water."

"Please yourself."

The yard is the classic design of old-style Kingston houses. A verandah attached to the kitchen overlooks a rectangular space, across which are the servants' quarters. Invariably thin rooms with one square of window.

I am brought up not to think about such things, to be content with paradise.

There is something about Patsy as she stands against that wall, her foot bent back like a great sea bird. I say this now, describing her image in my brain. But then? Then I was probably glad of the quiet, of the absence of the other woman, her tongue.

The water trickles into the enamel pan, finally filling it. I return to the kitchen.

Miss Girlie awaits, with a flowered teapot, a riot of pansies and forget-me-nots fading with time and the hard water of Kingston. I take the pot from her and put the measly handful of leaves into the stained inside. She puts the water on the kerosene stove.

Who were the Misses Small? For these are real women I have been talking about. Down to their names. They are long gone. Girlhood chums of my great-grandmother, they cluster together in my mind with all the other mad, crazy, eccentric, disappointed, demented, neurasthenic women of my childhood, where Bertha Mason grew on trees. Every family of our ilk, every single one, had such a member. And she was always hidden, and she was always a shame, and she was always the bearer of that which lay behind us.

Down the Shore

NEPTUNE. Long Branch. Navesink. Sea Girt. Manasquan. Atlantic Highlands.

Pinball. Boardwalks. Saltwater taffy.

"Don't dwell on the past so."

Cabins in a rectangle. Wading pool in the center. Knotty pine inside a cabin. Lying on a cot, a girl can't sleep; she is counting the knots. The pine smell is overwhelming. She gets no comfort from it. She connects it to the disinfectant they use at school. What is happening, has happened?

What is she wearing?

Why can't she sleep?

Where are the grown-ups?

Getting loaded?

Fighting?

Maybe she's not alone?

Driving past such a place thirty years and thousands of miles later, she feels a sudden dreadfulness.

"Don't dwell on the past so."

Outside STEAKS & CHOPS is flashing red/dark, red/dark. She tries counting the flashes on and off, on and off, but nothing works. She is wide awake.

Across the shore road. SEAFOOD. COCKTAILS.

Thirty years and thousands of miles later, a picture forms in her mind.

Those glass cases in the front of restaurants. After-dinner mints.

But mostly cigars.

Cigarettes are dispensed from mirrored machines in which women check if their lipstick needs repair, has smeared their front teeth.

The funny-house mirror in Asbury Park. Someone is giving her a quarter so she can see herself. The elongation of her; her body is waves. She is fluid, unsound. She could melt away.

Crimson cigarette ends die in clear glass ashtrays imprinted with a fisherman in a slicker. ORIGINAL HOUSE OF SEAFOOD. She can make out a sharp edge.

She sees a woman she recognizes at the table. A Kool lazing in the ashtray, ashening the fisherman's beard.

The woman is talking to someone.

The girl can't make out who it is.

Remember, this is thirty years and thousands of miles later. She is dwelling on the past; she has no choice.

None.

Cigar boxes embossed with exotic-looking women, or feathered savages, welcoming the after-dinner man to the pleasures of a smoke.

Hav-A-Tampa. Muriel.

"Why don't you pick me up and smoke me sometime?"

She is seven or eight or nine and peering into one of those cases. The woman with Kool has her by the hand. The woman is paying the cashier.

"I wonder how many of these you sell?" The woman indicates the Mason Mint in her hand.

The cashier smiles.

The picture is crystal.

It could shatter.

In the cabin the woman is nowhere to be seen.

Thirty years and thousands of miles later she feels like the girl in the Ringling Brothers sideshow her grandmother took her to. No arms or legs; a pen in her mouth. Her autograph. She has a pen in her mouth.

She is wetting the bed.

"Have this; it'll take the taste away."

The girl unwraps the sphere carefully and takes delicate bites from the Mason Mint. She folds the foil with care and puts it in her pajama pocket. The pj's are flannel, soft from many washings, with pink creatures dancing over them.

Thirty years and thousands of miles later a friend is saying she just assumed children had lousy memories.

That's how she's always felt. She can reconstruct the sixteenth century better than her own life.

The Store of a Million Items

As CHILDREN we had our seasons, apart from grown-up, growing seasons. Our own ways of dividing time, managing the elliptical motion of the Earth, life on a spinning planet. Our ways were grounded, uncelestial. Light years were beyond us; black holes not yet imagined. Our idea of a matter-destroying entity was the sewer under the city, stygian, dripping, where Floridian Godzillas survived on Norwegian rats.

No, our seasons were set by the appearance of something in The Store of a Million Items, on Victory Boulevard, between the Mercury Cleaners and the Mill End Shop. The store was a postwar phenomenon, promising a bounty only available in America. Everything we loved was there; there we flocked. As close to infinity as we dared.

The first Duncan yo-yo—the first to catch the eye, splendid, gold-flecked, *deluxe,* guaranteed to go around the world, without end, singing all the while—usually appeared sometime in March, brought by common carrier from the Midwest. It led the way, grand marshal of a parade of yo-yos, lined up in a corner of the store window, as less *deluxe,* less articulate yo-yos followed, right down to the twenty-nine-cent model, thick wood and flaccid kitchen string, unable to sleep or sing, promising no momentum at all. Its brand-new cherry-red face was deceptively bright, for the paint would soon enough crack, strip, even run in the rain, dyeing its master, mistress red-handed. Stamped MADE IN JAPAN, which phrase then signified nothing so much as inferiority, cheapness. The work of the un-American.

But—and this is important, the teacher stressed—you couldn't trust MADE IN USA either, for right after Hiroshima, a Japanese town had changed its name to USA (pronounced you-sah) and therefore MADE IN USA was suspect. The un-American was crafty.

"Too many people don't understand Hiroshima," Miss Clausen continued. "Make sure it's U-period, S-period, A-period," she cautioned.

Yet the child who couldn't afford a grander, made in U-period, S-period, A-period yo-yo (and was too chicken, or good, to lift one) would treasure even the Japanese version, determined to overcome its birthright and teach it to sleep. Fingering the wood in his pants pocket, rubbing it along the wale of her corduroy skirt, you could hear the call of the schoolyard, while the teacher's voice became white noise.

We stood in clusters on the concrete, surrounded by the whirr of yo-yos sleeping. In the shape of the world, the world on a string.

We were truly blessed, the principal assured us.

Behind the Iron Curtain were streets of empty markets, with nothing but shelf after shelf of noodles. That's what happened when people lived on handouts. Everybody had cardboard in their shoes, not just the poor kids or the kids whose parents had better use for their money. Behind the Iron Curtain they sold *Uncle Tom's Cabin,* stamped 1955, with the words "first edition" on the title page.

We knew better.

On August 28, 1955, Emmett Till's body was dredged from the River Pearl. But teachers weren't responsible for telling us about things that happened in summer.

Behind the Iron Curtain everything was gray—people, cities, skies. The sun didn't shine there. They were deprived of Happy Tooth, while Mr. Tooth Decay dogged their tracks, like a villain in a silent two-reeler. Even the children had false teeth, if they were lucky.

In 1956 we passed around a special edition of *Life* devoted to the Hungarian Revolution. We were about to receive a refugee classmate. Some of us were foreign-born, but he would be our first refugee. Gray tanks rumbled through streets page after page. People were squashed. For some reason the refugee went to Chicago instead.

The years moved on. Jacks. Marbles. Jump ropes. Peashooters.

Water pistols. My personal favorite. Coming at the end of spring, the verge of summer vacation, when we watched the green canvas shade, drawn down against the sun and against our eyes, drawn by the warmth of the outdoors, trained on long evenings. The shade flapped gently, but any breeze was trapped.

Black Lugers. Silver derringers. Translucent ray guns. One blast and your enemy would disintegrate before your very eyes. We'd all seen *The Day the Earth Stood Still. The Thing. It Came from Outer Space.* Pods landing in a California valley.

Earth Versus the Flying Saucers.

"Will they be back, Brad?"

"Not as long as we're here, Sally."

Saturday mornings in the children's pit of the local movie house, the matron, whom some of us would come to remember as a stone butch, patrolled the aisles during the show. She collected water pistols at the door, those she could detect, or tried to remember the children who were likely to be armed.

We hated her with a feeling as natural as what we felt for Messala in *Ben Hur.*

"C'mon, Ben!" we cheered during the chariot race and thrilled as Ben's nemesis was dragged bloody through the sand of the Circus Maximus.

Of course some of us eluded the matron's once-over, and we blasted her again and again, water running over her ducktail, droplets bouncing off her Vitalis'ed strands, soaking the nurse's uniform they dressed her in.

"Bas-tuds!" She swore at us, calling us chicken, threatening to stop the picture and raise the lights.

When the water ran out, we pelted her with Goobers and Raisinets, Good-and-Plentys, and Milk Duds.

Then she brought out the heavy artillery, the ticket-taker, for one final warning: "Now, boys and girls." To which we either feigned good behavior or began a rampage, depending on whether we knew the ending of the movie or cared. We were in that dark pit gloriously leaderless. Anarchy for the most part prevailed.

In school we declared War! (what else?) on each other. The-girls-against-the-boys, the-boys-against-the-girls, ancient compound nouns, spoken in one rapid breath, running back and forth during recess, reloading our sidearms in the girls' room, the boys' room. There was a rumor a boy in 5-3 peed in his.

Even Gerald O'Brien, who draped pop beads from The Store of a

Million Items around his waist and pretended he was a mermaid—like Ann Blyth, he said—armed himself. Gerald wouldn't have been caught dead at the movies on Saturday morning. He said he preferred solitude, hated crowds, and watched his movies in peace on *The Early Show,* in the time between the end of school and his parents' return from work. He drank tap water from a stemmed glass he'd bought in The Store of a Million Items, into which he dropped two cocktail onions, calling himself a Gibson Girl. He would have preferred to have used his water pistol as a prop in high drama or melodrama, *The Letter* or *Deception,* the first frames of *Mildred Pierce,* the final scene of *Duel in the Sun,* not as the rest of us did, in gross displays of force.

"Boys and girls, boys and girls, hold your partner's hand," we were told, as we were marched from one place to another, to the schoolyard, gym, auditorium for assembly on Friday mornings, to the lunchroom, which always smelled of alphabet soup no matter the entree of the day.

Seated in front of a plate on which sugary Franco-American ravioli and sauce has congealed, a girl suddenly pulls a derringer from a pleat in her plaid skirt and lays waste to her lunch partner.

"Drop it!" The lunch marshal swoops into action, confiscating the gun, huge tins (fallout shelter size) of cling peaches bearing witness on a shelf behind her, SCIENTIA EST POTENTIA etched in tile above her head.

A visit to the Brooklyn Botanical Gardens, where exotica have been gathered, labeled, staked. Where armed children descend in the glass-enclosed re-creation of a tropical rain forest, heavy mist thickening with their excited breath, the City's rising humidity. We are running, tripping over metal stakes, tags identifying tree ferns, bromeliads, orchids, flesh wet with scent, the place as lush as the Hanging Gardens of Babylon, which we've memorized as one of the Seven Wonders of the Ancient World and can only imagine.

The tropics have seized us. The teachers have not seen anything like it since some seventh-graders escaped from the star show at the Hayden Planetarium and occupied the war canoe at the Museum of Natural History.

They scream for order.

"Hey, Jesse, this make you homesick for Puerto Rico?"

Does he mean the chaos or the foliage?

"Man, you don't know nothing."

"I like to be in America . . ."

The guerrillas are swarming. Thin streams from our pistols whip the mist further. We have created our own fog. A wall lies ahead of us.

Someone, off by himself, hidden, is tracing in the glass of the greenhouse: VITO WAS HERE.

The steam will dissipate, the letters disappear.

"Death doesn't make sense in summer," one girl tells another. "Last summer, when Marilyn Monroe died, I just didn't get it."

"Yeah."

"Maybe it's not summer. Maybe it was being at camp. You don't expect bad things to happen."

"Yeah."

There was a vacant lot about two blocks up the hill from school. Traces of a former structure could be detected in the ground, but what dominated the lot and drew some of us into it were several huge boulders we named the Mexican Rocks, lending the exotic, the untamed, to a common urban terrain, making it strange.

One day Gerald O'Brien is taking a shortcut from school to *The Early Show* through the vacant lot. He hears a moan, then the sound of something scraping against the rock, the granite that is the bedrock of the island. He looks into the bushes. Suddenly he is afraid of what he will find. He sees the thin arm of a girl, charm bracelet dragging in the dirt. Zodiacal fishes, Eiffel Tower, Statue of Liberty, Sacred Heart, each displayed in clear plastic trays at The Store of a Million Items, are visible, beside the bulk of a man in a business suit, who is moaning. Gerald wishes he were in The Store of a Million Items right now, browsing.

Or at home, in front of his flickering images, hearing "The Syncopated Clock," heralding *The Early Show.*

"Hey, mister! Quit it, mister! Quit it!" He screams at the back of the man.

"You wanna crush her?!"

The man doesn't seem to hear him. Gerald picks up a discarded Pepsi bottle and, knowing only he wants this to stop, shuts his eyes and cracks the man on the back of the head.

"What the fuck?!"

Gerald has the man's attention. He moves back a few steps, afraid of what is coming next. "Oh, shit," the man says, under his breath, as if this were nothing.

He gets up and begins to walk away, down the hill toward the schoolyard, brushing his suit as he goes.

The girl just lies there, uncovered, her plaid skirt up, bright red stains her upper leg. Gerald is afraid to touch her. He lays his pullover over her. The wool scratches her. She starts; cries. "Stay here," he says.

"Please; don't leave me."

He sits with her until another grown-up comes by, a woman loaded down with groceries. He does his best to tell the woman what happened. He stares at the ACME stamped on her bags as he speaks.

"Why, you're a little hero," she says.

Gerald is commended at the next assembly. He never sees the girl again. No one does. She disappears down the Jersey shore with her mother and father, who pray it will not follow them. Gerald's father tries to reconcile his pansy of a son with the hero of the Mexican Rocks.

The PTA chips in and buys Gerald a glove embossed with Mickey Mantle's signature.

At The Store of a Million Items baseball gloves, cards, bats, balls, caps give way. School approaches. Marbled notebooks, Crayolas, pencil cases, rulers, erasers, compasses, protractors, things vital and unnecessary lie side by side under BACK TO SCHOOL.

Time passes. Seasons change.

Soon enough it is nearing Christmas and "Silver Bells" is piped to the sidewalk from The Store of a Million Items. We're getting in the mood. We watch as a whole window is cleared for the Flexible Flyers—surely the most beautiful name anything was ever given. They are arranged like fallen dominoes, one resting against the next, Eagle trademark echoing behind the glass.

There is a loud explosion. A huge clap over the City.

A fireball follows, rolling in the early dark of the December afternoon, above the last-minute shoppers, the schoolchildren looking to the holiday. Some of us think: "Russia," "Communism," "Sneak attack." We duck and cover and wait for the all clear.

There is no sound.

Outside it begins to rain people. Arms and legs catch in the ailanthus, the ginkgo trees. Torsos bounce from awnings. Scraps of metal shine through the slush. Airsick bags dissolve in the streets. Samsonite jams a storm drain. It's unbelievable.

No one will forget it. Nobody doesn't talk about it. I heard this, I heard that. In the halls, on the line in the lunchroom, over trays heavy with Weissglass milk and Dinty Moore beef stew. "I seen a head rolling to the Colonial Lanes."

"You're full of it."

"My mom's a nurse. You probably wouldn't believe her neither. She said they had to put the pieces together, just so's they could bury them. There must have been millions of pieces, she said."

"I bet."

"She said you couldn't tell if they were a man or woman, or colored neither."

That gets someone's attention.

"Isn't that a sin?"

"What?"

"To bury people all mixed up."

"I guess."

A woman on the radio says she dreamed it before it happened. "That's right. I dreamed there were sugar packets falling from the sky. Some said TWA, some said United. That's when I knew. I just didn't have the flight numbers."

"Have you had this . . ."

"Kind of experience before? You bet."

"They didn't know what hit them," is spoken all over the City as benediction.

The Store of a Million Items shifts the display of Flexible Flyers, moves the mechanical Santa bowing to passers-by, cuts off "Silver Bells," and on snow made from Ivory flakes, sets two black-shrouded model planes, assembled by the owner's grandson.

The collision, the crash, the manmade thunder and lightning, the rain of people, this was horrible enough, and then came the news that a kid had caused it.

A girl and her father are sitting at a kitchen table. The tabletop is Formica, gray with pink flamingos, covered with a striped tablecloth. The table is a gift from generous in-laws; the mother prefers the table covered. "No taste," her rationale.

The man is wearing a freshly laundered breakneck shirt, his name embroidered over his left nipple. It's his bowling night. He's taking time out to talk to his daughter.

"You know why those planes collided and all those people died?"

"No," she responds; but she does. The teacher told them during current events that morning. Finding irresistible the news that a boy playing with his transistor interfered with the planes' communication with the tower at Idlewild and BOOM!

"What does that tell us, boys and girls?"

The girl knows her father wants to be the first to tell her; so she lies, and feigns surprise as he gets to the point.

"A kid."

"I didn't know that." The woman at the sink, carefully soaping the dinner plates, comments.

"Didn't you hear me?"

"Yes, Dad."

"Well?"

"You need help, Mom?"

"Stay put, young lady."

"Okay."

"Don't 'okay' me. I want you to hear this. A kid caused the whole thing."

"How?" She plays along.

"He was playing with his transistor, that's how."

Maybe it was hearing it a second time, being weary of the adult version, the blame attached to this dead boy. Maybe it was remembering Jesse Moreno whispering in her ear, "Better he shoulda been playing with himself." But a smile was starting and she was desperate to erase it.

Too late.

"You think that's funny?"

"No, Dad."

"Well, then. That's not all. You know what happened to him?"

"No."

"He landed a few blocks from his grandparents' house in Bay Ridge. He was visiting them for the holidays."

She is biting her bottom lip, hoping to bring on tears, avoid laughter. She hates crying in front of her parents but would welcome the embarrassment right now.

Her mother only makes it worse.

"What were his grandparents?"

"Catholic." He is adamant in his knowledge of these strangers.

"From Naples, originally."

"Poor things."

"Irony is what you call that."

"Honey?"

"What?"

"If they're all dead, how come we know this?"

"Know what?"

"That the boy caused the crash."

"The papers said he confessed before he died. Said he didn't listen to the stewardess when she asked him to stop. It was in all the papers."

"Poor thing."

"What poor thing? He took all those people with him. All because he wouldn't listen."

"Imagine how his people feel."

When we went with our mothers to buy shoes, in the back of The Store of a Million Items, the shoe salesman had us stand on a pair of metal feet and we were x-rayed. They thought they saw right through us; tissue, muscle, tendon became transparent and the bones beneath the skin, the skeleton of our feet was bared, cast in negative, like the Mr. Boneses hanging in the window around Halloween time.

Stan's Speed Shop

"DON'T YOU THINK the sound of men's voices raised in harmony is a holy sound? You know, like the Beach Boys."

I was lying on the grass in the July sunlight, reading. The voice was coming from somewhere above my head.

My aunt had warned me that the son of a rich man she knew was crazy; although harmless, she insisted.

Once you're told someone is crazy, anything they say may be used to support the claim. Here was a case in point. His ecstatic question unsettled me.

I looked up. "Hello."

"Hi."

He was not dressed as another rich young man on a warm summer afternoon might be. He was wearing a khaki shirt and pants, and his hands shone with a film of oil. *Stan* was embroidered over one pocket of his shirt.

"I guess you've heard all about me."

I wasn't about to say. My aunt said the finest families had their skeletons. In some cases, she said, refinement existed in clear relation to strangeness. Look at our own family. We had enough skeletons to supply a medical school. Like a great uncle once incarcerated in New York City's Bellevue who kidnapped his nurse to the roof and suggested they take a lover's leap. The nurse said, "Oh, everyone jumps off the roof; let's go down and jump up."

Poor Uncle Billy. He fell for it.

We originated in the place where the sun never set and the blood never dried. Fragility was almost a point of honor, evidence of our delicacy against cruelty. Whatever happened, we weren't to blame, nor were we to make any change.

My aunt said that Stan was about twenty-five and that he chose to live in a room over the garage. In her words, "like a servant." Outside the windows to his room a sign hung, hand-lettered: STAN'S SPEED SHOP.

The shop was a space at the back of the six-car garage, decorated with girlie posters, calendars with half-naked women elongated against crushed satin backgrounds, their breasts as sharp as a medieval weapon. The girls hung from cords, above shelves of coolant and antifreeze, fan belts framing them on either side. There was a desk of sorts, with one of those spikes for impaling bills, and a glass ashtray from the Piping Rock Club.

"He's more to be pitied than censured," my aunt said. "Who in their right mind would think of looking for a car repair shop behind a great house on Long Island?"

"What are you reading?"

I held up my book for him to see.

"Oh, yeah, I heard about that one."

"It's very interesting." I was only twelve so a lot of *The Great Gatsby* was lost on me, but I liked what I could get out of it. Out of Gatsby especially. I had plans of escape. I kept a map of France over my bed and a jar where I saved money for my passage. I wanted to be different from the people I was related to. That meant breaking away.

"I guess I don't read much, except for car stuff. I hated school so I hate to read, except for car stuff."

I didn't mention that car stuff lay at the center of Fitzgerald's novel.

"I hate school too," I said, although I didn't.

He lowered himself to the ground beside me. "Okay?" he asked.

I nodded okay.

Then I sat up, keeping my finger in my place in the novel. Gatsby was about to pay the price. It was almost over.

Beyond the well-kept lawns on which we sat, and the crescent of a garden planted with strawberries and ancient roses, thick with time and scent, was the house, huge and brick, with only a suggestion of columns in front. Behind the house was the garage. Behind that were the tennis courts. And beyond them were the woods, which edged the property, which my aunt forbade me to explore. In the woods I could see an opening between trees, suggesting water. Without saying much my aunt allied the woods, and the water dividing them, with death and the maiden. I was properly frightened.

Stan and I and my aunt were the only residents at the moment except for a German couple who lived in and spoke only to each other.

Stan's mother was away for the summer, drying out in what my aunt referred to as a French hospital. Why I have no idea, except the word *French* attached itself to things one should be ashamed of, at least in our world. French letters, etc.

Stan's father was in Southeast Asia, protecting some investments against a possible coup.

I was there because my aunt was a friend of Stan's father and had been asked to look after things. That's what she told me. But there was really nothing to look after. The Germans saw to the house and grounds, and Stan kept to himself and the family cars for the most part.

I did not suspect the real story until later that summer. In a letter from Stan's father saying he was going to be delayed "due to sudden unrest" was a check made out to my aunt, drawn on the Banque d'Indochine. Stan's father had written "companionship" in the space explaining the check. It was a nice touch.

I was acting as her beard.

The letter was as formal, as courtly as the check. The check was on heavy pale blue paper, the letter on thin hotel stationery. Each was scented with another time, a colonial grace note.

She had been sent here to wait on his return, whenever that happened, to catch some time with him before his nice dry wife reemerged. I didn't want to believe it was only a money arrangement, but maybe it was. The letter gave nothing away.

While she waited she did her best to entertain me. We went to Sagamore Hill, where she and I read the legends about Teddy Roosevelt. Looking back as I write this, I remember only a dark hall and a room filled with the heads of dead animals and their skins.

My aunt and I took our meals in the breakfast room, which looked out on a fishpond. Stan didn't eat with us. During the daytime he ate among the cars. In the evening he went into the village to a greasy spoon. My aunt and I had seen him there once. We were taking a stroll and spotted him from the back, hunched over the counter at the Kozy Korner.

"Poor devil," my aunt said, "like Montgomery Clift in *A Place in the Sun.* What's wrong with him, acting like a poor relation?"

"You said he was crazy," I reminded her.

"There's crazy and then there's crazy," she said, and I wasn't sure what she meant.

We walked on, away from the Kozy Korner, and turned toward what each of us had called "home" at least twice, when nothing could have been further from the truth.

When the German couple retired for the evening, my aunt and I explored the kitchen, which she called the "autopsy parlor."

"Why?" I asked her.

"All that stainless steel. Everything. Whoever heard of caging a light bulb? Like a bloody institution. From the refrigerators to the counters. I used to work in a hospital, you know."

I commented on the size of the two refrigerators. "Space for a few bodies," I said.

"They used to entertain a lot," my aunt said as she rummaged through bricks of dark chocolate, cracking one with a steel mallet, licking the crumbs from her hand, catching her face in the convex shine of steel. "Mind we leave things as we found them," she said, "or there will be hell to pay."

We tidied up the place, running a chamois over the steel counters.

"Those bloody Germans," she said as she switched off the light. "Bloody spies."

"Do you know who the aborigines are?"

"Yes."

My early schooling had been drenched in the repetitions of Empire. The aborigines lived in what Captain Cook had christened *terra nullius*—no man's land. The details were returning as they had been learned, in single file, by rote.

"I saw them once."

"How come?"

"My father had to go there on business. He took me along. It was long before now."

"Oh."

"Yeah. It's like the surface of Mars maybe."

I wasn't sure if this had anything to do with singing, with his original question.

"The dreams of the people. It's where the aborigines go to get away. Sometimes they sing the dreams. I was remembering hearing them."

He started to get up. "Come with me to the garage. I want to show you something."

Every warning I'd ever been given about the danger of being female repeated itself. But I followed him anyway.

We walked through the side door out of the July sun. It was dark inside. I'd left my sandals on the grass along with *The Great Gatsby,* and the concrete sent a chill up through me.

Stan switched on the lights. The cars were lit from above. A green-shaded hanging lamp cast its shadow across his desk.

"Wait'll you see this." He went over to the desk and pulled out a side drawer. "I got this on the same trip. We made a stop in South America. Do you know what it is?"

He thrust a small dark object toward me. "Look."

It was hard to make out the details of the thing in his hand, even with the lights on.

"Do you know what this is?"

"Not really."

He smiled. "It's a shrunken head, from up the Amazon. Scare you?"

Without a skull the head folded in on itself. That it once was attached to a human body was unbelievable.

The thing itself didn't frighten me.

"Look at the hair on this thing, the eyes." He swung the head back and forth in front of my face by its long lank hair.

"You're getting sleepy, very sleepy," he joked; I hoped. "When I snap my fingers, your mind will go blank." Now he twisted the hair around his fist and thrust the head forward at me.

I backed up. "I better get going," I said, retreating farther. "My aunt will be wondering where I am."

"Okey-dokey," he said and rocked back in his swivel chair. "Catch!"

The head made an arc toward me. I let it bounce off my chest where it hit, then turned and walked out of the garage. I shaded my eyes before I came into the brightness of the out-of-doors.

I was afraid he would come after me. In my mind's eye I was being dragged into the woods. But he didn't, and the last sound I heard from the garage was the noise of a car radio broadcasting a baseball game.

That night in the steel kitchen I wondered if I should tell my aunt what had happened.

She'd say I was lucky. It was my own fault for following a madman. Her declarations of his harmlessness would be forgotten. It was my fault and I was bloody lucky bloody worse did not transpire.

"What's that on your blouse?" she asked me under the steel-caged lights.

I looked down. There was a smudge where the head had made contact, a stain like chocolate. "Dirt, I guess."

"Well, leave it in the hamper for the German woman."

The German woman who did not speak to either of us silently removed our laundry once a week and returned it folded and pressed the next day. She just as silently served us our meals in the breakfast room overlooking the fishpond. We always said thank you. She said nothing.

Her husband, skimming algae off the surface of the pond, occasionally glanced through the window at us, nodding his head ever so slightly.

"Okay," I said.

"Sometimes I think this place looks more like an abortionist's clinic behind the Iron Curtain than an autopsy parlor."

"What?"

"Nothing. Let's make some popcorn and see what's on the television."

"When can we go home?"

"I thought you liked it here. I thought this was an adventure."

"I just wondered. When?"

"Soon enough."

She turned out the lights and we ascended to the sitting room in the guest wing. *The Million Dollar Movie* was showing *While the City Sleeps.* We settled in to watch.

I touched the place on my chest where the head, unrecognizable, human, had touched me.

Wartime

THE YEAR WAS 1974. I was walking on a dusty road above Cherbourg, wasteland on each side, on my way to the D-Day museum. There's not much to do in Cherbourg. Last night I saw *The Poseidon Adventure* dubbed in French.

A man is following me in a *deux-chevaux*. About ten yards behind me. As I go faster, so does he, but he maintains a distance, the pursuit. I can hear Cat Stevens on the radio. I worry that this is a wasteland. I hope he's only playing.

He persists, coming closer, and I turn and we make eye contact. He says something I don't get.

"Fool!" I yell at him, needing to say something, not wanting to set him off with something stronger.

"The French are so stunted," a friend of mine is fond of saying, ever since her lover went off with one of them.

Would that it were only the French. I remember the train from San Sebastian to Madrid, a man with a chicken in one hand, the other running itself under my skirt as I passed through the corridor. I turned; his wife, standing beside him. Both with gold teeth and smiles. I am well traveled.

The Frenchman suddenly blasts his horn a few times, U-turns, sending dust spiraling into me. Then gone. Just like that.

"Thank God," I say out loud.

Soon enough I reach the museum. I can see the cloud raised by the *deux-chevaux* at the foot of the hill.

No other company except the odd salamander.

The museum is divided into two parts. On the top floor, D-Day; downstairs, the Deportations. I am the only visitor. The curator, an older man with rosy cheeks, takes me by the hand. He leads me through the hodgepodge of the surroundings. The D-Day exhibits seem to consist of mementos scrounged from lost knapsacks. Canteens. C rations. Snapshots. A flotilla made of children's boats sits on a blue-paper-covered table in the center of one room. Another table is covered with sand leading to precipices made of papier-mâché. I could be in someone's finished basement.

My father set up a Lionel train on a sheet of plywood he painted green. I was not allowed to touch, but I was allowed to watch and to drop the smoke pellets into the locomotive's smokestack, one by one.

The curator leads me downstairs to the Deportations. The departed are memorialized by a gaunt statue, some newsprint and some photographs, and a list of names with numbers next to them, typed on an ancient machine, with much x-ing out.

The curator asks me if I am a Jew. When I say no, he beckons me back upstairs. He asks me if I am American. When I say yes, his eyes light, and he speaks of the *gloire* of June 6, 1944.

But I turn back down the stairs, trace my hand over the list of names.

My mind starts to wander. I am recalling my senior year in college, when I worked as a receptionist in a tax preparer's office on Victory Boulevard and became acquainted with a Jew who had left both of his legs behind on Omaha Beach.

Almost everyone smoked in that office. Almost everyone smoked back then.

Jack Costello, the head accountant, took his place on a barstool next door to the office. It was the beginning of his daily routine. Eight A.M., and the owner was sweeping out the trash of the night before. Butts skated across the sidewalk in front of the broom, taking the slope of the concrete and tumbling into the gutter.

Jack sat with a shot of Scotch in front of him, the sun raking the plate glass window and his brain, gilding the liquid in the shot glass, showing up the infinity of rings within rings on the surface of the bar.

Jack was the first person I knew who treated alcohol like insulin, dosing himself steadily through the day, maintaining equilibrium enough to add column after column of figures, as his long fingers flew across the adding machine. As his left hand worked the keys of the machine, his right hand held a Pall Mall, and the blue smoke of unfiltered Turkish tobacco haloed his desk.

To look at him you never would have suspected he was a drunk.

He was, for one, impeccably turned out. Shined. Ironed. Brilliantined. Always in a three-piece suit, even when the City was suffering a wave of spring humidity and heat. Always decorated with a gold watch fob. Always with exactly one inch of gold-linked cuff showing.

If he liked you, he'd tell you all about the war and what a bastard Patton had been. And crazy besides. "The deranged son of a bitch believed in reincarnation. Thought he was Alexander the Great.

"And that was no accident," he said, referring to Patton's death. "His men did him in."

Jack claimed to have proof.

"The only proof Jack has is eighty proof," Fred Silvers said.

Fred was Jack's opposite. For one thing he never touched a drop.

"They put the son of a bitch in traction, with fishhooks through his cheeks."

For Fred the war seemed a lifetime ago. For Jack it was yesterday.

Fred couldn't remember which leg it was that had a scar from belly-whopping down Benziger Avenue, ending up under a milk truck, where a piece of the truck's exhaust tore through his pants and into his kneecap.

Fred wasn't an accountant. He leased space in the office during tax season and tried to get people to invest their refunds with Dreyfus. For the future, he told them. For security. Some of them barely glanced at the brochure he handed them, the lion emerging from the subway. Others gave him their attention, thought of security, but they were paying for what had passed, never mind what was to come.

Fred's interest in the future was newborn; he wanted to spread it around.

According to the way Jack told it, Fred had spent twenty-odd years in the back bedroom of a house in Levittown, his prosthetic legs propped against a chest of drawers. The legs changed over time, becoming lighter, more flexible. "Lifelike," Jack said, "if you weren't alive."

Fred's wife and their family doctor kept up with the latest models. Fred's wife changed the socks and shoes regularly. She kept the legs within his line of vision from the bed, where he was propped on pillows.

She wanted to make the legs irresistible, so he would ask to strap them on, make her call the doctor to fulfill his desire to walk.

Her tender washing of the legs, oiling the knee and ankle joints, slipping the feet into argyle socks in winter, white cotton in summer, was ritual for her. "Like Mary Magdalene at the Last Supper," Jack said, speaking from his Catholic-addled brain.

When she put black executive hose and Thom McAn oxfords on the feet, Fred took her dancing. When she put on white tennis shoes, they strolled the beach, the boardwalk, rode the Ferris wheel.

"It was so goddamned sad," Jack said. "She went into debt for those legs. The VA would only cover the cheapest models, especially for a guy who refused to use them. Forget that. She needed them."

Fred's life might have ended there, had the Veterans of Foreign Wars not intervened, in the person of Jack.

"I just showed up one morning to talk to Fred," Jack said. "It was part of the program at the post.

"I told him he was wasting away."

"Why should you care?" Fred asked.

"There's a whole new world out there."

"So?"

"So why don't you go take a look?"

"This suits me fine."

"Television will rot your brain." *As the World Turns* droned in a corner by the legs.

"Maybe."

"Besides, soap operas are for housewives."

"It's only noise."

"I was there, too, you know."

"I figured."

"You want to know where?"

"No, thanks."

Jack admitted he needed to regroup.

"Excuse me a second."

"It's down the hall."

Sitting on the throne, Jack took a long draw from his flask, leaned back, and closed his eyes. "It came to me right there," he told me.

"Look, I'll make a deal with you."

"And what might that be?"

"Think of your wife."

"I do. All the time. It's really none of your business. Not that any of this is."

"We haven't forgotten you."

"You can't forget someone you've never known."

"I disagree. Look, if you give it a try, I'll take you to the track."

"What?"

"You'll love it."

"You must be nuts."

"There's nothing like it. We'll start small. Maybe Monmouth Park. Then the Big A. Aqueduct. How about it?"

And that brainstorm, Jack promised, was how he got Fred into the legs. "He was ready, that's all. I just provided the incentive."

Wherever the truth lies, Fred allowed Jack his story.

One Saturday afternoon in March 1969 is imprinted on my memory.

The door opens and a man staggers into the office.

There's a lull today, so Jack has his bottle of Johnnie Walker Black in full view. Fred has stopped by with lunch, which Jack barely touches.

"You can't live on whiskey alone, you know."

"I can try."

"You want to end up . . ."

Their conversation stops as each realizes the man standing just inside the door is wearing camouflage and his hands are trembling violently.

Jack looks him over.

"We don't keep any cash here."

The man only stares.

Fred pours some Scotch into a paper cup and offers the straggler a drink.

The man shakes out his hands three times, quick awkward motions, stopping the tremors long enough to take the cup from Fred.

"Thanks," he whispers. "Mind if I sit down?"

"Please." Fred balances himself on his legs and pulls out a chair for the man.

"How can I help you?"

"I came to get my taxes together. I have a letter from the IRS somewhere."

"Sixty-eight?"

"Since sixty-six, I think."

"Well, let's get you started." Fred is speaking softly, taking on my usual job, filling out the top parts of the tax forms.

"Name?"

"James Franklin."

"Address?"

"You can reach me at the VA. I don't have the address on me."

"That's okay. I'll fill it in."

"Thanks."

"Occupation? Army?"

"Surgeon."

That gets everyone's attention. A silver caduceus that none of us noticed before is pinned to his fatigues.

"Something wrong?"

"Nothing," Jack speaks up.

"Back for good?" Fred asks.

"I think so. Not sure."

"Working at the VA?"

"Taking the cure."

"Tell him about the time Eisenhower stopped by your bed, Fred." Jack's intake appears to be out of whack.

"Don't mind him."

"I'll try."

"Tell him, Fred. If you don't I will."

"You know what, Jack? That never happened. It's just a war story."

"Don't kid a kidder, Fred."

I might as well be invisible. In fact I wish I was. A girl, one who marched against the war and probably will again, I feel ashamed, out of place.

"Hey, honey?" Jack startles me.

"Yes?"

"Here's twenty bucks. Go get me a fifth, will you? And keep the change."

"Come on, Jack. Enough is enough."

"Johnnie Walker got his gun, Fred. It's not just for me. It's for the doctor here. Don't forget, honey. Johnnie Walker Black, that's important. We don't want to insult the doctor."

Dr. Franklin makes no sign he's heard anything.

"I served under Patton." Jack has seized the floor. "The worst son of a bitch you ever want to see. Every son of a bitch has to come and bow down to that son of a bitch."

"Dr. Franklin?' Fred asks.

"Yes?"

"Did you really come here to get your taxes done?"

"It's almost time, isn't it?"

"Okay, then. Did you bring your documents?"

"Documents?"

"Lots been happening here since sixty-six," Jack says to no one.

"I guess I'd better come back."

"Do you have a way to get to the hospital?"

"I'll be fine."

"How'd you get here in the first place?"

"Cab."

"Let me call one for you."

"It's okay. Maybe I'll walk.

"Promise to come back."

"Right."

"No way in hell he took a cab. Who'd pick him up?" Jack says.

Dr. Franklin shoots him a look but says nothing. He gets up and leaves.

I'm still standing there with Jack's twenty in my hand.

"Well, honey, what are you waiting for?" There's a panic beneath the edge in his voice.

"I'll take that." Fred slips the bill from my hand and lays it on Jack's desk.

"You go home now. Make the rest of the day a holiday."

"Thanks, Mr. Silvers," I say, not exactly sure what he means, eager to be gone.

I turn and walk toward the door.

"Just imagine, Fred. A colored surgeon in the army. That wouldn't have happened in our day."

"No. It wouldn't," is Fred's reply.

I leave them through the glass door with the gold lettering.

My back is turned to the curator. I am looking out the window down at the Channel, and the beach, thinking about the decomposing of bones.

"La Manche," the curator says.

"Yes. I know."

He has a document in his hand. The folds of years threaten its integrity. It has a seal at one corner. He's holding it up against the window in the afternoon light. I can make out a watermark, a brown stain. The head of a helmeted female.

He points to a name. Points to himself. He folds the document along the same lines, tucks it into his breast pocket.

I thank the curator and leave the museum.

Outside the sun is high, pounding the dust on the hillside. I walk slowly toward the town. I feel like I've been away. Like leaving the dark of a Saturday matinee. The movie inside of me, not wanting to let it go.

Art History

I

I PICK UP the *New York Times* sometime in 1992 and find your name. My heart catches. We are twenty years from a summer filled with each other, and now I hear you laugh, and I sound foolishly romantic, now death is around us.

The first winnowing, a doctor said, cold. And if she is right, who will be left standing? This feels like a rout.

Riding uptown in a cab one spring evening in 1990—it's important to get the years right; so much is happening, so fast—passing a bar called Billy's Topless, Angela musing, "I wonder if his mother knows?"

Arturo laughing.

Me between the two of them. She and I get out in the thirties, Arturo heads farther uptown. He's convinced the hotel's haunted by the ghost of Veronica Lake.

Two years later both he and Angela are dead.

"I'll call you when I'm in London."

His huge eyes. "We need a party."

But talk of this is for another time.

That summer you were subletting the apartment of an art historian in a brownstone just off Park, verging Spanish Harlem. Almost the top of the City, where the streets begin to broaden, becoming lighter, darker.

The art historian sent you a postcard from the Bomarzo, showing a picnic table between the legs of a gigantic stucco, stone, or terra cotta female. Her message was all business, then, underlined, "My favorite place to dine when in Italy." You showed it to me without a word.

The color in my cheeks rose higher and higher.

You were smiling. "Just once?" you asked.

I turned away, to the windows at the front of the apartment, overlooking the street, a playground, and some tenement walls plastered with Colt 45 and Newport ads in Spanish, and one wall that stood apart. On it shreds of a couple dressed in evening clothes framed a portrait of Bessie Smith. Someone had cast the Empress across brick, across ancient lettering advertising Madam's Rosewater, worn into "adam's Rose," elixir disappearing into her ermine wrap.

The light of the summer evening set the street to glowing, bathing the girls and boys in the playground, the men leaning against the anchor fence, the brown bags housing Ripple or Night Train or Thunderbird. Bessie Smith watching over them all. For a minute everything was golden, and then the evening shadows crept in.

"There's nothing like summer in New York," I said.

I turned around and kissed you good-bye.

"Why don't you stay?"

I was living downtown, in the Village, house-sitting the townhouse of a former boss, whose copper-topped cocktail table I kept polished, whose mail I collected, and whose very gray portrait hung over the mantelpiece. She was perched on the edge of a chair, leaning forward, out of the plane of the picture, almost to launch herself into the room.

Her eyes were the same color as the suit she was posed in, close to charcoal, oddly missing the pinpoints of white, the light captive in the eye.

The painting was signed by her husband.

"Bill so much wanted a son," she told me as she showed me around the house, "and look what he got." We had ended up on the top floor of the slender building, in her son's room, painted black, with a purple ceiling, without furniture. "Absence," she said.

About a year before she had taken me to lunch at the Algonquin for my birthday. Because, she explained, they had the driest martinis in a five-block radius. I'd revealed to her that I'd never had a martini, and she said, "My God, you can't call yourself an American and not have had a martini."

She meant well and went ahead and ordered for me.

After she had drunk about three of them, she told me about her boy, actually a man, who set fire to the brooms at the Montessori where he worked as an aide. She talked about his need to fall from higher and higher places. She thought he was trying to fly, she said. "To leave himself behind and rise from the ashes.

"But it was no good."

After years of high places, and the places beneath, he fell from a window in Macy's, where he worked as a stock boy.

"One of those rainy New York nights," she said, "in November."

All of a sudden I thought of the Thanksgiving Day Parade and in my mind's eye caught a boy entangled in the guy wires of a balloon. Popeye's tattooed forearm floated by. I wanted to smile. It must have been the gin.

"I had to identify him. The morgue people didn't know what to do with me. They just stared, as if to ask, what kind of a woman has a son like that?"

I tried to engage her eyes but she was staring into her glass, into the bluish tinge of good gin.

"I didn't actually see what the fall had done. They had covered his face. I identified him from the nametag on his smock. But they told me."

I didn't know what to say to her, except, "I'm sorry." It was one of those moments when I felt ignorant of some secret female gesture, something traditional I had never learned.

"Thank you," she said, "but I've only myself to blame."

For what? I wondered. Not breast-feeding him? Being a "career-woman"? Not wanting a child in the first place?

"Why should you blame yourself?" I asked, using the same tone I had learned to use with my father when he drank too much and became maudlin. I hated the sound of it, matching the unrealness of the drunken voice note for note.

"I should never have listened to them."

"Who?"

"The doctors. My husband. You have no idea how difficult artists can be. The last thing he wanted . . ."

"Oh," I said, unable to ask what.

"It was the fifties." She paused. Specters crowded in. "I like Ike." Betty Furness opening a sparkling white Westinghouse. *I've Got a Secret.*

"I didn't have a hell of a lot of options. Punishment and reward. That was the prescription. Please don't tell anyone about this."

"Of course not."

I wasn't sure what I'd heard.

I went back to my office, closed the door, and fell asleep.

We were standing in his room, at the top of the slender house, the door open to the fire escape, the perfect perch for a boy who wanted to fly.

In the purple ceiling and black walls were thumbtack marks, and I wondered what he had pinned there and what they would tell me if I knew.

She broke the silence in the room.

"There's one other thing about house-sitting this summer. I probably should have mentioned this to you before."

"What is it?"

"If my son calls here, you are under no circumstances to tell him where we are." She was cold sober, and her voice was unwavering although gathering speed. "And, if he asks to come here, you are to tell him *no,* in no uncertain terms. If he persists, or tries to get in, first call the precinct—they know all about the situation—then call us."

It had started to rain, a summer shower, sounding on the roof right over us, pelting the railing of the fire escape. The hot scent of summer mixing with rain came into the room, and she went on about the dead-alive boy.

I was, as they say in old novels, nonplussed.

"Damn, Bill and I better get going. He hates to drive in bad weather. The number in Wellfleet is by the phone in the kitchen. This is the first time in years Bill and I have had a place without room for Billy. There's no place for him with us anymore, there just isn't. Here, there, anywhere. You do understand, don't you?"

Hardly. But I nodded anyway, and when I found my voice I assured her, "Yes." I knew enough not to ask.

"Oh, and I'll leave a photo of him by the phone. It's a bit out of date, but it's the only one left. For God's sake don't fall for his poor soul routine."

"I won't," I said, and felt horrible.

As soon as they drove off I went into the kitchen. On a bulletin board next to the wall phone, between a postcard of a lighthouse and the takeout menu from the Good Woman of Szechuan, was the photograph of a boy. Dark, as if it had been taken at night with a flash. Crew cut, striped shirt, two-wheeler, vintage 1955 or so.

The landscape around the boy was nondescript. It could have been anywhere a boy like him might have been. Central Park, maybe. Just some bushes and trees. In the darkness it was hard to tell much more. No suggestion of water, no shadow of a city skyline.

When I showed it to you, you thought he might be standing on the grounds of the place in *I Never Promised You a Rose Garden* or some other upper-class madhouse. Like Cascades in *Now, Voyager.* Ice cream, tennis, Claude Rains.

"Where rich people send their kids," you said.

"Then why did she say . . . ?"

"She'd had a lot to drink. Maybe she has a drunken version and a sober version. Maybe she wishes he would."

"Jump?"

"Umhmm."

"Or maybe he's been standing by these bushes for twenty years."

I had no idea what I would do should he try to get in touch. I put the photograph away, in a drawer with playing cards and flashlight batteries.

I took the portrait from over the mantelpiece and hid it in a closet.

It was no use. Their shadows overwhelmed the place. I began spending more and more time uptown, returning to West Eleventh only to erase the tarnish from the copper-topped cocktail table and collect the mail.

One day there was a bill from someplace in the Berkshires, stamped *dated material, please respond,* and the mystery seemed to be solved.

No matter.

I slept with you in the art historian's bed, under a print of Michelangelo's *Night.* We slept like children at first.

But soon I woke to find my hand in the small of your back, linger there, becoming aware of your skin and mine. The evenness of your breath. The only sound in a room in a city with the windows open.

"What are you afraid of?" you asked me in the dawn.

"I want your mouth on me."

"Oh, that." You laughed in half-sleep.

Drawing me closer.

. . .

The art historian sent a postcard from a bar called Elle Est Lui. "I hope you've met my neighbors by now." Then: "*Toujours gai!*" signed Mehitabel.

Downstairs, in the garden apartment, were two painters, Judith and Alberto. She from Grand Island, Nebraska. He from a hilltown near Siena.

The art historian had not mentioned that Judith was dying.

As Alberto cooked, Judith talked almost nonstop, as if silence was a passage into the dark.

At first she entertained us with art world gossip. "Louise? Forget her. She just calls the foundry now. Doesn't even bother to stop by."

One of us mentioned the name of another woman artist, exploding into posters, calendars, note cards, threatening even Warhol with her promiscuity.

Judith smiled. "What's next?" she asked. "Sheets and pillowcases? A shower curtain with one of her wretched cow skulls?"

"And she's never been sick a day in her life. Imagine. Just imagine."

As Judith spoke, the colored lights around the fountain in the back garden flickered. The water sprayed through the lights from the wide-open mouth of a dolphin, creating tiny, constantly changing patterns. The relentless exchange of form and color, light and water, helped take her mind off the pain, which the painkillers did less and less to mask.

We began to stop by there almost every evening.

"Here," she said suddenly, "this really belongs to you. I want you to have it."

She handed me a copy of *Wide Sargasso Sea*.

I looked at the jacket. A sad-looking young woman stood in the middle of an explosion of tropical lushness. She held a red hibiscus blossom. "Why?" I asked Judith. I didn't know the book at all.

"Because it's about your part of the world," she said. "How amazing to come from a place like that."

I only nodded, not having the heart to tell her what I actually thought of paradise. On the back of the book jacket was a familiar sight, the great house about to be swallowed by the green.

"Alberto and I were there once."

"Really? When?"

"A long time ago. Kingston was one of our ports of call on a voyage way back when. We took a freighter. We were only allowed to spend one afternoon ashore. When we got back the decks were piled high with bananas. And we were off, doing the bidding of United Fruit. I remember the mountains as this green approaching blue and the sea, my God . . . in the harbor dolphins skated by us. I was sitting on a pile of bananas, sketching like crazy. What must it have been like being a girl there?"

I always become wary when someone not of my ilk speaks of Jamaica, especially if I like the person. I wait for smiling or sullen natives, simple or crafty market women, paradise lost on its inhabitants.

"It *is* a beautiful place," I said.

"I'm only sorry we weren't there long enough to get a real sense of it. We did see the boys diving for coins alongside the cruise ships. That was distressing."

I remembered those boys. There, as if they should be. Like the coconut palms, Her Majesty's sailors on leave, the maze at Hope Gardens, the viciousness of peacocks. Nothing was said in that part of the world when I was a girl. A truckful of market women falling into a ravine. Screams into a Saturday night, then silence. I remember the headlights shining from below. People spoke of how the roadway was haunted, nothing else.

I was about to let her into a sliver of my girlhood, then I realized she had dozed off.

Judith didn't want any of her old friends or rivals "to see me like this," or so she said. Maybe she was afraid to ask them. I wondered if the remark about Louise not bothering to stop by referred to the foundry after all.

She said she was content with our company. "My new friends, my girls. You know, I don't believe anyone dies of cancer. Not as long as you have company."

"You're probably right," you said.

"Yes," Judith said. "You have to be alone to die."

My mother had been. Maybe Judith was right.

I allowed myself the chance to look at you, your amber eyes rapt with her blue ones. I watched you take her hand, your fingers cradling hers, resting on the thing that covered her. She sighed. She gripped you tightly.

We sat there until the terror passed. For now.

"We should probably be going," I whispered, and you nodded, and that afternoon under the print of *Night* I made love to you, lifting and parting, lifting and parting, drinking you to my heart's content.

The next day we met for lunch in midtown and afterwards strolled through the Morgan Library. A guard showed us the murals in the ceiling over the old man's desk. Angelic or pagan forms gaped down, colors fading into wormed wood but for bright gilt around the borders. "From Lucca, Italy," the guard said, as if it were his ceiling, "I can tell you anything you want to know."

Judith sat across from her water and lights as Alberto cooked us chanterelles he'd gathered behind the reservoir in Central Park.

"Alberto goes mushroom gathering every day the day after it rains," she said.

The City had been washed clean the day before, that kind of hot rain that falls in August.

"Isn't this marvelous?" she asked us, holding up a tumbler. "They gave it to Alberto at a gas station."

GIANTS was stenciled on the side of the glass in dark blue along with a football helmet.

"Alberto goes mushroom gathering, and he also digs potatoes and onions. Guess where."

We both looked blank.

"Give up?"

"On one of those truck farms on Long Island," I guessed.

"Nope." She couldn't wait to tell us. "On the grounds of the Cloisters," she paused. "Honest."

"I kid you not," Alberto attested.

"Someone's kitchen garden from a long time ago. When the place was rural, before they put that pile of stones there. Imagine. Who were they? Whatever remains concealed in the middle of some bushes. The sweetest onions you've ever tasted. And the potatoes! My God. A kind from before all the crap they put into the ground. Some gnarled, misshapen, dented where they grew against rock. Nothing perfect."

"How did you find them?" I asked Alberto.

"I smelled the onions one afternoon. Very strong. I followed my nose to them. In Italian, *cipollini*."

"And garlic," Judith said, "and thyme and sage. Lavender. Don't you love the City? I find it very moving. Chamomile coming up through cobblestones."

"All through the City you find things like this," Alberto said.

"Anyplace people have lived a long time," Judith said. "There are vineyards in the depths of Staten Island."

It was a beautiful vision. The City as garden. The traces of others.

"Please come to dinner on Sunday," Judith invited us.

"Prego," Alberto said.

"Alberto has promised to trap a rabbit in Westchester—not as crazy as it sounds—and roast it on a spit in the fireplace for us. We'll put on the air conditioning full blast and pretend we're in the middle of a Russian winter instead of a waning New York summer. We must each choose someone to be. Someone who doesn't have cancer, that is."

"How about TB?" you asked, and Judith smiled.

"Yes, poor wretches, they all coughed, didn't they? All through those interminable novels—that or epilepsy, the Idiot and all that. No, we must be healthy Russians. No bloody handkerchiefs. Picture Catherine the Great, robust as hell, I have no doubt."

"Can we bring anything?" I asked.

"Just yourselves. You may choose to be lovers."

She smiled up at us from her place on the couch.

"It's the drugs talking; you must excuse her," Alberto said.

"It is not, my darling; not at all."

You bent over her and kissed her, we said good night and turned to go upstairs.

"Just steer clear of Anna and Vronsky. Talk about the wrong side of the tracks." She laughed.

I stood at the bedroom window for a long time, looking out over Judith's fountain, the lights playing through the water, the water flowing from the dolphin. As long as there was light and motion, I felt safe for her.

And then Alberto turned out the lights, shut off the flow of water, and I knew Judith had fallen asleep. That's how it would be. I hoped as much.

"Were you surprised?" You had come up behind me, your arm was around my middle.

"A little. Is it that obvious?"

"I do think she cares about us, you know."

"I just don't like having my mind read, that's all."

"Don't read disapproval into what she said, unless it's your own."

Boom! There it was, and I couldn't say anything.

You were looking into the darkness as the night breezes swung into the art historian's bedroom, lifting the corners of *Night*. The traffic noises, the breaking glass across the way seemed to back off, and instead we heard Bessie Smith, her fine sounds, her blues.

The night with its half-asleep sounds, then the suddenness of the human voice raised in caress.

Sunday, as promised, a rabbit turned slowly on the spit, its fur wrapping to one side, folded in anticipation of another use.

Alberto wasted nothing.

He was at the sink blending a wild berry mixture into some yogurt.

Judith was all dressed up. Not as a Russian; that scheme had been forgotten, or discarded. She was dressed as if for a gallery opening, all in black with a bright scarf wrapped around her burned head.

Around her, facing her on the tile of the kitchen floor, was her life's work.

One canvas was yellow. A bright chrome yellow. In the middle the painting seemed to tear and an underlayer of paint was revealed. Apparition of black beneath yellow. Dark behind light.

II

Judith died that September. In the middle of an Indian summer heat wave when there was a power failure and the lights around the City went out.

Stars were visible. The moon hung over the men in the playground.

The art historian returned from her travels with a woman she'd found at the Sound and Light show at the Colosseum in Rome.

My former boss sent a postcard of Highland Light and asked if I'd guard the townhouse one more month. "Bill and I have found each other again," she wrote. "Who knows where it might lead? P.S.: We're thinking of adopting."

I ignored her request and called the precinct to tell them I had been called away and left the keys to the house with Captain January or whatever his name was.

Rubicon

THE RUBICON sported but one neon sign in the window, advertising a locally brewed beer that no one within memory had ever ordered. Underneath the sign, in the right-hand corner of the glass, was a printed notice, WE RESERVE THE RIGHT TO TURN ANYONE AWAY.

The name of the bar was painted over the front door, the letters forming an arc above the entry.

This was the quiet end of the island, away from the skyline, the Statue of Liberty, the Quarantine Station at Ellis Island. This end of the island imagined another history. The Rubicon sat on a stretch of dead-end road between what was said to have been an Indian burial ground and the ferryboat to Perth Amboy. The burial ground was the terrain of high-school students, who tracked rats among the grassy mounds and necked in fin-tailed cars.

Some of the regulars at the bar came from the New Jersey side, crossing the Kill after work, catching the last boat back. Sailing, after hours, a passenger could make out beacons, pilot lights crowning the refinery drums like St. Elmo's fire, like the Lady carrying her torch. Beacons lighting ordinary houses, laundry pinned to the line in all seasons, against Esso, Shell, Sinclair encircling a brontosaurus.

The building that housed the bar was long and low, somewhere between wartime Quonset hut and postwar Levittown, tidy, nondescript. It stood solitary on its stretch of road, the nearest neighbor the Conference House where George Washington signed some papers. That was a half-mile away, at night lit by the occasional pass of a watchman's flashlight, by day the province of schoolchildren led by their teachers and a couple of parent (always mothers) volunteers.

If anyone entering the Rubicon expected a likeness of Julius Caesar, a map of Gaul, assuming the name came from someone's passion for ancient history—like the elegantly suited Latin teacher who stopped in now and then for Scotch, neat, who'd been attracted by the name in the first place—they soon realized their error. The Latin teacher glanced about the room, whispered to herself, "All hope abandon, ye who enter here," relieved no one heard; no one seemed to pay her any mind as she slid onto a barstool and ordered.

An eight-by-ten glossy taped to the wall over the cash register, autographed "Straight from the Heart," informed everyone that the name of the bar derived from its owners—Ruby, Billie, and Connie—onetime girl singers with a big band.

The only Latin these girls knew was Xavier Cugat.

In the photograph the girls wore matching evening gowns as they had on the bandstand, perched on gilt chairs (like the kind people rent for weddings), their hands gloved and folded in their laps, waiting for the bandleader to signal them with his baton and for them to "Take it away!" in three-part harmony.

The bandleader was Phil Gardner—he called the band the Philharmonics—and the circuit they traveled meant they would never collide with Artie Shaw or Tommy Dorsey, either on the charts or on the open road. Their bus, a pink curtain draped in front of the last couple of rows, flimsy privacy, took them through small towns as far west as Iowa, as far south as Kentucky, where they played in lodge halls and at county fairs.

"Those county fairs were something else," Connie said, tending bar one night. "The stories I could tell you. Not someone's pickles and preserves and flower arrangements. No. I learned about hookers at a county fair in Indiana. Honest. They kept the girls in a tent behind the midway. Who knows where they came from?"

"Made a change from pigs and sheep, I guess," Ruby said.

"Probably girls on the run," Connie said.

"Don't tell your father I brought you here," a woman was saying to a girl in a parochial uniform, the shield of St. Lucy over her breast pocket.

"Promise?" the woman asked.

The schoolgirl nodded.

"Please say it out loud, honey."

"I promise."

It was about four on a Thursday afternoon. The girl smiled briefly, as if to reassure, then turned her attention to her Coca-Cola, drawing it through a waxed paper straw, trying to trap the maraschino cherry on the end, then releasing it, drowning it once again.

"Okay," her mother leaned forward, "I'll be back in an hour or so, sweetie. Do you have something to occupy yourself while I'm gone?"

"Homework."

"Oh, well, here's a quarter for the jukebox in case you get bored."

The woman placed the coin next to the girl's school bag and got up to leave, turning toward the stairs at the right of the front door. Before she took her ascent she turned back to her daughter, mouthing "Promise?" which the girl, intent on her Coke, did not see.

The room upstairs was bathed in blue, the effect of a lampshade draped with a silk scarf. A dim winter light cast by a snow-promising sky barely grazed the window beside the bed. The bars of a space heater glowed red in one corner. A bunch of anemones, dead-of-winter extravagance, were opening in a glass jar on the windowsill, slowly, for the light was scarce.

Two women lay side by side on a chenille bedspread.

"Tell me."

"Not again. Hold me, please."

The jukebox sat at the far end of the bar, away from the front door, and featured selections from the heyday, such as it was, of Phil and his Philharmonics, with vocals by the Rubicon Sisters. "Collector's items," Billie liked to say. "Real museum pieces, honey. They couldn't have pressed more than a thousand, if that. We never saw a dime."

The schoolgirl had devised a game like Concentration to go with the display of song titles. But since the display never changed, at least it hadn't during the time her mother had been bringing her here, she soon committed it to heart and gave up her game. She wouldn't dream of playing the musical selections advertised—what was her mother thinking?—so the quarters accumulated in a jar in the top drawer of the girl's bureau, under a map of France on which she charted her future and imagined herself gone from that room.

Now, finished with her Coke, she wondered what to do next. Her mother's promise of an hour was never an hour. The girl stared at the hands of her wristwatch, trying to detect movement. She finally got up and walked over to the window, looking out into the street, noticed she hoped by no one. None of these women ever bothered her, but she felt conspicuous, odd.

The only person sitting at the bar that Thursday afternoon was Patty, nursing a gin and tonic. A summer drink in the dead of winter. Close your eyes and you were at a backyard barbecue surrounded by regular Americans, some of whom you were related to. Ye gods. She shivered.

"Someone just walked over my grave," she said, addressing no one.

In the back of the room, to the back of the girl, a few couples were scattered at tables with parchment-shaded lamps on which red-coated hunters chased a fox. Smoked yellow light raked each tabletop. The walls around the tables were hung with memorabilia, handbills, and posters, in the dark like the past, future.

The place was quiet but for the hum of the cooler.

The TV over the bar was tuned to *The Edge of Night* with the sound off. Patty preferred it that way. And since she was the only one at the bar it was her call.

Someone was on trial. The judge banged his gavel. Someone was pointing at the front row of spectators in the courtroom.

The girl turned from her view of the empty street and glanced up at the silent screen.

"You are my heart urchin."

"What's that?"

"A sea creature."

"I wish there was somewhere else we could go."

"Ever try to figure out what they're saying?" Patty spoke in the direction of the girl.

"Sometimes."

"It's fun, isn't it?"

"I guess."

A slope-backed Chevy takes a turn, moves down the street toward the building in late-afternoon winter light. The light makes the day colder.

Makes some people long for the dinner hour, when they will be inside, safe, the driver thinks, TV tuned in, minute steak or fried chicken or spaghetti on a table set with a tablecloth. The radio in the car is tuned to the news, but the driver is not paying any attention. The car slows, slides next to the curb, idles. The driver cracks the window, takes a deep breath of cold air. Everything is gray, upholstery, dashboard, sky, building, the afternoon. But for the car, which is black, and the end of her cigarette glows red.

"Hey, Patty?" Connie emerged from the back room, a case of Seagram's about to slip from her arms.

"Yeah?"

"Give me a hand, will you?"

"Sure."

Patty stood down from her barstool and went over to Connie. Between them the two women hefted the box onto the surface of the bar.

"Thanks, hon. Let me get you one on the house."

"No, I'd better not."

"Plans?"

"God, how I hate going out that door."

"Can I get you another Coke?" Connie had turned to the girl.

"No, thank you."

"There's cheese and crackers, if you're hungry. They're free."

"I'm not hungry."

"Okay. Well, if you change your mind, it's right here. Just help yourself."

"What a life," Patty said.

"It'll do," Connie responded.

"Why don't you let me get you a cup of coffee before you go?" Connie asked. "It's awful raw out there."

"Okay, thanks." Patty settled back on her barstool, not ready to leave, not just yet.

The Edge of Night had given way to *The Secret Storm*.

The driver of the Chevy is in danger of running down the battery. She turns the key in the ignition, the engine revs up, and the car pulls away from the curb and continues slowly down the road.

Through the gray, snow starts to fall. Lightly. Lightly coating the branches of birches at the side of the road. The driver turns on the wipers, turns the car around, and makes her way to Hylan Boulevard. She turns left at the corner and heads down the boulevard toward the ferry to Perth Amboy. She passes Wolfe's Pond Park and remembers a picnic some years back. She and some other high-school seniors, cheerleaders all, entertained a group of boys from the Mount Loretto Children's Home. She remembered her boy very well. Olive-skinned with curly brown hair, he was about eight, and she gave him a baseball glove. He said to her, "I'll have to ask Sister to put this away for me." From the boy the chain of memory takes her to one particular girl, who got pregnant and was expelled and disappeared from all their lives the fall of their senior year. The driver later met her in a supermarket but nothing was said.

The car stops at the edge of the Kill, and she turns around and heads back to the bar, where she will sit for a while and wonder what is on the other side of the door.

"Waiting must be pretty boring," Patty says.

"It's okay."

Like most rituals—and Thursday afternoon has become ritual—boredom is one aspect.

Each Thursday afternoon her mother picks her up at school and says, "I have to make one stop on the way home. Okay, sweetie?"

And the girl says, "Okay."

And the ritual continues with the question her mother asks her in the bar, and her promise.

As long as this remains ritual, as long as whatever happens upstairs does not come downstairs, everything will be as it is and has been. Ritual contains.

So the waiting is okay.

Apache Tears

Apache Tears is a small community thirty miles east-northeast of downtown Los Angeles. Unlike most of the communities that impinge on the city, Apache Tears is discrete, the secret of a canyon as the desert begins, set out by a railwayman who longed for his hometown and worshipped the orderliness of a grid.

Apache Tears is the kind of place where, at the end of the twentieth century, milk is delivered to the front door, placed on porches in wooden boxes stamped in red APACHE TEARS DAIRY, contained in glass bottles with cardboard stoppers stamped in black HOMOGENIZED.

Not a silhouette of a missing child in sight. No "Have you seen me?" (And what would you do if you had?) next to a lost face. Rather, the bottles are etched with a herd of Jersey cows standing on the deck of a clipper ship heading around the Horn in the nineteenth century. Brave cows, lashed to the mast in a gale.

Cream, eggs, orange juice, and butter are also available, and the milkman with the teeth of a puppy and a black plastic bow tie leaves a pad and pencil for the lady of the house to communicate her wishes.

He visits in the dark, ending his tour of Apache Tears just as the sun begins its rise. Few have seen him, but many lying between dreamtime and waking have heard the gentle rattle of milk bottles being exchanged. This lends them comfort and allows them another few moments of rest.

WELCOME TO APACHE TEARS, the sign says at the edge of town, IF YOU'RE QUIET, YOU'LL NEVER HAVE TO LEAVE. Some believe this motto had its origin when Alfred Hitchcock scouted the town as a location for *Shadow of a Doubt* only to settle on Santa Rosa up north. Others have their doubts.

The town of Apache Tears is entirely self-contained. Along with the dairy, there's the Apache Tears Agricultural Project, the Apache Tears *Clarion,* Apache Tears College, the Apache Tears Bach Society, the Apache Tears Medical Center, and what some consider the crown jewel, the Apache Tears Museum, presided over by the town raptor.

The Museum is at first glance unassuming, kept in a residence on one of the many tree-lined streets. Apparently just another Victorian, one of many on streets past clean, fronted by lawn so green, cut so close, they might have been painted (as Santa Barbarans were forced to do in the years of drought). Water tells the story of much of the West, and Apache Tears owes its well-being to an underground river, diverted by means of dynamite and careful planning. This is the edge of the desert after all. Desert scrub, creosote mountains blacken the horizon. Joshua trees stark as a lynched hombre, rattlers that go straight for the nervous system, chasing the victim into unconsciousness.

None see past the danger of the desert into its tender nature. It blooms at its heart.

It surrounds them.

Small black stones mark the town's perimeter.

Perfectly folded newspapers lie each at the same angle on the flagstone walks, while lines of porch swings move gently in the clear morning air. Doors are opened, greetings exchanged, the day has begun.

The town raptor is a woman, a natural-born collector. She has been drawn to collecting since childhood. Of course many children collect, have collected. The usual things: baseball cards, seashells, rocks, bottle caps, dolls from around the world. The raptor stands apart from the usual. Her specialty since childhood has been the possessions of the dead.

And she's a natural.

There is very little gossip in Apache Tears so it's hard to tell where the raptor got her enthusiasm for death, and back issues of the *Clarion* shed no light.

In the depths of her walk-in closets upstairs is an extraordinary array. Clothes of every age, type, but also accouterments, medicaments, passports, cigarette lighters, diaries, tie clasps, canned goods, bridgework, handkerchiefs, watches, eyelash curlers, moisturizers, corkscrews, car keys, bracelets, lockets, stacks and stacks of ticket stubs, bowling shoes, golf balls, catgut rackets.

From the expanse of those closets to the public rooms on the first floor, the heart and soul of the museum, the raptor has proved herself the best at what she does. But who's to compare?

She dresses herself from the upstairs closets and descends to greet visitors at the front door. She is in a way the first exhibit, a taste of what is to come.

One day she may sport the leather jacket of a dead lover, lean on the shooting stick of a departed Jesuit, wear the eyeglasses of a cleaning woman stricken on the job, drape her neck with a locket containing the hair of an infant found in the trash behind the Apache Tears Motel (the *Clarion* reported an outbreak of measles), paint her nails with the savage choice of a long gone (but not forgotten) actress.

She will tell visitors to the museum about the dead she wears that day after a fashion. They expect from her the unexpected, the strange, never knowing who will greet them, interrupting their dailiness. This is prologue.

She will lead them into the public rooms and tell them again how she circumvented everyone, from local police to U.S. Customs, transporting bits and pieces from the burial places of Sumeria and Crete, the graves of Hittites and Etruscans, the inner chambers of Egyptians, and, closer to home, with only reservation cops between her find and her station wagon, the leavings of Hopi and Acoma, bones that sing.

From one wall, in what would be the dining room were this an ordinary place, the feathered burial robe of a Hawai'ian elder threatens flight. Illusion.

In her guide to the collection, the raptor goes into great detail about the process of acquisition. The guide covers everything from the beginning of the raptor's passion, excising childhood. The raptor, whose face is not reflected in the hall mirror, quicksilver worn away in a nun's cell, explains that her mentor was her first and only husband, a necrologist who led her by the hand from her freshman year at Apache Tears College into the days of the dead of the rest of the world.

She left him behind once she was expert, she says, and when she found him pissing into the embalmed mouth of a Javanese princess, which remains unsaid.

. . .

The artifacts are confused. Restless.

A Sumerian beanpot intended for the next world is lost in southern California on a shelf at the edge of the desert in a place with its back to the desert, encircled by small black stones.

pots shards rattles gourds urns
words pictograph
petroglyph message
code allusion poetry quip devotion
gods they know gods who make love
to them
who make fun
of them
outlines of the ghost-dance on a buckskin shirt
dance them into the sea
dance them off
when grasses are high
into the Great Silence.

on a beach thousands of miles away a female is tossed up
slashes across her breast lines etched by iron
trace of a braid face
the sea was not responsible for this for you
some someone was sweetheart
echoes collide in this silence
unheard by the raptor, who looks at these things, strokes
them, relies on their company, but cannot imagine their
awful noise.

Loneliness.

Like the aboriginal child waking at twenty-five to no memory. Is she not fortunate?

Their properties may drift. Cut from their gods as they are, their dreamtime. They may become corrupt. Then what? What may be summoned?

This place is not the toy shop after dark (Toyland, Toyland, wonderful girl-and-boy-land, Follow the bouncing ball!), after the Gepetto has gone home and the marionettes and tin soldiers and porcelain ballerinas make merry.

Things linger.

In the back room under lock and key, in the chamber where the raptor works, in what would be the butler's pantry were this an ordinary place, something bobs in a jar of spirits. The liquid turns bloodred as the sun drops.

Outside the town limits, in the desert proper, beyond the stone circle is a settlement known to outsiders as Cactusville.

Cactusville consists of a few motels, a gas station, a taquéria, a convenience store that once had a million-dollar winner. Like the infant found in the Dumpster behind the Apache Tears Motel, a million-dollar winner seemed an anomaly in a dried-up place like Cactusville.

The motels are from the forties, fifties, miniature Mission revival, small adobe rooms facing a central courtyard. The residents of those rooms come from across the border, down Mexico way, and travel to the fields in school buses with portable toilets strapped to the back of the bus.

At the border, behind the streams leading from the *maquilladoras,* there is an outbreak of anencephalic children

The lottery winner left behind a snapshot, which the convenience store manager displays over the lottery ticket dispenser. He has drawn a jagged outline around her, fixed false roses at each corner, and cut a crescent moon from cardboard that he has placed at her feet. A line of red glasses with white candles stands in front of her, on top of the lottery ticket dispenser, and *milagros* hang like earrings around this apparition of *Nuestra Señora de la Lotería.*

Outside the convenience store, out back in the arroyo once coursing with water from underground, where wild grapevines coiled around telegraph poles, a Mojave rattler draws circles in the dust, knowing his protective coloring cannot save him.

A Public Woman

IN HER ROOM she saw what she thought was the apparition of a knight dressed in silver, with a plumed helmet. The plume appeared black in the black-and-white of midnight but could have been crimson or indigo. The figure did not vanish when she opened and shut her eyes, and she reckoned—however much reckoning anyone can do in the dead of night, suddenly woken—he could not be inside her mind. He must be in her room.

Slowly the silver coat, glinting in the dark of the small bedroom, the one she kept for herself, marched toward her and she could make no difference.

Under its thrall she could make no sound.

No one would ever know her real name, her point of origin.

Among her effects were:

1 blue plaid silk dress
1 red moiré dress and cloak
1 gold hunting watch
1 silver cup, inscribed J. C. B.
1 silver brick, marked with the same initials
1 jet breastpin

A filigreed ivory cylinder carved with bearded monkeys and split pomegranates, extraordinary work, very fine. Inside the cylinder, like a curled prayer, was a piece of parchment coated with a sticky substance. At first glance, black characters dotted the parchment, underlining the apprehension that here was some sort of text. Silk ribbons hung from the top of the cylinder, which the coroner had untied from inside Jule's drawers. The whole gadget was the size of a fountain pen.

A mystery in the middle of a mystery until a closer look revealed the black characters were not a Chinese prayer for the dead (the thing had an oriental look to it, the investigator thought), or the last will and testament of a public woman, but trapped fleas. The investigator remarked that he had heard of such things (he couldn't call it an ornament despite the delicacy of its design), but he'd never seen one up close, much less handled one.

The flea-catcher made the two men, coroner and investigator, smile.

There was no escaping the ignominy of sudden violent death.

Next to the bed, next to her body, on a deal table she'd ordered all the way from England, was a framed tintype. The background of the picture appeared to be painted, like the backdrop on the stage of Piper's Opera House in Virginia City. She'd gone there one afternoon for the phenomenon of Jenny Lind and noticed the scenes of the Comstock, the advertisements over the singer's head (Lafayette Beef & Veal & Pork; Star Restaurant; Davis Master Stationers; Imperial Hotel) and above them, dead center, a portrait of William Shakespeare.

The wealth of the Comstock drew all manner of unimaginable beings to it, like the Swedish Nightingale, like Jule's silver knight.

The background of the tintype had a garden urn mounted on a carved pillar beyond which was a tree with hundreds of small oval leaves. To one side of the two human figures in the foreground was a drawn-back curtain, apparently brocade, either real or trompe l'oeil, it was hard to say. The floor on which the two figures stood was covered by a carpet with rings and rings of roses.

The two human figures were another mystery. Neither was recognizable as Jule. One was a dark-skinned woman in a taffeta (or what looked like taffeta) dress, but not African, dark from somewhere else. And next to her stood a man in a morning coat and striped trousers, light-colored mustaches dripping at either side of his mouth. A pickax in his left hand, against which he rested.

The investigator studied the tintype, could draw no conclusions except the obvious: the man was a miner, the studio portrait perhaps to commemorate a strike.

The investigator laid the picture beside her other effects.

On a writing desk in a corner of the room was a page facedown on the blotter. The investigator carefully turned it over.

January 20, 1867

Paid O'Hara $5 for squaw-washing.
Burning sensation, outweighed by relief.
Brandy. Then bed. No company.

January 21, 1867

Egg passed safely. No ill-effects of the washing.
Fed a group of hand-carters who came to the door.
Awful late for emigration I said.
Said they'd had enough and were headed back.
Don't know how they pitched up on this side of town, amongst all us female boarders.
Didn't ask anything.
Directed the women to the public baths.
Men stayed behind to rearrange the goods on the carts.
No children with them. I know enough not to say anything.
Gave the men some Sazerac while the women were gone.

"Never heard of a whore keeping a diary," the investigator said.

From time to time the investigator visited the parlor houses overseen by madams, the lowdown hurdy-gurdy houses, the rows of cribs—called stockades—inhabited by girls on their own.

All women were hard to know, to be sure; whores, the "fair but frail," the most opaque of all. There was an apparent boldness to women who called themselves Big-Mouthed Annie (and not because of her volubility), the Big Bonanza, the German Muscle Woman, but who were they really; where had they come from? The streets of this and every other boomtown were filled with women from all parts, each covering her trail.

And when the mines began to fail, as they must, and the towns became skeletal, the women faded. Tokens for their services encrusted with the cryptobiotic desert, embossed with their monikers, Dianne the Queen, Skidoo Babe, Jew Ida.

Julia Bulette, known as Jule, was one of these.

Her name had not been given her; like the others, she'd taken it.

Her place of origin was said to be London, or New Orleans, or Istanbul. Or all three. Her closest friend was believed to be Glorious

Holmes, neighbor and whore, with whom she took breakfast and lunch, to whom Jule read aloud (but the investigator would not suspect this). Glorious Holmes claimed to be a renegade Mormon, turning the life of a plural wife inside out, a price on her head by the busy little bees.

On a narrow shelf bordered by a slender brass rail at the top of the writing desk was a silver tray in which a *carte de visite* lay, inscribed *Jule,* in black italic script, printed by Davis Master Stationers, who'd advertised their services above the head of Jenny Lind.

Jule worked alone. Her only employee was someone known as the Chinaman who came to her house early each morning to build a fire. It was he who found her body, was questioned (although he spoke almost no English), and was released to the Chinese side of town where on his own he warned the Chinese whores of his discovery.

In the center of the bed the body lay, a counterpane covering her face. Underneath the covers was her slit throat, her blood collecting, draining into the mattress, running onto the carpet into the floor.

The trouble with the murder of a whore, the investigator said to the coroner, is that the number of suspects grows according to the popularity of the whore. And since whores don't keep very good records, well then.

"If a married woman is murdered, you have a number-one suspect right there, who usually turns out to be the culprit. Same with a girl who's spoken for. But with whores, well, you know."

"Indeed I do," the coroner said.

They finally did arrest someone. An illiterate Frenchman with the name (given or taken) of Jean A. Villain, who was caught peddling a blue silk dress with the initials J. C. B. embroidered inside the neckline. Glorious Holmes affirmed that the dress belonged to Jule, and Sam Rosener, the local dry goods merchant, testified he'd sold the cloth to Jule.

That was that.

Villain hanged for Jule's murder in front of a crowd of three thousand, including Mark Twain, a reporter for the *Territorial Enterprise,* who attended with his colleague William Wright (pen name Dan De Quille).

. . .

Some weeks before:

To the Estate of Julia Bulette

1 Mahogany Coffin	$75.00
1 Plate & Engraving	10.00
1 Merino Shroud	20.00
1 Wreath of Flowers	3.00
1 Escort in Attendance with Hearse	25.00
	$133.00

Payable to J. W. Wilson

EVERY VARIETY OF FUNERAL EQUIPMENTS
EXHUMATION & SHIPPING A SPECIALTY

Her burial took place in the rage of a snowstorm.

We are left with the mystery of which the investigator and coroner were unaware, but neither could imagine the dream of a public woman, or the last thing she saw. Nor should we blame them.

The man in silver in her room whom she apprehended as a knight with a plumed helmet.

Glorious Holmes paid the funeral costs. “It’s the least I can do,” she said.

Eventually the street was razed. Under its ruins, washed up by winter rains, was a glass douche, patented 1857.

Publication History

"Then As Now" was first published in *Bomb* (Spring 1999).

"Crocodilopolis" was first published in *Bloom* (July 2004).

"Ecce Homo" was first published in *Small Axe* (2000).

"Carnegie's Bones" was first published in *Southwest Review* (Fall 1999).

"Columba" was first published in *The American Voice* (Spring 1988).

"Election Day 1984" was first published in the *Voice Literary Supplement* (November 1988).

"Transactions" was first published in *Tri-Quarterly* (Fall 1996).

"Monster" was first published in *American Voice* (Summer 1999).

"Contagious Melancholia" was first published in *Women: A Cultural Review* (1993).

"Down the Shore" was first published in *American Voice* (Winter 1991).

"The Store of a Million Items" was first published in the *Voice Literary Supplement* (October 1992).

"Stan's Speed Shop" was first published in *Agni* 47 (1998).

"A Public Woman" was first published in *Southwest Review* (Summer 1996).

Born in Kingston, Jamaica, **Michelle Cliff** has lectured at many universities and was Allan K. Smith Professor of English Language and Literature at Trinity College in Hartford, Connecticut. She is the author of *If I Could Write This in Fire* (Minnesota, 2008) and of the acclaimed novels *Abeng, No Telephone to Heaven,* and *Free Enterprise*. She lives in California.